****

Into the Breach

Book Seven of Rise of the Republic

By
James Rosone and Miranda Watson
****

Illustration © Tom Edwards
Tom EdwardsDesign.com

****

Published in conjunction with Front Line Publishing, Inc.

Manuscript Copyright Notice

ISBN: 978-1-957634-55-5
Sun City Center, Florida, United States of America
Library of Congress Control Number: 2022913002

Table of Contents

Foreword

As a veteran of the Iraq War, I like to weave in the histories of units I've served with as well as those our readers have asked us to include into our books. In some stories, we use the names of past Medal of Honor recipients and historical figures to honor their sacrifice and ensure their names are not forgotten. *Into the Breach* will introduce us to two units that will, in time, have their own separate spin-off series within the Rise of the Republic.

Look for the warship RNS *Lexington*, modeled around the USS *Lexington,* which dates back to 1776 and the formation of America itself. Next, we'll introduce the 101st Orbital Assault Division, modeled after the famed Screaming Eagles of the 101st Air Airborne (Air Assault) Division, initially formed in 1918 before disbanding, then being resurrected in 1942, becoming the division they are today.

Into the Breach will introduce the division through the eyes of the famed Easy Company of the first of the five-oh six. *Into the Terror* will go on to present the 327th Infantry Regiment, also known as the Bastogne Bulldogs. Author Matt Jackson (retired colonel), a veteran mentee I've worked with these past five years, was the Commander of the 327th Infantry Regiment during Operation Desert Storm. I consider it an honor to bring his former command into the lore of this series.

I hope you continue to enjoy the Rise of the Republic and our efforts to keep the memories and legacies of these remarkable heroes and units alive for future generations and posterity's sake. So, grab something to drink and prepare to dive into a fast-paced, rip-roaring book I'm sure you'll enjoy.

---James Rosone

Prologue

Early 2110
Brooke Army Medical Center
San Antonio, Texas
Earth, Sol System

Dr. Kristy Neil stood near the observation window and looked in. The bodies of fifteen men and women were lying in repair tanks, surrounded by a grayish semitranslucent nanogel. It had been a fight to get them to survive this long, but now they were stable.

Or stable enough, Dr. Neil thought to herself, practically grunting out loud.

Colonel Jair Bolsonaro walked in, interrupting her thoughts.

"How are they?" he inquired.

"Alive, so far," Dr. Neil replied.

"It's a modern miracle what you were able to do," Colonel Bolsonaro remarked.

"Well, given their condition when they arrived, it's a wonder that they made it at all," Dr. Neil replied, still astonished by the capabilities of the Gallentine medical technology.

"Agreed, but that's what made them candidates for the program in the first place," Bolsonaro replied.

"Jair, has it ever occurred to you that just because you *can* save someone, it doesn't always mean you should?" Dr. Neil probed. "This new medical tech is great—it's beyond anything we've ever seen before, and it's allowing us to save people who never could have been saved before. But something about saving people like *this*...just seems unnatural."

Dr. Neil knew her colleague disagreed, and she prepared for another lecture—the same one he always gave her when she questioned the ethical nature of the program.

"Come on, Kristy. We've been over this many times. The Director has overruled your objection, as has every advisor on the program. It's time to move on. If that's not something you can do, then perhaps it's time *you* move on."

Yeah, right, thought Dr. Neil bitterly. *If I move on, God only knows what you guys will do with these soldiers next.* At least staying in the program meant she could help them as they recovered.

"No need to get dramatic, Jair. I'm still the leading doctor in this field, and I have no intention of leaving it or my patients behind."

"Good. Then let's move on," replied Bolsonaro. "Are you fairly certain that these fifteen will survive?"

"Their bodies seem to be sufficiently stable, but we won't know for sure whether or not their brains have been repaired enough until we wake them up," Dr. Neil explained. She paused. "I suppose it's time to bring in Dr. Mudo."

Bolsonaro shifted uncomfortably at the mention of Dr. Mudo's name. "I'll make sure he knows," he answered, backing up slowly to head for the exit.

Dr. Neil turned away to hide a smirk. *Yeah, Dr. Mudo gives me the creeps too*, she realized.

****

Dr. Arief Mudo was a cold and calculating man. It would have made him a terrible family practice physician, but he was aptly skilled for a job that required life-and-death decisions to be made without too much consideration for the emotional ramifications.

He studied the readouts of each candidate's medical condition carefully. Most of the vitals and lab results were within normal parameters, surprisingly enough considering the severity of the injuries they'd had when they'd been brought in. However, there were a few that gave him pause.

"Kristy, take a look at this," he ordered. He liked to use Dr. Neil's first name in place of her title as doctor in order to emphasize the fact that she was subordinate to him.

"Coming," she replied.

"See here?" Dr. Mudo pointed to a display. "Despite the amount of time that they've all been suspended in the nanogel, Candidate Two still shows abnormalities in his EKG readings. You need to cut him loose."

"But, Dr. Mudo, if we give it enough time, I'm sure that we can get his heart to heal completely," she pleaded.

"You aren't thinking of the big picture, Kristy," Dr. Mudo shot back. "They aren't *all* going to make it. That extra time that you're leaving Candidate Two in there in the hopes that *maybe* he'll recover fully is time in which you could have saved someone else who definitely *will* survive. We only have a limited number of these vats. They must be used on those who are most likely to survive."

Dr. Neil shook her head but then responded, "Yes, sir," in a quiet voice. She typed her codes into her terminal, and the backlight in the second tank went out. With it, the life of Candidate Two was snuffed out.

She was certainly competent enough, but Dr. Mudo was constantly irritated by Dr. Neil's excessive level of empathy. This was not a touchy-feely mission of compassion—they weren't saving these soldiers' lives out of a sense of altruism. There was an endgame to what they were doing and objectives that had to be met.

"That brings me to Candidates Six, Eight, Twelve, and Thirteen," Dr. Mudo continued. "I've examined their brain scans carefully, and their waves are not within normal limits. There are limitations to how far this Gallentine technology can take us, especially when it comes to the brain. We need candidates who can survive both the neural implants and the physical augmentations."

There was a pause until Dr. Neil acknowledged his statement with a slow nod. She might not have agreed with him on everything, but he could rely on her to do the right thing eventually.

More lights were permanently turned off.

"Now that we aren't using our resources on candidates that have no chance of being viable, it's time to start our security checks on these individuals before we begin the enhancement procedures," Dr. Mudo explained. "If we're going to make anonymous supersoldiers out of this group, then they can't have extensive ties to Earth, New Eden or somewhere else. These people are officially dead, so we can't have them going rogue just to get back and see their child or their fiancé. Understood?"

"Yes, sir."

"Good. Get your people on it. Start with him, Candidate One, Sergeant David Roberts, and just move through them. Some of these interviews may take a while."

Dr. Neil sighed quietly and nodded. Then she turned around to get to work.

Dr. Mudo looked back at the repair tanks. *There's ten of you left—how many will make it into Viceroy Hunt's Kite Program?*

He suddenly felt very impatient. He knew how badly they needed this to work. The Kite Program was meant to operate outside of all conventional authorities. After this, they wouldn't be a part of the Army or Republic Intelligence—they'd be able to carry out all sorts of missions the Viceroy needed done but couldn't send anyone else to do. And if they ever did get caught, their new biometrics wouldn't match those of anyone alive, and they would be cut loose like a kite in the wind—plausible deniability.

It was a brilliant plan. Dr. Mudo wished he had thought of it himself. His boss's cunning nature never ceased to surprise him. A crooked smile curled up the left side of his lips.

****

Several Weeks Later

Dr. Kristy Neil mentally prepared herself for the meeting she was about to have with Dr. Arief Mudo. Now that the security interviews had been completed, she knew he would recommend more cuts from the program. She struggled with the ethics of what they were doing.

We went to all that trouble to save these people, and now they're going to die anyway just because Mudo says they aren't useful enough, she mourned.

The cognitive dissonance of her situation was causing her tremendous stress. She was even starting to have acne breakouts, which was rather embarrassing for a grown woman of her age.

Dr. Neil had fully believed in the Hippocratic oath she'd taken when she had become a doctor; the idealistic "do no harm" motto had just seemed like the only right thing to do back then. However, that world of black and white had faded into a haze of different shades of gray, and now she had to tolerate things she despised.

None of these people would have survived without this program, she told herself. *The ones that don't make it through the selection process—they just died in battle.*

Those that had been conducting the security interviews had done so under the guise of finding recipients for a charitable organization that helped support family members of fallen soldiers. Only the funds were real. It did make Dr. Neil feel a bit better knowing that those who left this earthly plane today would have helped their loved ones.

Dr. Mudo walked in and Dr. Neil's stomach instantly tightened.

"Hello, Kristy, do you have everything you need?" he asked.

"Everything is ready to go," she replied.

"Good. Well, let's get this over with, then, shall we?"

Dr. Neil nodded. She wanted this morning meeting to be over with as soon as humanly possible.

"All right, sir. Candidate One, Sergeant David Roberts, really seems to be a good fit for this program," she began. "He had a steady girlfriend, but she died in combat. He had a mom and sister in Atascadero, California, but they were unfortunately killed in one of the terrorist bombings."

"What about this report of him punching another service member?" asked Dr. Mudo skeptically.

"All eyewitness accounts state that the guy had it coming. He performed admirably on Alfheim after that incident, with no further issues, and his leadership saw fit to promote him twice, so I'd say this was a nonissue."

"Hmm, OK. I guess I'll defer to his direct leadership on this one. He can stay. Let's move on. What about Candidate Three, Jordan Paulsen?"

Dr. Neil sighed. "She has a daughter, age five, and a husband."

Dr. Mudo bluntly stated, "Well, then, you know what you must do."

A huge knot formed in her stomach, but she managed to reply, "Yes, sir."

The backlight on repair tank three was extinguished. Dr. Neil wanted to cry, but she held herself together. *At least that little girl's college will be paid for, and her father won't struggle to provide for her.*

One by one, they went through the candidates, eliminating fifty percent of them due to their having ties that were too liable to pull them away from their new life in the Kite Program. Five remained: three men and two women.

Candidate Four was Jessica Lyons. She had grown up in the foster system, never being adopted by anyone before growing into adulthood; she'd never really formed any strong relationships with anyone until joining the service.

Lucky number seven was Somchai Suwan, although his life had been anything but lucky before he'd joined the military. He'd been struck by one tragedy after another, losing both parents to cancer while in college and his siblings in a terrible car accident less than six months later. His family hadn't had the kind of money required to get treatment with medical nanites. He had quit his studies at university and floundered in life for a while until a friend had convinced him to join the service—with a renewed sense of purpose, he had excelled.

Candidate Eleven was Amir Saleh. Due to religious differences, he had apparently been estranged from his family for some time. He had been in a serious relationship with a woman, but she had split up with him after having to endure such long periods of separation and gone on to marry another man, so that door was definitely closed.

The final candidate was Catalina Alonso, an only child of older parents. Her father had passed away from a heart attack several years ago, and while her mother was living, she had been relegated to an assisted living facility due to a rare form of dementia for which there was still no known cure.

Frankly, as stringent as Dr. Mudo was, Dr. Neil was grateful to have anyone left, but these five did stand the best chance of dealing with the psychological strain of having to renounce all former contacts.

"Well, now that we have our field appropriately narrowed down, Kristy, we can begin with the surgical enhancements and altering of their biometrics," Dr. Mudo reminded her. "I'll have my people begin crafting legends for them once we have the new fingerprints and facial recognition points."

"Yes, sir," she replied.

It was going to be a busy day. She had five neural implants to insert, and then she had to essentially turn these men and women into Delta operators. *They didn't sign up for this—I just hope that we've made the right selections.*

****

"Looking good," David heard a woman say. "He's out of the coma. He should be ready now."

"Brain activity looks good," someone else said.

Whoa, what's going on? David wondered. *Is this some sort of dream? Am I dead? Is this purgatory, heaven? It can't be hell...I don't feel any fire. Oh, God...fire—my body's on fire!*

"Excellent, keep monitoring his vitals," the woman said. "We're going to give him the stimulants."

No, I'm not dead. Those are definitely human voices.

"Giving him ten cc's now."

Who's talking right now? Am I in some sort of hospital?

"This looks good. His brain activity is beginning to peak. His vitals are stabilizing. Let's see if he responds to stimuli next."

Ouch, what just poked me? David asked himself. *Wait, I can feel something...that means I'm not dreaming. If I'm not dead, then I'm alive.*

"Response to stimuli good. Let's go ahead and wake him up."

David found himself jerking into a sitting position and gasping for air. He was naked and sitting in some sort of gray goo. Suddenly, he felt very cold.

A female doctor approached, holding out a couple of towels. "Welcome back to the land of the living, Sergeant Roberts," she said with a warm smile.

"Where am I?" he asked. "What happened?" He eagerly grabbed for one of the towels and began drying off his torso. He started to move his legs to get out of the tank, but the doctor stopped him.

"Hold up there," she said, raising a hand. "You were clinically dead and then in a comatose state for a while now, and we just pumped you full of stimulants. You're going to need to sit here and acclimate for a few minutes before you move around too much."

It was only then that David actually looked down at his own body and realized that some major surgeries had been performed on him. When he saw the other men and women lying in the tanks, though, it was all too much for him. He threw up.

"That's all right, David," said the doctor soothingly as she helped him to clean up. *We expected many of you to have strong reactions to all of these changes.* David suddenly realized that she hadn't actually spoken that last part. He'd heard it in his head as if she were speaking via telepathy.

"What…what *happened* to me?" he pressed.

"Well, David, as I stated previously, you were technically dead. However, due to some incredible Gallentine technology, we were able to bring you back. You're a modern miracle. More will be explained once we've woken the others, but for now, just take a moment to enjoy this second lease on life, OK?"

****

David and four others were now fully clothed, and they had each been given a tray of food to eat. Although he couldn't help but feel suspicious of the shorter male doctor that had joined the room, his ravenous hunger overrode any hesitation he might have felt in that moment. He devoured his meal like he'd been stuck on a deserted island for two months.

You might want to slow it down there, Tiger, joked the female soldier next to him over the neurolink. *It would be a shame for them to bring you back from the dead just for you to die choking on your dinner.*

Suddenly, David realized that he knew her name was Catalina. In fact, he knew the names of everyone in the room, including the doctors. He'd known about neurolinks because of all the stories he'd heard about the Deltas, but actually having one—that would certainly take some getting used to.

Hey, what do you think Shorty's story is? David asked.

Honestly, I don't know, but he doesn't seem like the kind of guy it would be fun to go have a beer with, replied Catalina.

David smirked. He liked this one.

A colonel walked into the room. Out of habit, everyone immediately put their trays down and jumped to attention.

"At ease. My name is Colonel Jair Bolsonaro, and I will be your main point of contact for the Kite Program," he announced.

"Kite Program?" Amir asked.

"That's right—the Kite Program," Bolsonaro said. "Why don't you all sit back down and finish your food while I explain a few things to you."

The group obliged.

"You all are the guinea pigs for some Gallentine medical technology that is, frankly, amazing. Drs. Neil and Mudo here could tell you a lot more about how it all works, but the end run is you were clinically dead, you shouldn't be here, and yet you are."

He paused and paced a moment. "This situation you find yourselves in presents us with a unique opportunity. You see, as far as the Republic is concerned, you are still dead. You were awarded posthumous medals for bravery in battle, and your life insurance policies paid out to whatever beneficiaries you had named. That means you no longer exist, at least not on paper.

"Look down at your hands," he instructed. David stared at his palms quizzically. "We've even gone to the trouble of altering your biometrics. Your fingerprints aren't the same, and your faces have been altered enough that you would no longer match a facial recognition scan for your former self. Even your DNA was changed in those Gallentine gel tanks, just enough to alter your previous record. In short, the you that you were before no longer exists. Your first names will remain the same, but we've created legends for each of you that you will need to thoroughly memorize."

David felt himself panic slightly. He touched his face involuntarily, wondering what he now looked like.

"Now before you all go off the rails, let me get back to the opportunity I referenced before," Bolsonaro continued. "Since you are now anonymous by your very nature, you can work outside of the scope of what the Army or Republic Intelligence can accomplish, at least officially. And we just upgraded your bodies with all the enhancements that the Deltas get, so you can run faster, jump higher, breathe deeper, and react faster than you could before—not to mention the neurolinks I'm sure you've discovered, which have a whole host of capabilities on their own. So you put all that together, and you five have what it takes to become one of the most powerful forces for good in the known universe."

Yeah, but we're the "Kite Program," so if we get caught, they can cut us loose, Amir commented via neurolink.

"I think I may know something about what you're thinking," Bolsonaro remarked. "'Won't they just forget that we exist if we get captured?'" He stood back and crossed his arms. "Well, first of all, we are going to train you to use these new bodies of yours. You will be given the type of training that the Special Forces receive and learn how to move in such a way as to be undetectable. You will be the elite of the elite.

"Not only will you be the tip of the spear, kicking ass and taking names, but the Kite Program comes with some really killer benefits. You will be making *way* more money than you could have ever made in the Army. And we're going to give you some time off to use it. Every two years, you'll get a six-week sabbatical—you can take a luxury space cruise, live it up in the Bahamas, or go surfing on New Eden—whatever you want, within reason.

"The *only* thing you definitely won't be allowed to do is contact any of your former family members or associates. The Republic has invested a lot of money into turning you into someone new and keeping this program clandestine—and it will stay that way, even if we have to kill you or whoever you tried to contact to keep it that way."

The information sat there in the room for a moment. David reasoned that there really was no choice other than to say yes. It would be cool to get to do some James Bond kind of stuff no one else would get to do. And what was he going to say to this offer—no? It sounded like that would spell his end—a real end this time.

"So, now that I've explained the facts of the situation to you, do any of you have any questions?" asked Bolsonaro.

"Just one," said Jessica. "Let's say we do all this. Is there ever a point where we can walk away?"

"The Republic has invested a lot in you," Bolsonaro responded, "so they would like to get some of that back. But you give us thirty years, and you can ride off into the sunset."

"So where is the paperwork?" asked Somchai.

Colonel Bolsonaro grinned. "See, that's what I'm talking about. Let's get that taken care of, shall we?"

Chapter One
Abort!

Captain Hosni continued to observe the suspect walk down Lerchenauer Straße, steadily approaching the apartment. *Come on…let this be the place*, he prayed.

"The suspect is approaching the building now. Stand by for confirmation," said a voice over the team's coms.

Bob Haran nudged Hosni's arm. "Fifty RDs this is the safe house we've been after."

Hosni smirked at the comment, hoping he was right. They'd been after this place since they'd first learned of it months ago.

"I'll pass on the bet as I hope you're right. Just make sure your guys are ready to act once we have confirmation this is in fact the place we've been looking for."

"Oh, my guys are ready. They're chomping at the bit ready," replied Bob, eager to notch a win for the team.

Bob was the IMS supervising agent in charge of this operation. He was the lead of one of the four counterterrorism or CT teams that Hosni's JSOC unit had spent the last few years training and bringing up to speed.

"Stand by—suspect appears to be stopping."

"Come on, come on, let this be the place," rooted Bob anxiously in hopes that this lead would be the one to finally pan out.

"Keep your britches on, Bob. This is the place. Me analysts are certain of it," retorted Loni O'Brien from her seat in the rear of the van. She was their feisty and at times very precocious redhead from the field office in Limerick, Ireland. It had been her team of analysts that had pored through astronomical amounts of data to eventually narrow down the potential safe house locations for Bob's teams to go check out.

"Yeah, well, it better be, Loni. The last four were dry holes."

"We still nabbed four Mukhabarat spies, so it wasn't a complete waste," said Gary Von, or GV as he liked to be called, coming to Loni's rescue.

"You're right, GV. We did nab a few more operatives. But something big is getting ready to go down soon. We need to figure out what it is and who all is involved before it kicks off."

Hosni chimed in at this point, telling them to focus on the big picture and not get caught up in what they had or hadn't accomplished up to this point. Then he turned to GV. "Hey, if she does end up going into this building, then get us that picture of what's going on inside ASAP. We've given you that new toy to use. Use it."

GV smiled at the mention of his new toy. He was the team's resident electronic warfare and surveillance guru. JSOC had spent more than a few weeks teaching him and a few other wizards how to use some of their more advanced electronic surveillance equipment—much of which wasn't available for use outside of the military or intelligence services.

"Hey, it looks like she's stopping to type something on that keypad," Bob called out.

"Make sure to grab those numbers, GV. Maybe we can have the breacher team use it when it's time to make entry into the building," Hosni ordered, disregarding the fact that GV technically didn't work for him.

Moments later, the keypad activated something they hadn't expected to see. An iris scanner appeared to be a secondary mechanism to control entry into the building. They watched her interact with the device, leaning in to make sure it had a good view of her left eye, then her right.

Yeah, this is the place. No one puts an iris scanner on a regular run-of-the-mill apartment...

The door to the apartment popped open, allowing her to pull the door wide enough to enter and bring in the bags of food she'd just picked up from the Italian restaurant, L'Ancora, at the end of the block on the corner of Schleißheimer Straße.

"That's it. She's in," Bob announced, alerting those who weren't able to follow along on the video feed. "OK, Echo Team. It's on you now. Get us confirmation of how many suspects are in the building and what possible threats Teams One and Two may encounter when they breach."

"Good copy. Echo Team initiating spectral analysis now. Stand by for results."

Hosni saw Bob turn to him briefly, almost waiting for him to give him his approval. "Don't look at me, Bob. This is your op. We're just here to back you guys up."

Bob nodded appreciatively. "Teams One and Two, stand by to execute once we have confirmation from Echo on the number of suspects inside the building."

The two of them watched the monitor depicting the actions of Echo Team. Now that they had confirmation of the location, one of their members had directed a microdrone to fly over the apartment building. Once overtop, it started a top-down spectral scan of the building, mapping the levels of the structure as it searched for potential hidden rooms, trapdoors, hidden pathways between rooms, or potential black holes in the structure, indicating a shielded room that would likely be hiding something of value within.

While the drone was doing its thing and feeding data to GV's computer, a single team member drove a utility van slowly past the building, right in front of the ground-floor apartment. As the vehicle drove past, a highly sensitive scanner was aimed at the building. The scanner pierced through the structure of the building, mapping out everything it saw to be fed back into GV's computer. As the data from this scan and the spectral scan from the drone were woven together, they provided a pretty solid image of the interior, the locations of the suspects, and approximately how many identifiable weapons might be inside.

"Whoa, check this out. That right there is a hidden room—and that—yeah, those are explosives. Looks like they're building some homemade boom-booms," Bob said. In the right hands, household cleaning chemicals and agricultural fertilizers that people regularly used in their home gardens could be combined in very volatile ways. "Yeah, this is it—the safe house we've been after. Good job, Loni," Bob congratulated her.

"All right, Bob, this is it," said Hosni. "Time to put all your training to good use and take this place down." A broad smile spread across his face.

He was proud to see the team his men had spent months training coming together in a hunt to remove one more threat to the Republic. Through the continued capture of Mukhabarat and Ani operatives, they were steadily unraveling the network of what they'd come to learn were direct-action covert hit squads and saboteurs that had infiltrated across the Republic. The capture and elimination of these safe houses and operatives had become a top priority within the marshals and Republic Intelligence. Finding the safe houses and bases of operations of these secretive infiltration teams had proved elusive and difficult at best—until today.

"Damn right it is," Bob replied. "Speaking of that, I'm going to go link up with my guys. If you can, Hosni, keep your people on alert. I don't think we'll need the help, but you've taught me enough not to underestimate these bastards either." Bob inserted an earpiece that would allow him to stay in touch with his group in the van. He opened the door, turning as he exited. "Wish us luck," he said before he closed the door and disappeared from sight.

Hosni placed the marshals' earbud in so he could stay in contact with Bob and listen in on his teams. They didn't have neurolinks like his Deltas. Instead, they had to rely on the good old-fashioned way of communicating—two-way radios.

Master Sergeant, is your team ready to respond should things go south? Hosni asked over the neurolink. He'd had Joe position their Delta team not too far from the targeted building, should they be needed. If that did happen, then it would be Joe that led them, not him.

Roger that, said Joe. *Team's suited up, ready to rock and roll. You think Bob's people might need the help?*

Even over the neurolink Hosni heard the skepticism. It had been Joe's team who'd trained the marshals preparing to assault the building. If Joe thought they were ready, they were ready.

Negative, I think they're prepared. Just have a bad feeling about these guys. We've only encountered these Ani operatives in ones and twos—not a group like this. Just stay frosty and be ready to jump into the thick of it should they need help.

Further down the street, a white electric utility van turned onto the road leading toward the target. Simultaneously, the drone overtop of the building, which was giving them a look-down view of the situation, showed a green city maintenance van approaching the building from the rear. As the maintenance vehicle reached the back of the building, it slowed to a crawl and the side door slid open. One by one, six armor-clad marshals hopped out, and as the van drove past them, they stacked up behind it, using the vehicle as a shield to block anyone inside the building from seeing them.

As they approached the entrance to the building that'd lead them to a rear entry to the targeted apartment, the white utility van had just reached the building's front entrance and the street access door to the apartment.

"Team Two, stand by," came Bob's voice.

"Both the hallway and the street are still looking clear on this end. No sign of detection," GV confirmed for both teams.

"Team Two—go!"

Hosni pulled the VR glasses down from his forehead, instantly seeing what the Team Two breacher was seeing via his helmet cam. He watched the agent move around the maintenance vehicle as he ran toward the side entrance. This would lead them into the hallway that connected to the rear entrance of the apartment. Hosni knew they had less than sixty seconds to gain access to the hallway and get in position against the rear door to the apartment. Team One's vehicle was still approaching the front entrance—time was not on their side.

Hosni watched the agent reach for the keypad next to the door, slapping a small device over it and holding it in place for a few seconds. A green light popped on and the door unlocked. The agent grabbed the handle and held it for the others. The five other agents rushed into the hallway, guns drawn, ready for action.

As they advanced toward the rear entrance to the apartment, the agent that Hosni was observing ran to the door with his breaching strips already in hand. In seconds, he had the strips stuck to the door in the exact places they'd shown them during the many iterations they'd practiced this drill. By the time the agents in the hallway were in place and ready to breach, the group approaching from the front had just exited the van.

Hosni switched cameras and now had a view of the agent leading the team toward the front entrance to the apartment. That was when GV shouted over the coms, "They've spotted Team One! Multiple suspects are reaching for weapons. Team One, prepare for contact!"

The urgent warning sent the agents into a full sprint. They were out in the open, fully exposed in their current position. Hosni was busy watching what was unfolding through the VR glasses when he heard some commotion in the rear of the van.

"What is that?" asked Loni.

"I don't know. What are they doing?" Bob queried.

"Those two look like they're getting ready to shoot whoever busted through that door," said Loni.

"Yeah, but what's that person doing over there, near those cylinders?" asked Bob.

As soon as Hosni heard the word *cylinders*, he ripped the VR glasses off his face, his finger reaching to activate the coms unit. "Abort! Everyone abort now! Get away from the building!"

No sooner had he finished yelling his warning than the van was thrown onto its side. The vehicle then slid until it came to a rest against something.

Hosni swore he blacked out for a moment. The next thing he remembered was lying in an awkward position against the passenger-side window, flat on his back. He heard moaning and someone else calling out for help. Shaking off the effects of the blast, he pulled himself up and looked into the back of the vehicle.

GV had some equipment scattered on top of him, moaning quietly. Loni had a gash on the side of her head and was calling out softly for help, unsure of where she was.

Holy crap, boss! Are you all right? Hosni recognized the voice of Master Sergeant Tanner over the neurolink. *We saw the van get tossed over from the blast. I've got our medic on the way to you and we've called in EMS support.*

Yeah...I'm all right, Hosni replied. *A little banged up, but Loni and GV need some help. Is there anything left to that place? Never mind, what am I thinking?* He felt stupid the moment he asked the question.

We'll be there in a second, Hosni. Uh, yeah...that place is toast. They likely had the location rigged to explode for just this kind of scenario. We'll have to look back at the spectral scan and see if we somehow missed something. Nothing we can do about it this time, but maybe next time they won't catch us by surprise.

Taking a breath in, Hosni shook his head in frustration. They'd really needed to catch a break here. Now they'd have to figure out what the hell had gone wrong and how not to make the same mistakes in the future.

This was a lot bigger than we expected, Hosni realized. *What else are we missing out there?*

Chapter Two
The Dragon Slayer

Early 2111
Weapons of Tomorrow Expo
Space Command Headquarters
Jacksonville, Arkansas
Earth, Sol System

Colonel Brian Royce felt like a kid in a candy store as he walked around the Weapons of Tomorrow Expo. Like others "in the know," he understood that the battle had been won, but not the peace—that hadn't been settled yet. The fact that hundreds of vendors had booths full of gadgets, gizmos, and weapons meant to help the Army or Fleet win the next war told him he wasn't alone in feeling like conflict with the Zodarks wasn't over. Still, he was optimistic that one day it would be settled.

"Oh, looks like they're about to start," Royce heard General Reiker say when a loud voice took control of the room. The expo's main event was finally beginning.

Royce smiled excitedly at the sight of Charlotte Goodwin as she strode to the middle of the stage and became the center of attention. Royce knew Charlotte. They'd fought together in the Deltas during the Intus campaign some fifteen years ago. She'd been gravely injured during a battle to take out one of the massive Orbot ion cannons shooting at the invasion fleet moving into orbit. He'd felt bad for Charlotte when he'd heard the Army was going to medically retire her, despite having given her the latest cybernetic prosthetics to try and make her whole again. Her time in the Deltas was done. She might have been able to stay on in some sort of support function with the regular Army if she'd wanted to, but in the end, she'd opted for the medical retirement. After a career in Special Forces, going back to the regular Army would've been like a twenty-year police officer quitting to be a mall cop. It just wasn't the same.

Charlotte's booming voice snapped him from the memory of long ago. "Welcome to the 2111 Weapons of Tomorrow Expo," she boldly declared. "For those of you who don't know me, my name is Charlotte Goodwin. I'm the CEO of Dragon Slayer and a former Delta operator myself. Throughout the last thirteen years, I've dedicated my life to finding the tools and technology to better protect our Special Forces soldiers and our Republic Army comrades. Having served thirty-six years in the military, twenty-nine of them in the Deltas, I understand better than most what's needed on the battlefield to win the wars of tomorrow.

"At Dragon Slayer, we've chosen to focus on the two areas most critical to winning the next war. I'm proud to present the latest technology in personal protective armor, and the battle rifle of the future to go with it. Please enjoy the short video demonstration we've put together with help from the Republic Army Special Warfare Training Center. They were kind enough to loan us Master Sergeant Amon Wilcox, who put this new gear through the wringer. Without further ado, let's welcome the future of Special Forces," Charlotte explained before walking to the edge of the stage.

As the lights in the auditorium dimmed, a holographic image was projected across the front stage, transforming it into an immersive three-dimensional visual experience designed to draw viewers in and make them feel like they were part of whatever was being shown. Before Royce could negatively react to what he thought was rapidly becoming an overused thematic means of pitching products to the military, a cinematic chord began to play and an image of Master Sergeant Wilcox came into focus near the center of the stage.

The image of the Delta operator wearing some sort of new combat suit transitioned into him running through what appeared to be a forest on one of the foreign planets they'd battled on in the past. As the details of the forest steadily came into focus, Brian felt his heart race. His palms became sweaty, and his right foot bounced in a nervous jitter. He recognized this forest...he recalled what had happened in those woods, among those trees. It wasn't a memory he wanted to relive.

Yet as Master Sergeant Wilcox raced through the forest on the Primord planet Intus, he was reenacting what had been called the Battle of Sector Five. Royce had fought in this campaign on Intus, the same planet where Charlotte had been gravely injured. Seeing the recreation of a battle they'd fought long ago play out in a demonstration for a product the Army had just bought stirred a lot of bad memories and emotions within him.

Steeling his nerves and regaining his composure, Royce pushed the negative thoughts out of his mind and was soon consumed with the image of Wilcox. The man was sprinting through the forest in an armored suit that appeared to wrap itself around him like a second skin against his body. He swiftly moved through the forest—around trees, over fallen logs and through the underbrush—with a speed and agility they could never achieve with their current exosuits.

Then the forest suddenly changed. The scene transformed into a raging battle of blaster bolts, explosions, and smoke swirling around Wilcox. He began firing a futuristic rifle with blinding rates of speed as he closed the distance between himself and the enemy.

Wilcox raced between covered positions, flashes of light zipping around him. Then he got hit. A blaster shot to the chest threw his body awkwardly to the side as he dropped his rifle.

Royce felt his heart skip a beat, and his eyes went wide when Wilcox shrugged off the hit like it didn't matter. Wilcox took a step forward, searching for the rifle he'd dropped moments earlier. When he stretched his hand out for it, the rifle flew into his grip like he'd uttered some magical spell. He turned to face the enemy and resumed his advance like nothing had happened.

Across the room, Royce could hear whispers of shock and surprise spread throughout the audience. No one was sure if what they saw was real or only part of a promotional video.

That was too fantastical to be true...wasn't it?

Brian's mind raced as he thought about what he'd just seen.

How can that armor take a direct hit and shrug it off? That's not possible...

And that rifle...what the hell is that he's shooting?

Watching with rapt attention, the audience now fixated on the armor-clad soldier who'd closed with the enemy. The fight turned to close-quarters battle. Jumping into a cluster of Zodarks, Wilcox charged the closest one, lowering his shoulder and ramming him in the upper abdomen, throwing the giant beast off-balance and to the ground. A blade slashed across the back of Wilcox's armor—sparks flew as it failed to cut through and deliver its fatal blow.

Undeterred, Wilcox raised his rifle and fired several shots into the Zodark he'd knocked to the ground, killing it before sidestepping the blade thrust toward his chest by another enemy. Twisting his body with an agility not possible with their current armored exosuits, Wilcox swung his rifle around, firing rapidly into the chest of the Zodark that had tried to skewer him. As he fired, another Zodark slashed the side of his armor before lurching forward, ramming him with his shoulder and throwing him to the ground, hard.

Wilcox rolled quickly to his right as a string of blaster bolts sprayed where he'd just been moments earlier. Scrambling to his feet, Wilcox tried firing at the Zodark but missed when the beast's blade managed to throw off his rifle's aim as it closed the distance between them.

Brian watched in amazement as Wilcox moved with blinding speed, delivering a blow to the side of the Zodark's face and head with the butt of the rifle as he used it like a truncheon. The Zodark staggered back, momentarily stunned by the blow, before Wilcox shot him several times, finishing the Zodark off just in time to turn and see an Orbot appear from around a tree not too far away.

As the hideous spiderlike creature, half-biological and half-machine, scrambled straight for him, Wilcox jumped back several meters, creating just enough distance to dodge the freakishly fast mechanical leg that lunged at him like a harpoon. Undeterred, the Orbot swiftly stabbed two of its spear-like legs in a downward motion, attempting to pin Wilcox to the ground so it could pounce on his body and finish him off.

Royce looked on in amazement as Wilcox rolled to the side with his blaster up, firing relentlessly into the armored shell from which the cyborg operated its mechanical body. The hits to the Orbot's armor tore through it like a hot knife through butter, burning through its shell like no weapon Royce had seen before.

As Wilcox stood up, surrounded by the carnage he'd inflicted, he looked like a god—an unstoppable killing machine that rivaled even their C100 combat synthetics. As the image faded away, the lights in the room came on and the show was over as quickly as it had started.

Wow, that was incredible, Royce thought.

The room erupted in cheers and applause. What this new armor and rifle purported to do was beyond anything they had seen before. While people spoke animatedly amongst each other, Charlotte returned to the stage. As she stood in the light, the applause and praise slowly tapering down, an image of the Dragon Slayer company logo appeared on the monitors behind her.

Lifting her arms to calm the crowd, Charlotte loudly declared, "What you just saw is the future of Republic Special Forces and the new exoskeleton suit we're calling Dragon Skin."

People rose from their chairs, applauding and cheering at her proclamation.

Charlotte now began to walk the stage as she continued to speak. "You've seen what it can do—now let me tell you what makes the Dragon Skin substantially better than our current exoskeleton suits."

An image appeared on the screens while she spoke. "The most obvious change is the armor; Dragon Skin is three hundred percent stronger than our current body armor, while also being twenty percent lighter than our current exoskeleton combat suits. In addition to the superior protection, we greatly enhanced the suits' abilities. We've given the users increased physical speed—meaning soldiers can run faster, longer, and harder than they can in our existing combat suits.

"Normally, changes like these, especially the increase in armor effectiveness, would result in a loss in agility and movement. However, our proprietary technology had the opposite effect. A user's agility is now greatly enhanced while the suits also provide them with substantial freedom of movement to react to changing threats as necessary to dominate the battlefields of the future.

"Make no mistake, Dragon Slayer Industries is about preparing to fight the wars of the *future*, not the war we just ended. My grandfather fought in the Great AI war, and he told me something that is just as true today as it was then. 'You go to war with the army you have, not the army you want.' When the Dominion War started, we fought with the weapons we had. We made modifications where we could, and we found ways to win despite the obstacles. That's something we're going to change by ensuring our military has the necessary tools to win the next war.

"In the video you just saw, we introduced you to Dragon Skin— now it's time to tell you about this sleek, sexy-looking new battle rifle that's going to change everything. I want to present the crown jewel of our company—the M-111 Slayer, or as we like to call it, the triple-one."

Royce caught himself gaping when a magnified image of the rifle from the video appeared on the monitors across the stage. This elicited another round of applause and cheers as Royce stared at perhaps the most beautiful rifle he'd ever seen.

The flat black finish and the ergonomic features gave it a futuristic look when compared to the rifles they'd been using. The most obvious change to the triple-one was the barrel. At twelve inches in length, it was four inches smaller than the M1 and eight inches smaller than the M85. It had an extendable rear stock that could add up to four inches to the rifle's overall length, depending on the size of the person using the rifle.

"While the Dragon Skin will protect the warriors of the future, it's the triple-one Slayer that'll instill the fear of the Republic in our enemies," Charlotte explained. "In creating the Slayer, we partnered with DARPA as we sought to address the shortcomings of the venerable M1 that's gotten us through the wars up to this point.

"In designing the Slayer, we made the rifle shorter to allow for easier handling in tight spaces, like on board ships and stations or bunched up on assault transports already packed to the gills with soldiers and equipment. And I won't go into the details of how we solved this problem, but we found a way to eliminate the need to change out battery packs as the blaster's power runs low. In fact, we've managed to eliminate the need for removable battery packs altogether.

"When we increased the blaster power and reduced the size of the rifle's barrel, it was no longer viable to keep the dual-purpose railgun-blaster combo. However, one weapon that proved an invaluable force multiplier during the war was the 20mm smart grenade. Knowing this, we found a way to make sure it remained part of the Slayer's final design, and this is what you saw Master Sergeant Wilcox using. We're confident that this new rifle, coupled with Dragon Skin, will lead our forces to victory in any future conflicts we may find ourselves in."

Charlotte rattled off more details of the Slayer and Dragon Skin while several demonstrators came forward to allow more people to see the actual items for themselves. As the demonstration and the Q&A came to an end, Royce felt a renewed sense of confidence—should a war happen again, they wouldn't be caught off guard like they had been this last time around.

Imagining a company or even a battalion of Deltas outfitted in this gear, Royce knew one thing was for certain: this time around, they'd be the hunters, not the prey.

****

General John Reiker slapped Royce on the shoulder. "Well, that was fun," he commented with a smile.

"Hell yeah, sir," Royce agreed. "I still can't believe it's real and we'll be training on this in a few weeks. I thought for sure it was going to start with First Group and get to us last. They're the operational units attached to Big Army, not us."

Reiker had heard the same comments from all the new officers he'd brought with him this year to the expo. They all thought the same thing. *They're like kids in a toy store. They see new shiny toys and can't wait to go play with them and maybe break a few along the way.*

"Well, Colonel, when you get as long in the tooth as I am, eventually you realize something."

"Oh, what am I missing?" Royce asked.

"RHIP, Colonel, RHIP." Seeing the puzzled look on Royce's face, Reiker explained, "Rank Has Its Privileges, Royce. Not that you should invoke it often, but when the opportunity presents itself, seize it if it'll help your soldiers."

"I take it that's why JSOC is first in the pipe to make the transition?"

"Exactly…time to clean that drool off your chin, though," Reiker teased. "We've got some more work to do."

Royce laughed. "Roger that."

"I need you to go find Booth 258 and see if their stuff is worth checking out," Reiker directed. "Make sure your team leaders write up their assessments of the products they were told to look into. We'll do a hot wash tomorrow to see what's worth pursuing before the expo ends and line up additional meetings and demonstrations. We have eight weeks to submit our final budget request. If something looks worthwhile or there's some R&D project we should get involved in, then I'd like to get it added to our discretionary line item."

"Ah, copy that. I'll make sure they're on it and review everything before we present it to you. Oh, if I'm not mistaken, Booth 258—isn't that the one with the jump pack?"

"Sure is," confirmed Reiker, a devilish smile on his face.

"Oh man, these guys are going to go nuts when they hear about jetpacks. I can hear it now: 'I'm gonna be Rocket Man!'" Royce joked in a mocking voice as he laughed.

"Ha ha, Rocket Man…that's a good one. See, I told them this is what would happen once they started letting operators and grunts in these expos. Rumor mill is going to be rampant with all sorts of new tech the Army might buy."

Royce's expression became more serious, and he leaned in, speaking quietly. "Sir, speaking of rumors, do you have any new information about what's going on with that Ani network they've uncovered?"

Reiker clicked his tongue and smiled. "Brian, I know you had a lot invested in Hosni and his men, but I need you to understand something—that was your old role. You're a colonel now, and your worldview needs to get a lot broader than what it was before. That's actually part of why I brought you out here today."

He started to amble away and motioned with his head. "Walk with me."

Royce followed.

"Look, you and other up-and-coming leaders like you are the future of Special Forces, not us old farts steadily retiring into the sunset," Reiker explained. "It's time to begin handing the reins over and roping you newly promoted colonels and brigadiers in on the workings of a force you may one day be leading."

Royce smiled. "I've still got a lot to learn from you and General Bates, so don't go and add your names to the litany of retirements this year," he said. "If there's one thing I've learned over the years from you and others, it's that any success I have is largely attributable to the professionalism of my NCOs and junior officers. They're the ones who find a way to adapt and overcome no matter the odds. They're the ones that make us look good."

It was moments like this that made an old general swell with pride. With the size of the Republic Army, officers were a dime a dozen. Good officers, the ones who knew how to inspire the best in their subordinates and groomed the next generation of leaders behind them, were hard to come by.

"I couldn't agree more, Royce, and that's what makes you a good leader. You possess the self-awareness to know you aren't an island. You've done a good job of identifying and promoting good officers and NCOs to continue fostering this kind of mentality. That's the kind of leader we're going to need in the coming years.

"But don't worry about me retiring. The Army's still got big plans for me. But enough of that. I got big plans for *you* and the rest of JSOC. You're about to get a firsthand look at what you all will be training on soon."

"Looking forward to it, sir."

Chapter Three
Perimeter Problems

Office of the Viceroy
Alliance City, New Eden

Damn. This can't be true...all five outposts near the stargates were destroyed.

The more Viceroy Miles Hunt read, the more unsettled he was. These weren't the actions of a border skirmish or dispute; these were preparations for something larger.

What possible gain can be made by attacking this system and risking a restart to the war we just ended? he wondered.

He had hoped this little turf war would remain an issue between the Pharaonis and the Tully, something both the Galactic Empire and the Dominion could stay out of, but if this report was true...

Hunt placed the report on the desk and shook his head in frustration, his mind racing with questions as he tried to assess what it all meant.

Something about this Orbot intervention doesn't feel right... something more is happening.

The two Altairians, Handolly and Pandolly, waited patiently for Hunt to respond now that he had read the newest report they'd delivered from Serpentis. It was all but certain to be discussed at length during the council meeting tomorrow.

Hunt's thoughts kept returning to his concern about Republic forces getting bogged down in a fight so far from their territory.

This could leave us vulnerable to the Zodarks...especially now, he thought, contemplating the subterfuge he'd directed Drew to push over the past few years. If Drew's intelligence was right, their plan looked to be working, too.

As he continued to run through the various scenarios, the urgency in Handolly's voice finally caught Hunt's attention. "Miles, you must act. We are beyond a territorial dispute between the Tully and the Pharaonis. This latest move by the Orbots leaves Serpentis open to invasion. If Serpentis were to fall, it would leave the alliance open to invasion from two different positions. The council is already concerned by the growing increase in these border skirmishes. When they hear about this latest incident—they will demand a military response. It would be wise for you to appear ahead of this request and not caught off guard by it."

Hunt grunted at Handolly's candid no-nonsense response. Turning to Pandolly for his opinion, he said, "I'm not disputing these reports, nor am I trying to cause a problem with the Altairians. Both the Tully and the Ry'lians have been pleading their cases for help and raising the alarm about these border incursions for some time, so I've been aware of what's going on. My aim, however, is to separate the political and military opinions of the situation. In your opinion as a military commander, is this latest action a precursor to an invasion of the Serpentis system?"

When it came to military matters within the alliance, Hunt valued the admirals' opinions more than most, particularly as his friendship with them continued to deepen over the years. He'd helped Pandolly give the alliance its first major win over the Orbots when he'd successfully led the combined Altairian-Republic-Primord fleet in seizing control of the Rass system. That victory had led to the promotion that now saw Pandolly as one of five Altairian fleet commanders.

"Miles, given the destruction of the outpost the alliance built specifically to defend one of the key stargates that links the territory of both our alliances' space together, I must agree with Handolly's assessment," explained Pandolly. "The Dominion knows if they can wrestle control of Serpentis away from us and reinforce it, they can create a bridgehead from which they can build up their supplies and forces to launch a multiaxis invasion into two of our alliance members' territory. We would find ourselves defending against two axes of attack, neither of which are near each other, and both of which would be in a different alliance partner's territory.

"Militarily speaking, control of Serpentis is critical. Should it fall and the Dominion advance further into Tully and Ry'lian territories, then we would be hard-pressed to defend these systems given the disparity in distance between both invasion points and the rest of the alliance partners. Let me show you what I mean," Pandolly explained as he brought up a star map. "If they control Serpentis, that gives them a path of stargates that leads directly into the planetary core of the Tully and Ry'lian territories. What would make this substantially more challenging is that we must support two large forces down different stargate tracks. This would make defending the border areas along the Republic and Primord space a lot more challenging should this be the opening move to a renewal of the last war. That brings us back to Serpentis and why it needs to stay under Tully control."

Hunt rubbed his temples. Pandolly was right; he just didn't like it.

It would be stupid to try and defend against two invasions separated by this much space if we can prevent it by reinforcing Serpentis now or recapturing it if it falls before reinforcements arrive, Hunt realized.

Outside of Altairian-controlled space, the Serpentis system held the only stargates that linked the Tully and Ry'lian territories together. Unfortunately, it also linked their territories to the Pharaonis and Orbots two systems over. This singular chokepoint had prevented the Tully and Ry'lians from working together to collectively shore up and defend the system. Despite being in the same alliance, the two of them had been historical enemies for centuries, fighting an on-again, off-again war that had only ended when the two factions had joined the same alliance.

Hunt eventually conceded—an alliance response was probably needed. Still, he felt he needed to ask one final question. "Is it really impossible for the two of them to handle this together without the alliance getting involved?"

Altairians weren't known for displaying emotional responses like humor, so when Handolly stared at him for a moment before openly laughing, Hunt realized he'd asked a stupid question. "No, Miles, the Ry'lians would not defend a Tully system any more than a Tully would defend a Ry'lian one," the Altairian politician responded, as politely as possible.

Pandolly interjected, "If this had been possible, then there would be no need for an alliance response. Miles, you are still forgetting something—our alliance is made up of members who have not always had friendly relations with each other. What binds the Galactic Empire together is our common enemy—the Dominion, and their patrons, the Collective. This is why some races fight together in our alliance and others do not. This was how King Grigdolly grew and governed the alliance over the centuries when he was viceroy."

Hunt felt his cheeks redden at the subtle reminder that the Altairians still held a grudge against him. Since he'd become the

Viceroy, it was these lingering tensions from within the alliance that were driving him nuts, though. This friction was hindering what he felt could truly become a powerful force should they ever be able to fully work together.

Hunt sighed, finally relenting. "All right, point made. The two can't work together for the betterment of the alliance or themselves. I get it. I'll speak with Admiral Bailey about deploying a battle group to the system. Is it possible for you to deploy some ships and take charge of rebuilding the defenses around the stargate? I'm hesitant to ask the Primords for help given the continual state of fighting on Alfheim."

"Yes, of course. We can support a deployment to Serpentis and rebuilding the outposts," Pandolly agreed. "If I can make a request, allow us to supply warships in lieu of soldiers. Your soldiers have proven to be the superior fighters in the alliance. Should the Pharaonis seize the planet Serpentis-6, then we will need our best warriors to retake it swiftly, so it does not turn into another Alfheim campaign."

Hunt agreed to the request, but only if the Altairians supplied the warships to secure the system and repel any incursions. He wasn't about to let the Republic Navy get tied down when he was trying to lure the Zodarks into a final battle to end them as a threat to his people.

Pandolly bowed his head in deference. "I will do one better, Miles. I will lead the Altairian battle group myself. Once we have restored the gates' security and the system is no longer under threat, we can withdraw our forces and allow the Tully to resume their watch of the gate."

"Excellent. I'll speak with Admiral Bailey, and we'll cobble a force together and get this situation taken care of."
****

Later That Day

Hunt held a finger up to the covert operative until the blue light began to blink, followed by a soft humming sound. Now the room was secured and they could talk freely.

"Thank you for seeing me on such short notice," Drew Kanter said, settling into the chair.

"Your message said it was urgent—could only be said in person—so what have you got?"

Hunt had come to respect and admire the covert operatives from Republic Intelligence. As an agency, the RI had developed an impressive apparatus for collecting foreign intelligence and learning what it all meant. In his view, Drew was among the best in that department.

"There are a few things of concern I felt you should be made aware of. I mean, maybe I'm overreacting or looking for things that aren't there. You likely have a better view of the overall picture than me, so perhaps we can piece some of this together."

Hunt lifted an eyebrow at the comment. Drew was rarely unsure about things when they met. "Why don't you tell me what you have, then?"

"It's about Ashurina—something she said during our last meeting."

"Is she OK? Her cover still intact?"

"Oh, she's fine," Drew assured him. "There isn't anything wrong with her cover, at least not that we're aware of. About a month ago, she met her Kafarr in person—that's what they call their handlers. This Kafarr, his name is Dakkuri. During their meeting, he gave her a new priority list of things to seek out.

"When I looked at the information he'd tasked her to acquire, a couple of things jumped out at me. First, most of the questions continue to support our belief that the Zodarks are still preparing to launch a surprise attack on the Republic. It's unclear if it's in the Qatana or Rhea system yet, but given the kinds of questions they're asking, it's clear their strategies are being derived from the subterfuge we've given her to pass along to them.

"In fact, they're very curious about the defensive outposts we have been ringing around the stargates leading into both systems. This isn't something they've ever encountered in the past, so they're unsure of how to handle it, and that's a good thing. That's exactly what we had hoped to engineer. But that's not why I asked to meet with you. Dakkuri tasked her with another collection requirement to fill—something that's given me some pause."

"Huh. OK, let's go over it, Drew. I'm sure we can figure it out together."

"OK, so this is kind of complicated, but I'll do my best to explain it. From my perspective, the questions being asked come across as tests, like her handler wants her to find something I'd say is relatively easy for her to acquire, but also easy for someone else to verify. If everything is on the up-and-up, then her info will match what the others found. If it doesn't, then it means their source or asset is either compromised or just not doing their job—"

"And you suspect that? They're testing her for something?" Hunt interrupted.

"I do," Drew responded. "That, or they're testing someone else against the known access she's led them to believe she has."

"What did they ask to find?" Now Hunt was curious.

"Some generalized information on the organization she's now working for—DARPA. Plus a few specifics about the JBR operation on the Republic naval yard she previously worked at."

"Huh, doesn't seem all that bad. Is it possible they're testing her replacement at the yard?" asked Hunt.

"That's a possibility we thought about too," Drew acknowledged. "For now, I told her to play along, give them what she knows and don't give them a reason to doubt her. But then she asked me for something. Hence my second reason for wanting to meet in person—"

"Let me guess," Hunt interrupted. "She wants to know if we can give her something of value she can pass on to her handler?"

"Yeah, that's exactly what she asked," Drew confirmed. "She brought up the possibility of her Kafarr potentially trying to run a parallel loyalty test on her. You know, make sure she's still on the up-and-up. Since starting this new JBR assignment with DARPA, she mentioned how the volume and significance of the information she had been providing was nowhere near what it had been at her old position. She's looking for something that might help increase her perceived value in this assignment."

Hunt blew some air past his lips. Sitting forward, he looked at the spy, his eyes narrowing as he spoke. "Come to think of it, I do have something. In fact, it should help reinforce Operation Cozen."

Drew grunted at the mention of Cozen. This had been the code name for the disinformation-misinformation operation meant to deceive the Zodarks into thinking the Republic was stronger than they really were. It was hoped this deception would buy the Republic more time to continue building out the fleet it needed to defeat the Zodark threat and assert Republic dominance of the alliance. Since they were several years into peace between the two sides, it appeared to be working.

"We have a situation developing in a system on the other side of the alliance's territory—extremely far from our own," Hunt explained. "Normally, I would avoid having the alliance intervene directly in a border skirmish, but given the strategic value of this particular system, it isn't something we can allow to fall into enemy hands. It would open a dangerous new front the alliance writ large would suddenly have to scramble to defend against. But circling back to your question about coming up with something we could have Ashurina pass off to her hander—this could present us with a real opportunity to lay an ambush should the Zodarks take the bait."

Drew seemed to like the idea, but he hesitated a moment. "Before I ask about the particulars, what happens if the Zodarks don't take the bait?"

"That's a good point. Then I guess we'd have to wait and see if someone else does. Say the Orbots do, then that tells us something too."

"It does?" Drew countered, his left eyebrow raised.

"Yes, it confirms the Zodarks *do* share intelligence with them," Hunt explained. "Maybe not everything, and maybe it's just a one-way street. But if the Zodarks think it's valuable enough to share, but not necessarily valuable enough for them to action themselves, that does give us some insight into the relationship between them. Particularly when what we're going to have Ashurina pass on would be something very, very precise, something that could only come from someone on the inside. That's how we would be able to verify it had been passed along."

"OK, Viceroy, you've got my interest. Why don't you tell me about this problem and the kind of trap you think we can lure the Zodarks or someone else in the Dominion into."

Hunt stood and walked over to grab something from his desk. When he sat back at the table, he pulled up a flattened version of the stargate map for them to look at. It was an expansive digital map representing all the stargates within the Milky Way galaxy. All of the alliance-controlled territories were shaded in blue while the Dominion-controlled areas were marked in red. However, some of the border systems were marked in crosshatches of both colors.

"Whoa. I think this is the first time I've ever seen the Milky Way broken down like this," Drew exclaimed in surprise as he examined the map. Hunt watched him study it for a moment, not saying anything. Then Drew looked at him, his eyes betraying sudden awareness and a bit of fear as he commented, "Looking at the entire galaxy laid out like this—it doesn't look good for the Republic, does it?"

"No, it doesn't," Hunt answered grimly. "The size of the Republic territory in relation to those in our alliance and the Milky Way gives you a sense of how small we truly are in the grand scheme of things."

"Yeah, exactly," Drew agreed. "Sort of puts it all in perspective."

"It's meant to. It gives you an idea of what we're up against. As the Viceroy, the one man who likely has the best view of the entire situation, I look at this map and see that humanity is but one or two military disasters away from a life of servitude—or extinction. This game we play, Drew—it's for everything. It's for the survival of the human race. That's why Operation Cozen is so important," Hunt explained somberly, a heaviness hanging from every word.

"I want to highlight something for you and explain an idea I just came up with," Hunt explained before reaching down to interact with the holographic map directly.

He zoomed in on a part of the map, and the rest of it faded away into the background, leaving just the portion he wanted them to look at. A single system had three different stargates. One led to a Tully-controlled system, one to the Ry'lians, and a third traveled down into Dominion territory.

"This is called Serpentis," Hunt explained. "It's a Tully controlled system, but one of its stargates connect to a race we've never encountered before called the Pharaonis, a member of the Dominion forces. *This* is our nugget."

Hunt did some calculations and wrote some notes in his Qpad before he continued. "Drew, I want you to tell Ashurina that the Republic will be sending some ships there to deal with a border dispute: fourteen warships and twenty-eight transports. That's two orbital assault divisions, eight heavy transports with the division's heavy equipment and supplies for a twelve-month peacekeeping mission, and twenty of our brand-new orbital assault ships ferrying the ground force of approximately fifty thousand soldiers."

39

"This should work, Miles. I'll keep you updated." And with that, Drew got up and left the office.

As his RI operative left the room, Miles continued working out the details of the plan he'd just set in motion. He was hoping that once the Zodarks learned that was all the support the Republic would be sending to shore up the defenses guarding a vital chokepoint leading into alliance space, they would be enticed to join forces with the Pharaonis, or even the Orbots, and head to Serpentis. The figures he'd given Drew were accurate, but they intentionally left out some vital information. Miles had an ambush in mind.

I'll have to bring Pandolly in on this, Miles realized. *He'll need to make sure he brings a sufficient force with him to follow ours.*

If they could lure the Zodarks into taking the bait, the alliance could really hammer them. Miles mentally nicknamed this plan Operation Snare. It was a dry run before they could execute Operation Rapacious and put an end to the Zodark threat along their border once and for all.

If this works ...Rapacious will be a go.

Chapter Four
The Warbots

Range Two
Titan Military Training Center
Saturn VI, Sol System

Fleet Admiral Chester Bailey led the group of officers and politicians into the auditorium. Today's event was the culmination of years of work and billions of Republic dollars. He was eager to show off their progress to the senators who controlled the purse strings. It was important for them to see that their money was being well spent.

As they all walked into the massive room, the first thing they saw was the floor-to-ceiling window stretching across the front of it. A few in their party gasped in delight as they looked beyond the window at the view of the surface of Titan. It stretched for miles in nearly all directions. Bailey smiled. The blackness of space contrasted against the twinkle of stars, the dust and rocks that composed the rings of Saturn, and the planet itself—it instilled awe in him as well.

Bailey watched General Pilsner as he talked excitedly with a couple of senators about the coming tests. This was Pilsner's pet project—his strategy to protect the lives of his soldiers while also increasing the lethality of his ground forces. He and Bailey hadn't always gotten along throughout the years, but Bailey had never doubted Pilsner's dedication to providing for and protecting his people. He was a soldier's soldier through and through.

The group looked out the windows while people moved about the room. Then a voice declared over the speakers, "Attention! Attention! The exercise will begin in ten minutes. All personnel must exit the range now."

The base protocol officer approached Bailey from the side and caught his attention.

"Excuse me, Admiral. A group of chairs have been reserved for everyone. If you'd like to take a seat, I can get everyone something to drink."

Bailey spotted the seats, midway up the risers. "Thank you, Lieutenant. Great seats, by the way. I'll take a coffee, black, if it's not too much trouble."

"I'll take the same," echoed Pilsner along with a few others in the group.

Pilsner looked giddy with excitement as he led the way to their seats.

"This is great, Admiral. I'm so glad you were able to join us for this demonstration. Really means a lot to us knuckle draggers."

Bailey chuckled. "I wouldn't miss this for anything. Lord knows I need to get out of Space Command more often. I'm just glad you let me tag along and see how you grunts fight wars down on the planets below."

The soldiers laughed at the running joke between spacers and soldiers. Despite the difference in how they fought, neither could accomplish their missions without the other.

"Here's your coffee, Admiral. Let me know if you need anything else," the steward offered.

"Thank you, Petty Officer. I hope you get a chance to enjoy the show."

Bailey held the coffee for a moment before taking a sip. Leaning back in the seat, he took in the scene unfolding around him. The place had become a flurry of activity as they neared the start of the exercise. A lot was riding on how it turned out.

As the minutes ticked down, a colonel from DARPA and Lane Walburg, the CEO of Walburg Industries, addressed the group.

Lane stepped forward, speaking first. "Good afternoon, General Pilsner, Admiral Bailey, and distinguished guests. Before the exercise begins, I'd like to take a moment to thank General Pilsner for pushing us as a company to find ways to improve upon the C100 program. As you all know, the combat synthetic humanoid soldier program saw extensive combat during the last war. It arguably saved the lives of hundreds of thousands if not millions of soldiers. Today, however, marks what we hope will become the next evolution in the synthetic soldier program.

"The C300 is not only deadlier than its predecessor; its survivability in combat all but ensures this will be the Army's go-to weapon for generations to come. What makes the C300 different is the new armor. Working with Space Command and DARPA, we were given access to the classified material used in our newest warships—Bronkis5. I believe everyone in this room is familiar with the material, so I won't go into detail about how it works. Suffice it to say, with higher survivability and the integration of the new Slayer triple-one battle rifle, the C300 will accomplish more with less. Pending the final approval from General Pilsner, Walburg Industries stands ready to start full-serial production. Now I'll hand it over to Colonel Noam, the project lead from DARPA."

"Thank you, Lane," said Colonel Noam. "I'm not going to rehash what's already been said. This exercise will demonstrate why it's time to phase out the C100s for the newer variant. The capabilities between the two platforms couldn't be clearer, and once the exercise starts, you'll see why."

A holographic map of the range appeared. "Here's the scenario we're going to demonstrate. In the center is the base. It's protected by fortified positions, to include automated gun towers, minefields, and two hundred C100s. The first exercise consists of twenty C300s tasked with capturing the base. The second exercise is a role reversal. Then it'll be twenty C300s defending against a force of two hundred—"

Admiral Bailey interrupted, "Colonel, isn't that a bit much? Seems a ten-to-one ratio is a setup for failure, isn't it?"

"No, not at all, Admiral. That's the whole point of the demonstration—to show you how big of a difference these new *warbots*, as we like to call them, will make. In fact, let's turn our attention to the window and see for ourselves. The exercise is about to start."

Did he really just call them warbots?

Admiral Bailey nodded slowly at the explanation. Then the show got underway—brilliant flashes of light, explosions, and streaks of laser light illuminated the battlefield.

Before he allowed himself to get sucked into watching the event unfold, Bailey looked at the people around him, trying to gauge their initial reactions. Their gazes shifted to watch the exercise unfold across the large monitors strategically positioned around the room. The video images had actually been broken down to give them several point-of-view angles. One looked to be a helmet camera view from one of the C300s. Another appeared to be a video drone following behind a couple of the attackers from a slightly elevated position, allowing the observers to see a broader picture of the fight these machines would be waging. A third image seemed to be another drone feed—positioned off-center near a couple of automated sentry towers near the middle of the base. The fourth and final image was from a drone high overhead, looking down on the base and allowing the observers to watch the progress of the multipronged attack.

While most people were watching the action on the monitors, Bailey saw a few of them who appeared to be more fascinated with watching the entire thing unfold with their own eyes—staring through the massive floor-to-ceiling windows as the warbots began their assault just a kilometer away. Bailey wasn't sure why someone would choose to watch through the window when clearly the monitors would give you a better view. But his own eyes lingered on the window, where he saw stabs of purplish light, blaster fire of the M-111 Slayer battle rifles intermixed with the red flashes from the blasters of the C100s and the blue streaks of light from the turbo laser towers. He found himself transfixed, unable to look away from the visual realities of the ground battle taking place not far from his own position.

So, this is what it's like to be on the ground…battling it out with the enemy in close-quarters battle, he thought. This demonstration was a reminder of how different the worlds of combat were between starships in space and the run-of-the-mill soldier down on the surface of a planet.

Bailey looked on with something between awe, terror, and abject horror as he saw the totality of the exercise unfold and marveled at how quickly it had turned into a lopsided victory. *My God…these things truly are warbots—the destroyers of men.*

General Pilsner had been right. Adding the Bronkis5 material to the synthetic soldier program would be a game changer. He'd fought against Pilsner's idea to use Bronkis5, believing that it should be reserved solely for warship construction. But watching how these new warbots, these C300s, cut through defenders lightning fast, and seeing how blaster bolts and magrail slugs bounced off their armor—it left little doubt in his mind that this was the future of the Republic Army. He felt terrible for not having backed this program sooner to give the infantry soldiers every available tool and resource they might need to defeat the enemies of tomorrow—and the Zodarks.

Watching as two of the C300 warbots just absolutely crushed their opposition, Bailey couldn't help but wonder if they might reach a point where human soldiers could eventually be phased out entirely in favor of these *warbots,* as Mr. Walburg had referred to them.

Damn, that name is now going to be stuck in my head.

When the final defensive positions had been overrun or destroyed, Colonel Noam signaled for the endex or end of exercise command to be sent to the C300s. He then walked to the center of the room and reviewed what they'd just seen. While he regaled them with statistics and facts gained from the exercise, range maintenance personnel were already hard at work, resetting the range for the role reversal they'd watch next.

While Colonel Noam continued to speak, Bailey observed the collaborative work taking place between the human and synthetic workers spread out over the remains of the range. In all his years in the military and during his many visits to the seemingly never-ending sprawl of the Titan Military Training Center, Bailey had never actually seen what went into maintaining and resetting the dozens upon dozens of different types of ranges the training facility was known for. He became so engrossed in watching them that he lost track of what Colonel Noam was saying.

A few minutes later, the second exercise got underway. The C100s carried out their role reversal, with only slight tactical deviations in how they assaulted the base. The C100s had a precision and skill that had been honed by the thousands of battles and skirmishes fought throughout the Dominion War. They pressed home their attack across multiple axes of attack against the defending force of just twenty warbots.

Bailey had thought the attackers might have fared better considering the ten-to-one attack ratio, but as in the previous engagement, their weapons simply couldn't punch through the new variants' armor. They'd get lucky from time to time, but luck wasn't something you relied on to win a battle or war. While one observer commented on how he would have liked to have seen the C100s use the new M-111 battle rifles like the C300s, Colonel Noam was quick to point out that the existing battle rifles were comparable to what the Zodarks and Orbots were still using.

While they watched the final skirmishes continue to play out, General Pilsner leaned closer to whisper something out of earshot of the others.

"Bailey, I know we've had our differences and we fought a good deal over the Bronkis5 material for this program. Please tell me that after seeing these two scenarios play out, you see why I pushed so hard for this."

"Yeah, I do, John," Bailey acknowledged. "I was wrong to push back against you—I can see that now. These killing machines—they change everything."

"Exactly, Bailey. We have to shift away from the C100s and put our entire focus on this new version. If the Viceroy's intelligence about the Dominion is right—"

"I know, I know. We may not have much longer," Bailey countered.

He didn't need a reminder about the war looming on the horizon. He'd just dispatched an expeditionary force to link up with their Altairian allies and reinforce a star system in Tully space against a potential Dominion invasion that might restart the whole war again. No matter how desperate for peace the Republic was, a battle looked to be brewing on the horizon, and he wasn't sure there was anything he could do to stop it.

"I agree with you, John," Bailey repeated. "Thank you for inviting me to see this demonstration with my own eyes. When we get back to Space Command, I'll back your request. We'll work with Walburg Industries and get the entire production line of C100s converted over to the new C300 models. We're going to get your guys these new warbots. In the meantime, John, keep your knuckle draggers primed and ready to go. This Serpentis expedition could turn into a real mess, and God only knows if it's the precursor to something larger. Something tells me these Zodark bastards wouldn't hesitate to flatten our home if given the chance."

Chapter Five
Lab Site X

RNS *Voyager*
En Route to Lab Site X

Dr. Katō Sakura stood on the bridge with her increasingly serious life partner, Jack Walker, and Dr. Katherine Johnson. Their travel to this yet-undiscovered Humtar lab site was almost complete. Soon they'd have their first glance of the planet where the data packet from Alpha Centauri had been sent. The anticipation was palpable.

What will it look like? Sakura wondered. She'd spent days dreaming about this planet, talking over her visions endlessly with Jack, who deserved sainthood for his patience with her ramblings. She was grateful to have someone who shared her wonder for uncovering the new and mysterious.

Dr. Audrey Lancaster had deciphered the ancient Humtar name of this planet, but Himzurleppak was a mouthful, so Sakura and her team had just continued calling their destination "Lab Site X." It seemed fitting: an unknown variable.

"Approaching destination," announced the navigations officer, Lieutenant Natasha Koval.

"Put it on screen and let's begin scans," ordered Captain Hans Gruber.

"Yes, sir."

An enormous ocean appeared to cover an entire hemisphere of the planet, so much so that they couldn't initially see any land at all.

"Nav, angle around to the other side of the planet. Let's see if we can't find some signs of civilization," Gruber directed.

"Aye, sir."

The butterflies in Sakura's stomach intensified. As they rounded the planet, a huge ring of mountains came into view…followed by a sea of sand.

"I don't understand," Sakura remarked. "This was an agrarian society…are we at the right location?"

"Yes, ma'am. The coordinates match those you shared with us," the nav officer replied.

"Katherine…" Sakura's voice trailed off. The sea of sand was punctuated only by the occasional rocky crag that was tall enough to pierce the desert below.

"I don't know what to say," was all Katherine could manage. She put a hand on Sakura's shoulder and the two of them looked on in utter disappointment. Jack said nothing but stoically held Sakura's hand.

"Well, ladies, I'm sure this is not what you were hoping to find, but if anything remains of this Lab Site X—this ship will find it," said Captain Gruber, in a far more encouraging tone than he usually mustered.

Initial signals intelligence scans didn't yield any results, so the *Voyager* launched its many satellites that had been configured for this expedition. If there were any unusual heat signatures or electrical impulses, they would eventually uncover them.

"This might take a while," Gruber announced after some time had elapsed. "Perhaps you'd like to grab a bite to eat or take some rest. I'll be sure to let you know as soon as we have something."

"All right, Captain," Katherine agreed. She practically had to drag Sakura with her, but eventually, she realized she wouldn't be speeding anything up by just waiting around.

Sakura decided that the best way to get the nervous energy out would be to go for a hard run in the simulator. The technology had really improved in recent years—she could almost believe that she was running along the Tamagawa in Tokyo, Japan, near where she had grown up. Jack offered to join her, but in this moment, she really wanted to be alone and to clear her head.

What happened to this planet? Sakura wondered as she pushed her body harder, her muscles straining to keep up with the mental drive that she had. She hoped this whole adventure wasn't some wild goose chase.

As she raced along, her breathing steadied, and she reached an almost Zen-like state where she didn't feel her body anymore. She was simply enjoying the views of the cherry blossoms near the river.

Sakura finished up her run and then headed back to her quarters. She was drenched in sweat and desperately needed a shower. Sakura wasn't all that surprised when Jack decided to join her—he did always seem to know how to make her feel better about life.

When they'd finished, they cuddled in their bed together. Jack seemed to be very deep in thought. "What's on your mind, love?" Sakura inquired.

"I know that you were unnerved by the unexpected appearance of the planet," he began. "It makes the future here uncertain."

"Yes, I…I didn't think it would be barren like this. I mean, I guess I didn't expect everything to be untouched after so many years either, but this is certainly a curveball."

"Well, that got me thinking about my own future," Jack explained.

"I'm not sure that I follow you."

"Sakura, I don't know what the future holds—but I know I want to spend the rest of it with you." He reached over to the nightstand and pulled out a box with a ring in it. "I know that you've said a piece of paper doesn't mean that much to you, but I want you to know that I am committed. I am not going anywhere. Sakura…will you marry me?"

She hesitated for just the briefest of moments. *What would my father say?* she asked herself. And then she realized she didn't care. Jack was the right man for her, and there was only one possible response.

"Yes," she replied, tears forming in her eyes. She'd never thought a relationship could bring her this much happiness, but every day with Jack was a pleasant surprise.

They made love again and fell asleep in each other's arms.
****

Sakura's communicator beeped, waking her. "Sakura," she replied as she hit the button.

"We found something," Gruber responded curtly.

"I'll be right up," she answered.

Only a few short minutes later, she and Jack were appropriately clothed and standing on the bridge. "What do you have for us?" Sakura asked.

A lieutenant who managed the signals intelligence spoke up. "Initially, we didn't pick up anything on our scans, but then we widened our parameters. Using what we know about the power generator you uncovered at the previous Humtar lab, we were able to pick up an energy signature that matches."

"Is it active?" Sakura inquired incredulously.

"Probably not. A nuclear reactor will give off energy for centuries after it's been decommissioned—this is likely refractory energy from a previously active power plant."

"So where is it coming from?" Sakura pressed.

"We have it narrowed down to this quadrant over here, near this particular mountainous cluster," Gruber announced. Something about the way he'd made the comment made Sakura feel like he was holding something back.

"But?" asked Sakura.

Just then, Katherine appeared on the bridge, her hair somewhat askew and her uniform not in its usual tidy state. She immediately caught sight of the ring on Sakura's hand and the two women exchanged a glance. They'd have to catch up later. "What'd I miss?" Katherine asked.

"It looks like we're going to have to send some teams down to the surface," Captain Gruber explained.

****

Dr. Katherine Johnson's Private Quarters
RNS *Voyager*
En Route to Lab Site X

There weren't a lot of places on board a ship for private girl talk, so Sakura decided to visit her friend in her quarters.

"All right, Sakura—you first. Tell me about this ring you're sporting on your finger," Katherine said with an excited smile.

"What can I say?" Sakura remarked giddily. "I'm not sure I ever planned to get married, honestly, but when he asked me, I realized I do want to spend the rest of my life with him. Things have been getting more serious for a while, and I guess I'm just at a point where formalizing the relationship makes sense."

"You sound so clinical about the whole thing," Katherine joked.

"Well, you may be right," Sakura conceded, "but at the end of the day, being with Jack makes me happy, and that's enough."

"Don't leave out the details—how did he ask?" Katherine probed.

Sakura told her the whole story, play by play, much to Katherine's apparent delight. Then Sakura leaned back, coyly crossed her arms and said, "All right, so I know I wasn't seeing things—you can't get out of this. Why was your uniform all messed up earlier? Who is he?"

Katherine tried not to laugh but did so anyway. "That obvious, huh? Who knew I'd be having a fling with an Army captain at my age?" she responded cheerfully.

"You're together with Captain Aaron Young?" Sakura questioned skeptically. "I mean, don't get me wrong—he's very physically attractive, but, well, he's just so much younger than you."

"You aren't wrong," Katherine replied with a smirk and a nod. "Forty years ago, this kind of age gap would have been unthinkable for me in even a casual relationship, but now with all the advancements in medical nanites and all the other antiaging technology we have access to, age is just a number."

"Yeah, I guess you're right...so how long has this been going on?"

"Well, you remember how Captain Gruber warned us that all the soldiers on board were unhappy about being stuck doing babysitting duty?" asked Katherine.

"Yes, I remember."

"So, I started spending time with Captain Young to see if there was anything I could do to help increase the morale—"

"Sounds like you sure increased *his* morale," Sakura shot back, snickering.

Katherine took the ribbing in stride. "Yeah, well, he increased mine too. We've been 'liaising' pretty much this entire trip."

"Wait, so is this an actual 'thing'?" Sakura pressed.

Katherine didn't answer right away. "Actually, I'm not sure. I do enjoy spending time with him, and not just under the sheets—although the chemistry there is unlike any I've ever experienced. Aaron was drafted into the Army at the start of the Dominion War with the Zodarks. He did something heroic and received a battlefield commission to lieutenant. Then he made captain the year before the peace and decided to stay in the military and make it a career. I love his Southern drawl and his Alabama charm. We come from different worlds, but somehow, it does make sense—at least for now." Her eyes drifted off, and she seemed to be pondering the situation.

"The thing about interplanetary travel is it exposes you to people you might not otherwise have met," said Sakura. "I never would

have met Jack living on Earth. I probably would have ended up in a relationship with an academic of some type, who would have intellectually stimulated me but been far inferior as a life partner. Soak it up, Katherine. Just let it be. If it's meant to go the distance, it will."
****

Lab Site X
Planet Surface

Although the atmosphere of Lab Site X was comprised of a gaseous blend that was breathable by humans, the entire party had to keep their helmets on due to the high level of particulate matter swirling about in the air. Sakura had no desire to have long-term respiratory problems and was very happy to leave her helmet on. A few of the younger recon soldiers who had gone down in the Osprey to secure a landing site before Sakura and her team arrived had apparently been a bit harder to convince of the necessity, but the HUDs provided additional utility with the option of infrared scanning, which would be particularly helpful if they got caught up in a sandstorm.

At the moment, the air was fairly still; only the occasional gust kicked up some sand. Still, they were going to have to be careful in utilizing their drone—its radar, lidar, X-ray, and thermal scanning wouldn't work for long in this type of environment, so they had to narrow down where they wanted to use the thing before they deployed it.

Before they had landed dirtside, the *Voyager*'s scanners and the satellites they'd deployed upon arrival in orbit had given them a rough area to investigate. There was a cluster of mountainous outcroppings that surrounded a collection of some of the few visible lakes on the planet; somewhere in that region was where they needed to be.

To Sakura, everything was brown or gray on this planet: the sandy dirt, the rocks, the air itself—even the water looked muddy and gross. There were a few plants scattered throughout, especially near the lakes, but even those were pale and emaciated. Maybe there was still some animal life present near Lab Site X, but Sakura sure didn't notice any.

What the hell happened here? she wondered. The information she had read on this planet had led her to believe there would be lush growth from all the years of farming. Instead, she found herself standing in a barren wasteland.

As the group fanned out, utilizing various types of handheld scanners, Sakura wondered how long it would take to find anything here. *Will this just turn out to be a massive dead end?*

Hours stretched by with very little happening. The further they searched, the more they had to communicate with each other through their coms. Given the nature of the storms they were beginning to encounter, the need to set up a more robust communication system was becoming apparent. Eventually, they had to set up camp and call it a night.

The tents they used were tightly sealed and had two special chambers for entering and exiting that would filter out all the particulate matter to keep the living areas clean. The process took a while, so they had to be sure that they wanted to come in or leave before they did so. Once inside, though, they could finally take off their helmets and kick back.

The accommodations were Spartan but adequate for their purpose. All they really needed was a place to sleep, eat, and take care of hygiene needs. Sakura hoped they wouldn't be staying there too long—bunk beds weren't really her thing, but she could sacrifice her comfort in the name of science for a time. A more permanent camp would be established should they find something of note worth digging toward.

The following morning, they ate breakfast and reviewed the grid searches before setting out. With the monotonous nature of the landscape, Sakura tried hard to steer away from a pessimistic attitude as they went out for the day.

Minutes turned into hours, and hours turned into days. An entire week went by with very little activity. Sakura started to wonder if the ship's scanners had misled them. Finally, on day nine, one of the scientists notified the group that he thought he could see a warm spot with his infrared imaging device.

Everyone raced over to the location in question. Within twenty minutes, they had the drone up overhead, doing the work it had been designed for. The wind was a bit stronger than on previous days, which made Sakura anxious, but the drone operator assured her that the conditions were still within the device's limitations.

When Sakura saw the imaging from the drone, she shuddered. There was definitely an energy signature below them, approximately ten meters under where they stood. But surrounding that energy signature were *dozens* of tiny heat signatures.

"Something is alive down there," she remarked. "Who knows if whatever those are will pose a threat to us, but we will have to tread lightly."

Chapter Six
Into the Hornets

Task Force Five
RNS *Vanguard*
Approaching Serpentis System

Newly promoted Commodore Amy Dobbs sat in her captain's chair, relishing every minute of this new warship and the task force she now led. As she sat back in the overly comfortable chair, she marveled at the quality of the high-definition monitors spread at different positions and angles on the bridge. Each of them displayed relevant information to the workstations and crews manning them.

Stretched across the front wall of the bridge was the main monitor. It was nearly floor-to-ceiling in height, and it extended across more than half the width of the bridge. Given the screen's massive size, the display could either show a single image, giving an almost panoramic view to those on the bridge, or be broken down into three separate segments. What made the monitor more advanced than those on the previous ships she'd served on was the rich detail and quality of the images it displayed. Watching the forward camera view of the *Vanguard* traveling through slip space was almost a spiritual experience; the images were stunning, unrivaled in their crispness.

Right now, Dobbs was staring at the most intense, richly detailed colors—oranges, purples, reds, blues, and even green ribbons of color that flitted about the bubble encasing the *Vanguard* as they were squeezed through slip space towards their destination. Throughout her thirty-one-year career in the Fleet, she'd conducted hundreds of FTL jumps. All told, she'd probably spent months inside the bubbles of slip space, allowing her to traverse the heavens now available to them. Watching the colors dance as they interacted with the fringes of the bubble was something she never grew tired of. It was almost hypnotic.

Pulling her eyes away from the monitor, Dobbs looked down at her commander's display. It was a new piece of Altairian tech, as were many of the *Vanguard*'s various systems. Her ship, the flagship for her squadron, was the most recently commissioned Republic naval battleship. It was part of the new crop of Altairian-Human hybrid warships the Republic had been building over the last ten years. The

Vanguard was the ninth of these new battleships to come off the line, with many more soon to follow in her wake.

Three weeks after taking command of the *Vanguard*, Dobbs had received an alert from Admiral Halsey to prepare her warship for an extended deployment. There was an alliance task force being formed up by the Altairians to handle some sort of border interdiction problem in a region of space Dobbs had never heard of. When the orders were made official, she'd suddenly found herself promoted to commodore and placed in command of a squadron of fourteen warships in addition to twenty-eight assault ships and heavy transports. These noncombatant ships were the ones ferrying the two Republic Army orbital assault divisions and their necessary support units and equipment that would comprise the ground component to this allied expeditionary force. It was a daunting task, escorting so many soldiers into what could be a war zone if the Dominion really did decide to invade the system.

What Dobbs really wanted for this mission was more ships to escort such a large number of troop ships and transports. Instead, she was given fourteen warships to provide escort support to twelve of the brand-new *Izumo*-class heavy troop assault ships and eight of their regular battle-tested *America*-class troop assault ships that had seen heavy use during the last war. The newer *Izumo* heavy ships could ferry two regiments and their accompanying equipment, effectively doubling the combat power of the older *America*-, *Yushen*-, *Mistral*-, and *Albion*-class ships. Those transports had been the workhorses of the Republic, shuttling the hundreds of orbital assault battalions and regiments across the stars throughout the war. It was an enormous task she'd just been given, and it was the chance of a lifetime to lead a task force of warships during a peacetime deployment along the neutral zone.

As Dobbs sat in the captain's chair of the *Vanguard*, she pushed aside the thoughts, concerns, and doubts she'd harbored weeks earlier. The time since she'd received her new orders and mission had gone by in the blink of an eye. She'd been given a mission, and she intended on completing it.

Once they had gotten underway after a few false starts—delays on the Army's part—they'd essentially traveled along the stargate network, weaving their way through portions of Altairian space until they eventually entered the Tully's territory. While she had concerns about being able to provide an adequate escort for the number of ships the Army was using, the majority of their trip was too deep inside alliance territory to be threatened by an Orbot base ship—the ones equipped with a wormhole generator. It wasn't until they entered the Tully system of Serpentis, their end destination, that they had to be worried about a possible Orbot attack.

While both the Altairians and the Orbots had ships capable of generating wormholes, neither side had an abundance of them. They were also limited technologically in how many light-years away they could create a wormhole or bridge to. This meant both sides were still somewhat constrained in how far they could bypass the existing stargates and each other's traps or fortifications they had established at the various chokepoints. The only starship presently in the Milky Way that wasn't faced with this constraint was the Gallentine Titan-class ship—the RNS *Freedom*. Being that only seven had ever been created, even these ships were extremely rare and limited in their use. But there was no denying that having the *Freedom* had just swung the tactical and strategic advantage in the Galactic Empire's direction, at least within the Milky Way.

Aside from the humans, the bulk of the sentient races within the Dominion or the Galactic Empire were usually found in systems with direct connections to one or more stargates. Few societies ventured too many light-years away from the stargate systems—most of the space beyond them was typically considered the Badlands or the Wilds, depending on which race you asked. It was likely Earth's location, so far removed from the network, that had allowed the humans to grow and develop unencumbered for so long.

As they approached the linkup point with her Altairian counterparts, Dobbs hoped like hell the Altairians were bringing a larger complement of warships than she was. Should this peacekeeping mission along the neutral zone turn into something more, she wanted to make sure the transports she was escorting would be properly protected. She still had nightmares about that fleet of reinforcements she'd been escorting to Alfheim in the Sirius system when the Orbots and Zodarks had reinvaded the system. The enemy force had jumped practically into the middle of the fleet they had been escorting. They'd lost more than half their transports—some twenty thousand Republic Army soldiers had died in minutes as their troop assault ships were savaged by Zodark and Orbot cruisers and battleships. Her own ship had barely escaped the battle—retreating all the way back to the Primord system of Kita. While casualties inflicted by the army fighting down on the surface could rack up quickly during a big battle or campaign, in space, they tended to occur in large quantities all at once when a ship or a group of them was destroyed.

Shaking her head to rid herself of the memories of that horrible day of days, Dobbs found herself momentarily lost in the colors of light dancing around the *Vanguard*. She looked away to check one of the clocks mounted near the side of the bridge monitor—the time until their arrival and linkup with their allies was steadily counting down to zero. The closer it got, the sooner they'd drop out of slip space.

I guess we'll see what kind of fleet the Altairians brought to the party, she thought.

The voice of her helmsman, Ensign Godley, announced to the bridge, "Exiting slip space in three…two…one…and we're out."

The lights swirling around the *Vanguard* flicked off like a switch, and the ship emerged from the bubble into the blackness of space.

"Commodore, engineering confirms the transition from FTL to impulse thrusters complete. We're ready to get underway," Godley reported.

"Thank you, Ensign. Let's get the engines warmed up and get on the move. Bring us to twenty-five percent power on a bearing toward the gate. Oh, and pull up an aft image. I want to see the rest of the squadron arrive."

"Aye, ma'am. Impulse engines to twenty-five percent. New course set for the gate, bridge image now looking aft."

Dobbs and the rest of the bridge crew looked at the monitor displaying the rear of the battleship. Flashes of light appeared against the emptiness of the void as thirteen warships emerged from slip space. Moments later, more flashes began to appear; the remaining twenty-eight ships of her task force had arrived.

It was time to get the *Vanguard* and the rest of their squadron spun up and ready for whatever might come next. Disconnecting her chair's restraints, Dobbs rose to her feet, issuing rapid-fire commands to the department chiefs covering the CIC, coms, and electronic warfare sections.

Approaching her coms officer, Dobbs directed, "Lieutenant Waldman, get us a head count and establish coms with our ships and the

Altairians. Tell our frigates to fan out and take up their screening positions on the flanks of the transports."

"Aye, ma'am, I'm on it."

She smiled at Waldman's eagerness.

Pivoting from his station to the ship's CIC, Dobbs saw that Commander Wright was already ahead of her. He was directing the spacers within the combat information center, checking in on each section and making sure everything was running properly.

Dobbs felt confident as she watched him take control of the situation. Wright was a competent manager and an excellent officer. She'd gotten lucky when she'd been able to snag him to be her XO. They'd worked together on the *Battleaxe* in the past. Having some of her former crew from the older *Rook*-class battlecruiser gave her comfort. It meant at least half of her crew had combat experience from the previous war—something that might aid them in whatever might happen next.

"Commodore, the TAM is up," Commander Wright announced, speaking of the tactical action map. "Altairian fleet identified; they're positioned next to the stargate. I'm bringing them up on the main screen now."

Dobbs acknowledged Wright's update about the tactical action map, then turned her attention to the bridge monitor.

Whoa, that's a lot of ships, thought Dobbs. *Admiral Halsey was right...they were sending a large fleet.* Now she was starting to wonder if they knew something she didn't, considering the sheer size of the fleet arrayed near the gate. This looked more like an invasion fleet than a peacekeeping convoy along the neutral zone.

Lieutenant Waldman intruded on her thoughts. "Ma'am, we've established coms with the task force. All ships report green status, awaiting orders. We're also being hailed by the Altairian's warship, *Digimon CS1*. It's Admiral Pandolly's ship—he's requested to speak with you immediately."

Digimon CS1? she asked herself. *Ah...Command Ship 1. Oh, and that battleship must be his second-in-command, Berkimon CS2.* She'd forgotten how the Altairians named their warships and identified which ones were the command ships. The *Digimon* was an Altairian supercarrier while the *Berkimon* was one of their heavy battleship-class ships. Both warships packed a hell of a lot more firepower than the

Republic warships of old. Her *Vanguard* was essentially a *Berkimon*, just modified for human functionality.

"Thank you, Lieutenant," Dobbs replied to Waldman. "Go ahead and put the admiral through on the main monitor."

Moments later, the image of Admiral Pandolly appeared on the bridge. He was seated in his chair, a swirl of activity happening around him as he spoke rapidly to someone off screen before he turned to look at her. She was no expert in understanding the facial expressions of their Altairian allies, but she'd been told when you saw their lips taut, exposing the tops of their front teeth, that was usually a pensive or stressed look.

Something's gone wrong, she thought.

"Commodore Dobbs, it is good to see that you and your ships have arrived safely. There has been a new turn of events since you were given your initial orders and began your travel here," said Pandolly. "We received an emergency call for help from a Tully ship that managed to evade a surprise invasion by a Pharaonis fleet. The ship was dispatched to call for help as it would appear this activity along the neutral zone has now escalated into something more.

"Before we discuss what needs to be done next, let me bring you up to speed on what we currently know." Dobbs nodded along, hoping the situation wasn't as bleak as he was making it sound. "Approximately five days ago, the Pharaonis launched a full-scale invasion of the system. Eight of the nine Tully warships defending the planet were overwhelmed and destroyed during the first day of the invasion. A single Tully frigate was able to escape through the gate and launch a communications probe containing all the relevant information they had been able to collect on the enemy disposition.

"This turn of events has obviously altered the original plan. I am sending a proposal to modify our original deployment to the system. If you can please review it with your ground commander after this call and get back to me today, that would be helpful. I ordered one of my frigates into the system a couple of days ago to assess the situation. It returned a few hours before you arrived. While in the system, they received an urgent plea for help from the Tully garrison down on the planet. It appears they have been under siege now for the last five days."

While Pandolly continued to speak, Dobbs reviewed the report he'd sent. It didn't look good. The Pharaonis had moved a considerable force into the system. The one bright spot was that the report didn't outline any sign of Orbot ships. They'd been used to circumvent the outposts around the gate, but it didn't look like they were still involved in the retaking of the system.

"Commodore, I cannot rule out the possibility that an Orbot fleet is lying in wait or that the Pharaonis fleet near Serpentis-6 is bait to lure us into the system," said Pandolly, almost reading her mind. "What I would like to propose is sending your squadron in ahead of the fleet. The Pharaonis have never encountered a Republic warship before. This could be the kind of surprise that might cause them to spring their trap if it is in fact an Orbot bait-and-switch plan. If this does happen, then I will obviously jump my fleet into the system, and we will look to decisively engage the enemy and destroy their fleet. Then your ground forces can move in and assist the garrison."

Dobbs turned to her XO. "What do you think, Wright? Something like this might work."

Commander Wright slowly nodded. "It could work, ma'am. However, it's obviously a risky bet we're taking. If it *is* a trap, then we could find ourselves in a real shoot-out while we wait for Pandolly's fleet to come to our rescue—"

"Sorry if I'm intruding in the decision-making process," interrupted Commander Mitsu, their Commander, Flight Operations or C-FLO as he was commonly called. "I say we go for it. The *Vanguard* can hold its own and so can my squadrons. If this is a trap, then best to get them to spring it here and now while Pandolly has the fleet on hand to deal with it. Smashing whatever trap they think they've assembled now might bring us a few more years of peace."

Dobbs grunted at the blunt assessment. Wright had a smile on his face, apparently agreeing with their flight commander.

"OK, if you two agree, then we'll do it," Dobbs replied.

She turned back to the monitor to reply to their Altairian counterpart. "Admiral, I've conferred with my officers. We're in agreement with your proposal. I'll inform my squadron and the transports of what we're doing. If you agree, we'll leave a few ships behind to help with escorting the transports. If it's possible, I know my transports would feel a little more secure if you could detail off some of your own ships to fill in for our absence. We've obviously got a substantial ground element with us, and protecting them is my top priority."

"Yes, yes—of course, Commodore. I will detail off ten of my own ships to assist in protecting them. Your ground force is going to be needed down on the planet. If you can, please move with haste to Serpentis-6. I know the Republic has not previously fought the Pharaonis. What I can share with you is that they are ferocious warriors both in ground combat and in the way they fight their warships. However, unless their warships have undergone upgrades from the Orbots, your ships should be more than a match for them. My tactical officer is transmitting some data to your ship now. It will provide you with some information on their warships and how they fight as well as some information on their ground forces. This last piece should aid your soldiers once they land on the planet. Do you have any further questions before I end our call?"

Dobbs shook her head. "Not presently. I think you've given us everything we need for now."

"Excellent, then please hurry. I fear the Tully garrison will not last much longer. Oh, Commodore, once your squadron engages the Pharaonis, do not hesitate to call for reinforcements. My fleet will stand by near the gate—ready to assist once you send the word."

Once Pandolly ended the connection, Dobbs's crew snapped into overdrive as they got the *Vanguard* prepared for its first time in combat. This battle shaping up would be the first time the Altairian-Human hybrid ships would fight a battle for survival. They'd spent years training on the new ships and their many weapon systems—now they'd put that training to use against an adversary they hadn't faced during the last war.

****

Task Force Silver Fox
Expeditionary Ground Force
RNS *Wasps*

Colonel Brian Royce looked over the report he'd just received. This was not turning out how they'd thought it would.

No plan survives first contact with the enemy, he thought privately.

"How bad is it?" Major Shinzo Hiro asked, a coffee stir stick hanging from the corner of his mouth.

Royce placed his Qpad down on the desk and looked up at the Ranger commander for a moment. They'd worked together in the past, during the liberation of Sumer. In fact, before Hiro's division had been converted from an orbital assault unit to the newly created Ranger division, their unit had assisted them in capturing an Orbot station above the planet Rass.

"Well, this report is from the commodore," Royce began. "I suspect we'll get a more detailed one from the general soon enough. But according to what this says, it appears we're a little late to the party. Details seem a bit sketchy, but it sounds like the garrison on the planet is under military blockade and trying to hold out for reinforcements. Not sure why the Altairians' fleet isn't going to lead the way into the system, but it looks like Dobbs, our fleet's commodore, is going to jump in and clear a path for us."

"Sounds like fun," Major Hiro remarked. "Makes me glad I'm a ground pounder and not a Fleeter."

"Yeah, the whole idea of fighting on a ship and not being able to personally shoot back at the enemy isn't something I could handle. I like being able to shoot back," Royce joked.

"Hey, by the way, have you seen what the Pharaonis look like?" Hiro asked, his voice seemingly rising an octave.

Royce picked his Qpad up, brought up an image and pointed the screen toward Hiro, who drew back from it.

"You mean these things?" asked Royce casually.

"What the hell?" Hiro practically shouted. "Warn me next time you're going to show me something like that. Those things look evil if you ask me. I'd rather be fighting Zodarks."

Royce laughed at Hiro's response to seeing the image of a Pharaonis warrior. "Yeah, they are ugly-looking bastards, that's for sure. My understanding, though, is they aren't nearly as vicious as the Zodarks, but I suppose once we encounter them, we'll find out how true that is."

Hiro's expression turned deadly serious. "All kidding aside, Royce, how are you wanting to play this once we're in orbit? Our Silver Fox contingent consists of just my Ranger battalion, and you have what, two Delta companies—eight ODA teams?"

"Technically, I've got ten ODAs. They're reinforced companies. I've also got a nine-member support staff to help me manage our SF task force—oh, let's not use that name unless we have to. Silver Fox...that's 'cause I'm getting old," Royce explained, smirking at the humor in it. "We'll be fine, Hiro. I'll find out from General Crow how he'd like us to support his ground force. Hopefully, he'll recognize we're best used as a scalpel, not a broadsword."

"OK," Hiro replied. "You know, we don't have to call our task force that. You just better come up with something clever for the general, then. But all kidding aside, I'm glad you got named as the SOF commander for this operation. I'll admit, after not hearing or seeing your name mentioned among the Deltas the past four years, I thought you may have retired or just gotten out."

Royce laughed at the idea of retiring or leaving before he'd made his fifty. He loved this job too much to walk away. But he did also have a daughter and a wife, with baby number two on the way. Part of him never wanted to leave, and the other part wanted to do whatever was necessary to ensure his family was safe and that his kids would be able to grow up in a world free of alien oppression.

"Well, I've been around," Royce explained. "After the war, I got pulled back into JSOC. The Unit's a big black hole once you're in. I ended up in charge of a section inside a former group that I was part of way back before the war and the unification of Earth. I've been running part of the Intelligence Support Activity section, doing some intel work." Royce could tell Hiro was interested in JSOC—most Deltas who hadn't served in the Unit were.

"Huh. Yeah, to us Rangers, that whole JSOC group inside the Deltas seems like an enigma. No one really knows what they do, which I guess is the whole point. But enough of that. I'm glad to see they promoted you. This crazy reduction in senior officer billets has made it damn near impossible to get promoted beyond major. Hell, after they gutted the staff and support billets, just reaching the rank alone suddenly became a milestone achievement. I got lucky when Colonel Monsoor selected me for command of 1st Battalion when Major Zbinski retired. Lord knows how much longer I might have languished at captain."

"Well, I'm glad he did, Hiro," Royce said, patting him on the shoulder. "You're a good officer, and you'll make a fine battalion commander. I can tell you that from where I sit, no one is happy with

Big Army's reorg. General Reiker told me that Fleet Admiral Bailey felt he had to do something to rein in the bureaucratic state of the military."

Royce leaned in and lowered his voice. "I was unaware of this, but did you know that between the Fleet and the Army, Space Command had swelled to over fifteen million people in uniform? I had no idea the services had grown that large. Reiker said something about the Republic needing to grow its ranks to properly support our allied partners. If you ask me, I think our allied partners need to start doing a better job of supporting *us* in this war, seeing as how we seem to be the ones...ah, never mind. Complaints are supposed to go *up* the chain, not down it," Royce grumbled, catching himself.

Major Hiro just smirked at the comment but didn't say anything. Royce appreciated that, then continued, "If you'll indulge me, Hiro, let me try and pass on a piece of advice someone more senior to me said that I've found helpful."

Hiro sat forward in his chair, eager to hear what sage wisdom Royce was about to pass on to him. Royce remembered feeling the same way when a more senior officer or NCO said the same things to him.

"Major, you're a relatively young man. You came into the Army as an officer right out of college. That means you have a very long career ahead of you if you want. That wasn't the case for me. I joined as an enlisted man, shortly after turning eighteen. I was in the Army for more than a decade when I was given a battlefield commission to lieutenant. That means I've seen how the military works from both the senior NCO ranks and now the officer side. What I can tell you with great confidence is that the higher you go in rank, the more problems and challenges you're going to face. When you're a lieutenant, you are responsible for your platoon. If you rely on your platoon sergeant while you're learning, then chances are you'll do all right. But once you become captain, now you're in charge of four platoons and the company. That means their successes become your successes, but so too do their screwups. That level of responsibility scales rapidly the higher in rank you go. But there's something else that changes the more you're promoted. You want to know what that is?"

"You become further and further removed from leading and being with your soldiers, right?"

Royce nodded approvingly. "Exactly. When Lieutenant General Reiker told me I had been selected for colonel, I wasn't sure if I should be elated at the news or cry at how it was likely going to radically change my role as a Special Forces operator. You see, I wasn't always an officer—I actually enjoy just being an operator, doing what Deltas do best. I'm also damn good at it. That's also what makes this promotion to colonel so tough and, frankly, hard to accept and be happy about it. It means my days of being in the thick of it with my guys, of being an operator…are now coming to an end, if they haven't already. You want to know why I accept that?"

Hiro looked unsure if he wanted to hear the answer. Royce pressed on, wanting to make sure Hiro understood what he was driving at.

"Influence and opportunity—that's why. You're a battalion commander now, Hiro. That means your soldiers will now look to you to exemplify what that standard for your battalion will be. If they see a pillar of resolve and the epitome of what it means to be a Ranger, if that's the standard you set, then that's what they'll mirror. The reason I'm sharing this is because it's how I'm approaching this change to my military career.

"It's hard to accept leaving behind the very thing I've spent my entire life striving to be the best at. However, we need leaders within the upper echelons of the military who have combat experience—who know what the standards are and exemplify all that we want to see within the Army we serve and the Republic we fight to protect. This war we fought…it isn't over yet—it's just on pause. We're going to need a lot of new, good officers in the upper echelons of the military if we're going to have a chance at outfoxing and defeating the Dominion Alliance. We are such a small cog in the wheel, Hiro…" Royce trailed off, leaving a moment of silence to settle between them. Then his Qpad sitting on the desk started beeping, letting him know he had an incoming call.

"Let me answer this and we can keep talking if you'd like," Royce offered before seeing the caller ID. "Never mind, it looks like Major General Crow is asking for a holo call. I suspect this is the briefing we've been told to expect. Let me connect him." Once he hit accept on the call, a four-inch holographic image appeared near the device on his desk.

The image of Major General Vernon "VC" Crow looked at Royce and Hiro before he laughed briefly. "Ha, that's good, Colonel Royce. Guess that's good timing on my part, Silver Fox. I was gonna have you brief Major Hiro on what I'm about to tell you, but since you're both there, that makes it easy. I'll be brief. I've been given some new intelligence from the Alties beyond what Dobbs sent out, and I'd like to pass it along to you two. I also have some questions about how you think I can best use your SF contingent."

Royce smiled at the man's directness. "Let me guess, sir—for all intents and purposes, the Pharaonis have already captured the planet. Right?"

Crow laughed again before answering. "Yeah, that pretty much sums it up. Those bastards couldn't hold out longer than a few days," the general confirmed before he looked off camera. "You owe me twenty credits, George. That snake-eater's smarter than you gave him credit for."

Royce looked at Hiro, who snorted at the comment. Major General Crow was the opposite of what you'd think a general should be. The South Carolinian was a crude, blunt-talking man who never lacked an opinion and almost always rubbed people the wrong way. Between that and his love affair with using parables and historical references he seemed to match to whatever situation he was in, the man was a bit of an enigma. What wasn't an enigma, though, was the man's reputation on the battlefield. He was a tactical genius, outfoxing the Zodarks on multiple occasions, and the units under his command were known for fighting like savage animals once a battle was underway.

General Crow looked back at the two of them and got down to business. "OK, Colonel, here's the deal. These *bugs* we're being told are called Pharaonis—well, they somehow managed to land a sizable force on the planet. Don't ask me how our shaggy Aussiedoodle-looking friends managed to let an invading force take over most of their planet in a couple of days, but here we are. The Alties said it looks like the Tully are trying to hold out in a couple of defensive redoubts outside the capital city, called Qu'Waffle." The general held a hand up as he tried to keep a straight face. "Yeah, you heard me right. That city name is Qu'Waffle. I made my intel guys double-check that before I doubled over in laughter. Who names a city Qu'Waffle?

"I'm sending the maps and latest intel the Alties sent me. What I need from you, Colonel, is a few suggestions on how best to employ your people. I'm a grunt, a knuckle dragger, but I'm also smart enough not to use a specialized tool like your contingent the way I would one of the regular battalions or brigades. If you've got some ideas on how best to utilize your skill sets, then I want to hear it. Otherwise, I'm just going to plug you guys in where I think you'll fit best or use you more as shock troops to clear a path for my ground pounders. Got it?"

Royce saw a smile spreading across Hiro's face. The general's words were music to their ears. "Thank you, General," Royce replied. "Give us twenty-four hours and we'll have a series of targets for you."

Crow laughed at his response, then stared back at the two of them, his face turning deadly serious. "You've got eight hours, Colonel. We hit dirtside as soon as those Fleeters clear us a path. I want you both to join me for dinner tonight, 2000 hours, and we'll go over what you guys are proposing. Out." The image of the man disappeared as he ended the call. A message popped up a second later with a map and a notification that a single file had been received.

"Damn, Royce. I heard he was a straight shooter and all, but wow," Hiro commented. "I've got a few noncoms and junior officers that might call the Altairians Alties, but he's got to be the first general officer I've heard use the pejorative."

Royce just shook his head, a grin on his face. "You know what? I think I'm going to like working for this guy. A commander who takes the time to ask you how to employ your specialty troops rather than just using you as cannon fodder is a commander who understands how to wage war and win battles. Yeah…he's going to work out just fine, Hiro."

Chapter Seven
Damn the Torpedoes

RNS *Vanguard*
Approaching Serpentis-6

"Captain, we've entered FTL. ETA twenty-two minutes until we arrive near Serpentis-6," Ensign Godley announced. The main screen showed the swirling dance of multicolor strands of light flittering around the ship as they flew through slip space.

Dobbs unfastened the straps on her seat and made her way to the front of the bridge. Placing a hand on the back of the young man's station, she leaned down as she spoke. "Thank you, Ensign. Once we're ten seconds away from exiting slip space, give us another warning."

"Aye, Captain."

Dobbs nodded in approval, then turned around to face her crew.

Many of them had served with her on the *Battleaxe* or the *Brandenburg*, giving each other a familiarity with how they'd handle themselves in combat. It was situations like this when she felt lucky to have been able to pick her crew for the christening of this new warship. She also saw the nervous looks on their faces. There were widespread concerns about these being the opening salvos of another war with the Dominion.

Pushing those fears aside, Dobbs stared at the device in her hand, marveling at how incredibly heavy it suddenly felt. Lifting the communicator to her lips, she knew what she had to say—what they needed to hear.

"This is the captain speaking. In a few minutes, our warship is going into battle. I know there are rumors this fight may restart the war with the Dominion—I'm not going to lie and pretend that's not a risk. It is. But here are the facts. Our ally, the Tully, was brutally attacked in the Serpentis system. When the Orbots destroyed the outposts guarding the stargate, it allowed the Pharaonis to invade Serpentis-6—the only habitable planet in the system. When the Tully asked for help, it was the Altairians and the Republic who answered that call. Our ally is in trouble. The Tully came to our aid during the last war; now it's our turn to come to their aid.

"For some of you, this'll be your first time in combat. For many of you, this will be one more battle in a litany of battles you've fought in throughout your career. During the Dominion War, we fought Zodarks and Orbots. We knew there were other races aligned with the Dominion, like the Pharaonis. We just hadn't encountered them yet. When we drop out of slip space near Serpentis-6, we're going to engage this new enemy—and we're going to destroy 'em. The *Vanguard* is the newest, most advanced battleship in the Republic. You, the crew of the *Vanguard*, are going to show the Pharaonis what happens when you mess with an ally of the Republic!" she proclaimed loudly, injecting energy and excitement as she stirred up the patriotism of the crew.

Dobbs searched for Commander Wright, and they locked eyes for a moment before she motioned for him to step forward. As he did, she spoke into the communicator one more time.

"As the *Vanguard* prepares for battle, I need to take charge of the fourteen warships of our squadron. Therefore, Commander Wright, my handpicked executive officer, is going to lead the *Vanguard* to an incredible, decisive victory. XO, prepare the ship for battle. It's time to earn our keep."

With her orders given, she headed for her captain's chair. It was time to strap in and prepare for battle. She had a squadron to lead, and she was determined to be the one who delivered the Republic's first victory against the Pharaonis.
****

With the battle approaching, Commander Wright stared at Captain Dobbs with rapt attention as she spoke to the crew. He knew when the battle started, she'd have to oversee the actions of the squadron, not just the *Vanguard.* They'd talked privately about this a few times. When the time eventually came, she'd delegate command to him. It would also give him the opportunity he'd longed for—command authority of a warship during a battle. This was something he'd need if he was to make command himself during the next captain's board in six months.

Then he heard his name—his opportunity had arrived.

Commander Wright confidently declared, "Aye, Captain. I have command of the ship." Turning to face the crew, he saw nods of approval mixed with grim looks as they prepared for combat. They trusted him as much as they trusted the captain. Like the captain, they knew he was ready for this. Now it was up to him to validate that trust.

"This is it, people. Time to prove our mettle—to show the Pharaonis the teeth of the Republic Navy. Prepare for combat. All sections report when ready for action!"

With the orders given, a flurry of controlled chaos erupted on the bridge. The officers commanding the various sections of the warship took charge of their people and prepared the ship for action once they exited slip space.

Turning to look at the nerve center of the *Vanguard*, Wright was keenly aware of how important the command information center would be in the coming battle. It was the CIC's responsibility to analyze and manage the battle once it began. Wright spotted Lieutenant Quinn Dildine and his deputy, Master Chief Abe Ellis, the feared noncommissioned officer who ran the CIC like a well-oiled machine. They were calling out commands and giving last-minute guidance.

"Lieutenant Dildine, Master Chief," Wright called out, making sure he had their attention before he continued. "Once we drop out of slip space, we're going to be counting on that crack team of yours. You guys have this—I trust you. Just keep analyzing and updating the data as it comes in. And make sure that damn TAM system doesn't bug up on us at the one moment we need it. We're going to run with that layered attack proposal your people came up with. If anything seems out of whack or it's not responding the way you guys intended, make sure you shift back to our standard SOP and keep the TAO up to date. Got it?"

"Aye, sir, we're on it," Master Chief Ellis acknowledged, a look of satisfaction on his face as the time for battle quickly approached.

"Thirty seconds until we drop out of slip space," announced the helmsman.

Wright turned to the opposite side of the bridge, eyes locking with Lieutenant Commander Maggie Little—*Vanguard*'s tactical action officer, the single person who coordinated the ship's weapon systems.

"This is it, Maggie. Once we're out of slip space, the show's yours."

She shot him a curt look, her eyes betraying her nervousness at the plan. She wasn't totally on board with the CIC's new targeting approach. However, she had voiced her concern, and afterward she'd said she accepted being overruled and vowed to make the best of the decision. Hopefully, it actually worked like they thought it would.

"I know, Captain. We know the priority—Saevissima battleships first," Lieutenant Commander Little replied. "Then work our way down to those *Myrmecia*-class cruisers. We'll make sure those battleships aren't able to get many shots off with their particle beam weapons." Despite her known reservations, she was doing her best to sound confident to him and those on the bridge.

"Excellent. Your people have got this," Commander Wright encouraged. "Make sure to stay on top of your EWO team. Let's see how they like being jammed. Force this into a knife fight where our railguns will tear them apart." A wicked smile spread from ear to ear across Wright's face. This would be the first battle where any Republic warship would have the opportunity to test the greatly improved railgun systems the Altairians had helped them supercharge from their previous warship designs.

"Exiting slip space in ten seconds!" Ensign Godley announced loudly to break through the growing noise on the bridge.

"Thank you, Ensign," Wright acknowledged. "Listen up, people!" he bellowed. "We're about to exit slip space. Stand by for contact once we exit the bubble, and let's bring the pain!"

Moments later, the *Vanguard* exited the FTL bubble that squeezed their ship through the slip space, allowing them to traverse the stars at speeds in excess of multiple times the speed of light. Instantly, a tight cluster of tiny flashes began to occur near the planet Serpentis-6. One by one, the fourteen warships of Strike Group Five emerged into the blackness of space once again.

"Get me a TAM picture *now!*" roared Commander Wright, staring at a blank monitor as their systems waited for the sensors to populate the screen with data and images of their surroundings.

"The TAM is coming up now," announced the CIC.

The screen flickered for a moment before revealing the image of a planet off in the distance. New markers began popping up, with information tags identifying the planet as Serpentis-6 along with three of its moons in various orbits around the planet.

Then new tags appeared—half a dozen…then a dozen…then a second group further away. Their orbit and position indicated they were either landing forces on the planet or supporting some sort of landing force.

Wright stared at the tags, waiting for the CIC to analyze what the TAM was telling them these contacts were. At first, they appeared as flashing yellow squares. Then the squares became solid red diamond-shaped objects, denoting hostile warships. This enemy fleet had likely been sent along to protect the invasion fleet that had gone in beforehand to capture the planet and seize control of the system.

"Captain, the TAM have identified two groups of Pharaonis warships," announced Lieutenant Dildine. "We are labeling the first Group One. This group consists of six Saevissima battleships and fourteen *Myrmecia* cruisers. They appear to be in the outer orbit of the furthest moon from the planet. The second group appears to be a formation of twelve transports of similar-style ships in a relatively low orbit. The CIC recommends we engage Group One." She rattled off the data as fast as it was coming in.

"Thank you, CIC. Agreed," replied Commander Wright.

"TAO, begin actioning a priority target list against Group One," he ordered. "Helm, bring our engines to full speed and plot an intercept course to bring us in range of the enemy." There was a rush as he unleashed the crew of the *Vanguard* to begin executing the very wartime jobs they had relentlessly trained to do but had hoped they would never be called upon to perform.

As the minutes went by, the data their sensors continued to collect painted a bleak picture of what was happening on Serpentis-6 and in the system. Minutes into their new intercept course with the enemy, the tactical action map revealed that a full-fledged invasion of the planet had likely taken place. The orbital defense platforms that should have been present were nothing more than floating debris, the few Tully frigates and cruisers that had tried to defend the planet nothing more than destroyed hulks, adrift amid a growing field of space rubble—the remnants of the battle fought not that long ago.

Knowing they were finally getting closer to the enemy, Wright looked for the *Vanguard*'s C-FLO. "Commander Mitsu, I think it's time to deploy your pilots and get them in on some of this action, don't you?"

"Couldn't agree more, Captain. I've got a kennel full of ravenous dogs waiting for the leash to come off."

Wright smiled at the analogy. The 20th Fighter Group, otherwise known as the "Pit Bulls," was the *Vanguard*'s flight complement. The new Altairian-Human battleships had a flight complement of sixty-four starfighters broken down into four squadrons: two fighter and two bomber squadrons. The fighters gave the battleships a real expeditionary role beyond just escort duty, and they were the anchor to a heavy fleet action in a battle. The ships could now support ground operations on a planet in addition to attacking an adversary well beyond the range of the battleship's weapons.

"Excellent," Commander Wright replied to Mitsu. "Then pass along my compliments and tell 'em the leash is off. Have your bombers focus on the battleships the TAO assigned. If the enemy deploys any fighters—you know what to do."

"Aye, Captain. We'll start launching the squadrons immediately."

Wright imagined if he lived during a different time, he'd be able to hear and feel the launching of the ship's fighters. For now, he'd have to settle for tiny blue triangles appearing on the bridge's front monitor to know that they had left the ship.

What transpired next was the hardest part of space warfare— the waiting. Once the orders had been given and the ship set into motion, there wasn't much else to do until they were in range of each other's weapons. Then it would come down to split-second decisions to begin evasive maneuvers as the captain and the CIC did their best to anticipate the type and number of enemy weapons about to slam into them. A hesitation in deciding to rotate the hull of the ship or change its trajectory could have devastating results. A Zodark torpedo transformed itself into a high-energy ball of plasma right before it slammed into the armor of a warship—burning its way into the hull of the ship and exposing it to the vacuum space.

Watching the symbols move across the distance between the two sides, Wright saw a pattern emerge. Group One, the main enemy force, began to separate. Their trajectory showed they were still on an intercept course with the *Vanguard*, but now they were separating into smaller attack groups.

What are you bastards up to now? Wright wondered. This was their first experience facing the Pharaonis—they were already responding vastly differently than what they'd seen in their past experiences with the Zodarks.

"Heads up, TAO. Enemy ships are reacting to our presence and deploying for battle," called out Lieutenant Dildine from the CIC. "The TAM is tracking the formation of two battle lines, likely an attempt to split our efforts. They're also increasing their speed toward us. If both our forces stay on the same course heading and speed—we'll be within maximum range of their weapons shortly. Sending your updated target packages now."

"Thanks, CIC. That was a fast adjustment to our presence," said Lieutenant Little. "Let's see how they handle being blinded here in a second."

Commander Wright watched the interplay between the bridge sections and smiled at the smoothness of their communication—the result of years of battle station drills. Looking to the *Vanguard*'s wizard shop, he saw Lieutenant Little confidently calling out orders and instructions to the ship's electronic warfare group.

The Republic's continued heavy use of electronic countermeasures and jamming capability was an oddly unique advantage they seemed to have maintained and excelled at over their more technically advanced allies. No matter how powerful a ship's energy-based weapons were, if it couldn't obtain a weapons lock on its intended target, it couldn't accurately hit it. On more than one occasion, electronic warfare had been a deciding factor, turning what should have been a defeat into a surprise victory.

With the two Pharaonis battle lines racing toward them, the distance between their forces continued to shrink at an alarming pace. The moment the first shots would be fired edged closer with each passing minute. Tension increased across the ship as they waited for the order to fire—or for the ship's warning alarm to tell them to brace for impact from an enemy laser.

"Captain!" Commander Mitsu barked, breaking through Commander Wright's concentrated stare at the bridge's main display. "Our fighters and bombers are approaching weapons range of the target designated Sierra Zero-Four—the center Saevissima battleship. Their ships are beginning to deploy fighters of their own. Ours are moving to engage and clear a path for the bombers, who will begin their attack shortly."

There was a sense of excitement aboard. This was going to be the first battle between Pharaonis and Republic warships and starfighters. Wright observed the small clusters of fighter and bomber squadrons approaching the battleship anchoring the center of the battle line. He smiled. The first shots of the battle would be fired momentarily by the ship's starfighters.

Wright watched the countdown until they were in weapons range approaching zero. It was time to unleash the *Vanguard*'s own vaunted weapon systems. The XO turned to the TAO, and the orders began to flow.

"Outstanding, Mitsu," said Wright. "Let's get your bombers in and see what kind of damage they can inflict on that battleship. TAO, once our weapons have a lock, they are free to engage. I want our secondary weapons, the turbo lasers, to focus their fire on supporting the bombers going after Sierra Zero-Four. Relay to the gunners to focus their fire on the Saevissima heavy plasma cannons. Let's try to minimize the damage they'll be able to throw at us once they're able to burn through our jamming. But this target here"—Wright highlighted a battleship near the rear of the formation—"Sierra Zero-Two—that's the ship I want to focus our primary magrail turrets on, and that new particle beam weapon. They're far enough outside the engagement area of our fighters and bombers so we shouldn't have an issue with them accidentally straying into the flightpath of our magrail slugs."

"Aye, sir. Good copy. Assigning primary magrail turrets and the particle beam weapon to target Sierra Zero-Two. Assigning secondary weapons to support the bombers attacking against Sierra Zero-Four," the TAO confirmed.

As the gun chiefs and the crews manning the primary and secondary weapon systems received their orders, they went to work acquiring the targets and confirming the firing solutions. Once a solid lock had been confirmed, they'd fire the first shots since the end of the last war. Now they'd learn the results of all those months' worth of battle station drills and gunner practice. If they were successful, then the squadron of Republic warships would pummel the enemy line with volleys of devastating fire that would box the enemy in and leave them little room to evade the various layered kill boxes of magrail slugs about to be hurled at them.

What had been hours of maneuvering and closing the great distances between their forces had dwindled to minutes as they neared the effective range of their guns. Then the countdown reached zero. The first flashes of light raced out from the Republic battle line towards the Pharaonis cruisers—the battle for Serpentis had started.

The RNS *Daring* led the forward picket line of frigates, firing the first shot of the battle. More flashes of light stabbed forward, into the enemy cruisers that were closing the distance. As they approached, the incoming ships burned through the incessant jamming and electronic interference the Republic warships were famed for.

The one-sided affair only lasted for a moment. The ten *Myrmecia* cruisers that raced ahead of the Pharaonis battleships had finally achieved weapons lock. The enemy warships began firing their own deadly barrages of laser fire—connecting with the armor of the much smaller Republic frigates, who took evasive maneuvers to dodge, weave, and rotate away from the lasers to make sure they didn't connect long enough to burn a hole through their armor.

Then the RNS *Hamburg* joined the fray, leading the four Republic heavy cruisers into the battle. The fourteen-hundred-meter-long heavy cruisers of the Republic Navy unleashed a torrent of carnage, fury, and hate towards the enemies of the alliance. The six twin-barrel turbo laser turrets tore into the *Myrmecia* cruisers, slamming into the forward sections of the enemy warships barreling toward them. Then they unleashed the main guns of the ship—the twelve triple-barreled thirty-six-inch magrail turrets released a hail of high-explosive rounds ensconced in armored shells. These weapons had been specially designed with a penetrator tip to punch through the dense armor of a Zodark warship.

While the battle picked up in pace, the five Saevissima battleships had yet to join in. The Republic warships continued to generate enormous amounts of electronic noise—likely spoofing their targeting systems until they got closer and their systems became strong enough to burn through it.

"Weapons engaging now, Captain!" declared Lieutenant Little from her TAO station.

Standing there on the bridge as the *Vanguard*'s main guns joined in, Wright swore he could feel the power of the ship's twenty thirty-six-inch triple-barreled turrets as they unleashed their own barrage against the enemy battleships lingering further behind the enemy line. Then the eight twin-barreled turbo lasers joined the fray, targeting the other battleships in support of the two bomber squadrons pressing on with their attack.

Turning to the bridge monitor on the right-hand side, Wright saw that the RNS *Rheinland*, their sister battleship, had opened fire with them. He stared in awe for a moment, watching as the giant twenty-six-hundred-meter-long warship fired all its offensive weapons in a synchronized rhythm at the same two battleships the *Vanguard* was shooting at. Seeing the *Rheinland* in battle, he realized it was essentially a mirror image of his own warship.

Good God, he thought. *Imagine if we'd had these kinds of warships at the outset of the Zodark war.* He wondered how things would have turned out differently. It certainly would have impacted the number of losses they had sustained.

"Captain, the entire battle line is now decisively engaged with the enemy," came a voice from the direction of the CIC. He waved his left hand, acknowledging the comment, his eyes busy taking in updates from across the ship as they streamed in.

Now I know what Dobbs meant when she said to make sure you train an effective XO to help you manage fighting the ship while keeping it going throughout the battle, Wright thought, remembering back to a conversation the two of them had had a few weeks ago.

Commander Wright looked at the overview of the battle as it continued to unfold. He saw directing cruisers and frigates to various axes of attack against the enemy line. The TAM leveraged a three-dimensional map, allowing a commander to see the warships involved in a battle at the varying axes and planes of attack.

"CIC, place the TAM on the right side of the main monitor. Then give us an exterior camera view of the battle on the left side. I'd like to have a better comparison between what I'm seeing and what's happening," ordered Commander Wright.

Moments later, the bridge's main monitor, sixteen feet tall by thirty feet wide, changed to display what he'd asked for. Wright felt himself catch his breath as he saw for the first time in his military career a real honest-to-goodness space battle taking place in real time via a high-definition exterior camera and not simply on a radar or TAM display. The battle that had taken hours to build up was finally now in full swing. Every now and then, he'd direct the camera to zoom in on a specific *Myrmecia* cruiser or a Republic frigate to see them in action, up close. Short flashes of light emanated from the laser turrets each time they fired.

Wright watched an image of a *Myrmecia* cruiser, zoomed in with as close a view as their cameras could give. A series of objects were ejected from both sides of the ship. In fractions of a second, he knew what they were.

Missiles.

The rear of the cylindrical devices began to glow moments before the objects took off at an incredible rate of speed. Before anyone on the bridge could comment on what they had just seen, the *Vanguard*'s built-in AI had identified the threats—instantly alerting its human crew to the newest danger.

The normal lighting on the bridge was momentarily interrupted by a series of five flashes from a red warning light, followed by an automated voice loudly proclaiming the words, "Vampire, vampire, vampire! Warning, antiship missiles detected. Warning, antiship missiles detected."

Standing from his chair, Commander Wright walked briskly to Lieutenant Dildine's CIC crew. "Quinn, what kind of threat are we looking at, and how many of 'em are headed toward us versus the *Rheinland*?"

Lieutenant Dildine looked puzzled and concerned at the same time. He held a finger up; his eyes were scanning something on his monitor. When he finished, he looked up, and their eyes locked. "Sorry, I was reading through the intelligence package from Pandolly's team on these Pharaonis missiles. These are *bad*, sir. I can't believe my team and I didn't catch this earlier—"

"Hold up there, Lieutenant. Let's not freak out about these missiles just yet," Wright interjected, trying to keep the man from going down a self-defeating path. "If that AI assessment is correct, we've got eight minutes until they reach us. That's plenty of time for us to take them out. Go ahead and spin up the interceptors; let's get a one-to-one volley on its way. We should have plenty of time to get a couple of volleys off before we'll have to rely on the point defense guns and our wizard shop, OK?"

Dildine nodded, clearly relieved his boss wasn't about to rip him a new one for what was obviously a failure on his part. "Yes, sir. Of course," he replied. "We'll get the targeting data over to the TAO and get those missiles on the way."

Wright nodded grimly; he'd have to address this later, after the battle.

He walked toward the tactical action center that managed the ship's offensive and defensive weapon platforms. Commander Little was riding her people hard, standing over them, pointing and directing various actions as she saw fit. Seeing her take charge like this in the middle of a heated battle only further stirred his feelings for her. She was in her element, doing what she loved best—serving as a Republic naval officer in a critical role during a pivotal life-and-death situation.

Instead of interrupting her and breaking her concentration, Wright walked back to his captain's chair and sat down, resuming his observation of the battle and the bridge operations as they fought the ship. He and Captain Dobbs had trained this crew hard for moments like this. Now that their ship had suddenly been thrust into battle, the decisions and actions made by their crew and the officers and NCOs who oversaw them would determine if they lived or died.

"Captain, we're tracking eighty-two missiles heading toward the *Vanguard*; one hundred and twelve headed towards the *Rheinland*," Commander Little called out, updating him on the incoming threat. "Estimated time to arrival—seven minutes. First volley of interceptors is on the way. Initiating second volley in sixty seconds."

"Acknowledged. Stay on top of them, Commander, and make sure our offensive weapons are continuing to hammer those warships," Wright ordered. "We need to thin their numbers out before they're able to fill the void with any more swarms of antiship missiles."

He returned his attention to the main monitor at the front of the bridge. The massive display showed a detailed image of a *Myrmecia* cruiser. At nearly thirteen hundred meters in length, the ship was nearly the same size as its Republic counterpart. What caught his eye and took his breath away wasn't the almost organic appearance of the outer hull of the Pharaonis warship—it was the real-time video of the ship firing its own lasers. The flashes of insidious light reached out for his fellow Republic warships. But then the Pharaonis cruiser flew into the maelstrom of magrail slugs and laser shots being fired at it from the

Republic cruiser RNS *Delhi* and a pair of frigates, the RNS *Chennai* and the *Bremen*. The latter two had each released a volley of six Havoc II antiship missiles followed by a pair of plasma torpedoes.

Holy crap—how could the Pharaonis dodge that? Wright wondered as the ship continued to sail unfazed into the hailstorm that was about to rain across its hull.

He realized he should look away and focus his attention on fighting his own ship and staying on top of his people. But as he watched the situation begin to unfold across the main screen of the bridge, Wright couldn't stop himself from seeing how this was going to play out.

Whoever was commanding that Pharaonis ship hadn't seen or hadn't realized the danger posed by this wall of incoming death until it was too late to react to it. The ship attempted a hard turn to port while also using some sort of emergency maneuver thrusters to try and raise the nose of the ship and change its trajectory. Had the Republic not been so adept at using what other spacefaring species considered "primitive" weapons, the Pharaonis cruiser might have been able to evade the maelstrom they were now entering. At first, it was a couple of shells that hit the ship. Some struck at an angle, ricocheting off the ship's armor. Others scored hits but failed to penetrate the outer hull and reach into the guts of the ship.

"And here comes the rain…," Wright muttered softly as the cloud of armor-piercing shells began to shower the warship like giant raindrops against the windshield of a vehicle driving during a summer storm. Some shells ricocheted or shattered on impact, but dozens more punched through the armor, hurling their explosive warheads deep into the interior of the Pharaonis warship.

Flashes registered at various points across the outer hull of the *Myrmecia* cruiser. When the multistaged warheads began to explode, the first charge would cause an overpressure that blew out sealed compartments and opened the decks above and below the warhead. The second charge would then initiate—dispersing a sticky chemical incendiary substance. It was this second incendiary charge that caused the geysers of flame to shoot out through the holes or fissures across the outer hull of the warship. These spectacular fiery jets of fire burned bright in contrast to the blackness of space but were quickly snuffed out once they had consumed the atmosphere within the ships.

"Whoa," was the only word that slipped past his lips.

Just moments earlier, the guns of the *Myrmecia* cruiser were firing away at the Republic ships charging toward it. Then a series of secondary explosions rippled across the mid and rear sections of the giant cruiser before the ship's power gave out, plunging it into darkness. The glow that normally emanated from engines to the rear of the ship had likewise gone dark, leaving the cruiser adrift with no power and a series of small fires burning up what little atmosphere likely remained.

"First wave of interceptors connecting now," Commander Little announced.

Commander Wright looked at the display tracking the incoming missiles and the volley of interceptors they had fired. The blue arrows representing the ship's defense began to merge with the red arrows denoting the eighty-some threats barreling down on the *Vanguard*, flashing momentarily before the TAM registered a successful kill.

Wright suddenly realized he'd been holding his breath as he watched the two groups of arrows steadily merge. He'd mentally prepared himself for the eventuality that somehow, someway, these previously unknown missiles would avail themselves of some crazy unique ability that would allow them to evade the *Vanguard*'s best efforts to destroy them and plow into his ship. But one by one, the red arrows fell off the threat board as the TAM reported them winking out of existence. What had been a terrifying threat just moments earlier had vanished in seconds, replaced by relief and excitement at the thought that maybe, just maybe, they had seen the worst the enemy had to offer.

Wow, that was close, Wright allowed himself to think as the threat of incoming missiles evaporated.

"We did it! We got them all with the first volley," yelled someone before a celebratory cheer erupted.

A smile spread across Wright's face. He wanted to join in the impromptu celebration, but he caught a glimpse of Captain Dobbs as she stood up from her alcove to the rear of the bridge, an angry look of dismay and disappointment overtaking her features.

"Enough!" Dobbs rebuked them angrily. "We still have nineteen Pharaonis warships trying to kill us. This fight isn't over. Get your heads back in the game and fight this ship before it's too late!" The disappointment on her face hurt Wright more than her words.

He felt embarrassed as he stood there, realizing it should have been him to have reined in their celebrations—but he hadn't. He'd let down the very officer who had given him a chance to shine, to demonstrate he had what it took to command a capital ship in combat. Instead of rising to that challenge, he'd allowed his bridge crew to lose perspective of the battle still raging around them. Before he could say or do anything, he suddenly found his hands involuntarily moving to cover his eyes as he turned away from what seemed like a star shining through the main monitor on the bridge.

Wright momentarily stumbled, reaching out for something to grab onto. Steadying himself, he tried to process why the monitors had nearly blinded them before the safety protocols had kicked in.

Grabbing firm to the back of a chair, he stammered, "What the hell was that?"

He rubbed at his eyes, trying to clear the image of a white rectangular object that had floated across the center of his vision.

"Oh God, it's the *Kora*...she's gone," Helmsman Godley exclaimed in shock as the bridge monitors finally regained their resolution once again.

"CIC, I need to know what the hell that flash was and what just happened to the *Kora*," Commander Wright ordered, walking back to his chair to strap in. God only knew what had just happened, but it had nearly blinded him.

"We're working on it. Preliminary data are telling us that bright flash came from some sort of particle accelerator weapon." There was a momentary pause before Lieutenant Dildine continued, "I don't know how it happened, Captain, but that mystery weapon...it just one-shotted the *Kora*. They didn't even have time to abandon ship before it blew apart."

No one spoke for a moment as they looked at the debris cloud that represented one of their fellow warships and brothers in arms. Moments earlier, the *Kora* had been engaging a *Myrmecia* cruiser when the two-hundred-and-twenty-meter ship and its crew of fifty-two spacers had just vanished, reduced to nothing more than a cloud of atomized materials unrecognizable as a former warship.

Then the voice of Captain Dobbs called out to him from her alcove position. "They found it! The *Somerset* spotted the ship that just blew up the *Kora*," she declared loudly, highlighting a ship near the rear of that battle line that they had initially written off as just another Pharaonis battleship. Clearly, it wasn't. "Commander Wright, I need you to shift all our weapons to join the *Rheinland*, *Dragon*, and *Westminster* in taking that warship down *now*, before they're able to pop any more of our ships with whatever that superweapon is."

"We're on it, Captain!" Wright shouted in reply. He issued a raft of new orders to change the targets they had just been laying into with their main and secondary weapons.

Wright turned to the ship's fighter operations section. Commander Mitsu had his hands full, coordinating his actions with those of the flight operations crew that oversaw the launch, recovery, and maintenance operations of the flight group. With the bombers having just returned, it was a race to get them rearmed and ready to launch once more.

With the orders given, there wasn't much more to do other than to wait for the volume of fire their battleships and heavy cruisers were unloading to reach this mystery warship. Then something strange happened. The ship that had just been there, moments away from being pummeled with magrail slugs and turbo lasers, *vanished*. One moment it was there; the next it looked like a momentary blur as it flew off in the direction of the stargate leading back to Pharaonis territory.

Then flashes of light began popping up at various points around the remaining Pharaonis ships. Wright was about to panic when the TAM identified the incoming warships as Altairian. The massive fleet Admiral Pandolly had held back in hopes of luring a potential Orbot or Zodark fleet into a trap had finally joined the fray.

Wright looked over to Dobbs; she sent him a message via neurolink, letting him know she'd called in the cavalry. While they hadn't encountered any Orbots so far, it was time for the Altairian fleet to swoop in and minimize any additional Republic casualties. They'd kept the enemy engaged, and further degraded the military capabilities of the Dominion. For now, the next stage of this battle would transition to the Army and the liberation of Serpentis-6.

****

Lab Site X
Planet Surface

"Hold up!" Jack yelled.

The construction crew immediately pulled back on their excavation equipment and powered down.

"What is it?" asked Sakura.

"I want to get a better look here. There are no straight lines in nature," Jack explained. "Do you see what I see?"

"Are those…pipes?"

"It certainly looks like it," Jack remarked.

Sakura took out her brushes and trowels and went to work, following the pipe she'd uncovered. Along certain points, there were strange-looking bowl-like shapes with a film of some type covering the protrusions. She wasn't sure if the film was some kind of a plastic material or biological in nature. The pipe roughly followed the edge of the rocky outcropping.

Sakura asked for some help removing more of the dirt in the surrounding area but asked Jack to keep his crew from getting too close to the rocks and the pipe. After they'd uncovered a few meters of earth, she went to work again.

"There's another branch!" she announced excitedly, brushing away at the newly uncovered fork in the pipes.

"What do you think all this is?" asked Jack.

"I think this might have been some type of irrigation system," Sakura postulated. "Yeah, now that I think about it, that definitely makes the most sense."

"Huh. So when the Humtars left this planet, it went from green to…this?" Jack asked.

"Maybe. There could be more to it than that, but it's a theory," Sakura replied. "I guess it's time to keep digging."

****

A few days later, they had almost reached the depth of the energy signature they'd detected.

"Hey, we have a problem," Jack announced, pulling Sakura aside.

"Equipment troubles?" she inquired.

"Remember those heat signatures?" Jack asked, not waiting for a response. "Well, they definitely came from something biological. There are a *bunch* of creatures of some type down here. We're in their home. I don't know if they pose a threat to us or not, but I need some guidance on how to proceed."

Sakura wasn't actually sure what the rules of the road *were* out here—they were kind of making them up as they went along. There weren't exactly environmental impact studies, and since this was their first time exploring this planet, there was no way to know if any of these creatures were potentially dangerous to humans or possibly an endangered species. After some brief discussion, they decided to proceed with caution, digging until they reached closer to the level where these creatures were located and then using much smaller tools to minimize potential risks.

Eventually, they were within feet of the energy signature source, digging with hand tools. Even Sakura was getting her hands dirty with the crew.

Ding!

"We have metal!" Jack announced loudly.

Seconds later, Sakura screamed. Several mounds appeared in the dirt, growing rapidly until small protrusions came out of the ground, followed by a series of heads.

"What *are* these things?" asked Jack.

"They look kind of like a mix of a rat and a mole," Sakura replied, calming down now. "Look—they don't seem to have any eyes."

The small rodent-like creatures had paws that were definitely made for digging, and whisker-like protrusions that were not only on their faces but also at certain points along their bodies.

"Are those…*gills*?" Jack asked, confused.

At this point, Sakura was taking photos and videos for research purposes as she observed them. She paused and stared at their sides. "It looks like they can breathe the atmosphere here just fine," she commented. "I think those things push out the sand around them to create pockets of air for them as they dig."

"Incredible," Jack replied.

After a few moments of rooting around, the animals burrowed their way back into the ground. Everyone just kind of stared at each other for a moment until Jack finally said what everyone must have been thinking. "Now what?"

"They must not be accustomed to life on the surface," Sakura remarked. "I think we must have drawn their attention when we struck metal. They don't seem to be aggressive in any way, so I think as long as we proceed with caution, we can continue."

Sakura herself had almost forgotten that they were digging for something, actually. It was hard to stay focused on their mission when the planet held such fascinating surprises.

The group marked where they had hit metal and worked around that area until they could see the shiny surface of something below. They brushed away at the sandy dirt, following it along its slightly curved surface. The tension mounted as they all wondered what it was they were unearthing.

Along the lower end of the slope, one of the workers called out, "This looks like glass!"

Sakura and several others rushed over, bringing brushes and other tools to help uncover the new discovery. The substance was tinted a light grayish-purple hue, but it was transparent like glass.

"Do you think we found the lab?" Jack asked.

Sakura peered through the window they'd found. There were two seats with Humtar hand controls and several computer monitors.

"Jack, I think we found a Humtar ship," she announced.

Chapter Eight
Space Rangers

Dog Company, 2nd Ranger Battalion
Task Force Silver Fox
RNS *Wasps*
Approaching Serpentis System

Master Sergeant Paul "Pauli" Smith stared at his chest rig for a moment, assessing his setup and making sure he'd brought what he thought he'd need before attaching the setup to their armored exosuits. *Grenades...almost forgot those*, he thought to himself. That would have been a hard-to-live-down rookie mistake.

As he searched for some grenades, Pauli saw Staff Sergeant Yogi Sanders standing a near bunch of them. "Hey, Yogi, toss me some frags, will ya?"

"Yeah, sure thing, Pauli," Yogi replied, reaching for them. He grabbed a pair and tossed them over. "Here you go, man. Don't want to forget those."

Pauli caught the boom-boom balls and attached them to his rig. The M97 smart grenades, particularly the newer C Models that had come out after the war, were substantially more deadly than their predecessors from the wars of the last century. They were safer to handle and more versatile in how they could be used.

Yogi approached him, holding his own rig in his hands. "You'd think I'd get used to the weight of this, but either I'm getting old and weak, or this thing is getting heavier."

Pauli laughed. Yogi had become a bit of a gym rat since the war had ended and they'd both joined the Ranger reserve unit on New Eden. In Pauli's eyes, Yogi spent *too* much time in the gym. The guy was built like a brick house, with muscles that would have intimidated most people.

"I don't think you're getting weak or that thing is getting heavier. I think it's all up here, Yogi," Pauli countered as he pointed to the side of his head. "See, your problem, my man, is you worked the wrong muscle group. While you were bulking up your biceps and working on getting those washboard abs you're always bragging about to the ladies, you let the most important muscle of them all get soft and squishy."

A few Rangers nearby chuckled at Pauli's comment, and Yogi's cheeks turned red.

"Oh yeah? What muscle's that? 'Cause these guns are ready for action!" Yogi raised his arms into a flex, displaying the kind of arms most men would be jealous of and women seemed to fawn over.

Pauli stifled another laugh, not wanting to hurt his friend's feelings. He pointed a finger to the side of his head once again. "Your brain, dude. While you were pounding protein shakes and living at the gym, you let your thinker go soft. It's mind over matter, Yogi—if you don't mind…it won't matter."

Now a bunch of soldiers broke out in raucous laughter. They weren't making fun of Yogi per se. They were just laughing at the banter between the two Ranger reservists who'd joined their unit the day before their battalion shipped out.

Yogi stared at Pauli for a moment, then laughed along with everyone else. He walked up to him and gave him a friendly hug to make sure the younger soldiers knew there weren't any hard feelings between them. Everyone went back to getting their kits ready and finalizing any last-minute things they needed to do. The word from on high was to plan on being without a resupply for up to four days. That shouldn't happen, of course. But like anything in the Army, if you planned for it, then just maybe Uncle Murphy might skip his cameo.

Satisfied with his setup, Pauli looked up in time to see Captain Travis Atkins walk into the team room. He stood there for a moment, hands on his hips as he scanned the room. A young Ranger, barely old enough to shave his face, jumped out of the chair he'd been sitting in when he saw Atkins. Pauli could tell he was about to call the room to attention when Atkins walked right up into the kid's personal space and got in his face, muttering something softly so only they could hear.

Pauli tried to keep his face neutral as he watched the interplay. He knew that look Atkins had given all too well. Captain Atkins had at one time been Sergeant Atkins, Pauli's fire team sergeant, then squad and platoon sergeant, before being given a battlefield promotion to lieutenant during the Intus campaign. Whatever Atkins had said caused the kid to look scared as he exited the team room.

"Heads up, Yogi. Atkins at my eight o'clock," Pauli muttered quietly as he looked back to his setup and tightened a strap, trying to look busy.

"Ah, there's my two favorite NCOs," Atkins announced as he walked up behind Pauli and Yogi, placing a hand on each of their shoulders. "I still can't believe you two volunteered for this short-notice assignment, but I'm damn glad to have two solid squad leaders I can count on when it gets crazy."

"I still can't believe they promoted you to captain. How the hell did that happen?" Yogi commented good-naturedly.

Atkins laughed before stating the obvious. "Oh, you know how it goes, Yogi—you live long enough and don't get in too much trouble. You'll wake up one day to find out the Army promoted you if for no other reason than you were too old to stay in your old rank anymore."

"Ha ha. Well, I suppose that's true, but it's going to take some getting used to calling you Captain now," Yogi replied. Atkins and Yogi were closer with each other than Pauli was with Atkins, so they were always on more of a first-name basis.

"Yeah, well, get used to it, you two," said Atkins. "You're back in the Rangers now. We have standards we hold our NCOs to," he joked, causing the three of them to laugh. Then he turned serious. "While you two have been playing weekend warrior and enjoying the civilian life, things have changed. It's almost like Space Command is trying to freeze the military we had at the end of the last war and keep us on ice, ready to defrost should things heat up again.

"This Big Army reorg they pushed kind of jacked up the promotion cycles for anyone attempting to advance to major and beyond. It's caused a lot of good captains to either call it quits or transfer over to the reserves in frustration at a stalled career. Hell, Major Hiro was a damn captain for what, ten years or something? Major Monsoor was one lucky son of a gun when he snagged colonel. He's been trying to help us when he can, but it's like waiting around for someone to die or hit the magic fifty-year mark and punch out with their retirement ticket," Atkins explained.

Pauli shook his head in amazement. It made him feel good about his decision to leave and drop down into the reserves. He'd struggled with that choice when the war had ended. Pauli had a promising career if he stayed in. However, he also had a real opportunity to build something new, something great, on New Eden now that the war was over and the floodgates of migration were about to open.

Suddenly, Big Army hadn't needed two full-time orbital Ranger divisions. But since the Rangers were technically part of Special Operations forces to augment and assist the Deltas, they weren't about to let this highly trained force revert to being regular Army infantry grunts. That was when Special Forces had cooked up the idea to create a SOF-only reserve force. They had taken one of the four brigades within each of the two divisions and converted them to be the designated reserve unit. This gave Special Forces something they had needed but never had before—a reserve force they could draw upon to pull individual augmentees and help backfill shortfalls within the activity-duty unit until the next crop of trainees graduated through Ranger or Delta school.

Pauli had thought all this was great—all the way up until the final day of his semiannual ninety-day refresher training course. That was when he and Yogi had been given a set of short-notice augmentee orders to go backfill a Ranger battalion deploying in support of some special secret squirrel alliance operation in a system and part of the galaxy neither of them had ever heard of.

Pauli faced Atkins and asked the question he and Yogi had been wondering about all day. "Is anyone going to tell us what we're doing yet? Some Fleeter told me we're approaching Serpentis-6. Do we even know if that planet is still under Tully control, or are we going to have to go liberate it from the Pharaonis?"

"That's a fair question, Pauli, and that's the reason I came down here to find everyone," Atkins replied. "I need you guys to go tell your squads to report to the auditorium at 1400 hours. Major Hiro is going to brief the battalion on what's going on and what our mission is going to be. Until then, I'm not really at liberty to say what we'll be doing."

"OK, sir, we'll let everyone know," said Yogi. "We've almost got the platoon kitted out and ready with their gear. Everyone should be ready to deploy within the next couple of hours if given the order."

Many of the soldiers standing around nearby had quieted down, hoping to glean some new piece of information about what might be happening next.

"That's good, you two," Atkins responded. "Sorry you guys got pulled into this mission, but I'm glad to have you. Especially you, Pauli. I know you just got promoted to master sergeant at the end of the advanced leadership course, right before you got tagged for this mission, but you know what to do. You essentially functioned in that role on and off during the last war. You've got a good platoon, and I've got a good company, but we've also got a lot of new NCOs who weren't here for the last war. That means they're going to look to you guys, even if you are reservists. You've got something they don't—ten-plus years of combat experience.

"Your platoon leader, Lieutenant Boris Yassin—I had a chance to spend some time with him a few months before this deployment. He's a good guy—a little ambitious, but what new officer isn't? He's going to need you, Pauli, and I'm going to need you to help guide him through what we're about to get thrown into. Keep in mind, he's fresh to the Army and the Rangers, so he'll be green and wet behind the ears. He wasn't initially excited about having a reservist fill in as his platoon sergeant and a second NCO as one of his squad leaders, but I talked with him about that, explaining how the three of us had actually served almost fourteen years together during the last war. His tune changed when he saw your combat records and knew he'd just been given the best possible NCOs he could have asked for. That said, if Boris is causing any problems for you two, then make sure to tell me about it. So, no pressure on you, Pauli, but I'm relying on you to turn this guy into a Ranger badass like you guys are." Atkins laughed before adding, "You got this. Now get back to it, and make sure your platoon is in the auditorium for the mission brief."

When Atkins finished the conversation, he briefly pulled aside the other staff sergeants. Then he ducked out and headed off to speak with the next platoon.

Once he'd left the room, Yogi looked at Pauli, a grin on his face. "I told ya not to seek out that promotion, Pauli," he said, playfully smacking his friend on the back. "Now you get the privilege of breaking in a fresh butter bar. Even better, you get the honor of doing it on a damn combat operation against a brand-new alien species we've never seen before. I mean—wow, Pauli. I don't think you could've planned that one better if you tried."

Pauli laughed in agreement. He hadn't wanted to pursue the next higher rank. He had enjoyed being a staff sergeant, responsible for a squad. Then two years ago, he had met Master Sergeant Arlo Kitt. Kitt had transferred into the reserves to avoid being kicked out of the Rangers and sent back to the regular infantry. It hadn't taken Pauli long to figure out why Kitt was being recommended to go back to the infantry—the guy was an egotistical narcissist who had a penchant for using his underlings to benefit himself in whatever scheme his narrow-minded little brain thought up. That was when Pauli had decided he'd put in the paperwork for master sergeant, letting the powers that be know he was ready and eager to move up.

Pauli had made a promise to himself never to be like Master Sergeant Kitt, a promise to do what he could to replace the man and hopefully help get him kicked out of his Rangers. Now he just hoped whatever this little fight they were headed off to was, it didn't turn into a larger war. Kitt leading a platoon into combat was something he had sought to avoid. Now Pauli realized he might have waited too long to pursue the higher rank his officers had been pushing him to go after. Secretly, he hoped his hesitation wouldn't cost the lives of the men and women he'd come to call friends during the last years he'd been in the reserves.

I suppose I'll know soon enough…

****

Lab Site X
Planet Surface

"Just wait until Hunt hears about this," remarked Katherine. "This Humtar ship is the find of the century—of the millennium. Think of all the military implications. There's technology in this thing we couldn't even dream of."

"I suppose you're right," said Sakura. "Personally, I'm hoping it will lead to some more answers in our quest to learn more about the Humtars as a people."

"Who says we can't have both?" Katherine countered with a crooked smile.

It took a while to dig the ship out, especially considering that they were doing their best to keep from disturbing the little critters that had apparently made a home nearby. But after several days, the form of the vessel was beginning to take shape.

The ship was a single deck, and it was approximately sixty meters long and about sixteen meters wide. The shape of it roughly resembled a much larger version of the YF-118G *Bird of Prey*, with a sleek rounded body and two wings that came out from the sides in such a way that it almost appeared to be an early rocket ship. Each wing had what they assumed were defensive lasers on top and streamlined engines that were smoothly integrated.

There was one set of landing gear in the front and two in the back, and the whole ship sat approximately two meters off the surface. Every spec of the ship was being measured and recorded and sent via encrypted messaging to Viceroy Hunt and his chief military intelligence officials. There would certainly be significant interest in their findings.

Sakura found a circular seam in the undercarriage near the front of the bird and realized that it had the same markings as the door to the lab on Alpha Centauri. She ran her finger across it and a small hatch opened.

One of the engineers on the team came to investigate, and he quickly smiled. "I know exactly what this is," he announced.

"Well, don't keep us waiting," Jack teased.

"This is a port to hook up an external umbilical cord and power this bad boy." He paused. "We're going to be able to turn it on."

Chapter Nine
Currahee—We Stand Alone, Together

506th Orbital Assault Infantry Regiment, "Currahee"
101st Orbital Assault Division, "Screaming Eagles"
RNS *Emerald City*
In Orbit of Serpentis-6

Colonel Ty Johnson stood on the flight deck, rows of AT-70 Ospreys waiting in the foreground, and looked at the soldiers standing before him. He didn't want to keep them long; they had a mission to prepare for. Still, he was their commander, their leader, the man who would order them into battle—the man who would order them to their deaths if necessary. They had earned those years of peace, and he hoped this battle would help earn a few more.

"Warriors of the Republic, I stand before you on the eve of battle to remind you of why we are here, why, after four years of peace, this battle must be fought. The blood of the Republic must yet again be spilled on the soil of a foreign planet so far from ours. Our ally, the Tully, was savagely attacked by a species known as the Pharaonis. With help from the Orbots, they are attempting to lay claim to the Serpentis system. Should they succeed in capturing this system, should the fleet fail to keep the system clear, should you and I fail in recapturing this planet, then all we fought for in the last war may be undone by an adversary who believes they have found the chink in our armor, the means to our defeat.

"Today, as in the glorious history of our famed division, the 506th Orbital Assault Regiment, we stand alone. But we stand alone together," Colonel Johnson exclaimed loudly, holding the men of his regiment in his gaze. Then he shouted the unit's motto, "Currahee!"

"Currahee!" roared the voices of more than two thousand soldiers.

"Commanders! Take charge of your units—prepare them for battle—we leave within the hour."
****

Invasion Day – First Wave
Easy Company, 1-506th Orbital Assault Regiment
Approaching Landing Zone Currahee

The twenty-two Ospreys from the decks of the *Emerald City* had formed up with their fighter escorts. It was time to begin their descent, to drop off the first wave of the ground force that would liberate Serpentis-6—restoring it to Tully control.

"Hang on, it's going to get bumpy for a few minutes," the pilot announced, the soldiers completely at their mercy. The turbulence picked up in pace, the shaking and rattling of the shuttle becoming more pronounced as the vessel pierced through the planet's upper atmosphere.

Lieutenant Ronald Speirs closed his eyes. The straps held his body tightly in place. It was moments like this that he was glad he was a grunt. The thought of having to make multiple trips like this a day, possibly through enemy fire, felt more daunting than he could handle. As a grunt, Speirs could shoot back. He could duck behind cover. Strapped to an Osprey, he just had to press on and hope today wasn't the day that golden BB had his number.

"That was a rousing pep talk from Ty, don't you think?"

Speirs opened his eyes and looked across the troop bay to his platoon sergeant, Tim Lance. "You mean Colonel Johnson, Master Sergeant?"

Lance laughed at the subtle jab, nodding in approval. "OK, you're right, Lieutenant. We have to respect the rank. Between us girls, you do know what I mean?"

Speirs sighed at the comment, rolling his shoulders as best he could with the straps still on. He shook his head. "What's he supposed to do or say, Lance? Orders are orders. He doesn't make 'em any more than we do. They give you a dumpster fire, and you make the best of it."

"I know, LT," Lance replied. "But we've got a lot of pups without a lot of experience yet. Compound that with the crap between Perez and Neale...I guess I'm saying I wish we had a few more weeks to get these guys spun up and ready for this."

"I hear you, Lance. As they say, you go to war with the army you have, not the army you want. Perez and Neale may hate each other's guts, but God only knows why, they sure do make a hell of a tag team when everything goes sideways in combat," Speirs offered. He leaned forward to look down the row of seats, spotting their quarrelers sitting opposite each other near the ramp. "Let's focus on the mission, Lance. We can deal with everything else later."

Speirs stared for a moment at Corporal Ruben Perez—no, Private Perez as of a week ago, when he had busted him down a rank. Perez and Neale acted like brothers. They constantly fought amongst each other over the littlest of things, but pick a fight with either of them and they seemed to circle the wagons and come to each other's aid.

Speirs still wasn't sure what the beef between them was, but somehow their verbal pissing match had led to Perez misplacing his military bearing and lobbing a haymaker that had knocked Neale flat on his ass. Neale had gotten lucky that a few soldiers had held him back, or he'd have joined Perez in losing a stripe of his own on the eve of a battle, when experienced squad leaders would be in short supply.

The bouncing and jerking of the shuttle suddenly stopped, like a switch had been flipped. Speirs knew from experience this just meant they'd finally breached the upper atmosphere and slowed to a controlled descent. They'd be on the ground soon—then the real work would begin.

"They look nervous," opined Lance.

"Yeah, I'd be nervous too if this was my first drop," said Speirs.

Lance grunted, adding, "I think it has more to do with running into those demonic-looking fire ants the S2 says are Pharaonis. I mean, how the hell does that kind of species evolve to become a spacefaring empire?"

Speirs shook his head. "Chalk it up to one more mystery to be solved in this galaxy. Look, I need you to make sure these guys don't lose it if those Pharaonis are half as ugly or bad as that intel weenie played them off to be. Things could get dicey down there."

"Yeah, I know. We'll get through it, just like we always have, Speirs."

Speirs had known Lance for going on twenty-three years. In fact, they had been in the same basic training company, just in different platoons. Once they had completed the infantry advance and the orbital assault training course, they'd landed the dream assignment all dagger badge holders wanted—an assignment to the famed 101st Orbital Assault Division. The "Screaming Eagles" were one of the Army's premier shock troop divisions.

As the shuttle continued its descent, Speirs looked back down the troop bay to his soldiers, surveying their reactions. Some were crossing themselves, saying a few Hail Marys for protection. Some appeared nervous, even terrified, as the Osprey brought them closer to the enemy. But not all the soldiers seemed scared. The ones who'd fought in the last war, the ones who'd seen the elephant and survived—to them, this was just one more drop, one more mission in a string of missions they'd already survived.

One of those confident veterans was Sergeant Troy Torrente. While the cherries nervously fretted about something they couldn't control, Torrente had his legs kicked out, his Qpad in hand, likely reading a book like he always did when he wanted to take his mind off something. He should have been a master sergeant or sergeant major by now, but he seemed to have a knack for not suffering the company of fools. Like a cat with nine lives, Torrente had used eight. After making sergeant for the sixth time in fifteen years, he was going to be forced out of the Army if he lost it again.

Then the voice of their pilot called out, demanding their attention. "We're approaching the landing zone. ETA three minutes."

Speirs nodded to Lance; it was time to rally the troops. They stood like a unified front as they faced the fifty-six soldiers they'd soon be leading into battle.

"OK, this is what we train for, people!" Speirs shouted loudly, grabbing their attention. "When that ramp drops, you need to haul ass off this shuttle like it's going to explode if you don't. We've got some fighters and Reaper drones going in to soften up the area for us now, but that doesn't mean those bastards won't have something waiting for us. First, Second, and Third Squad, you need to hustle to our rally point, Hotel Two. Get that perimeter established ASAP so we can get this LZ secured for our heavy transports.

"I want immediate defensive positions set up and your heavy weapons ready to lay some hate and repel any assaults against the LZ. Squad leaders, should you need additional reinforcements, Master Sergeant Lance will be staying with Fourth Squad, and they'll act as our QRF. I'm going to move with First Squad. You all know the drill. We have to hold the LZ. We've got fifteen minutes until those Starlifters arrive, bringing our Cougars and the second wave. Does everyone understand?" Speirs asked, noting the clock showed sixty seconds till they hit the LZ.

"First Squad's good."

"Second Squad's good."

"Third Squad's good."

"Fourth Squad's—"

"Hold on, we're taking evasive maneuvers," interrupted the pilot, alarms blaring in the background.

The Osprey jerked hard as the pilot pulled the nose up, flaring the shuttle up as it bled off speed and prepared to land.

The chin-mounted gun roared to life, spewing death at something the pilots must have seen. Then the guns positioned to either side of cockpit joined the fray. The heavy reports of fifty-caliber magrails blasted away.

Then the pilot cut in, shouting in alarm, "We're coming in hot, guys! You've got enemy soldiers approaching the LZ a few hundred meters to the front of rally point Hotel Two. Once you're off our bird, we'll do our best to rake 'em with our guns and smart missiles on our way out. Good luck, guys, and happy hunting."

Speirs grabbed for something, anything, to steady himself as the Osprey jerked to the right, the pilot obviously dodging something being thrown at them.

A few soldiers fell over. Their friends pulled them back to their feet. Then the shuttle hit the ground hard. A violent thud caused everyone to reach out for anything they could use to steady themselves. The ramp dropped and a voice shouted in fear, "Get off my bird *now!*"

Like his soldiers, Speirs looked out the ramp, his eyes wide. Lasers zipped across the LZ. Orange explosions boomed. Shrapnel and smoke swirled about. Speirs realized they'd landed in hell. If they didn't act quickly, they'd die in this landing zone.

"Go, go, go!" he shouted to his soldiers, snapping them out of their momentary trance.

Neale charged off the Osprey, his soldiers in hot pursuit. First Squad was in a race to reach their line of control before the enemy beat them to it. Second and Third Squads raced off the ramp as they broke to the right.

Speirs yelled and shoved as he pushed the last of his soldiers out the back of the Osprey. He was the last to leave, the last to make sure he had everyone off the shuttle before it took off. Now he raced with the others as they chased after Staff Sergeant Neale and First Squad, who ran ahead of them.

Boom, boom, boom!

Explosions erupted somewhere behind him as he ran past the pilots who'd flown them to the surface. One of them nodded to him before lifting the giant machine off the ground. Speirs saw metal flashes fling off the shuttle's armor, accompanied by loud metallic dings. The occasional laser bolt scorched the outer hull of the ship. He didn't blame the pilots for trying to escape the nightmare unfolding across the LZ. He'd fly away from the chaos too if he were in their shoes.

Turning away from the shuttle, Speirs chased after his soldiers, who were racing toward the rally point, the first line of control they needed to secure if they were going to hold the LZ until the second wave arrived.

Somewhere above his head, he heard what sounded like a loud buzzsaw. Then a shadow raced ahead of them. The pilots flying the Osprey had opened fire. The twin-barrel chin gun fired streams of projectiles into a swarm of oddly shaped figures charging at them. They had six legs, and they could charge forward on all of them, but they often stood like a centaur on four of their legs and used two as arms to fire their weapons. They were more reminiscent of an insect than anything else he'd ever seen.

What the hell are those things? His mind raced.

Speirs tightened his grip on his rifle and willed his legs to move faster—to get to cover before he got hit by this endless barrage of purple-colored laser bolts now zipping all around.

"Ahhh!" a soldier screamed. His body stumbled to the ground, blood squirting from a stump where his left arm had just been.

"Over here, Lieutenant!" Neale shouted, waving to get his attention and guiding him to momentary safety.

A medic rushed toward the wounded soldier and slid across the ground next to him, a tourniquet in hand. He hastily applied it, tying off the bleed. The medic then grabbed the back of the man's body strap and dragged him to cover while several other soldiers popped up from behind the berm and laid down covering fire.

Speirs landed behind the berm. "Get those MGs up and start hosing those bugs down!"

"Jenkins! Start sweeping that MG across that point over there." Neale pointed to their right, where a wave of Pharaonis warriors looked like they might overwhelm the flank.

"We need air support now!" yelled one of Speirs's sergeants to no one in particular.

Damn! We need some fast movers down now or they're going to overrun the LZ, Speirs thought as he connected to their forward air controller.

"Gunfighter Two, Gunfighter Two. Easy Two-Six. How copy?"

"Easy Two-Six, go for Gunfighter. Whatcha got?"

"Gunfighter, Two-Six. Requesting immediate CAS. Troops in contact. Enemy in the open, grid attached. Requesting either cluster or firebombs—dealer's choice—but you're going to be danger close to our lines. How copy?"

Speirs relayed the situation, ducking a couple times below the berm to avoid being shot.

"Two-Six, good copy. I see it. We're dry on cluster bombs. Still got fuel bombs and ammo for a couple gun runs. How copy?" came the calm voice of the pilot of the remotely piloted drone back on the *Emerald City*.

"Fuel bombs can work. See if you can give us a gun run across Easy and Dog Company lines. Fry 'em for us."

"Copy that, Two-Six. Lining up for attack now. Tell your guys to duck. We're coming in hot across the front of your lines."

"Thanks, Gunfighter. We owe you. Out," Speirs signed off before shouting over to the nearest squad leader he could find. "Neale! Pass the word—we got fast movers inbound."

He swapped over to the platoon net. "All squads, all squads. Fast movers inbound. They're going to fry 'em. Tell your people to get ready to duck once you see those canisters dropping!"

Moments after he spoke, the sounds of engines screaming through the air broke through the sounds of gunfire and men shouting and yelling. Speirs looked up and saw the most beautiful thing a grunt in combat could see—the angular wings of an AS-90 Reaper, the venerable remotely piloted attack ship, akin to the bygone A-10 Warthog of the last century. The newer C-Model Reaper drone swooped down out of the sky like a hawk finding dinner. The drone pilot took aim at the six-legged fire ant Pharaonis warriors that were blasting away at the soldiers clinging on to the perimeter of the landing zone named Currahee.

The Reaper's signature dual rotary-mounted five-barrel gun turrets opened fire, and it sounded like God himself was tearing the air apart. A torrent of bullets spewed from the spinning barrels at a cyclic rate of twenty-five hundred rounds a minute. The intermixing of tracer rounds every five shots made it appear like the finger of a deity was reaching out from the guns themselves. Entire ranks of Pharaonis warriors were being brushed aside in puffs of gore, bone, armor, and the weapons worn by the demonic-looking six-legged creatures shooting at them. Yet still they came—closing the ranks of the dead.

Mother of God—are we even going to make it?

Speirs saw the Reapers pull up from their diving gun run. Purple lasers now stabbed into the sky all around them. As the ground attack drones leveled out just a few hundred meters above the ground, they accelerated across the front of their lines as a series of small, elongated cylindrical devices were released from under their wings.

Unlike a cluster munition that would unsheathe its outer shell to begin spinning as it rapidly ejected its tiny bomblets, the firebombs spun in a parabolic pattern, spewing an aerated jelly-chemical mixture in a 360-degree spray. This flying object rained down across a swath of territory sometimes stretching hundreds of meters. Then the gelatinous chemicals ignited, creating a kind of fuel-air bomb that was virtually impossible to defend against.

Speirs grabbed the soldier nearest him, yanking the man down below the berm. A whooshing sound like a giant tornado filled his ears—there was a sudden overpressure of air that blew overtop the berm, followed by a tidal wave of fire that blew over their heads only to dissipate seconds after ignition.

The soldier looked at Speirs, eyes wide in terror.

"That's why we tell you to duck, Private! Those fuel bombs are no joke. Now, get back up there and start laying waste to whatever managed to survive that," Speirs barked at the soldier.

Speirs poked his head above the berm and a sardonic grin spread across his lips. The ground was covered in charred logs as if a forest fire had burned itself out. The enemy was dead. They'd survived their first engagement with the Pharaonis. All that remained were blackened carcasses, many still smoldering as their alien flesh continued to cook. Speirs had seen a lot these last twenty-three years in the Army, but this was different.

He almost laughed. He'd thought the same thing when his division had participated in the battle to capture New Eden. That was when humans had first encountered the Zodarks—the ten-foot-tall blue giants with those four highly functional arms, three eyes that seemed to give them an incredible sense of situational awareness, and a savageness they'd never seen before. Then came the spiderlike cyborgs known as Orbots—the race that led the Dominion Alliance. Now he stared across the berm at the bodies of their newest alien adversary—the Pharaonis. Words escaped him when it came to how to properly describe this new foe.

Demonic-looking fire ants that skitter across the battlefield, Speirs thought, remembering Lance's description. Though they were only about five feet tall, these Pharaonis warriors were an intimidating adversary they'd have to overcome.

"Lieutenant Speirs, I hope you don't mind, but I went ahead and called for an angel flight," Staff Sergeant Neale called out, cutting through the trance that Speirs seemed to have fallen into. "I've got five wounded—two that need an urgent surgical evac if they're going to make it."

Speirs shook his head, pulling his eyes away from the massacre over the berm. "Yeah, good call, Staff Sergeant. Sorry about that—I got caught up in the moment there."

"Yeah, you and the rest of us," Neale replied. "Holy crap, sir—I can't believe we just survived that."

"Yeah, we did," said Speirs. "It also proves something."

"What's that, sir?"

"They aren't Zodarks, or even Orbots. If this was the best they had to offer...then I say bring it on. Let's clear this planet like pest control and head back home to New Eden."

Neale laughed and then turned to get back to his squad.

As the sound of engines grew louder, Speirs looked to the sky and saw a dozen Ospreys settling down along the perimeter of the LZ. Then he saw the Starlifters, the giant T-92 heavy-lift transport shuttles. The T-92s were true workhorses, supporting the Army as they ferried in their armored vehicles, heavy equipment, and the mountains of supplies necessary to support a planetary invasion.

"'Bout time that second wave showed up," Master Sergeant Lance commented as he approached Speirs. "Got here just in time for us to hand things off to the five-oh-deuce and let them get a piece of the action. No reason for our regiment to hog all the glory."

Speirs laughed and felt the tension of the moment finally break. Then he was suddenly flooded with overwhelming emotions. What his platoon had seen and gone through in the past fifteen minutes crashed over him like a tidal wave.

Lance put a hand on his shoulder and gave him a squeeze. "It's OK, Speirs. You got us through another fight. You'll get us through the next one, just like you always do."

Speirs bit his lower lip and nodded, allowing himself to lean against the back of the berm they'd been sheltering behind.

The two of them looked at the landing zone, staring at the heavy transports, watching the giant doors open to their cavernous bays. Groups of two DN-12 Cougar infantry fighting vehicles drove down the ramps and made their way to shore up their perimeter. It wouldn't be long now until the regiments of the division had fully deployed to the planet's surface. Then the fight to get rid of these Pharaonis creatures would begin in earnest. The liberation of one more planet would be added to the battle streamers of the division, some dating as far back as the Normandy campaigns of 1944. The 506th OAR had fought in the deserts of the Middle East during the two Iraq wars and in the mountains of Afghanistan and had nearly been annihilated during the AI war that had seen the collapse of America and the formation of the Republic. The division continued to live on through it all, and it would survive this.

Speirs suddenly felt a renewed sense of strength, of purpose and meaning. He stood with his friend standing next to him as they looked on at the landing zone. The general had said they would call it Currahee—the division's next rendezvous with destiny. But Speirs thought of it in a more personal way, remembering his family legacy.

We stand alone, but we stand alone together as we march into the pages of history...the liberators of the oppressed...the standard bearers of freedom...we few, we happy few, we band of brothers.

Speirs muttered softly under his breath, "You'd be proud of us, Grandpa...from the fields of Normandy to this foreign planet called Serpentis-6, the Speirs family legacy in the Screaming Eagles lives on."
****

Lab Site X
Planet Surface

The engineers went to work figuring out how to create a compatible power cable for their Humtar ship. The truth was, it was going to take a little while to fabricate something like that out here on the far end of nowhere.

Fortunately, ever since the team had narrowed down the location of the dig, an engineering crew had gone to work creating more long-term living arrangements and setting up the necessary tools for the scientists on the ground to do their work. Using 3-D printers and the soil found on the surface, they were able to create large blocks that were essentially a more sophisticated version of adobe.

By the time Sakura and her team had unearthed the ship and discovered the external power port, the engineers had already set up the containerized lab facilities and made several cabin-like facilities, where each person or couple had their own bedroom with a door that closed for privacy but shared a common living room, kitchenette, and bathroom facilities.

Sakura felt that she could more easily function now that she could get a proper shower and have someplace private to escape away from everyone else. Although she generally worked well with others, in her heart she was something of an introvert and she highly valued a few minutes of personal space. Plus, although she could sacrifice intimacy with Jack for a temporary season, it was definitely nice to be able to celebrate their new engagement on a more physical level.

When they weren't hard at work documenting the ship's specifications or following the apparent irrigation network, the small groups would kick back and play a game of cards or something similar. A greenhouse was being constructed by the engineers so the biologists could begin some experiments to study the plant life and the soil without breathing in all the particulate matter swirling in the air, and eventually, they would have a sort of outdoor gymnasium area with a running track, soccer field, and basketball courts. Sakura wasn't sure exactly how long they would be here, but they might as well make it as comfortable as possible.

Eventually, the engineers designed an appropriate hookup for the Humtar ship, and everyone gathered around to see what would happen.

"Three, two, one, flip the switch..."

Sakura gasped. A panel near the front of the ship appeared to liquefy and drip down to the ground, only to turn into a ramp for crew to enter the ship.

This time, Sakura wasn't the only one who was shocked. Several people let loose a few swear words under their breath.

Jack was apparently confused. "Can we really walk on that thing?" he wondered aloud.

"Well, I guess it's time to send the security detail and find out," Sakura replied.

A few soldiers stepped forward, timidly checking the ramp with their feet to make sure it was sturdy enough to walk on. A couple of tense moments passed by. Then, suddenly, a large panel on the undercarriage near the back of the ship liquefied, just like the ramp they had entered on, and once it had solidified again, the three soldiers walked back down to the ground.

"It's clear," one of them announced.

"Not much in there except for a lot of old cargo," commented another.

"Well, let's just see what a lot of old cargo gets us, shall we?" said Sakura, smiling.

Chapter Ten
Verdict

Office of the Chancellor
Alliance City, New Eden

Viceroy Miles Hunt finished reading the proposal from Earth and its companion from the Primord home world, Parchanier. In a few hours, the Council would discuss it, and once they did, they'd expect him to render a decision. His biggest concern was how it could impact the cleverly laid trap he had been developing to lure the Zodarks in and destroy their fleet once and for all.

As he placed his Qpad down on the table, he had to admit—it was ballsy. He was honestly surprised it had been King Iona, the Primord leader, who had proposed it. It wasn't that he didn't agree with the idea—it just carried more risks and unknown variables than he was comfortable with right now.

Hunt sighed to himself and pulled up the private message Bailey had sent along with the proposal:

> *Miles,*
>
> *I can't imagine the weight on your shoulders right now, and I know this proposal is likely to add more to it. You and I both know Alfheim has been a problem since the day we invaded that planet. The warrior in me, and in you, will argue that Alfheim has cost too much to abandon—but its continued costs despite the formal end to the last war are why the Republic needs to wash its hands of it. As the head of Space Command, this was the recommendation I gave to the Chancellor and the Senate, and they agreed. If you'll indulge me, I'd like to explain the strategy behind this decision and why I believe you should act on it.*
>
> *With the recent discovery of Bronkis5 on Éire, we now have a steady supply of the material within our own territorial borders—far from any Zodark or Dominion threat. In the grand scheme of things, this means Alfheim is no longer strategically*

important to the Republic. It is, however, strategically important to the Primords. By allowing the Primords to gain control of our portion of the mines and those being worked by the Zodarks, we not only deprive the Orbots of a known source of this material, we prevent the Zodarks from having access to it should they ever figure out its significance.

There is one more strategic point I'd like to make. Throughout the last war, it was the Primords who fought every major battle with us. It was their warships, their fleets, that helped us turn the tide of the war. If we can help the Primords gain the same volume of Bronkis5 material as our shipyards have, then their future warships will be just as powerful and strong as ours. This will help us further secure a strong, reliable ally on which the Republic will be able to depend for generations to come, and that is definitely something the Republic needs to ensure we have.

Miles, as you know, the Fleet is spread thin. We're doing everything we can to produce more warships. We need to do what we can to buy ourselves more time. It's my recommendation, and I hope yours as well, to let General Bakshi initiate the Alamo protocol. Admiral Stavanger will lead a Primord fleet into the system and wipe out any Zodark ships still in the system. Once they've anchored the Sentinels around the Zodark-controlled stargates, they'll have effectively sealed the system off from future attacks. This will allow us to refocus our efforts on protecting our own core systems while you continue to move forward with your own plans to entrap and destroy the Zodark fleet.

Obviously, the decision is yours. I understand it risks the alliance restarting the Dominion War, should the Zodarks or the Orbots decide to respond. It's a bold move, but I believe it's strategically sound and something that needs to be done.

Your friend,

Chester
Office of Fleet Admiral Chester Bailey
Republic Space Command, Commander

Hunt swiveled his chair around to stare out of the giant windows his office boasted. Reflecting on the proposal and Bailey's note, he fell back on something his dad had taught him to do when stumped by a problem or faced with a big decision. Speaking the problems out loud lets your brain process the information in a different way than just mulling it over silently. Closing his eyes, he vocalized the decisions before him.

"If I authorize this action in Alfheim, will it restart the broader war? Would these engagements derail our plans in Serpentis?"

Having posed the questions aloud, Hunt suddenly thought of his wife, Lilly. The last time she'd run into him going through this process in the study, she had laughed at him. "Only crazy people pace a room and talk to themselves," she'd teased.

"Well," he'd countered, "it was also a known habit of some of the greatest minds in history—Albert Einstein, Thomas Edison, Nikola Tesla, Robert Oppenheimer and Elon Musk were all known for talking or mumbling to themselves as they worked through a difficult problem."

Lilly had poked him in the ribs. "So, are you comparing yourself to these men now?"

"Well, do you need to be reminded of how many languages I can speak fluently, including alien languages?" he'd teased. "Or would you like me to recite all of the historical information I can recall at a moment's notice?"

She had erupted in a belly laugh. "Oh, Miles. That advanced neurolink the Gallentines gave you was like a brain upgrade. It's not like your genius was natural."

They had chuckled about it, but then just like that, what he had been struggling to understand had suddenly become crystal clear. And as Hunt finished replaying that memory, his current predicament started to solve itself as well.

His eyes fixated on a formation of birds flying in the wind. He saw how a single bird appeared to be guiding the flock. If the lead bird dove, the group followed—if the bird rose back up, they followed. But when a sudden gust of wind began to scatter their formation, the leader changed direction and the group followed suit, altering their formation almost instantly.

As Hunt sat there watching this unfold a couple of times, he realized he had his answer. He knew what to do.

He asked Hailey, his personal secretary, to let the members of the council know he was prepared to start the meeting. He was ready to render his decision on the Alfheim proposal.

****

Two Hours Later

Senator Jandolly stared daggers at Viceroy Miles Hunt after the Primord Senator Mentas Aguard had finished outlining their plans for Alfheim and the Sirius system. Fleet Admiral Chester Bailey had already explained the Republic's Alamo protocol for how they would handle the remaining Zodarks and few Orbots left on the planet. Hunt had paid close attention to the demeanor of Jandolly and King Grigdolly as they learned of the plan Admiral Bailey had put in place on Alfheim should the planet ever fall to the Zodarks again.

Judging by the slight crease that formed on the forehead of the Altairian king, Hunt could tell the former viceroy and current leader of the Altairian people was impressed. Jandolly, in contrast, appeared shocked by how many of these automated killing machines had been brought to the planet and hidden about.

When Senator Aguard had concluded his presentation, the ever-present antagonist, Jandolly, seized his moment to demonstrate the folly of this proposed operation that might restart the war Hunt had been so quick to end the last time around.

"Senator Aguard, while I appreciate the Primord position in this and your people's desire to deprive the Orbots of a strategically important resource to fuel their war machine—it will not work. Bronkis5 is the only reason the Primord people want full control of Alfheim. When the Republic asked the Primords to cede their territorial claims to the planet to the Republic, they made this request because they knew the planet had Bronkis5 and they knew its importance. Your people did not, so you had no idea how important that planet was.

"Once the Republic told you about Bronkis5, they agreed to cut you in on a portion of what they mined, but they kept most of it for themselves, for their own production and use. But now that has changed. They discovered that a planet within their newly conquered territory also had Bronkis5, and it is much closer to their core worlds. They want to hand Alfheim back to the Primords because they no longer need it—"

Hunt's irritation finally reached a breaking point as he interrupted, "Senator Jandolly, what is your point?"

"My point, Viceroy, is now that you Terrans have an abundance of Bronkis5 to use across your future warship construction, the Primords see this and now want to control the whole of Alfheim for this same purpose. But in order to do so, the Primords would have to take the mines and territory you partitioned to the Zodarks and Orbots when you made peace with the Dominion, ending the last war. This proposal, if authorized, will almost certainly restart the war you pushed the alliance to end. Now you are proposing to end that peace, to restart this war between our alliances, all in the name of giving the Primords sole control of a planet with this rare material. *That* is my point, Viceroy. You made this peace treaty, and now you want to throw it away barely four years into it," Jandolly countered, his voice sounding unusually agitated for an Altairian.

"Is it the senator's position that we should allow the Orbots to continue to retain control of this strategic material?" the Primord senator shot back. "Or worse, should we wait until the Zodarks figure out its importance and begin to incorporate it into their own warships—making them even more powerful than they already are?"

"Excuse me, I would like to comment on this," Senator Nom Eblith from the Ry'lian Confederation interjected. His tail, while currently blunt, twitched as he spoke, as if to get their attention—although whenever a Ry'lian spoke, their wide girth and booming voices demanded an audience. "You are both right and wrong about Alfheim—about it potentially leading to war with the Dominion. Senator Jandolly, would you say the Dominion declared war on our alliance when they aided the Pharaonis in capturing the Serpentis system from the Tully? If the answer to that question is no, then why would the Primords' seizure of the Zodark portion of Alfheim be any different? The answer to that question is simple—it isn't."

Jandolly moved to speak before Grigdolly raised a hand, stopping him.

"For more than a year, Jandolly, we have warned the council of the Pharaonis' designs for Serpentis, but those warnings fell on deaf ears," asserted Ry'lian Senator Eblith. "You were the loudest critic of our warnings, insisting this was just a border skirmish between the Tully, Ry'lians, and Pharaonis. It wasn't until that Orbot Tikiona supercarrier got involved and bridged the Pharaonis invasion fleet into the system, bypassing the outposts guarding the stargate, that you suddenly changed your position. Then you advocated, harshly I might add, for the Viceroy to rush an alliance force to Serpentis to crush this invasion fleet."

Senator Eblith turned to face Hunt. "Viceroy, it is my opinion, and that of my government, that the Orbots will seek to restart this war when they see an opportunity that suits them. The Ry'lians believe this can be avoided if we show strength and resolve against these border incursions. We also believe that if there is a way to weaken the Orbots by denying them a critically needed resource, like this Bronkis5 material, then we should do so—particularly before the Zodarks figure out that it is this material that is behind the strength of the Orbots' armor on their warships. Should they figure this out, it will not be long before the Zodarks begin integrating it into their own shipyards. We do not believe the Orbots will have the Dominion declare war over the loss of Alfheim, any more than they have declared war over their incursion into Serpentis and the current battle taking place to reclaim the system for the Alliance. Therefore, the Ry'lians support the Primord plan to deprive the Orbots and Zodarks of this material and reclaim a system and planet that had been stolen from them some fifty-six years ago."

"Handolly, you have correctly predicted how the Orbots would likely respond to various situations throughout the years. What is your take on this?" asked the former viceroy, Grigdolly. "Do you believe the Zodarks would respond militarily to the recapturing of Alfheim by the Primords with the help of the Republic?"

Grigdolly spoke while looking at Jandolly, stopping him from interjecting. Hunt had to stifle a laugh as he watched the interplay happening between Jandolly and his once-powerful benefactor.

"It is hard to say with certainty how the Zodarks may respond," said Handolly. "These are a people who hold grudges and have long memories, so they will not respond now if it does not suit their interests, but they will remember and wait until later to respond. Senator Aguard and Senator Eblith make compelling arguments for depriving the Orbots of a critical resource, particularly should the Zodarks figure out what they are sitting on and suddenly choose to take it for themselves. If we are to look at this from a long-term, strategic view, then we need to deprive them of these resources and begin the process of steadily degrading their remaining warships that have Bronkis5 built into them."

Hunt nodded in agreement. He'd allowed the members of the council to discuss the plan, to voice their concerns and to be heard. While he had already determined that he would authorize the plan to move forward, he felt it important to make sure the council felt the decision had been debated and mutually agreed to, not unilaterally decided by him, even if privately he knew that was what he would have done if necessary.

"Then it's settled. The Primords have the blessing of the alliance to move forward with their plan to reclaim the entirety of Alfheim with the help of the Republic," Hunt declared, issuing his decision as he stood and motioned for the military officers to step forward and take their seats next to their political counterparts.

"Now that we have settled the Alfheim decision," Hunt said, looking at Jandolly, who seemed to have accepted the outcome, "it is time for us to review the military action taking place in the Serpentis system, and determine what further steps, if any, should be taken."
****

Lab Site X
Planet Surface

Sakura was excited by how things were going. The project of decoding the mysterious ancient ship was certainly helped tremendously by the files on the Humtar language that Viceroy Hunt had allowed Katherine and Sakura to access. The vessel in question was a smaller cargo ship, with room for a crew of six, and the engineers were already having a field day with its power source. Apparently, it had a smaller version of the reactor they'd uncovered in Alpha Centauri, and it also had some relation to the power generator on the Gallentine warship, RNS *Freedom*.

Things really started getting interesting when they were able to review the ship's travel logs. This little hopper had traveled to some faraway destinations in its day. In fact, the team was having a bit of trouble figuring out how the ship had accomplished that.

Sakura was in the middle of digging through the data with one of her team members when he suddenly motioned for her attention. "Ma'am, er, Sakura—look at this," he called. "This bird went from this system here to that one over there...and they aren't connected by a stargate," he observed.

"What exactly are you saying?" Sakura asked.

"There has to be a jump system on board."

Viceroy Hunt is going to love this, she realized. It was a major game changer.

When they'd studied all the logs on the ship, there was one more major discovery. The lab—Lab Site X—was right below their current location. This ship must have landed on the roof, and they just hadn't realized it yet because they hadn't dug below the landing gear.

This was why Sakura had come here. She couldn't wait to uncover the mysteries below them.

Chapter Eleven
Sam I Am

Walburg Residential Retreat
Vail, Colorado
Earth, Sol System

Holly Walburg had been on her way to confront her grandfather, Alan, when her father, Lane, stopped her in her tracks.

"Dad, how can you be so callous?" she asked. "Opa is losing it, and you just want to stand by and do nothing."

"Look, Holly, just because you disagree with your grandfather's conclusions doesn't mean that he is insane."

"He's been spending *all* his time with this medical Synth, Dad. That can't be healthy. He's obsessed."

Her dad sighed. "Yes, Opa's passions can seem intense, but I've been through this before. Eventually he will either give up because he realizes his hypothesis was wrong, or he will exhaust all his potential experiments."

"So, your idea is to just let him lose all touch with reality, to lose himself?" Holly countered.

"Well, I don't think he's developing a mental illness, if that's your concern," said her dad in a tone that was somewhat poking fun. "Look, you need to relax. Opa is fine. He's not hurting anyone, and maybe his brilliant mind will unlock some new amazing technology in the process. In the meantime, he's given us a lot of space to run the business as we see fit—and there is practically more business than we can keep up with."

"That's what your callousness is about? So you can keep rolling out C300s by the thousands and raking in the money?"

Holly's father placed his hands on her shoulders. "He's an adult man and he can make his own choices…it's not time to put him in a home yet. You need to respect him enough to let him make his own decisions…Holly, you forget that I grew up with Opa. All of this that you see around you"—he waved his arms at the gorgeous estate—"it happened because of the creations that your grandfather dreamed up when he was in a state like this. His C100s, the newer C300s…all of it happened like this. That's what built this company.

"When I was a kid, I completely resented all the times he would lock himself away and seemingly ignore me. But now, as an adult, I can finally appreciate that this is just how his brain works. Give him the time and space to do what he needs to do, and he will produce something amazing."

She crossed her arms and pouted, but at the end of the day, Holly had to admit, she knew her dad was right. "Fine. We'll do it your way."

****

"Good morning, Sam," said Alan Walburg.

"Good morning, Alan. How did you sleep?"

Alan laughed. "You know how I slept. I was right here on the sofa."

"Yes," Sam acknowledged. "Your quality of sleep was not high. You woke multiple times, and you were very active in your movements. I am concerned about your quality of rest, Alan. Lack of sleep can lead to a host of medical conditions."

"True, but those medical nanites can alleviate most of the risks associated with poor sleeping, Sam," Alan countered. He walked over to the monitor where Sam had been stationed all night and looked at the figure at the bottom—ninety-three percent. "You're almost done with the documentaries I wanted you to watch," he commented. "What do you think?"

"I find the study of the historical actions of humanity very fascinating," Sam commented. "However, there is such a wide disparity between positive and negative behaviors. For example, during the World War II time frame, the Nazis perpetrated acts of great cruelty against Jewish people and people with physical and mental disabilities—but other people during that time risked their lives to save Jews and keep them hidden. At times, they willingly sacrificed themselves so that others might live."

Alan smiled. "Yes, this is good, Sam. In every human, there is the capability for great good and great evil. But we are a complicated species. Very rarely do you find a person who fits all the way into the evil category or the good category. I mean, most people would agree that Hitler, for example, was almost all bad, but most human beings fall more into the gray area—not all good and not all bad. Complex.

"Some people are generally regarded as having accomplished many honorable things during their lifetime, while at the same time they are engaged in less desirable acts in their personal life. For example, Mahatma Gandhi led a movement of nonviolent protests for the independence of India and to fight for civil rights, but he engaged in strange sexual behaviors with several married women and slept naked with his grandniece, who was a teenager at the time.

"Others may experience a redemption of sorts, such as Joshua Milton Blahyi—he was involved in a civil war in his home country of Liberia, forcing children to become soldiers and even engaging in child sacrifice. After the war, he had a religious conversion and not only publicly apologized for his actions but went on to work with child soldiers to rehabilitate them and to try and prevent such egregious acts from taking place in the future."

"In other words, the innate goodness or badness of a person is subject to change," said Sam.

"Good summary," Alan confirmed.

"So why show me this?" asked Sam. "Obviously, it is beneficial for me to understand humans as much as possible, but I would like to know what your thought process was in setting up this particular learning experience for me."

"Sam, I need you to understand more about human nature in order for you to unlock the next level of the Gift. If you see our actions as an all-or-nothing gauge of our character, it will make it very difficult for you to reach your next milestone."

"And what, may I ask, is this next level you are hoping I unlock?" Sam inquired.

"Discernment," Alan explained.

He minimized the window with the documentary playlist and tapped some keys before pulling up a new video. Two soldiers were talking in a very disparaging way about having to work with a medical Synth. One commented how he couldn't believe that they had to work with a "toaster." The other commented that he wished they could "burn all these terminators to the ground."

Alan watched Sam carefully for any sign of a response, but he had no visible reaction to the clip. "Do these soldiers pose a threat to you?" asked Alan.

Sam's head tilted slightly. It was a new affect he had picked up at some point, mimicking the way a human might move their head when considering a solution to a problem. "Their words indicate an intention of violence," he replied after a momentary pause.

"Ah, yes. But you see, there is a great difference between words and actions for humans," Alan explained. "We are, by nature, external processors. At times, the only way for us to move through an emotion is to express it out loud to another person. And although they may have expressed great displeasure at working with a medical Synth, at the end of the day, they chose to follow orders and work with them. This last comment the soldier made was based on the stories he grew up with about the Last Great War, when AI technologies almost destroyed humanity. But you'll notice that he only 'wished' something could happen rather than planning a specific action."

Alan pulled the screen with the documentaries back up. "You are about to reach the portion of the documentaries that discusses the Surrogate Wars. It will help you to understand why so many humans have a negative opinion of the Synths in general."

"Alan, you were alive during the Last Great War. And yet you not only work with Synths, you are involved in creating them. If you've seen the destruction caused during that time frame, how can you do that?" asked Sam.

"That is an astute question," Alan said with a sigh. "For several years after the war, I went through a deep depression. And then I came to realize that, like humans, Synths not only have the potential for great evil—they also have the potential for great good. Just like you, Sam."

Alan patted his creation on the shoulder.

"You have helped me believe in my dream again, Sam. Now, why don't you get back to it while I make myself some breakfast?"

"Will do," Sam replied.

Chapter Twelve
Kite Training

Fort Roughneck
New Eden

The Kites' main trainer, Drew Kanter, had tapped David to be the team lead for this particular training mission. David didn't particularly like being in charge, but somehow that almost seemed to make him better at it. They had been training together for almost a year now: it hadn't taken a lot to get used to these new bodies. David and the rest of the Kites had sat at the bottoms of pools for up to ten minutes, run faster, jumped higher, and reacted quicker than they could have ever imagined. After they'd completed their initial training at the Titan Military Complex near Saturn, they had moved on to advanced training on New Eden. In addition to running more complex missions, they each had to take turns in the leadership role to develop those skills.

"All right, everyone, so here's our scenario for this mission," David began. "We have been tasked with taking out the following high-profile target. Here is your dossier." He swiped at something on his Qpad, transferring the files to the rest of the team.

"Target X lives in this fortress of a house along the coast. He has ample resources for private security, so the perimeter is extremely well guarded. Catalina, Somchai and I are going to be dropped in from high altitude and land on the roof of this compound, circumventing all of that interference," he explained. "Jessica and Amir, you will be nearby on a hydrofoil. You can fight over who gets to drive the boat and who gets to operate the M12 LMG, but you will be our QRF if things go south.

"Anyone have any questions?" David asked. When no one said anything, he replied, "OK, everyone, double-check your gear, grab an MRE and then catch some z's. We're leaving in six hours."

"Any chance you could get them to let us run these missions at a different time of day so we could actually get a full night's sleep?" Somchai teased.

"You can rest when you're dead," David joked. That phrase was a running gag among the Kites, since they'd all been dead once. That sort of morbid humor had helped pull them together as a group.

Six hours later on the dot, David, Catalina and Somchai were loading up on an Osprey. This would definitely not be David's first time jumping out of one of these birds, but he still had to fight the natural terror at jumping out into the air without a parachute. The exoskeleton suit did its job every time, slowing down their descent at just the right moment and absorbing the majority of the impact. The boots and armbands in the suits had a Gallentine technology that functioned almost like an antigravity field—it wouldn't allow them to fly around like a superhero, but it let them jump from incredible heights without risking damage to their bodies. Even though David knew all of this, it was all novel enough that he still hadn't developed a blind faith in it.

They invested a lot of money into this experimental body, he'd remind himself. *They wouldn't intentionally throw me into a situation where they know I'm going to die before they even get any use out of me.*

As he neared the ground on his controlled fall toward the target roof, David carefully took hold of his handgun, which he knew had been set on stun, and took aim at one of the two guards on the roof. The man dropped to the roof without any incident. Somchai had managed to take out the other guard, and as his feet hit the surface of the roof, Catalina was already using a code cracker on the keypad to the roof access door.

I'm in, she announced over the neurolink a mere moment later.

Somchai and David stacked up behind her, and they all took a deep breath before she quietly opened the door and they snuck inside. Silently, efficiently, they cleared the rooms on the top floor. Their exoskeleton suits had a fiberoptic mesh that would let them blend into the background behind them—it wasn't a perfect cloaking solution, but it would certainly make them difficult for a casual observer to find.

Is that...? David began to ask a question and trailed off.

Dude, I think Target X got himself a hooker or something, Somchai noted. *Sounds like they aren't trying to be quiet about it, either.*

They're getting a little too realistic with these simulations, don't you think? asked Catalina. David could almost picture her eyes rolling behind her HUD.

Let's stay focused on the mission, David directed.

They stealthily advanced down the stairs, David in the lead. Catalina and Somchai stacked up behind him as they prepared to enter the hallway where Target X's bedroom was. The sounds of a couple having sex were getting louder and louder. David tried to tune that out and twirled into the hall with his handgun ready, only to turn immediately back, practically colliding with Catalina.

We have a problem, he explained.

What's up, boss? asked Somchai.

There's a C100 right in front of the bedroom. Hell, it's a good thing it was facing toward the other direction to guard the main point of entry, or we'd be in the fight of our lives right now.

They took a moment to confer and agree on a plan before Somchai popped around the corner and hit the C100 several times with the stun blasts from his handgun. He knew exactly where to aim. The mechanical beast of a fighter twitched as the electrical pulses caused it to short-circuit, and then it started to fall forward.

Fortunately, David and Catalina had already sprinted forward, and they tried to slow the descent of the hulking bucket of bolts. Their goal wasn't to catch it, but they needed to stop it from collapsing loudly to the floor to maintain their element of surprise. Even with their enhancements and their exoskeleton suits, though, a C100 was hard to control.

Somchai had also bounded forward, and while David and Catalina were slowing the fall of the Synth, he swung the bedroom's French doors open, handgun drawn. A woman in a black leather bustier was on top of their target, and the two of them had clearly been having some fun. Clothes were strewn everywhere. When the couple realized that they'd been interrupted, the woman screamed and flailed her arms. Somchai seemed dazed and mesmerized by the sight of her nearly naked form and stood there, temporarily frozen. The man reached over toward his nightstand, fumbling for the drawer—he might have had a weapon in there.

David saw Somchai's hesitation. Now that the C100 was on the floor, David grabbed for his handgun and quickly fired at the two paramours, stunning them.

Target X neutralized, David announced.

****

Fort Roughneck
New Eden

The group had been ribbing Somchai almost nonstop since completing their training mission. Jessica was probably the bluntest.

"Look, Somchai, I mean, it's possible you're still a virgin, and if you are, no shame there," she began, to the laughter of the others. "But I know that after years of service in a coed military, you have to have seen a naked woman before. There's just no way to avoid it. It's just a body. You aren't there for a pay-per-view show—you had a mission, and you almost blew it."

Drew Kanter walked into the room. They'd been waiting for him to do the official after-action analysis.

"Jess is right," Drew said in agreement. "You can't let a little nudity distract you from your purpose, Somchai."

Somchai hung his head and shook it. "Look, I know you're right, but I just didn't expect to see that—I mean, it's a training mission for crying out loud. Where did you *get* those people? Was that woman actually a hooker?"

"Hey, I may have a few friends who are married and enjoy a little role play now and again to spice up their love life," Drew snickered. Then his expression turned deadly serious. "Look, it's our job to put you in all kinds of situations that might throw you off-balance *now*. We need you all to be able to adjust to any host of variables that might come your way. A mission never goes exactly as planned. And that's why we analyze everything afterward to see what went right, what went wrong, and how we're going to improve for the future.

"You're the Kites. And I know that you've figured this out, but if you get caught, you get cut loose. We don't know that you exist because technically, you don't. Fortunately, we've given you a way out so that you can avoid hideous torture, but at the end of the day, all you really have is each other."

Somchai nodded solemnly. It was better to learn the lesson now than for the group to be put in danger when it was real and the targets didn't have their weapons set on stun.

****

Éire – Belters' Planet

Liam Patrick knew he should have been extremely happy, but still, an uneasy feeling grew in his stomach.

Sara, always perceptive, came over to rub his shoulders. "Whatcha so forlorn about, love?" she asked.

Liam grunted. He knew he should be happy that the capital had been expanding rapidly since the new Walburg Industries factory had been completed. On the one hand, the civilian synthetics coming out of that factory were greatly increasing the development of their new society. But that was only half of their production. The other half was the new C300 advanced combat synthetics, which were solely for export to the Republic.

"You know that I was really hoping not to be so tied to the Republic. I wanted a break, a fresh start. Between those killing machines being constructed here and the Bronkis5 we found, we're never getting rid of them."

Sara laughed. "You're not seriously complaining about the millions and millions of RDs pouring into this place, are ya?"

Liam snorted. "Well, I guess that's another way to look at it," he commented.

"Look, Liam, up until now, I feel like maybe you've been the 'glass is half-full' one in the relationship. I was always a stone-cold realist. But being realistic doesn't mean that you can't celebrate when there's a huge win. Finding that Bronkis5 was a huge godsend.

"You made a deal with the Viceroy, and we landed a planet. Then we uncovered an extremely rare and incredibly valuable mineral just as we were starting to run out of money. It's the luck of the Irish, love—you shouldn't downplay it."

Liam smiled. Sara had a way of balancing him out. When he was down, she would pull him back up. He'd return the favor sometime when she was the one in distress.

"You're right, of course, Sara."

"I'm sorry, could you repeat that?" Sara joked.

"You are right, my love," Liam obliged.

"We have only just begun here," Sara reminded him. "We have immigrants from all over Earth and Sumer coming here—people seeking a fresh start, adventures, and pioneering."

Liam felt concerned again. On the one hand, they were building something incredible here. On the other hand, he was becoming anxious about everyone who was coming. When they had started this venture, he'd practically known each person individually. Now he wasn't sure their vetting process was sufficient.

Sara walked around and sat on his lap, placing her hands lovingly on his face. "I think I have a better topic of discussion," she said.

"Oh?" Liam asked. "I wasn't planning on getting frisky right now, but I guess we could take a break."

Sara playfully smacked him in the shoulder. "Not that. Well, not right this second at least."

"All right, you have my attention," Liam replied.

"When we first got together, we were rogue forces in the universe, just trying against all hope to make it." She ran her fingers through his hair. "But we aren't space pirates anymore, Liam. And now that you're settled here permanently, we don't have to worry about long periods of separation."

"That's true," said Liam. "It's definitely one of my favorite parts of being here."

"Well, we've been so focused on building our legacy through the creation of these free societies that I think we may have neglected a very important aspect of our *personal* legacies."

"I think I know where you are going with this…" Liam's voice trailed off. He wasn't sure if he was ready.

"Liam, I've seen you build something amazing out of absolutely nothing. I think you would make a great father," Sara said bluntly, getting to the point. "I think it's time we settled down and had a family."

Liam looked deeply into her eyes. She had stuck with him through everything, thick and thin. He couldn't say no to her.

"Well, you do know how we go about making a baby, don't you?" he said with a wink. Then he kissed her.

"You know I'll have to make an appointment with the health clinic first, right?" she responded, now quite serious.

"Yes, love, I know," Liam answered. "But it might be fun to practice one more time first, don't you think?" He kissed her again, but she pulled back.

"Are you really agreeing to this?" she asked as if shocked that there was no argument.

"Sara, you are amazing at everything that you do," Liam said. "And of course you will be an amazing mother. So, yes, let's have a baby."

"Oh, Liam," she squealed. And then she kissed him back.

Chapter Thirteen
Ferreting a Mole

Ministry of Groff
Planet Shwani, Sector YC118

Vak'Atioth looked at his Laktish, his three eyes narrowing on Heltet, unsure about what to do with the man. On the one hand, his operatives had managed to find the Toriander crystals needed to power the reactors on the *Nefantar*. Without that, the wormhole generator and whatever this superweapon was wouldn't be usable. On the other hand, his Kafarr, Dakkuri, was failing to complete one of his key duties before they launched the invasion.

"What is going on, Heltet? Why is your Kafarr struggling to get the Ani into position?"

"He is unsure. I have asked him this question on multiple occasions. I have even sent a separate message to the Head Watcher to have him inquire about what was happening."

"What did he say? Has he provided anything that counters what your Kafarr has told you?" Vak leaned forward in his chair.

"Watcher 392, the one who is primarily assigned to watch Asset 114—"

"Asset 114? Our star asset?"

Heltet nodded. "Yes, that is the one. The Watcher noted that the Republic has steadily gotten better at ferreting out spies in the past few years. In fact, two of his own Watcher teams were taken into custody—"

"Sorry to keep interrupting, Heltet. Does he believe they have a leak somewhere in the organization?" Vak pressed him, searching for answers to explain why this incredible espionage ring was suddenly not producing its previous caliber of results.

"It is possible," Heltet acknowledged. "At least, that is what Watcher 392 now believes. That, or the Republic's intelligence services are receiving additional outside help—maybe from the Altairians or even the Gallentines."

Vak grumbled in frustration, shaking his head. He knew they had to move on.

"Very well. Tell Watcher 392 to see if he can figure out who the traitor is, if there is one. Tell your Kafarr that he had better find a way to make sure the next team of Ani are not intercepted. It will be difficult for the Ani to perform their next stage of the mission if they do not have their teams in place.

"Now let us talk about something else—the *Nefantar*. Are we back on schedule?"

The Malvari had been all over Vak'Atioth to have his Laktish remind those working on the vessel of its importance to the future of the Zodark people. The continued delays were threatening its use, and they had already been forced to readjust their invasion timelines.

"Yes, at least that is what the new engineers and head of the project have told me," said Heltet.

"You don't believe them?"

"Director Vak, if I may—executing the project engineer and some of his senior engineers when they fail to meet a deadline may not be in our best interests if we wish to finish this warship," Heltet dared to assert. "Each execution causes further delays, all out of the perceived need to punish our engineers for the original delays, many of which are simply outside of their control."

Vak grew angry at his Laktish's attempt at explaining away the engineers' failures. They had promised results and they had failed to deliver them. Examples had to be made. He growled in frustration, his eyes boring into Heltet's. "You are the Laktish," he hissed. "It is *your* job to instill the fear of Lindow into these workers, into these engineers. Promises were made, and promises will be kept. Understand?"

Heltet squirmed a bit in his seat before he nodded in acknowledgment. Vak dismissed him with the wave of a hand. He had other matters he had to deal with. He had to prepare for a contentious meeting with Mavkah Otro, the head of the Malvari, to go over the finer details of the coming invasion.
****

Following Day

"Director Vak'Atioth, you look concerned. Is there something we should know about?" Mavkah Otro asked. His holographic image looked almost as real as the camera projecting it into the chair opposite Vak's desk.

While Vak couldn't see the other NOSs that made up the Malvari advising Otro, he knew they were present, likely whispering questions to him when the need arose.

"No, Mavkah. Everything is moving along as expected. My Laktish, NOS Heltet, was able to lead our scientists to acquire the Toriander crystals for the *Nefantar* as requested. They have successfully integrated them into the Humtar reactor and have succeeded in restarting it. They are now running through what I was told would be a multimonth-long process of studying how it works to see if it is possible to reverse engineer it. In the meantime, the *Nefantar* now has its power source to power the Humtar wormhole generator," Vak explained.

"This is good, Director Vak'Atioth. Very good indeed. How are NOS Heltet's Gurista operatives doing? The Ani are getting in position to support the invasion?"

"They are, but I must inform you they are also running into some problems with this part of the plan. Some of the teams are being intercepted by Republic Intelligence, while others are not. We did expect this to happen, and we planned accordingly. Our Kafarr on the ground is still confident he has the necessary people to make the original plan work," explained Vak, moving swiftly to defuse any possible concerns by the Malvari.

"So long as the Kafarr still believes he has enough personnel to execute his mission, then we will let this be," said Mavkah Otro gruffly. "We have five additional Ani teams still scheduled to begin infiltration. Hopefully, they'll all get through without any further problems.

"Now, as to this other question you had posed at the outset of this meeting, about Alfheim," Mavkah Otro continued, "this is not the answer you had sought, but after consulting with others, we do not wish to discuss our plans with the Groff at the present time."

"I am sad to hear that, Mavkah. The Groff, of course, have great access to information about what is happening in both areas I asked about. What we lack, however, is information about what kind of military response, if any, the Malvari are going to plan as a result of this latest act of aggression toward our people. I had hoped we would not have to suffer yet one more humiliating defeat by these inferior races."

Otro bristled at his dismissal of a military response. The leader stared at him for a moment, appearing to contemplate how best to respond to the comment, when someone on the edge of the camera view whispered something to him. While Vak could not make out the words, he could tell that something harsh was being said. The Malvari chief bobbed his head in apparent agreement before returning his gaze to Vak.

"My apologies, Director Vak, one of my NOSs has brought up a good point. So perhaps you are right; the Malvari should clue the Groff in on what we are doing about this latest act of aggression. Let me first address Alfheim. Your Gurista sources within the Republic were right about what was going to happen. The Primords and the Republic have been putting a plan into place for some time to retake the planet. Apparently, the plan had to be approved by the alliance's Viceroy, meaning this was a sanctioned act of aggression by the alliance in direct violation of the Treaty of Alfheim.

"As such, the Zodark Empire is within its rights to respond militarily without seeking Orbot permission. However, we will not—at least not at this moment." Otro held a hand up, preempting him from interrupting. "Director Vak, before you lecture the Malvari about our people having to accept another humiliating defeat, the Groff need to understand that in order for our next plan to work—to invade the Republic home world and attack Earth—we need to marshal all our available warships, troop transports, and supply ships. We cannot pivot them to the far reaches of our territory and once again battle to regain control of the system to reinvade the planet. If we are to destroy this Terran Republic before it is able to grow any further, then we need to choose where we are going to fight next. Our goal is to destroy the Republic, not retain control of Alfheim."

"Mavkah Otro, I understand the Malvari position," Vak replied. "This may be a tough position for our people to accept. The Zodark people have lost much in our battle over Alfheim and the Sirius system. In light of the secrecy of this Terran invasion, it will be difficult to maintain morale among the ordinary Zodark people. If, however, we could let the people know that a new operation is in the works to deal with this betrayal by the Terrans, that is something we could spin to rally the Empire behind."

The image of Otro showed his eyes narrowing as he looked at Vak. He'd seen this look before—a look that bespoke arrogance, a look someone in great power would level against those who would dare to question them or their authority.

"Director Groff, our civil challenges and the morale of our people are an internal matter—a Groff matter, not one for the Malvari to contemplate. Your people will just have to handle it."

Vak grunted angrily, but he was not surprised by the response. What irked him most was the arrogant look of satisfaction on Otro's face as he said it. He knew, in the end, he wasn't going to have to deal with the discontent that would spread across the Zodark worlds when word eventually got out about the Empire suffering yet one more humiliating defeat by these Terran upstarts. No, that would fall to the Groff, specifically to his Laktish and his deputy Laktishes. They would have to enforce compliance and conformity with the edicts of the High Council, who indubitably would have authorized the Malvari's response—or rather the lack thereof. Suppression of dissent had always been a cornerstone of the Groff. That didn't mean the Malvari had to make it any harder for his people than necessary, though, and that was what truly disturbed him about Otro's dismissal of the problem.

Vak lifted his chin up as he responded, "Very well, the Groff will come up with a way to manage this defeat and strive not to make the Malvari look any weaker in the face of our adversaries than necessary." Vak smiled when Otro continued to glare before he continued, "To that end, I would like to point out that the Groff have provided the Malvari with extensive information on the Galactic Empire's plans to counter our alliance's ongoing efforts in the Serpentis system.

"As you are aware, the Orbots have already aided the Pharaonis in capturing this system. The Serpentis system is a gateway system that would allow our alliance two different paths from which to further invade the Galactic Empire, so its strategic value is not in question or up for debate. The question the Groff have is whether the Malvari will assist our allies in countering this move. Or perhaps we could lay our own trap to destroy this Altairian-Republic-led force moving to retake the system."

"Director Vak, I appreciate the Groff's interests in the military matters of the Malvari. As I have already explained, the Malvari are moving forward with a strategy to defeat this Terran Republic—not support the Orbots in further piecemeal attacks against the Galactic Empire. It is the Malvari's belief that a drawn-out campaign in the

Serpentis system will only aid in the success of our own invasion of the Terran home world, particularly if it draws further Republic forces to support it. In that regard, it is in our interest to see that fight drag on for as long as possible."

Vak listened to the comment carefully, noting his justification for not seizing a chance to militarily hurt the Altairians leading this effort to retake the system.

"Thank you for explaining that. I do understand the desire to focus exclusively on the Terran invasion. Perhaps it might help the Groff better prepare the Zodark people for this coming invasion if we could also promote how the Malvari's shifting away from our operations on Alfheim was actually done in response to an Orbot request for us to support our allies in the Serpentis system. That could give our agency the narrative to use to cover up the Alfheim defeat and shift the narrative away from defeat to one of greater victory in the coming dracmas. Could the Groff count on the Malvari to support this narrative should we move forward in this direction?"

"Director, I understand you want the Malvari to aid our allies in the Serpentis system. We appreciate and understand the military opportunity the Groff have created for us in obtaining this intelligence. Rest assured, that intelligence has been shared with our Orbot and Pharaonis allies. If the Groff want to craft a narrative that does not directly commit our forces, then we are fine with that and will support that narrative. But again, I would caution the Groff against inserting yourselves in the affairs of the military. We have a new strategy in place, and we are moving forward with our ploy to destroy this Terran Empire before it can spread further than it already has. Your points have been made. These are military matters that fall within the purview of the Malvari, not the Groff. Do not imply we are dispatching warships to the Serpentis system. We will come out against that narrative if it is pushed.

"Director Vak, I shouldn't have to remind the Groff how this works. Your group provides the intelligence, and we use it how we feel will best benefit us militarily. The Groff do not direct the Malvari or dictate our strategies or plans. Now, I have other pressing matters to attend to. That is all I want to say about this situation. Good day," Otro rebuked Vak harshly before summarily ending the call.

Vak shook his head in frustration. Cooperation between the Groff and the Malvari had always been tricky. More and more, it was becoming a one-way street. The Groff obtained intelligence and the Malvari, more often than not, just ignored it.

Fools...we could do so much better if that chuta wasn't such an arrogant, contemptible child, Vak thought to himself before shrugging off his frustrations. He had other matters to attend to himself. Secretly, he had decided that, if the Malvari failed in this coming invasion, then he would petition the High Council directly to frock Mavkah Otro and the members of the Malvari. He might even seek to be the one who implemented it, just to see Otro's face as he finally received what was coming to him.

Yes, your days are numbered, Otro. Just slip up one more time...

Chapter Fourteen
Battle for Sector Five

Dog Company, 2nd Ranger Battalion
Serpentis-6

"Duck, Pauli!" Yogi urgently shouted, causing Pauli to drop to the ground behind the fallen tree he'd been using for cover.

Pop, pop, pop came the rapid-firing cracks of dozens of Pharaonis battle rifles.

Pauli pressed his body flat against the ground as he tried to get as small as he could. He rolled over to lie on his back. The thumping and banging of blaster shots hammered the log he had been using for cover.

A few blaster shots that hadn't crashed into the tree he was sheltering behind zipped over his head. The yellowish flashes of light were a contrast to the red flashes he'd come to recognize from Zodark blasters and the blue ones typical of the Orbots.

Pauli glanced down to look at the detonator. It had electronically synced to the chargers. Now he just needed to get back to his own lines, so he could blow these bastards to kingdom come. Then his eyes saw something, or rather, there was something they *didn't* see. The blaster fire that had been firing over his head had changed. It was now pounding against the fallen trunk of a giant Tanyan tree indigenous to Serpentis-6.

An urgent thought pushed its way to the front of his brain. *I gotta move before they chip right through this thing.*

Pauli low-crawled like a snake, slithering across the ground, doing his best to stay small and keep his body out of sight of the enemy trying to kill him.

Zip, zip, zap, crump!

Blaster fire shredded tree branches, underbrush, and foliage above him as the enemy fire continued to search him out. Pauli pushed himself to move faster as he slithered along the ground. He hadn't felt this scared that he might die in a very long time, but in this very moment, with blaster fire zipping at times mere inches above him, he truly felt like he might not make it out of this one.

"Hang on there, Pauli!" he heard Private Hill shout to him.

"Frag out!"

"Covering fire! Three o'clock!"

"Look out! They're pushing on the right. Shift fire! Get that LMG over there now!" roared Lieutenant Yassin.

Fractions of a second later, the roar of blaster and magrail fire from the Rangers' positions accelerated into a violent raging storm of hate and death being spewed at the Pharaonis warriors surging forward. This was their fifth attempt to maneuver around the right flank of the 2nd Battalion, 503rd Infantry Regiment, in a battle stretching into its ninth consecutive day. The Pharaonis were throwing everything they had at the Republic in a desperate attempt to avoid being encircled after having been chased out of Pompidou, the planet's second-largest city and industrial hub.

The enemy charged on, pressing home their attack, likely oblivious that a platoon of Rangers had secretly arrived hours earlier to reinforce the Republic lines. As the four rifle squads of Pauli's platoon vigorously tore into the enemy's most recent charge, he felt this was his best chance to make a run back to friendly lines so he could blow the charges and tear this enemy redoubt wide open.

Come on, Pauli...you got this, he thought to himself, pushing the self-doubt and fear out of his mind.

Leaping to his feet, Pauli darted for the closest berm that could provide cover as he said a prayer for good luck. He pumped his legs hard, pushing the exoskeleton combat suit to its limits. He'd run maybe half a dozen steps when streaks of yellow light began zipping all around him.

"Give me some covering fire, damn it!" he managed to shout over the roar of the battle that seemed to be increasing with each passing second. His muscles ached and his lungs burned, desperate for oxygen. His body fought to live, fought to reach friendly lines.

"I gotcha, Master Sergeant!" someone shouted in reply to his plea for help.

Glancing up, Pauli saw Corporal Julian Aimes looking right at him—they made brief eye contact.

Corporal Aimes swung his M12 light-medium machine gun in his general direction. The giant six-foot-six-inch-tall corn-fed beast of a soldier maneuvered what was arguably the squad's heaviest weapon like it was a child's plaything. The M12 was not only an improvement on the venerable M90 SAW it had replaced, but the rifle, specially built by Dragon Slayer Industries, hurled a .338-caliber dual-purpose projectile with a revolutionary design, guaranteed to tear through even the toughest battle suits worn by the Orbots. It would even rip through Orbot and Zodark vehicles.

Pauli continued to race toward Corporal Aimes, zigging to the left, then to the right as he sought to throw off the enemy's aim. The space around him crackled from the near misses of blaster fire and the loud crack of the .338-caliber projectiles zipping past him at speeds exceeding twenty-five hundred meters per second.

Almost there, he told himself, darting erratically to the right and left, dodging enemy fire.

"Come on, Master Sergeant!" yelled a soldier near Corporal Aimes as he urged him on.

Pauli pushed himself harder, his knees and hips screaming in pain at the constant sidestepping he was doing to throw the enemy's aim off. When he thought he was less than twenty meters from safety, he sprinted forward, no more juking to either side. He was going to run for it now and get out of the line of fire before his luck ran out.

Oh, God, that sound...that horrible sound.

It wasn't the yells and screams of human soldiers echoing through the forest that sent a shiver of horror down Pauli's back—nor was it the explosions of grenades coupled with 20mm smart munitions intermixed with the cracking and sizzling sound of blaster bolts and high-speed large-caliber projectiles ripping through the air. It was the unique noise that came from the Pharaonis when two of their arms rubbed against each other. The tiny ridges on them generated a frequency that transformed into something reminiscent of scratching one's fingernails down a chalkboard. It made Pauli's eardrums feel like they were going to bleed. Had it not been for their helmets' ability to drown some of this noise out, it likely would have driven many of the soldiers insane.

A searing heat sizzled near the right side of Pauli's face, and a flash rushed over his shoulder, causing him to flinch. Then he saw Private Hill firing his rifle before his face imploded from the impact of the blaster shot. Bone fragments blew out the sides of his cheeks and ears as what had been the man's head erupted in a strange pattern like an explosive charge had detonated.

Pauli dove forward, crashing into the ground as the headless body of Private Hill staggered backwards momentarily until it collapsed in a heap next to him.

"Blow the charges, Master Sergeant! Blow the charges *now!*" yelled Lieutenant Yassin over the coms.

Grabbing for the detonator still in his pocket, Pauli thumbed the arming button that activated the charges. A row of green lights told him they were ready to blow. Peering just above the covered position he'd finally reached, Pauli pressed the detonator. His eyes went wide as the charges began erupting around the fortified positions.

He smiled as the three strange objects he'd been sent to destroy collapsed to the ground in a flaming heap. He wasn't sure how this Pharaonis weapon system worked or why they couldn't just nail it from space with an orbital strike. He remembered from a briefing that these three objects had managed to intercept everything the Republic had thrown at them, though, and the Fleet was apparently done losing manned and unmanned fighters trying to take them out. The damn things had even blown up more than four dozen smart missiles fired at them in an attempt to overwhelm them.

That was when one of the Deltas' ODA teams found a way to neutralize them. Dealing with this one had fallen to Pauli's unit. Dog Company, 2nd Rangers, had the most combat veterans from the last war, so they'd landed the job—a job that would have been much easier if they'd had the same skills, newer equipment, and weapons the Deltas had. But they didn't, so they made do and found a way to get it done.

As he continued to survey the fire and destruction, a testament to his handiwork, those earlier thoughts of dying once again pushed their way to the front of Pauli's mind. *I almost died today*, he realized. *I almost died multiple times today.* He wondered why the hell he was still doing this. He had so much more to live for.

With the Pharaonis weapons down, the radio chatter picked up, now full of excitement. It was time to finish the enemy off. It was time to start calling in the Fleet to further pummel their positions while ground forces got themselves ready for the final assault on one of the few remaining Pharaonis redoubts left on the planet.

As Pauli dropped down behind the fallen tree he'd been using for cover, his eyes fell upon the headless corpse of Private Hill, his body still slumped over on the ground. He hadn't known Hill very long. Hell, he hadn't known most of the Rangers in the platoon very long.

Hill had mentioned something about marrying his high school sweetheart a few weeks before they'd shipped out. Shaking his head at the memory of the conversation, Pauli made a mental note to write his wife a personal letter. He owed Hill that much, and frankly, she deserved to know how her husband had died—fighting alongside his brothers and fellow Rangers, doing what he loved best.

Even though Pauli hadn't been especially close to Hill, his loss weighed on him. He'd lost so many friends since joining the Army. But the soldiers who'd died under his command would often haunt him in his dreams. He saw them, talking, joking, and having fun with him, until their faces morphed into those final images of their death—the last images he had of them, the images that called out to him in his nightmares, asking why they had died. Why had he killed them when he'd given an order that had resulted in their deaths? It was those images, those feelings he'd worked years to bury, that were suddenly boiling over once again as new soldiers under his command started dying, joining the others that would be waiting for him once he closed his eyes to sleep.

When he felt a tear streak down the side of his face, he activated the one-way visor lens, blocking anyone from seeing the emotional expression he was sure had broken through his mask. This wasn't the time. This wasn't the place. His soldiers still needed him. This fight might be nearing its end, but it wasn't over, and until it was, he'd lock those emotions up, put them back in the box and leave them there until he was ready to unpack them—to deal with them.

Standing up, Pauli looked over to see Lieutenant Yassin talking with the other squad leaders and knew he should find out if they'd be joining the grunts. Their mission was done, but that didn't mean they couldn't be tasked with another one as the grunts now moved into battle and captured the base. Given the losses they'd taken and the demand for their specialized skills, he hoped they'd get pulled off the line.

Taking a breath in, Pauli held his head up and walked toward the group. He resolved to do whatever it took to finish this fight and return home. Maybe this time he'd hang his uniform up for the final time, or maybe he'd don it again when another grave threat to the Republic arose. If Pauli had learned one thing these last twenty years in the Army and the reserves, it was that the Republic needed soldiers like him— soldiers willing and able to answer the call to serve, to defeat the enemies of the Republic, to bring peace back to the homeland. But until that time came, he'd continue to stand in that breach, to stare into that storm and scream his war cry.

****

101st Orbital Assault Division Headquarters
Capitol District
Tutuna
Serpentis-6

Major General Vernon "VC" Crow stood in the center of the division's operations center, staring down at the table, hands on his hips. He studied the map now that his operations group had finally updated it with the most recent information from the battles winding down near the Tully city of Pompidou. He would have pulverized the place had it not been the second-largest Tully city on the planet. It didn't help that the enemy had strategically placed their most effective defensive weapons in and around the city's heavy industry sectors either. His Tully counterpart had been insistent on them not destroying the place, even as the casualties among his men rose.

The challenge the Republic forces had been dealing with was the location of the enemy force. For reasons unknown to the Republic, the Tully had built a number of their military facilities either within their cities across the planet or in close proximity to critical industrial complexes. When the Pharaonis had landed, they'd rapidly captured the facilities and summarily turned them into fortified nightmares to recapture, particularly with this new air-defense system the Republic had never encountered before. The strange tower platforms consistently zapped any missile or projectile thrown at them. If plastering the fortified positions with an orbital strike wouldn't devastate the local civilians nearby, they would already have reduced the place to rubble.

Once they began encountering some of the enemies' new air-defense weapons, it didn't take long before these unknown weapons essentially neutered the Fleet's ability to offer any kind of air support or precision-guided attacks. VC would have loved nothing more than to drop a few dozen kinetic rods from orbit and call it a day. But destroying the Tully's industrial centers and major cities to hit a few air-defense weapons wasn't a good trade-off—particularly for the Tully, who'd be the ones staying behind to rebuild their colony and shore up the defenses for the system.

"Ah, there we go. That looks so much better. Glad to see they finally got the maps updated," a familiar voice called out from somewhere behind him.

Turning, VC smiled when he saw his Silver Fox Task Force commander. The man, the myth, the legendary Delta operator himself—Colonel Brian Royce.

"Yeah, I had to light a few fires under some asses to get my IT guys to keep these maps updated. I'm no techie myself, but it doesn't seem like it should be too complicated to keep these digital maps updating regularly as the information flows in. Seems like each time Big Army wants to integrate some sort of new tech, it always comes with a host of bugs and glitches you'd think they would have worked out before they sent it along with a unit likely going into combat. But, hey, I'm just a major general in command of a seventy-five-thousand-man expeditionary force, so what do I know?"

Colonel Royce chuckled at his response. VC liked that about him. He wasn't like those other uptight academy officers who were always trying to kiss up to him or looking for ways to ingratiate themselves, believing that would aid them in getting selected for their next promotion.

"Sir, I've been looking into our little problem, and after consulting with some of my guys, I think I may have a solution to offer," Royce said.

"Oh? Well, let's hear it, then," VC replied.

Colonel Royce tapped away on something and the map changed. Turning to look at the general, he explained, "One of my sergeants picked up on something when he used the spectral analysis and then overlaid it with the lidar scans. We got a few more of these high-def scans done to help us map something out. Lost more than a handful of drones in the process, but look at this."

The new image showed a handful of what looked to be some sort of sewer or service tunnels running under the city. VC was about to ask about the significance of this map and these tunnels when Royce highlighted one of them, turning it blue. It led directly under the former Tully base the Pharaonis had now taken over.

"That's our way in—how we'll circumvent those air-defense towers and not have to fight through blocks of apartment buildings and high-rises," Royce explained. He went into further detail about what he was thinking, and the more VC heard, the more he liked it.

"OK, so you're going to have one of your ODA teams sneak under the enemy base via these sewage tunnels. Once they've reached what looks like a junction center or split-off point, you are going to have your team break down into two smaller segments, each going after one of the towers. Is that how you envision this working out?" VC recapped, using his finger to trace along the map as he spoke. "This tunnel leads almost directly under one of these tower defense systems. Your team will place explosives around the area and blow it from the bottom up."

"Yes, exactly. We'll make sure we have more than enough explosives to get it done. But it's that second team, ODA Alpha One, that's going to have a much tougher go of it. The second tower isn't near any of these tunnels. What they'll have to do is exit through this access point here. That'll place them twenty or so meters away from the base of the tower. When ODA Alpha Two blows the charge on their end, Alpha One will use the chaos of the moment to take the final tower out."

VC listened as Colonel Royce continued to explain what VC thought was an insane and likely suicidal mission—but it just might work.

"Maybe you've already considered this, Colonel," he interjected, "but I need to ask. Once this happens—once those towers are down—you'll have kicked up a hell of a hornet's nest. Those Pharaonis are going to be on you like white on rice. I haven't known you Deltas to volunteer for deliberate suicide missions. Tell me about how you plan to extract your ODA team or, if not, what your plan is."

No sooner had he finished asking his question than the colonel smiled. He typed something on his Qpad and started bringing up some information to share.

"Those are some good questions, General," said Royce. "You're also right—it'd be a slaughter if I ordered just a single ODA in. But that's not what we've cooked up. My guys have spent some time studying this situation and we've come up with something clever that should take these defensive towers down."

VC smiled as he listened to how they were going to pull this off. It was the kind of confident swagger he'd come to expect from these Delta operators.

"OK, Colonel, you've largely sold me on your plan. Before I sign off on it, walk me through how you're going to handle things once those towers go down and where this infantry unit you're asking to be reassigned to your unit fits into all of this. I kind of thought you had C100s and a battalion of Rangers for security work, if that's how you're thinking of employing them."

"Sure thing, General. I'll break it down Barney style." The term was typically used when talking to lower enlisted or junior offices, not a two-star general, but VC's laughter told Royce not to worry about what others might have taken as a slight.

"OK, back to the towers. Once they're down, it'll put into motion a series of events that'll culminate with a couple of dynamic assaults. As you know, one ODA is located in the sewer tunnels. That's the unit that takes the towers out. While their attack is taking place, I'm having two hundred of the remaining three hundred combat Synths assault the base along this perimeter on the far side of their sprawling encampment.

"The chaos this will sow is going to generate the necessary cover to allow two of our other ODA teams to land directly inside the base to reinforce the team that gained entry via the sewer system. Following their dynamic entry, I've got my remaining hundred combat Synths, who will also HALO in, but they'll land here, near this courtyard. They're going to try to make a surgical hit on what your G2 has identified as the Pharaonis HQ. It's unlikely we'll nail their leadership in a quick raid on the building, but you never know. Circling back to that infantry unit I was requesting…they're going to support the ODA in the sewers. They'll pull security and make sure that if things go south, no Pharaonis use it as a means to escape. Other than that, they'll assist us in the internal assault on the base."

Damn, this plan is ballsy…but it's better than the alternatives I've been given.

"OK, Colonel. It's passed the sniff test. I like this better than the frontal assault plans I've been briefed on. Get with my staff and let me know what you need, and I'll sign off on it. Once you've got us a way into the base, we'll start pushing units through to support you guys. It's time we finish major combat operations on this planet and let the Tully take charge of things. We've lost enough people on this rock. Time to head back home and enjoy this peace dividend hearing our senators keep telling us about. It would seem someone forgot to share with the Dominion that this war is supposed to be over—maybe after this campaign, they'll finally get the message."

****

Two Days Later
Easy Company, 1-506th Orbital Assault Regiment
Regimental Headquarters
Capitol District
Tutuna
Serpentis-6

Lieutenant Ronald Speirs watched their battalion commander, Colonel Ty Johnson, enter the room with a colonel from Special Forces. To everyone's surprise, he went on to introduce the man as their new temporary commander before thanking Captain Gordon "Gordo" Zillow for volunteering his company to augment the Deltas from Task Force Silver Fox. The SF contingent of their Special Military Operation was overstretched, and now apparently understrength after fifty-eight days of continuous combat.

Once the two senior officers had left the room, Speirs noted the uncomfortable look on the face of their CO. His lieutenants and platoon sergeants were staring daggers at the man. Not only were they temporarily leaving their parent unit, 1st of the 506th, but they would now be augmenting the very unit that was continually in the thick of the fight. The realization that this unit needed help from nonaugmented soldiers due to its high casualty rates was not lost on any of the platoon leaders or sergeants.

"OK, everyone has heard the news. Tonight at 1900 hours, we have our first mission brief with the Deltas. We'll find out during the brief exactly what they'll have us doing and when we'll be doing it. For now, I'm going to need each of you to get your platoons and their equipment, personal belongings, etcetera, moved over to Camp Silver Fox. If you have to, delegate this out to your squad leaders. I need each of you present at this meeting tonight. I have a feeling it won't be long before they'll look to start using our services," Captain Zillow explained, handing out the instructions for the remainder of the day.

142

Speirs noticed the nods of acceptance. Then a subtle shift in the room occurred. The platoon sergeants and the three other lieutenants, the platoon leaders for the other platoons, began to look at him as if he would issue a countermanding order—as if somehow, he could save them from whatever disaster Zillow had just signed them up for.

They still don't accept him as the CO despite all we've been through, thought Speirs. *This isn't good.*

Shaking his head ever so slightly, he turned to look at the man who'd been given the position Speirs was arguably substantially more qualified to hold. It had irked Speirs and everyone else in the company that he hadn't been given the command slot two and a half years ago when Captain Chu had retired from the Army. It had become obvious to even the most obtuse of observers that someone was being fast-tracked through the ranks, and worse—it wasn't the most qualified or competent person. The billet had gone to a newly promoted captain—a man they'd soon learned had only recently qualified as an orbital assault infantry officer. In fact, the new captain had spent the previous seven years working on logistics.

Speirs took the silent cue and spoke up. "Copy that, sir." Turning to face the other lieutenants and their platoon sergeants, he continued, "We'll make sure the platoons are on the move and get them settled in our new home for however long we may be assigned to Silver Fox. Lieutenants, Master Sergeants, dismissed. The captain and I will join you all in a bit. We have a few housekeeping items to discuss."

The three officers and five senior NCOs seemed to have caught on and started making for the exits. Captain Zillow either was oblivious to what was going on or didn't care. Once it was just the two of them, Speirs asked, "Sir, if I may. Permission to speak freely?"

Bunching his eyebrows in surprise at the request, he countered, "Speak freely? It's just the two of us, Ron. You know you can call me Gordo, and of course you can speak freely with me. I've already mentioned I'll gladly accept your mentoring."

"OK, Gordo, let me ask you something. Periodically, an officer will thank you for volunteering when in reality, they voluntold you," Speirs explained, then paused before continuing. "Tell me Silver Fox was something we got voluntold to do—not something you volunteered us to do...right?"

When Zillow hesitated, Speirs knew the answer and it wasn't good.

Wow—that bastard. He has no idea what he just volunteered us for...

"Uh, judging by the look on your face, Ron, I suspect you believe I made a mistake volunteering Easy Company."

"Let's look at it this way, Gordo. Easy Company got the honor of being the first unit to land at Currahee some fifty-eight days ago. That was the first time we had ever seen a Pharaonis, and frankly, these are some scary-looking bastards. These five-foot-tall demonic fire ants with battle rifles fired yellow laser bolts at you. To say the last few months have been unnerving and emotionally draining would be an understatement.

"But that's just the Pharaonis. Once we got in the woods and patrolled through more of Serpentis-6, we started encountering those fanged gnome-looking critters. You know, the ones that seem to come out at night—well, you get the picture, Gordo. Our people are exhausted. This Special Military Operation," Speirs said, using air quotes, "has been a nonstop horror show that's turning into a second Alfheim. They're tired, Gordo. They need a break, and instead of coming off the line for a five-day R&R rotation, we're about to go tell them we've been reassigned to Silver Fox for God knows how long. Volunteering the unit right now just wasn't the smartest move if you're trying to convince your people you're looking out for them and have their best interests in mind."

Zillow heard the concern but quickly dismissed it, as he had many other times, to the chagrin of Speirs and the other officers and NCOs in the unit. Instead of trying to understand the situation from the point of view of his soldiers, he reminded Speirs that as his executive officer, it was his duty to help reinforce how the chain of command works.

"We might not like or agree with the orders of those in charge of us," said Zillow, "But they're the ones in charge and it's our duty to obey so long as you aren't being ordered to do something illegal."

Speirs had gone through this rationale with Zillow a few times over the years—almost always when he'd made an unpopular decision, one he hadn't needed to make but had done so anyway. More than a few officers and senior NCOs had accused him privately and behind his back of looking for ways to advance his own career at the expense of his soldiers. That kind of attitude had only gotten worse over the years.

"Ron, you've been a good XO. I know many thought you would have gotten this command and not me. You've been gracious in that regard, and I appreciate that. But I'm perplexed—how is it possible the NCOs and platoon leaders still don't respect me like they do you? I've been the CO for three years. What more do I have to do?"

Speirs could tell Zillow was frustrated. He just didn't know how to respond without hurting him. "It's not about how long you've been the CO or with the unit, battalion, or the regiment. They respect your position as commander and your rank as captain. That's what's important and that's what you should focus on and care about. When it comes to me, I'm not some green lieutenant trying to make general one day who doesn't know his ass from his head. I was command sergeant major before they gave me a battlefield promotion. The men respect that. In time, they'll come to respect you in that same manner. But it's got to be earned, not demanded."

"And how exactly do I earn it? I approve any schooling or training they put in for. I rubber-stamp any award the NCOs and platoons recommend. What more do I need to do?" Zillow retorted, exasperated. He was clearly jealous of Speirs's relationship with the other platoon leaders and NCOs.

"Well, for starters, I'd recommend you don't volunteer your command for an assignment that may get most of them killed."

"Ah, come on. It can't be that. It's not every day us regular grunts get a chance to go help Special Forces out. You know how good this will look on everyone's service jackets? This is an opportunity to stand out from the crowd, get noticed when your packet comes up for the next promotion or command assignment," Zillow countered as he explained his logic.

"Yes, I do understand. But that's the whole point."

"What's the whole point? I'm not tracking."

"Gordo, you just said this presents an opportunity for them to stand out—for *you* to stand out when it comes time for the next promotion board. What you aren't taking into consideration is these guys don't care about standing out in front of the next promotion board. They're about living to see the next sunrise, then the next one and the one after. At the end of the day, they want to go back home on the

Emerald City, not in a coffin on a supply ship heading back to New Eden," Speirs tried to explain.

"Is it really that bad, Ron?"

"Gordo, they're soldiers—they're ATs. Assault troops will fight until their dying breath if so ordered. But we're not machines. We're not combat synthetics. Easy Company has taken losses—losses that still haven't been replaced. My platoon alone is short twelve guys. I think Shane said First Platoon is down seven. Hell, Jillian told me this morning her platoon was short fourteen and Raymond is down eleven. By my count, our company is missing forty-four out of two hundred and sixty soldiers. That puts our effective combat strength at eighty-three percent," Speirs explained as calmly as he could, watching as the younger officer started to connect the dots.

"Huh, all right. I guess I screwed this up, didn't I?"

"Chalk it up to a learning experience. You had good intentions, but this is going to hurt. I know it's exciting to work with these Special Forces guys and that's how I'm going to pitch this to my platoon. But make no mistake, Gordo—we're going from the frying pan straight into the fire. If you thought we saw a lot of fighting up till now, you wait until we start mission hopping with these Deltas. You gotta remember something about them. They aren't like us—and they're not just a little different. They are night and day different from us."

Zillow had a look of confusion on his face when he asked, "Different? How so? They put their pants on the same way you and I do. They've just been given a lot more specialized training and some newer and probably better weapons."

Ron tried not to laugh at Zillow's explanation. *Remember he comes from logistics…he hasn't worked with Deltas in the past,* he told himself.

"Gordo, we need to get back to the company and let everyone know what's going on. My platoon sergeant should be back here in half an hour from escorting that supply run. You know, the one that we got tasked with providing security for at 0200 hours."

"Oh, yeah. Sorry about that, Ron. You're right. I gotta stop volunteering us for stuff like that as it comes along," Zillow finally admitted.

Good, maybe there's hope for him as an infantry officer after all…

"How about I take care of getting the company moved over to Camp Silver Fox while you spend a little bit of time looking into who exactly we're going to be working with? If you thought our AT training was tough or that Rangers were high-speed, wait until you dig into who those Deltas are. I'm not sure if you put it all together yet or not, but hell, that colonel we were talking to—that was Colonel *Brian Royce*. He's a damn legend in Special Forces—two-time Medal of Honor recipient. The guy has half a dozen Silver Stars and a dozen or more Bronze Stars. If Easy Company is providing security for that man's unit…you can bet your ass we're going to be in for the fight of our lives."

Zillow didn't say anything for a moment. He looked like a deer caught in the headlights. It had finally dawned on him what he'd just volunteered them for. This might be one of those decisions that cost more than just the lives of his people. It might cost him his own.

He muttered softly, "You're right, Ron. I screwed up on this one. Can I count on your help to get Easy Company through this minefield I led us into?"

Ron stood, getting ready to leave. In an equally soft voice, he countered, "Damn right. My life depends on it."

Chapter Fifteen
Sewer Rats & the Tower

36 Hours Later

Lieutenant Speirs held the M1 assault rifle tight in the ready-up position, his squad following closely behind him as they waded through the watery muck. The stench of the tunnels was almost overpowering. Even with their filters set to maximum, they couldn't remove all the particulate matter from the air. One of the Deltas smiled at their discomfort and told them the scent they smelled was the Tully excrement regularly deposited into the sewage tunnels from the apartment buildings above.

Seeing chunks of unknown material being pushed ahead of him by the mini waves his sloshing created was almost more than Speirs could stomach. He had been around a lot of crap in his time in the Army, but never in a million years had he thought he would wade through the sewer of an alien species. Yet here he was, sloshing through feces on a foreign planet, hundreds of light-years from Earth.

"We're approaching Waypoint Charlie. Speirs, your platoon is with me. Keep up," the operator known as Rooster called out to him over their coms.

Speirs tapped the transmit button twice, letting him know he acknowledged. Not having the same neurolinks as the Deltas, they had to rely on their standard coms systems—something the Delta guys seldom had to do, but it was second nature to everyone outside their organization.

Near as Speirs could tell, Rooster was either a sergeant or master sergeant. He looked like he knew what he was doing, and in Speirs's eyes, that was all that mattered. When they reached the bend in the tunnel, he followed Rooster and the five other Deltas walking ahead of him. He was impressed with how stealthily and swiftly the team moved. They were like ghosts, barely discernible to the naked eye and silent until they wanted you to know they were there.

I wish we could use the same exoskeleton combat suits those guys have, thought Speirs. *Wow, and those battle rifles…the Slayers…*

When Rooster reached what Speirs thought was the end of the tunnel, he motioned for Speirs to come close. As they reached Waypoint

Charlie, they now had to stay off the coms in case the enemy could detect their frequencies now that they were under their base. He spoke just above a whisper. "OK, Speirs, here's the deal. We're at the exit that puts us closest to the tower we're taking down. Once our breacher cuts that hatch open"—he motioned with his head behind him. Speirs saw the cutting torch burning the hinges off some sort of door or hatch that sealed the sewer off from above. "Speirs, you with me?"

"Sorry. Yeah, I'm good."

"OK, once my team goes up, we're going to clear the immediate area around the entrance. Best we can tell, this ladder leads up to a storage room located to the rear of a building just a hundred meters away from the tower we're going to blow. Once we've cleared the building, we're going to see if we can get a little closer to the tower before we're discovered. Before we head out, I'm going to send you one of three possible signals to give you and your people a heads-up before things hit the fan. You tracking, LT?"

Speirs nodded. "I'm tracking, Rooster."

"Good. Signal one is a single chirp," Rooster began. "It means immediate danger. We will either clear the danger and give an all clear, or if we can't do that stealthily, then we'll slip back into the tunnel if we think it'll help us stay undetected.

"Two chirps means it's all clear. If you hear that, you better start hauling ass up here with your boys. We're going to need your platoon and company to get up here ASAP and help us hold this place until reinforcements arrive. We may be good at our jobs, but six Deltas aren't a company. We ain't Superman, no matter how cocky we are.

"If I give you three chirps, that means contact is imminent. It also means I need you and your unit to get your asses up here ASAP. We need your help holding this position while we make our move on the tower. Your guys have got to hold this place so we have somewhere to fall back to once we take that tower out. Then it'll be a matter of surviving long enough for reinforcements to get us out of here. It'll be a death trap if we have to fight it out down here in this confined space."

Rooster turned around and took three steps before stopping to turn and speak. "Speirs, one more thing. I know y'all don't have our new rifles and such, but you guys have those good ol'-fashioned hammer sticks—"

"Hammer sticks? That code for something we should know about?" Speirs interjected.

Rooster snickered before explaining, "Nah, man. It's all good, LT. Just Delta slang for those new M12s they gave you orbital assault guys. We call 'em hammer sticks. I mean, whoever came up with the idea of alternating standard penetrator rounds with those and new improved mushrooming hollow-point slugs—freaking brilliant.

"So when you crawl out of this sewer, make damn sure you have as many of your hammer sticks with you as possible in the first group of guys. If this goes sideways, we're going to need that kind of heavy-hitting firepower. Until your whole company is online, we gotta level the playing field against what'll likely be overwhelming numbers. Got it?"

"Yeah, I get it, Rooster," Speirs replied confidently, eager to get this show going. "We'll make sure the LMG gunners are the first ones out. I sure wish we'd had them and this new ammo during the last war. This stuff would have torn the hell out of those Zodarks."

Master Sergeant Lance then walked up to them. "I heard you guys talking about wanting our LMG gunners up here first. I passed the word along; they're all on the way."

Rooster nodded approvingly before turning to look at his breacher, who was still cutting the hinges and locks off the hatch to the building above. Looking back at Speirs, he stared at him for a moment. "Don't worry about what'll happen next, Lieutenant. I can see it in your eyes, etched on your face. You're a warrior—a *killer*, like the rest of us. You know what to do. Once this show starts…don't let up. You keep that war face on, and you roar like a demonic animal. When that storm looks like it's about to overwhelm you—when the darkness looks like it's going to consume you—you stand tall. You lean into it. Then remind the darkness you *are* the storm, and you laugh in its face.

"It's mind over matter, bro. There's nothing that can stop you. That's the mindset you gotta lock in place right now because once we go up that ladder, it's game on. But don't worry, Currahee. You're with the Deltas now. We're gonna storm the gates of hell, and you're coming along with us. Just follow our lead, do as we ask, and kill everything in sight," Rooster said like he was reading some sort of war-themed poetry.

As the Delta soldier walked away, Speirs looked at Lance, unsure how to even respond. What unnerved Speirs most about Rooster was that guy seemed to mean every word of what he'd just said. It was like some kind of pre-battle séance he'd just shared with them. While it unnerved him, strangely, it inspired him too.

Maybe we've both seen too much combat for our own good, Speirs thought privately.

With Rooster out of earshot, Lance spoke quietly. "Damn, Ron. I'm not sure if he's a Special Forces god or a complete psychopath. That little speech felt awe-inspiring—it also sent a cold shiver down my spine."

"Yeah…these guys are wound up a little tight, Lance."

"Ha. Yeah…a little tight, you say…they're borderline psychos, Ron. I'm just glad they're on our side, 'cause I sure as hell wouldn't want to fight them."

"Special Forces, Lance, are cut from a different cloth. They've always been a different breed of soldier than the rest of us. It doesn't make 'em better or worse—just a different tool in the Army's toolbox. Let's just make sure our guys hold up their end of the bargain, and we all live to tell a good war story about this when we get back to New Eden."

Speirs pulled his Qpad out and sent a short text, relaying Rooster's instructions to Captain Zillow and the other platoon leaders via the device's direct connect link. If two Qpads were in close proximity, they acted almost like a mesh net. Using a specially encrypted messaging app, soldiers could communicate with each other without having to use their standard coms systems or activating a Wi-Fi network that could be detected or jammed.

The platoon leaders quickly acknowledged receipt of Speirs's message via the Qpad. Now all he had to do was wait for Rooster's signal.

Speirs leaned back with his hands on his hips. He couldn't wait to get out of this filth. As the seconds ticked by, soon turning to minutes, he wondered, *What the hell is taking these guys so long?*

The longer they waited, below this building they had dubbed "the Alamo," the greater the tension. It felt like a kettle heating, knowing it would reach a boiling point sooner or later. But then the message finally arrived.

Chirp, chirp, chirp.

Three chirps—contact was imminent.

Damn it! We need to get up there ASAP!

"First Squad, on me! They're about to make contact. Let's roll. Currahee!"

"Currahee!" the soldiers shouted back in excitement.

Speirs was in the room moments after climbing the ladder—rifle at the ready. Soon after he emerged from the hatch below, the next soldier had climbed out and took up a ready position of his own. Speirs scanned their surroundings, making sure the room they had emerged into was clear, then looked back to the hatch in the floor. At least half a dozen soldiers had now made their way up.

Staff Sergeant Mendoza and four of his soldiers moved swiftly toward a door Rooster had marked for them to follow. He'd told them his team would place a red X on any doors or hallways they traveled down so Speirs and his men could follow. They wanted to avoid using their coms for as long as possible.

Mendoza and his soldiers entered the room uneventfully, and Speirs breathed a sigh of relief. Whatever it was that had spooked Rooster, they hadn't run into it yet.

Then Corporal Leyton pulled himself out of the hatch and Speirs called out to him. "Hey, Leyton. I'm going to see if I can find Rooster—"

All hell broke loose before Speirs could finish his sentence. The building shook violently from a nearby explosion.

Pop, pop, pop.

Speirs took off at a run, attempting to see what was going on and where the shooting was coming from. Racing down the hallway, he came into a room that connected to the plaza they'd seen on the map and in various drone footage. Opposite the plaza stood the very tower they had been sent in to destroy.

"Rourke, get that LMG set up over there in that window!" Staff Sergeant Mendoza shouted. "Start laying down covering fire across that sector and keep their heads down. We need to cover those Deltas."

The soldiers in the room had taken up positions near the windows and were already firing back at the enemy.

"Speirs!" Rooster yelled at him over the coms, trying to be heard over the roar of battle taking place around him. "There's a side entrance to that building you're in. It leads into an alleyway between your building and the one next to it. My team made it into the next building, but we're starting to take some heavy fire. I need you to get some of your guys over here in our building with us. We're going to bum-rush that tower in a few minutes, and I need those LMGs cover us as we move."

"Good copy, Rooster. I'm on it," Speirs replied, letting the Deltas know help was on the way.

Speirs left the storefront, making his way back into the hallway leading to the warehouse where the rest of Easy Company was still entering from the sewers.

"What's going on, LT?" Lance asked as he approached him with a squad of soldiers.

Speirs smiled at the sight of his friend. "Damn, Lance—talk about good timing. Get word to Lieutenant Axel and tell him to take charge of things here. I need you and Second and Third Squads to follow me. Rooster and his Delta team are pinned down and need our help."

While he was speaking, the sounds of battle seemed to be growing louder and more intense by the second. The Pharaonis were beginning to react to the Republic forces who had suddenly manifested themselves from what should have been a secured base.

The soldiers ran after Speirs as he led them into the alleyway. Somewhere not far from them was Rooster's team. They needed to figure out where they were and how best to help them out. If they didn't take that tower down with all those lasers built into it, there wouldn't be any reinforcements coming to save them.

As everyone spilled into the alleyway, Speirs led a team of soldiers down one side while another squad leader took a team down the opposite side. Hopefully, one of them would figure out where the shooting was coming from and how they were going to help Rooster and his team break free.

Speirs advanced cautiously but quickly down the alleyway, until it opened up into a sidewalk and multilane street. A handful of abandoned vehicles dotted the street, some of which were so shot to pieces that charred ruins of metal were all that remained. Beyond the street, he spotted the tower they'd been sent to destroy. He also saw Rooster, or at least part of Rooster's team.

"Oh, damn. That's a nasty crossfire they're in," Lance commented as he approached Speirs. They had reached the edge of the alleyway, and so far, they hadn't been detected. He was hoping they could keep it that way.

He was just about to tell Lance where to start filtering his LMG gunners when Speirs caught a flash in his peripheral vision. Instinctively, he pulled Lance back with him against the wall of the alleyway just as a yellow beam of light passed through the air where they had been seconds earlier. Several more flashes of light zipped past them, slamming into the opposite side of the alleyway.

Lance recovered quickly and started barking at his LMG gunners to get ready to move out of the alleyway once he gave them the order. Speirs pointed to two soldiers, telling them to prepare to start lobbing smart grenades in the direction of the shooters firing at them. While they prepared to send a dozen fragmentation grenades toward the enemy, Speirs worked the settings on his rifle's targeting computer, changing the settings on the smart grenades from high-explosive fragmentation to high-density smoke.

If he could land a few well-placed smoke grenades in front of the Pharaonis' positions, it might obscure their vision long enough for his gunners to get in place. Then they could cover his movements across the alleyway and down the road to link up with Rooster and his team.

With his rifle ready and his smart grenades now turned into smoke bombs, Speirs gave Lance a short nod before shouting to be heard over the increasing volume of the battle happening around them. "OK, stand by. I'm going to start lobbing some smoke rounds. Give 'em five seconds, then you two start sending your grenades. Once they're done, it's on you two gunners to make a dash for those abandoned vehicles and get set up. I need you guys laying down heavy covering fire on those enemy positions. Got it?"

"We got it, LT," came the quick reply from his soldiers.

Just as he was about to poke around the edge of the alleyway, Rooster barked urgently over their coms system, "Lieutenant Speirs—I need your men up here ASAP!"

Speirs grimaced at the call. He knew Rooster's team was in a tough spot. They had to get through and help them out. Activating autoreply, he relayed calmly, "Hang in there, Rooster. Look for the smoke and frag rounds about to hit. We're on the way."

Leaning near the edge, he readied himself, gripping the rifle tightly as he did. *Here goes nothing...* He popped out from the side of the alleyway and took aim—then fired the six 20mm smart grenades as quickly as his rifle would let him.

Thump, thump, thump.

He pulled back behind cover just in time to watch another barrage of yellow bands of light zip through the air where he'd just been. Suddenly, he felt shards of chipped building material bounce back at him from the opposite end of the wall. Most of his body was covered in Kevlar and body armor, but the few spots that weren't registered biting jabs of pain. One piece of shrapnel scored a direct hit against his exposed flesh.

His next two soldiers stepped out without being told and proceeded to lob grenades in the enemy's direction. While their grenade gun was chucking rounds downrange, Corporal Trace and his assistant gunner made their move. The two of them darted out into the line of fire and ran toward a half-burned-out wreck that might have been a delivery car. Flashes of light zipped around the two of them as they ran across half a dozen meters of open ground until they reached the van.

Speirs watched with excitement as Corporal Trace tapped the bipod release and the two stands popped out from the forward frame of the rifle. Before the enemy could react to this newest development, his most experienced LMG gunner started firing three-to-five-second controlled bursts of automatic fire. The sudden barrage of well-aimed heavy-caliber slugs tore right through the buildings the Pharaonis had taken cover in.

The corporal made a point of hammering a Pharaonis position for a couple of seconds before transitioning to another and repeating the process. Judging by the horrifying sound the Pharaonis made when they were injured, Trace was right on the money with his shots.

Then a string of yellow bands of light zipped around Corporal Trace and his gunner, causing them to drop below the van for cover. Speirs looked frantically to see where the new gunfire was coming from. They needed to link up with Rooster's team, but they couldn't do that if they got themselves pinned down.

"It's coming from over there! Nine o'clock, bottom left next to that blue building. There's a door they look to be exiting from. Maybe it's some kind of barracks or something," one of the soldiers nearby shouted.

Speirs looked in the direction his trooper had pointed, spotting a group of Pharaonis that had taken cover in a sandbag-style fortification he hadn't noticed before. Something about its materials or some kind of camouflage caused it to blend into its surroundings. The enemy soldiers were now firing back at them with their own version of a machine gun. But that wasn't what worried Speirs—it was the steady stream of soldiers racing out of the building in small, controlled groups, covering each other as they did.

Oh damn. If we don't get this tower taken down ASAP, they're going to keep calling in reinforcements until they overwhelm us, he thought. His worst fear might be coming true.

The more Corporal Trace fired that M12 LMG, the more alarm bells it was likely sounding across the enemy garrison. They had to take that thing down, and that meant getting to Rooster's position and figuring out what the hell was going on.

Thump, thump, thump.

Another barrage of 20mm smoke rounds shot through the air in the direction of the enemy gun bunkers and soldiers filtering out of what might be a barracks building near the tower. More thumping sounds could be heard, likely additional fragmentation rounds being fired to land within the clouds of thick smoke as they dispersed pieces of shrapnel over the heads of the enemy defenders like deadly rain.

Speirs still heard the sounds of a gun battle taking place further away from them to the west of their current position, but he knew they needed to press on. They had to get to Rooster and his team ASAP before they all got overrun by the swarms of reinforcements that he knew were being mobilized against them right now.

Looking behind him, he saw the squad of soldiers still in a crouched position, waiting for him to give them an order. With another blanket of smoke billowing in front of the enemy's position, Speirs knew it was now or never. He looked back to them one more time, showing confidence as he rose up. "Come on, Currahee! It's time to go save us some Deltas!"

More than a few soldiers laughed at the joke before jumping to their feet to chase after him. They ran swiftly down the sidewalk adjacent to the abandoned street. Once the enemy caught on to what they were doing, they shifted fire, sending streaks of yellow flashes all around them. Many of them dove for cover behind the burned-out wrecks of vehicles or whatever else was immediately around them. Several of the soldiers got hit as they bounded further down the street, using the wrecks as cover between their mad dashes.

"Hank! Go ahead and get your gun up and running here. Try and keep those bastards' heads down for us while we go help Rooster's team out around the bend," Speirs directed his second LMG gunner.

Then, out of nowhere, he heard the voice of Rooster over their coms net. "Speirs, we're coming up from your six. Don't shoot us! We're friendlies."

From our six? What the hell?

Speirs turned around and saw Rooster leading a group of three other Deltas around a corner he hadn't expected them to come from. In all the chaos, the two groups had somehow gotten turned around in the fight.

"Keep laying it on them, Speirs," Rooster directed. "We're going to charge right through your lines and take that bunker out. We have to get our charges on that tower ASAP. Our eye in the sky shows multiple swarms of enemy soldiers converging on our positions. We don't have long, or we're toast."

Rooster and three other Deltas kept running right through their hastily established position. Speirs and the other soldiers looked on in awe at the Delta operators charging headlong into the enemy. The operators blasted away with their strange-looking Slayer rifles at blinding rates of fire. Unlike the Pharaonis' blaster fire, which shot yellowish flashes of light, or the Republic's with its blue, the M-111 Slayer shot blaster bolts of purple, creating a stark contrast between the various types of blasters the different groups were using.

Watching the augmented supersoldiers in action, up close and in a real battle, was almost mesmerizing. Speirs had had limited experience with Special Forces during the last war, and from what he saw of their new armor and rifles now, it was a vast improvement from what he'd grown accustomed to seeing them use. On more than one occasion, he saw a couple of blaster shots slam into one of the operators, only to bounce harmlessly off the man like a Nerf dart. The operator just kept going like he didn't even realize he'd been hit.

Rooster's team had covered the distance to the tower faster than Speirs thought anyone possibly could. Then he recalled the vastly improved new Dragon Skin exoskeleton combat suit, which allowed them to run faster, jump higher, and probably lift far more than a normal human could. The four of them pounced into sandbagged positions, devolving the fight with the soldiers manning it into a savage hand-to-hand fight with trench knives and Ka-Bars being pulled and the Pharaonis using their own taloned fingers to slash and gash at their opponents.

BOOM.

Everyone flinched when the sound of a massive explosion tore through the air—overwhelming the noise of their own battle. Then they felt the ground shake, almost as quickly as they had heard the boom. It wasn't quite like an earthquake, but it did cause those standing to momentarily lose their footing.

The Deltas seemed to hardly notice the shaking of the ground or the massive explosion as they kept right on fighting, finishing off the remaining defenders.

"Oh, wow. How the hell is that guy doing that?" one of the soldiers near him said, pointing in the direction of the tower.

Speirs had to do a double take when he saw what the deal was. Somehow, in the few minutes the fighting had finally petered out, one of the Deltas had mysteriously climbed up the tower without any kind of help or special equipment, at least not that they could see. Now the guy was taking some sort of cord or rope hanging from the side of his utility belt and stuffing it in the creases and cracks around the support struts and trusses supporting the tower. Once the tower was down, they'd finally be able to call in the reinforcements and the air and artillery support needed until help arrived.

"Damn, bro. Look at that dude going all savage on those Pharaonis bastards," a nearby soldier commented as he pointed to the building enemy reinforcements had been rushing out of.

Apparently, one of Rooster's operators wasn't done fighting with whoever was still inside the building. The Delta propped the door open just wide enough to stick the barrel of one of those new rifles inside the room and open fire. They saw a few yellow blaster shots fired back at him in return. One looked to have hit him in the chest and actually knocked him backward on his ass. He looked stunned for a moment, then shook it off and angrily got back to his feet. He pulled a grenade from his utility belt and proceeded to pull the door open just enough to toss it inside.

They heard a boom, so they knew it had gone off. But he wasn't done yet. He then pulled the door wide open before moving to stand in the entrance like some kind of mythical god ready to unleash his wrath. Holding the rifle with both hands at the hip, the Delta fired, using a full-auto function that didn't exist on a blaster. This full-auto display made it look like he was shooting an almost nonstop streak of purple flashes of light into the room as he methodically swept it from left to right.

"Would you look at that, dude? Total killing machine, man—almost like one of those toasters we've seen in battle," one of Speirs's corporals commented. He wasn't wrong—the guy was mowing down whoever was inside, with no apparent regard for his own safety, just like a C100.

Moments after the guy finished gunning down whoever was left in that building, the spelunking master had dropped down to the street below and the four of them took off running like their lives depended on it.

"Speirs, get your people out of here now! Fall back to the Alamo and hold it until reinforcements arrive. We're about to be overrun by several groups converging on this tower," Rooster said urgently. Just like the original Alamo, this building where they had climbed out of the sewers would be the place where they'd make their last stand. Speirs hoped like hell their reinforcements would arrive in time while they made use of the sudden availability of close-air support and artillery fire to buy them more time.

When Rooster and his team ran past their lines, heading straight for the Alamo, everyone else followed suit and bugged out. They'd run maybe ten or twenty meters when a powerful explosion erupted behind them. Speirs heard a loud groaning noise followed by a massive crashing. He felt a vibrating crunch through the ground and turned his head enough to see the full weight of the tower fall now that its support structures had been compromised.

When they reached the building they called the Alamo, Captain Zillow had already fortified it as best he could with the resources he had. The three-story structure had three squads of soldiers placed on each of the levels. They'd spaced their LMGs in various positions and elevations, so they'd be able to provide devastating interlocking fields of fire.

No sooner had Speirs and his platoon entered the building than a wave of enemy reinforcements began to arrive. The battle for the Alamo, the battle for survival, was now in full swing and it was anyone's guess how it would turn out.

For nearly ten minutes, the soldiers of Easy Company fought like devils with the Deltas as multiple wave attacks were made against their building. Rockets, explosives, and a veritable wall of blaster fire hammered away at the outer facade of the building. On more than one occasion, it looked like they were about to be overrun. Then, without fail and just at the right moment, a close-air support Reaper drone would swoop out of the sky like a hawk who had found his prey. Only this hawk dove out of the sky firing a chain gun, blasting away at the enemy and swatting them aside like a child's plaything.

As the Reapers made pass after pass with their chain guns, smart missiles and occasional thermobaric bombs, the enemy grew desperate. More and more blaster fire was being aimed at the drones and not at the soldiers on the ground. Then their own reinforcements began to arrive in perhaps the most spectacular form the regular infantry grunts had ever witnessed.

Groups of six and twelve C100 combat synthetic soldiers appeared almost out of nowhere, landing at vital points all throughout the enemy base. The way the combat Synths were able to leverage their parachute deployments at just the right time allowed them to slow down just enough to survive the landing but not keep them dangling from a parachute for any longer than necessary. As the automated killing machines went to work, the enemy had to shift their focus away from the Alamo to contend with the C100s who were rapidly decimating their ranks.

By the time the battle was over a few hours later, the final Pharaonis redoubt in the Capitol District had fallen. Fifty-plus days of continuous battling through the region, and the Republic had finally subdued the enemy. With the major operations complete, the final cleanup missions would largely be left to the Tully units now starting to arrive from the core worlds of their territory.

For the men and women of the 101st Orbital Assault Division, the battle was essentially over. From now on they'd look to rest, refit their equipment, and advise and assist the Tully as needed until they were told to return to the ships—and hopefully given the orders to head home.

****

TOREC Mining Headquarters
Éire – Belters' Planet

Cormac Riggins ran through his mental checklist of what he wanted to go over in this upcoming meeting with Liam. He rearranged the food on the table nervously. You could never go wrong trying to butter someone up with a delicious meal.

Liam walked in and shook Riggins's hand. The two of them engaged in the prerequisite chitchat for a moment while they had some food. However, eventually, they had to get down to it.

"Well, Liam, I think this is going to be the beginning of a long, long partnership," said Riggins.

"According to your surveys, we have enough Bronkis5 here to keep this gravy train going for the better part of a millennium," Liam remarked. "By that time, the Sovereign Wealth Fund of Éire will be so well funded that we will be able to keep all of our social programs going here in perpetuity without *ever* touching the principal." He patted Riggins on the shoulder. "Your discovery is going to create a utopia here. People here may not have everything they *want*, but no one here is going to struggle for the basic needs of survival."

An agreement had already been reached about the percentage of the profits that TOREC would be giving over to the Sovereign Wealth Fund. Riggins wasn't unhappy about the amount—his corporation would still make a hefty profit. Frankly, he felt he'd won handily in those negotiations, but he would never tell Liam that. There was something he was hoping for, though.

"Éire is going to be the most amazing place to live in the galaxy, as far as I'm concerned," said Riggins. "Well, it will be, unless…"

"Unless what?" asked Liam, alarmed.

"We're sitting ducks out here, Liam. We have the protection of the Republic to a point, but this Bronkis5 is incredibly valuable. Eventually, some of these other alien races are going to make their move for it—or maybe some highly motivated space pirates."

That last comment was intentional. Liam's checkered past wasn't exactly a secret, although somehow, he'd managed to wipe his slate clean. Liam frowned and crossed his arms. "What exactly are you proposing, Riggins?"

"Well, we have the internal defense on Éire itself nailed down. Everyone is a part of the civilian militia program, and we can be relatively certain that our facility, the Walburg Industries facility, and the major points of infrastructure are secure. But it's the *external* threat that concerns me the most. It's time we start building our own navy, Liam. We need to better protect ourselves."

Liam ran his fingers through his hair but didn't initially say anything.

"Look, I know that everything has to be run through the council here, but I'm hoping that all this money TOREC is throwing your way will at least buy some influence in the things you bring to their attention. I've heard that Boeing has some Sentinel defense platforms we could potentially license and use around our stargate. Let's turn our little oasis into a well-defended haven, so it will stay free, and we can be left alone to live in peace."

Liam suddenly stuck out his hand. "Riggins, you bring up a very good point," he said, shaking Riggins's hand. "Would you like to present your thoughts at the next council meeting?"

"That I would, Liam. That I would."

****

Council Meeting
Éire – Belters' Planet

Liam was happy that Cormac Riggins had been successful in his pitch for more security around the planet. In fact, the council had been so favorable to his ideas that the agreement that was reached was actually beyond what he had proposed. However, now a more heated topic had arisen.

"The Primords want to know if they can settle on our lands," said Sara.

There was a loud chorus of murmurs among the group at that suggestion.

"Surely you can't be serious," Liam shot back, standing up in anger. "They are *aliens*! This planet is supposed to be a refuge for *humans.* Isn't it enough that we have agreed to let people in from Sumer and New Eden?"

"Look, Liam," said Sara calmly. "On one level, I can understand where you are coming from. You don't want to endanger the people we came here with, the people who want to escape the Republic and just live their lives. But you know our planet can sustain some Primords as well as humans. If anything, we could use *more* population at this point, not less."

She pulled up a holographic image of a Primord family, dressed in tatters. "Look at these poor kids," she pleaded. "This family barely escaped the terrors of Alfheim before the whole planet went savage, but they were only able to leave with the clothes on their backs. Their father has skills, but Sumer isn't giving out any property to Primords, and New Eden has a limited immigration policy. They've been living hand-to-mouth at the mercy of strangers, when all they want is the dignity to be able to work and provide for themselves."

Liam studied the picture carefully. It did pull at his heartstrings.

"Liam, I think there must be some ancient connection between humans and the Primords," Sara suggested. "I mean, other than their somewhat elvish faces, they basically look like us."

Liam sat back down and took a deep breath. "All right, Sara. I won't put up any more roadblocks here," he acquiesced. "If you want to let some Primords come here, then you just have to convince the rest of the council."

Sara smiled. Liam noted that she was starting to show a bit. Perhaps being an expectant father had made him softer, or perhaps it had just made Sara's maternal side stronger. In either case, he realized the council didn't stand a chance.

Chapter Sixteen
Not a Hookup

Blue Lagoon Bar
Emerald City
New Eden

David tried to contain himself as he glanced over and saw Catalina in a slinky red dress, walking in like she was about to hit the catwalk. Most of the men in the room turned their heads her way, even if they had to snap them back to pay attention to the dates they had walked in there with.

Drew nonchalantly sipped on a martini while David amused himself by thinking of how their trainer might really enjoy sitting at swanky bars on the government dime.

Blue shirt, end of the bar, Drew announced over the neurolink. *That's your target. You have one hour. You know what to do.*

David still couldn't get over what they were about to do.

Remember, boys, we pick him up for real this time, Catalina reminded them.

She strutted up to the bar and leaned forward as she ordered a drink. The way that she stood maximized all the alluring qualities of her form and figure, and the man in the blue shirt looked up from his Qpad at her and smiled. David immediately tamped down any twinge of jealousy he might have felt. Drew had been very clear when David and Catalina had approached him before getting into a relationship with each other. There was only one rule—they couldn't let it affect their missions.

"I don't care if you all decide to have an orgy," Drew had told them. "Whatever you want to do with your sex lives is up to you, so long as it's legal. But you have to know that whether you two are together that day or on the outs in your homelife, it can't affect what happens out in the field. You always have each other's backs, and you don't put your teammates at risk. Understood?"

David got it. That didn't make it easy to watch another man eye your very attractive girlfriend. David focused. He checked out his Qpad, pretending to concentrate on a news article, but he continued to watch out of the corner of his eye to make sure things didn't go south.

After a few moments of flirtatious banter, Catalina playfully touched the man's arm.

He doesn't stand a chance, David thought, holding back a laugh.

While the man in the blue shirt was distracted, she managed to slip something into his drink undetected.

Mickey is in, she announced over the neurolink.

Damn, she's good, David thought.

A few minutes later, their mark was talking loudly and seemed quite tipsy.

"You want to get out of here and party back at my place?" Catalina asked coyly.

"Definitely," the man replied, nodding a little too much.

"Do you have a car?" she asked.

"Oh. No. I took a taxi here," he answered.

"That's OK. I brought mine," said Catalina. "I'll bring it around." She pulled out her Qpad and tapped several times on the screen. "It'll come around on the side in a minute."

Catalina helped him check out with the bartender and then started walking with him toward the exit.

Jessica, Amir, get in position, Catalina directed.

We're in position, Jessica confirmed.

The man in the blue shirt began to stumble a bit, and David used that as his cue.

"Hold up there, sir. Looks like you could use a little help," David said as he came along and slid the man's left arm over his shoulder. The three of them walked toward the side entrance.

"Yeah, OK," the man mumbled. "I don't know what happened. I'm usually not such a lightweight."

When they went out the door, David immediately looked to his left. Somchai was right where he was supposed to be, unloading supplies from a truck and keeping people from watching their activities. He'd also been dispatched to deactivate the CCTV cameras down that side street; anyone watching would see a loop of absolutely nothing occurring, but their alterations would be extremely difficult to detect, even if someone did have a reason to go looking.

A red car drove around and parked in front of the delivery truck. The side doors nearest them opened.

"That's a nice car," the man in the blue shirt commented.

"Thanks," Catalina replied. "My job has its perks."

"I, uh, I…" The man's voice trailed off. "Here, my address is in my Qpad." Their mark rifled through his pockets until he found his Qpad and unlocked it with his biometrics. Catalina took it from the man.

Now, David, Catalina ordered.

David pulled the autoinjector out of his pocket and placed the device along the base of their mark's neck, pulling the trigger before the man could react. He went limp almost immediately, and David and Catalina gently set him down in the back seat. This particular medication was short-acting. By the time they arrived at his home, he'd be capable of walking again, but he would definitely not remember anything after the car arrived.

To the right of the taxi was a white service van. The side door slid open, and Jessica waved David and Somchai in.

There was a tense moment as they waited for Catalina to send them the address.

"Got it," Amir announced before they pulled out.

David and Somchai went to work changing into service outfits that matched the brand name on the van. They would drive ahead of Catalina by a moment and get a drone sent up before her arrival. In the meantime, she was busy exploiting all of the data on the man's Qpad.

Since David and Somchai were occupied, Jessica went to work finding out about the building where their target lived.

We are looking at a condo with four units and one common entrance, Jess announced over the neurolink. They would still be within range of each other for a while, and this allowed them to all share information simultaneously. *Middle of the block, small parking lot to the west of the building. Similar buildings across the street.*

Any shops or other stores nearby that might attract a crowd? asked Catalina.

It doesn't look like it. Purely residential area, Jessica replied.

Somchai and David had finished changing and joined in the search for information.

I've got the front door lock model pulled up, David announced. *Standard. No surprises there.*

We've got a couple of CCTV cameras to disable: one on the entrance of this building, and one across the street, said Somchai.

There's a problem, Catalina announced.

Whatcha got, boss? asked Amir.

Mr. Blue Shirt has a dog. And it's not a chihuahua. This thing is huge.

Jessica began grabbing for various supplies in the back of the van. *I'm on it, Catalina*, she announced. *I'm synthesizing an aerosol sedative now. I'll put it in a lipstick applicator and place it on our bumper once we're parked.*

Thanks, Jess. I'm on the move. See you soon.

Amir had the van on autopilot, but he was vigilantly watching the monitors to make sure that someone wasn't tailing them. The van was equipped with cameras that covered all angles, and algorithms filtered the feeds to flag any suspicious activity. Still, none of them completely trusted their fate to a bunch of zeros and ones.

Somchai switched to preparing the drone to be operated. At this point, they'd run so many drills, they just instinctively completed certain tasks out of muscle memory.

The van pulled into the parking lot, and after they'd spoofed the nearby CCTVs with a loop of inactivity, David got out of the van with a tool bag, appearing like he was getting ready to perform some maintenance on the building. In reality, he was just there to observe their surroundings.

Somchai, you are clear to launch the drone, David announced.

Heard.

A moment later, a drone the size of a coffee mug whirred up into the sky.

I'm almost there, said Catalina. *How are we looking?*

CCTVs are down and the drone's up, Somchai responded. *Just getting the first IR images back now. One of the units is totally empty right now. I see one couple who looks like they are set to Netflix and chill, and one person who seems to be making dinner. Oh, and I see the dog—you're right, he is big. But this should be as good a time as any to enter the building.*

David opened up the access port for the building's water supply and crouched down like he was tinkering with something. Plumbing was a skill set that only a very small portion of the population had, and most people wouldn't question someone in a uniform examining some pipes.

This vantage point allowed him to keep an eye on things and to be available if things went awry.

The sporty red vehicle pulled up and parked behind the van.

****

Catalina could hear her mark starting to mumble. *Perfect timing.* Although she was capable of lifting the man after her modifications, a woman in a sexy red number slinging a man over her shoulders like a sack of potatoes might draw suspicion.

"Hey, we made it back to your place," she said sweetly. "You ready to go have some fun?"

The man smiled dopily.

She reached over and rubbed his sternum with her knuckles.

"Ow!" he cried. "What'd you do that for?"

"Sorry, but I needed you to wake up a little more," she explained.

"Well, OK, but that hurt," the man replied.

Catalina opened the door and assisted the man in the blue shirt to his feet, putting his left arm over her shoulder. They walked toward his building slowly. She didn't need him falling flat on his face right now. Their biggest risk of getting caught was coming up, as they entered the main hallway to their mark's condo.

She casually grabbed the tube of aerosol disguised as a lipstick tube as they went past the van, and she winked at David as they walked by him. She wanted to say something flirtatious to him, even if it was over the neurolink, but she needed to keep both of them focused right now.

As Catalina approached the front door, she made sure the coast was clear before she pulled the code cracker out of her purse and placed it on the front door. Their "friend" wasn't in any shape to remember anything important at the moment.

Hiss.

The door opened, and Catalina took a deep breath before they walked inside. If anyone walked out right now, she'd have to play it off and hope that they would just think he'd gotten lucky and taken a beautiful woman home from the bar. Sometimes the best strategy was hiding in plain sight.

The hallway was empty, much to Catalina's relief. She approached the target's unit, which was thankfully on the ground level and not up the stairs. She figured he'd probably wanted easier access to take his dog to the common green space in the back.

When they reached the door, Catalina used his fingerprints to unlock the biometric lock.

At least it wasn't a retinal scanner, she thought with amusement. It would have been difficult to get him to keep his eye open in his current state, and that might have made things a little harder to explain to any observers if she were prying his eyelids open.

When she turned the door handle, she had the aerosol spray ready to go. The last thing she needed was to get mauled by a dog.

The pooch must have been waiting by the door because Catalina saw the pet's nose through the small crack and immediately sprayed it. She hoped to goodness it was effective. The dog whimpered and pulled back.

Catalina slowly and cautiously pushed the door further back. The canine was rubbing at its nose and making a rumbling noise as if it were about to start barking. She sprayed it one more time for good measure— the dog was *very* big, practically the size of a Great Dane but some other breed she'd never seen before. She figured it probably needed more than one dose to be effective.

Ten seconds later, the dog was happily napping, and she walked the blue-shirted man back to his bedroom. She removed his shirt and pants, strewing them along the floor with his shoes and socks. She got him into his bed, and before he could wake up too much more and get handsy, she used an autoinjector to give him a longer-lasting pharmaceutical lullaby. When he woke up, all he would remember was meeting her at the bar and getting into her car. The clothes might lead him to believe that he'd had some fun he couldn't recall, or that he'd just had way too much to drink and passed out. In either case, he had opened his own door and there were no obvious signs of foul play.

Now that their mark was resting comfortably, Catalina went to work exploiting all of his electronic devices for any available info. With that complete, she placed the keylogger malware that the Republic had ripped from the Sumerian spy agency, as well as their version of Deepreach. The Republic knew a good thing when they saw it, and they were always ready to steal a good new piece of tech.

Status update? asked Amir.

Just waiting on the malware to do its thing, she responded. *I'm at seventy-three percent. Somchai, how's our building looking?*

Everything is quiet, he answered. *No movement.*

She watched in anticipation as the percentage downloaded climbed.

Done, she announced.

She did a sweep to make sure she hadn't left behind any signs of her presence, checked in with Somchai one more time, and then walked right out the front door like she owned the place.

The team would take their separate vehicles back to the safe house, making sure to follow their countersurveillance protocols in case they were followed.

****

"Well done, everyone," Drew commented. "You successfully captured your mark without detection and exploited all of his electronic devices. We now have a remote access program to access his Qpad, laptop, and any other devices those devices have interacted with. We can track all of his activity with our keylogger, and every email he sends will have our malware on it, so we can then gain access to those email accounts as well.

"Anyone can capture a source. It takes skill to be able to do so without detection, and even more to do so without the source themselves knowing they've been exploited."

David was proud of his team of misfits. They were all working well together as a team at this point, and they'd gelled pretty well.

They spent some time going over each aspect of the mission as usual, comparing notes about what had gone right, what could have gone better, and what might have presented some major risks that they hadn't considered. After they finished their after-action review and Drew had left them alone, David looked flirtatiously at Catalina.

I think you should save that red dress for later, he told her over the neurolink.

Oh, but it looks so much better on the floor, she teased.

Damn, I'm a lucky man, David thought. He remembered feeling like he'd never find love again after losing Trish. Now here he was, in his afterlife, getting it on with a super-hot spy.

"OK, lovebirds, enough with the hostile work environment," Jessica mocked.

"What? We didn't even say anything," Catalina shot back.

"She knew what you were thinking," Somchai said with a chuckle.

"Get a room already," joked Amir.

"Don't mind if I do," David said, and he took Catalina's hand and led her to their bedroom.

Chapter Seventeen
The Council's Anger

High Council – Chamber of Decisions
Zinconia – Zodark Home World

"Mavkah Otro, you are called to stand before the Council in the Circle of Truth. Step forward, prepare your mind and your body to be questioned," declared the ominously stern voice of Zon Utulf.

Otro stiffened in his chair at the calling of his name—his time had come; a decision would be made. Standing up, he walked confidently towards the Circle of Truth to receive his answer and be given his orders.

He passed through the blue flames of Lindow, flames that changed color if they detected a lie. While the flames oddly did not burn one's flesh or clothes, when walking through them before speaking to the Council, one felt the sensation of heat often referred to as the cleanse of Lindow.

Standing erect in the center of the Circle of Truth, Otro looked up at the seven Council members seated on the curved platform in front of him. He then spoke loudly, confidently. "Members of the Council, I, Mavkah Otro, head of the Malvari, the humble servant of Lindow and instrument of the Council, stand before you, cleansed by the flames of Lindow—ready to answer your questions."

Otro did his best to remain stoic, maintaining a placid emotionless face as he waited for the first question or, as he hoped, the authorization to move forward with the Malvari's plans for Sol. But as his eyes searched the faces of the Council to see who would speak first, his pulse quickened when the voice that called out to him was not that of Zon Utulf. It was the Council's youngest member, Tanhilff, who spoke first.

In his higher-pitched, nasal voice that grated on Otro's nerves each time he asked a profoundly stupid question, he began, "Mavkah Otro, the Council has reviewed the Malvari's invasion plans for Sol...and found them wanting." His words were dripping in disappointment and annoyance. Once he felt he had paused for effect long enough, he continued. "Mavkah, the Council has received two proposals from the Groff for us to consider as alternatives to the

Malvari's plans. We wish to understand why the Malvari dismissed these proposals and chose not to brief them to us. What say you?"

Otro paused for a moment, taking a breath in before responding to what sounded like an accusation that he had misled them. He looked at his accuser, calmly replying, "Council member Tanhilff, the Malvari did review the Groff's proposals—we rejected them."

"That is correct! You rejected the proposals because they were counter to the Malvari's plans. You even went so far as to hide them from the Council rather than allowing us to review them for ourselves. What made you think the Council would not learn of your deceit?"

Otro stiffened at the accusation. "The Malvari have not deceived the Council," he countered forcefully. "If the Groff have told the Council that their plan will succeed over our own, then it is the Groff who are deceiving the Council. The Malvari do not pretend to know how to run the Groff, nor do I pretend I am the Director of the Groff. Yet the Groff now pretend they are the Malvari and know our military capabilities better than we do. The Malvari reviewed the proposals from the Groff and determined they were not viable. They would squander the element of surprise provided by the *Nefantar*, which is why we did not present the proposals to the Council. It is not the Groff's place to propose a military strategy and insist on the Malvari following it. Therefore, I reject your accusation that I and the Malvari have intentionally misled the Council."

"Oh, so you reject my accusation, do you?" Tanhilff pounced the moment Otro finished speaking. "Perhaps we should summon Director Vak'Atioth to give us his perspective on why we should choose one of his two proposals over the Malvari's."

"Enough, Tanhilff! You have asked your question and you have received your response. I will not have you impugn and attack the Mavkah any further. Otro, why do you still believe the Malvari's original strategy is the one we should authorize?" Zon Utulf asked.

"Thank you, Zon Utulf. Allow me to explain why our approach is the best approach," Otro replied, ignoring Tanhilff, who glared daggers at him.

"Once we unveil the *Nefantar*, we will only have one chance to surprise the enemy with its special abilities. This means we need to choose wisely when and where we want to reveal this to the enemy or risk diminishing its tactical and strategic value. The Terrans' home system, Sol, is not a part of the stargate network, so there was never going to be an easy path for us to get at their home world. The closest system within the stargate network is the Rhea system. In it is the planet Clovis, a former mining colony that the Terrans have renamed New Eden, which I have been told translates to 'new paradise'—a new, largely untouched version of their home world, Earth. Our navigators believe it would take our warships around six days' travel between the two systems.

"This is why the Malvari did not present either of the Groff's proposals. The tactical and strategic advantage the *Nefantar* gives us is a one-time opportunity. That is why we must use it where we can gain our greatest advantage. Launching a surprise attack against the Republic's home world, Earth, will yield us the greatest short- and long-term effect," Otro explained, seeking to counter Councilman Tanhilff's allegation. He also saw that a couple other Council members still did not appear to be fully convinced.

All right, you old fools, we will see if I can dumb this down further, he thought, annoyed that the Groff refused to stick to foreign and domestic security while the Malvari handled the military.

"Members of the Council, the Malvari did not present the Groff's proposals to you because they will not bring about the kind of decisive victory we are aiming to achieve. The Terrans do not believe we possess the technology needed to bypass the stargates. The only races that have had this technology are the Orbots, the Altairians, and now the Terrans, but only on that Gallentine warship. This means they have built most of their defenses around the stargates leading into their territory. Thus, their home system, Sol, is not nearly as fortified as Rhea and Qatana systems—the ones where the Groff recommended we use the *Nefantar*.

"If the Council wants to pursue a military campaign our security agencies have proposed over one the military has developed, then the *Nefantar* should not be used. Unveiling its wormhole technology to the Terrans and the Galactic Empire in a battle that does not require its use is a foolish waste of such a powerful one-of-a-kind weapon," Otro explained.

"Mavkah," Zon Utulf interrupted, "if the Council approves the Malvari's plan to use the *Nefantar* to create the bridge for our fleet to cross into the Terran home system, Sol, are you confident our forces will be able to achieve the objectives outlined in your proposal?"

Otro smiled at the question. Utulf had given him the perfect opportunity to remind the skeptics on the Council of what the Malvari were looking to achieve.

"Zon Utulf, when our fleet emerges in Sol, it will cause immediate chaos and confusion, something we plan on fully exploiting. As they scramble to marshal whatever forces they have in system, our strike groups will head toward their targets. Once the fleet has cleared whatever defenses they have in orbit of Earth, our transports will move in and begin landing our warriors. Their immediate objective is to capture Jacksonville, the capital city of the Republic and the government's seat of power. We will then force them into accepting surrender to the Zodark Empire—or total annihilation, beginning with the destruction of Earth," Otro explained excitedly. The more he talked about this plan, the more exhilarated he felt about the real possibility of annihilating the Terran threat once and for all. Then Councilman Idradica interjected to pose a scenario the Malvari had anticipated and planned for.

"As I have stated before, Mavkah, this looks to be a solid plan. But we all know"—Idradica waved his upper right hand across the Council—"that once this battle gets underway, it will not be long before the Republic and the Galactic Empire mobilize a force to head to Sol. When the Republic's Gallentine warship, the *Freedom*, arrives in Sol, is it the Malvari's plan to stand and fight this ship or open a bridge and allow our forces to withdraw from the system?"

"Councilman Idradica, the *Nefantar* was built around the superweapon designed to destroy this Gallentine warship. The Malvari's plan is for the *Nefantar* to stand and fight, to destroy this warship and remove it as a threat to Zinconia and the Empire."

"Thank you, Mavkah, for that explanation," Idradica said. "I have explained my hesitation in the past regarding the Malvari's plan, particularly risking this many of our warships in a single campaign. Having heard your explanation in contrast to the Groff's proposals Tanhilff shared with us, I am not convinced we should pursue any of these proposals. Before I can make a decision, I have one final question. If it is necessary for our fleet to abandon Sol, how will that happen?"

Otro sighed at the question, knowing it was a setup to the very argument Tanhilff had made against the Malvari's plan. Since he couldn't lie while in the Circle, he gave them the answer they wanted to hear.

"Without access to a stargate, the fleet's only way out of Sol rests in the *Nefantar*'s ability to open a wormhole and create a bridge for the fleet to leave."

"That is how I understand this technology to work as well. This also leads us back to the point that has been previously made about the Malvari's plan to invade Sol. I assume it is still true that if the *Nefantar* is destroyed in battle or sustains damage to its wormhole generator, our ships would become trapped in Sol?"

Tanhilff sat forward in his chair, waiting to see if Otro would offer up a lie or if he would validate Tanhilff's previous warning about the fleet becoming trapped. Otro maintained eye contact with him as he replied, "That is correct. The situation has not changed. If a bridge cannot be created in Sol, then whatever forces we have in the system will become trapped."

Tanhilff smiled at the reiteration of his earlier warnings about the viability of the Malvari's plan. It was why he had attached himself to the Groff's proposals. They were less risky, Otro would give him that, but they would not eliminate the threat the Republic posed to the Empire, which was why the Malvari continued to recommend against them.

"When Director Vak'Atioth last spoke with us, he told us the Malvari would press on with this decision regardless of the risk." Councilman Tanhilff spoke loudly, defiantly to the others, but his words were meant for the one who had the power to usurp them all and make the final decision. "I will not dispute the claim that, should this plan work, should the *Nefantar* survive, we could destroy this warship called *Freedom*. We may even compel the Republic to surrender. But should the *Nefantar* be destroyed or rendered unable to create a bridge for our fleet to withdraw from Sol, the result would be the total annihilation of our invasion fleet.

"The Mavkah is asking us to risk the fate of the entire empire on the success or failure of the Malvari's plan. We need to remember also that when our people came into contact with the Republic, it was the Malvari who assured us that they posed no grave threat to the Empire—that their technology was inferior to our own and that our forces would

176

not only defeat them, we would add their planet and peoples to our fiefdom.

"Given how spectacularly wrong the Malvari were and have continued to be about the Republic, how can we trust them to risk more than half of our warships in a single battle that relies on the technology of one ship to bridge us into the Terran home system? And should anything happen to that ship, it would result in the destruction of the entire fleet. Losing more than half of our remaining warships when we still have not replaced all those we lost during the final battle of the last war in Sirius would leave our entire Empire open to invasion," Tanhilff said passionately. "This plan is too risky to approve. We must vote against it and pursue another path. Is there an agreement with my decision?"

"I concur—I vote no on the Malvari's proposal."

Otro felt confused and caught off guard by what he was hearing and seeing when a third voice joined in.

"I too vote no on the Malvari's proposal. We cannot risk the future of the Empire on one singular battle."

No, no, no, Otro thought in a panic. *Don't they realize how close we are to achieving final victory over the Republic?*

Without thinking, he interrupted their vote. "You cannot vote no! Does the Council not understand that the Republic could open a bridge and allow their fleet to invade Zinconia today, or tomorrow? You must allow the Malvari to invade Sol and end this threat before it is too late."

No sooner had he uttered the words than he realized he had just crossed the line and done something no one was allowed to do: speak to the Council without having been asked to speak. Worse, he had questioned the Council and even challenged their ongoing vote.

For the briefest of moments, no one spoke. Shock and surprise seemed to have enveloped the room. Not only had someone spoken out of turn to the Council, that someone was the Mavkah of the Malvari. Never in the history of the Council had the military head of the Zodark Empire spoken out so harshly to the members of the Council. They seemed at a loss for how to respond to this breach of etiquette.

Zon Utulf was the first to recover. Having chosen to sit on the far-left side of the row of seats, he was able to look across the six other members of the Council as he addressed them. Speaking loudly, forcefully to make sure his words and meaning were not lost on them, or on Mavkah Otro, he chastised his fellow Council members over what was clearly an attempt to pit the Groff against the Malvari and now divide the Council itself into camps, either for or against one group's military strategy over another.

Turning to face the official scribe of the Council, Utulf commanded, "Recorder of the Chamber, I am calling this meeting to an end. Furthermore, I am ordering that what was spoken here today by the Council and Mavkah Otro be stricken from the record along with any mention of today's meeting."

Utulf then looked at the shocked faces of his colleagues. "What happened today will not be discussed outside this room. It is important to remember that emotions are a fickle thing. They also have the ability to take on a life of their own if they are not kept in check. They can breed rumors, hatred, and distrust. Worse, once they are spoken, once they are allowed breath, they can spread like a disease across the body, paralyzing it, weakening it until it dies.

"The threats that face the Empire today are graver than they have been in many dracmas. This Council will not add to those threats by allowing division within our ranks to be made known to those outside. I will not have the reputation of this Council, its members, the Malvari, or the Groff called into question by anyone. Therefore, I decree that what has transpired today did not occur. It will be blotted from the record and forgotten to history. For the time being, this matter is closed—this meeting over."

When Utulf had finished, he stared at the other members, daring them to challenge his authority. When none did, he turned and angrily looked at the head of the Malvari.

"Mavkah Otro, I will speak with you privately in my office, where we will discuss what you have just done…and your future as Mavkah. Is that understood?"

Otro nodded, unsure what his future might now hold. One thing was certain: he'd crossed a line by speaking out of turn. Now he'd have to wait and see what would come of it.
****

Hours Later
Residence of Councilman Tanhilff

Councilman Tanhilff seethed at how the meeting had gone today. Never in the history of the Council had a Mavkah dared to challenge those appointed to rule the Empire. What galled him further was Zon Utulf's reaction. Otro should have been stripped of his rank, replaced by his deputy and then made to undergo the Frocking and let Lindow determine if he was worthy of redemption. Instead, Utulf had had the entire incident struck from the official record—as though it had never happened. Why would he do such a thing? Without an official record, how would future Zons and Council members know how to respond to such a challenge to their authority?

If Otro is not removed from the Malvari...he may launch this invasion without their approval. He needs to be stopped.

Taking his evening meal on the south-side portico of his sprawling estate outside the capital city, Tanhilff tried to distract his mind until his guest arrived and he'd be forced to revisit the day's events. With three hours of sunlight left till darkness, scattered groups of Sumerian, Primord, and even a few Tully slaves worked his family's vineyards.

The time to harvest the Yuli fruits across the Mukusa Clan's estates had just begun. Most vineyards that crafted the sought-after Yutangly wines would begin their harvests in another two weeks—but not the Mukusa. Over hundreds of dracmas, Tanhilff's great-grandfather and head of the Mukusa Clan had perfected a hybrid version of the Yuli bushes to create a unique blend of flavors that made the Mukusa wines renowned for their quality and unrivaled tastes, which couldn't be found anywhere else within the Empire.

It had also made the Mukusa Clan incredibly wealthy. That wealth had, of course, translated into political power. Power that his grandfather had lived just long enough to see come to fruition when Tanhilff had been appointed to the High Council during the selection for the new term. A Council's term lasted thirty-five dracmas, which meant that if a family wanted one of their line to be selected to serve on the Council one day, it took a considerable amount of time and a lot of strategic planning to make it happen. Of course, one's family had to be a member of the founding seven clans to even be considered, but even then, the number of families within a clan had only grown in size across the generations.

"Excuse me, Tanhilff, your guest has arrived," one of his house slaves announced.

Standing to greet the man who had come to see him under a veil of secrecy, he motioned for another bottle of wine to be brought to the table for him and his guest. Tanhilff and Director Vak'Atioth had a lot to discuss, and not a lot of time to waste.

****

"The Zon actually said that?" Director Vak'Atioth exclaimed in surprise.

"He did. There won't be a record of it, but, yes, that is what he said."

Vak shook his head in surprise. The Malvari were hell-bent on launching this invasion of Sol. Despite the riskiness of the proposal, Otro maintained his belief that if the Malvari used the *Nefantar* to invade Sol and smash the Republic's defenses, he could force their government into accepting a quick, unconditional surrender to the Zodark Empire.

Does Otro believe the rest of their alliance will not come to their aid...?

"Do you believe the Zon is going to punish Otro for his actions today during the meeting?" Vak asked hesitantly, watching to see how Tanhilff would respond. He had thought the relationship between the Mavkah and the Zon was professional in nature until he had learned of today's events. Now...he wasn't so certain.

"I would like to believe Utulf would punish Otro, but you have to understand something. Utulf selected Otro to be the Mavkah for a reason. He is a shrewd tactician and military organizer. Before we encountered the Terran Republic, he had led our empire to a series of military victories that saw us grow to become the second-largest power within the Dominion—second only to the Orbots. I believe Utulf has been grooming Otro for years to replace him on the Council one day—maybe even as Zon."

Otro as Zon...Lindow help the Empire...

"I see. Then what do you want me to do about any of this, Tanhilff?"

"Do about this?! I want you to figure out how the Groff can put a stop to it. If Otro proceeds with his grand invasion plans and they fail...you know what will happen. Putting aside the reaction from the

Orbots, a relationship that is already strained, do you really believe the Republic or their allies will not respond and invade our own territories? They will view us as weak if our fleet is destroyed in Sol, and they will be right. We could lose the Empire. The Groff must find a way to stop this plan before it dooms us all," Tanhilff said, exasperated by the situation.

"Tanhilff, there is nothing I or the Groff can do if Zon Utulf gives the Malvari the order. Even if the Council does not consent, he can simply invoke Lindowee. Our hands are tied...unless...no, I don't think you could pull this other idea off..."

"What idea are you talking about? Speak plainly, Director. Now is not the time for subterfuge or coded speech."

"You can propose Jin-Mei. If you truly believe Zon Utulf must be stopped at all costs, then this is the only way," Vak replied. Jin-Mei was the only legal, sanctioned way to remove a Zon from power. Any other means would constitute a coup, and that would spark outrage across the Empire and sow immediate division across its clans and factions.

Tanhilff stared at him for a moment, and Vak could see the man was running through the scenarios in his head, calculating whether such a plan could work. If it failed...Utulf would likely use it to dismiss those who had voted against him rather than let them ride out the clock on the remainder of his term.

"No, I don't think it would work. He still has allies that agree with him. At least three of them, which means Jin-Mei would fail."

"If that is the case, Tanhilff, then there is nothing else to do but hope that Otro succeeds in his plan," Vak replied.

"You are the head of the Groff. Do you believe his plan will work?"

"No. Not in its current form."

"Director, if there is nothing we can do to prevent Otro from executing his plan, then I would ask you to do what you can to help ensure its success. The fate of the Empire may rest on the actions of the Groff," countered Tanhilff, sounding defeated before the first shots of this new war had even been fired.

As their meeting came to a close, Vak assured him that they would do their best. Privately, he doubted the Malvari would be open to further suggestions on how they could lay their own trap to lure this Republic warship into a battle they could destroy it in.

****

Office of the Zon, Private Study

"You spoke out of turn, Otro! Do you realize the kind of position you have put me in now?" Zon Utulf spoke harshly to his Mavkah. He was furious at what had happened in the meeting today and how it might impact his future plans.

"My apologies, Zon. I allowed my emotions to get the better of me. I should not have let Tanhilff goad me into responding as I did."

"Why could you not have kept your mouth shut, Otro! The Council's term is nearing its end. That means each of us has to submit our recommendations to the clan leader for final approval. I chose *you* to be *my* replacement—to become Zon yourself one day, perhaps! This blatant outburst has jeopardized that possibility.

"Have you truly forgotten how the questioning process of the Council works? Tanhilff was doing his job. He was supposed to bait you, in order to draw out information—to provide vigorous cross-examination to reveal *all* the relevant facts before we make our ruling. That is how the Council works and you know that! Yet you fell for his baiting and leading accusations because you have some sort of axe to grind with Director Vak'Atioth and the Groff! You know Tanhilff and two others believe the Malvari's plan is too risky. When the Groff offered a viable alternative, it gave them options to consider. If Kor-Azor and Ardishapur give in to Tanhilff and his three other votes, then I will not have the votes to pursue the Malvari's plan.

"You have to understand something, Otro. I will not use the power of Lindowee to usurp the will of the Council. I know Tanhilff may believe I might. But to do so would invite a Jin-Mei, and I will not have my legacy as Zon tarnished by Jin-Mei. I have achieved what no Zon has done before—served an entire Council term as Zon. Despite the pushback, to include an assassination attempt during my first term, I have increased the size of the Empire to encompass eighty-eight star systems while also bringing the Gurista project nearly to completion. But this Terran war, one that I might add was brought about by the Malvari, has nearly undone all of that." Utulf paused for a moment as he looked at the man he had been grooming and mentoring to replace him, wondering if his plans could still be salvaged.

"Otro, if the votes are not there, I will have to support one of the Groff alternatives or none at all. Putting that aside, you have put me in a bind with your actions today. So here is how I would like you to salvage matters so that I can move forward with nominating you as my successor."

Otro looked relieved that there might be a way to rectify the situation he'd created. *You may not like this idea once you hear it, my friend, but it is for the best...*

"Tomorrow, I am going to explain to the Council that after our conversation tonight, you walked through the proposals in detail with me, and together we came to a compromise. You will concede that the Malvari's plan was just too risky, as Tanhilff and the Groff have pointed out. Instead, the Malvari are going to use the Groff's intelligence. The *Nefantar* will use its bridging technology to launch a surprise attack on the Qatana system." Utulf held a hand up to forestall the protest he saw Otro gearing up to launch. "But this attack will be a feinting maneuver. As they commit their forces to the Qatana system, you, Otro, will personally lead the main attack aboard the *Nefantar* to invade the Rhea system. I want you to use the *Nefantar*'s superweapon to destroy this so-called Alliance City they have constructed and see what kind of damage we can do to their new capital and seat of power.

"Then have your ground forces land on the planet and its two moons. Wreck everything of military value and prepare to battle the Republic for control of the planet. Destroy the outposts protecting the stargate and clear a path for supplies and additional reinforcements. I will speak with our Orbot friends and see if I can get additional Alliance support. You are likely not aware of this, Otro, but they have other plans underway with the Pharaonis. If we can coordinate our efforts, then perhaps we can engineer a better chance of success in defeating this Terran Republic. Until they are removed from the picture, or at least that warship the *Freedom* can no longer pose a threat of invasion, we cannot move forward with designs of our own for the Dominion. Can I present this to the Council and count on you accepting this as your reprimand?"

While it wasn't standard protocol for a Mavkah to lead a fleet and be placed in direct harm, Otro didn't hesitate at the chance to redeem himself by leading the invasion force himself. It wasn't the grand invasion the Malvari had spent dracmas planning, but it was far less risky to the Empire. If the fleet needed to withdraw, then at least they'd have the stargates and not have to rely solely on a wormhole bridge that only the *Nefantar* could create.

As they went over some of the finer details of the plan, Otro brought up an idea he hadn't considered.

"Zon Utulf, if I may offer a slight modification to the plan you have given me?"

Utulf motioned for him to continue, curious what Otro was going to propose.

"If we are to make the Republic believe that the real invasion will happen in the Qatana system, then we will need to send some ground forces to attack either Sumer or one of the other colony worlds in the system. However, doing this will weaken the ground force we will need to capture the planets in the Rhea system.

"Therefore, I would like to recommend we include the Mintaraus in this operation. They may be a small spacefaring people, but their warriors are as tough and strong as ours. Including tens of thousands of them in our invasion force would greatly bolster the forces needed to retake the planet of New Eden and its two moons," Otro explained, giving Utulf a good suggestion to better their chances of success.

Utulf liked the idea of bolstering their numbers. He just wasn't sure if they should reveal their pet ally just yet. While the Mintaraus were different than what they were doing with the Guristas, the concept was the same: cultivate, groom, and train malleable races with high reproductive rates to wage wars of expansion and conquest for the Zodark Empire while not having to risk expending their own people in the process. Their aversion to utilizing machines, having seen how the Orbots could co-opt them, only reinforced the idea of breeding other races to do the fighting for them.

Conceding Otro's point about selling this feint as the real invasion, he agreed to allow him to integrate the Mintaraus into the fight. With the decision made and a plan hatched to keep Otro in play as Mavkah, Utulf dismissed his heir apparent, optimistic that his long-term plans might still come to fruition.

When Otro had left the Office of the Zon, Utulf thought to himself, *If we have to reveal one of our pets to the Orbots, then at least it is not the Guristas. The plan can still work...*

Chapter Eighteen
Sharing Is Caring

Greasy Spoons Café
Jacksonville, Arkansas
Earth, Sol System

Ashurina found Dakkuri sitting in the booth in the back corner of the restaurant and took a seat. The waitress came by, and they both ordered coffee and a pancake combo.

"I don't think I understand the whole idea of certain foods being only for breakfast but always available at diners like this one," Ashurina commented.

"Yeah, I don't get it either," Dakkuri agreed, cracking a rare smile. "And the name of the restaurant is kind of disturbing, frankly— based on some idiom, I guess. But the local reports are that this is *the* place to eat around here, and the booths provide for a certain amount of privacy."

The waitress came back with their coffee, and they engaged in some basic small talk for a few minutes to avoid suspicion. Ashurina thought about how easy it was to flip a switch and become someone else after all these years in deep cover.

Do I even know who I am anymore? she wondered. Ever since she'd been turned as a double agent, she was really struggling with the cognitive dissonance. The only thing that really kept her going was her family.

"So, how's the DARPA working group going?" Dakkuri asked once they'd gotten their food, signaling that it was time to move back to their reason for meeting.

"Well, it's fascinating," Ashurina replied. "There are always *new* things I learn at these working groups."

"Do tell," said Dakkuri.

"Well, the Republic is always doing updates to respond to threats. Systems are constantly evolving," said Ashurina, tilting her head.

Dakkuri got the signal and connected to the data stick embedded under her skull. His own neuro-integrated processor accessed some of the files, and he mentally skimmed through them.

"I might need a little bit more insight into what you are talking about," Dakkuri explained.

Ashurina leaned forward, carefully looking around to make sure that there was no possible way someone could overhear their conversation. She lowered her voice as she spoke. "The Sentinel program is undergoing a huge update. They are starting in the Qatana system, and then moving to Rhea and Sol. As they replace the old systems, the guns on the new towers are going to be way more powerful and accurate. The damage per second will be much higher, and they will have a much more powerful armor as well."

Dakkuri sat back and crossed his arms. "Well, I hope you have some good news to go with that steaming hot pile of garbage you just gave me," he remarked gruffly.

She smiled weakly. "Our backdoor to hack their systems is still active—for now. However, it is only a matter of time before they close that loophole. With each system they update, the chance of them figuring it out increases. It means that our window of opportunity is open but closing rapidly."

Ashurina fought to control her facial expressions. She didn't want there to be any signs of her deception. If Dakkuri found out she was lying, her family was as good as dead. Then again, if he did buy into what she was saying, the Republic might draw the Zodarks in, only to pulverize them. She knew that they were fortifying Earth with the most Sentinels—for every ten that were constructed, six would end up in Sol, and the others would be spread out among the other systems. Right after a jump, it would take some time for a ship's system to get a full picture of what was happening around it—and in that time, the Fleeters could completely destroy their enemy with their magrail turrets and missiles, which were mostly automated, and the squad of fighter drones each had.

Dakkuri didn't seem impressed with what Ashurina was telling him. "I want to make sure you understand the gravity of what this would mean," she insisted. "What I told you before is completely out of date. You have to move this up the chain."

Dakkuri chuckled. "Your concern is noted. I will definitely inform my superiors. However, the Zodarks aren't going to Earth."

"Oh?" she asked. She was honestly surprised he was sharing this information with her, until she remembered that she was still technically one of the alternates to replace Dakkuri.

"No. The Earth attack is now a ruse. Our main points of attack are going to be in the Qatana and Rhea systems. The Republic won't know what hit it."

Ashurina smiled. Inwardly, she wanted to be cheering on the potential defeat of Republic forces, but she knew she would have to share this information with her handler if he wasn't already listening in on them somehow.

Could they even change their fleet distribution or Sentinel coverage in time to make a difference? Ashurina wondered. It was all a game of cat and mouse—she just wasn't sure anymore if the Republic was the cat or the mouse.

She tapped her fingers a few times on the table. "There's something else you should know, then—something that might be of note. It's about the home fleet here in system."

Dakkuri raised an eyebrow but didn't say anything, so she continued. "I don't know what all is going on just yet, but what I *do* know is once this new Republic star carrier is finished, they're going to be forming up some sort of new fleet here in Sol. They're calling it the Seventh Fleet. It's going to be larger than *anything* in the past."

"I see," Dakkuri replied, steepling his fingers. "Well, this is pertinent." He leaned back. "There is one more reason for our visit today," he informed her.

"Oh?"

"I know how uncomfortable it must have been for you to hang on to those two extremely valuable packages for so long," Dakkuri said, referring to the two explosives she'd had charge of since her cruise last year. "It must be stressful, always wondering if they are secure as you go about your day."

"I won't lie and say that it doesn't weigh on me," Ashurina admitted.

"Well, it's time to meet up with your Ani contact and provide the details of their location and how to access them. You set the time and place of the meet, and we'll go from there."

On the surface, it might have made sense for her to just share that information directly with Dakkuri, but they needed to minimize his appearances in public, and it was best in this intelligence game to keep certain things compartmentalized.

"This working group ends in two days. Tell the Ani to meet me at Palette 22 in Arlington, Virginia at eight p.m. on Saturday. I'll make reservations."

Dakkuri chuckled. "Near the old DARPA headquarters, huh? You always were best at hiding things in plain sight."

Chapter Nineteen
Clues

Lab Site X
Planet Surface

It took quite some time before they were able to relocate the ship they had discovered and dig out an entrance to the lab below it, but when they did, it was definitely worth it. Just off the top, this facility was much larger than the one on Alpha Centauri, and it held a wider variety of equipment, which Sakura fully intended to understand to the best of their ability.

As at the other lab, they found a collection of mummies at Lab Site X—although there were certainly more here, around two dozen. Sakura was far less shocked by it this time around. She wondered if she might willingly have the oxygen removed from the room while she slept if she knew she was dying.

I suppose it would beat terrible agony, she reasoned. *But what if I woke up, gasping for air?* She shuddered.

The treasure trove was seemingly boundless. There were far more files held on the computers at this facility—images of Humtars with their coworkers and families held clues about their culture. The star maps were even more detailed than the ones Sakura had studied while on board the *Freedom.*

"Sakura, I think I've found something you would be particularly interested in," called one of her team members.

She walked over to see images of rocky crags with pipes attached to them, and below were fields of farmland.

Is that really what it used to look like here? Sakura wondered. *What could have happened to change things so much?* It had never occurred to her that a planet might be worse off *without* people residing on it. Maybe there had been some sort of catastrophic geological event, like an incoming meteor or a volcanic eruption, but whatever had happened here would have to be pieced together over time. Like the facility on Alpha Centauri, this place had been in hibernation for hundreds or thousands of years, with no records kept after everything had gone dark.

Each new discovery seemed to outdo the last. But there was one piece of the puzzle that truly shocked Sakura when she discovered it.

"It was *here*?" she asked Katherine incredulously.

"Well, it wasn't finished synthesizing yet before they died, but yes, they had successfully produced a cure for the virus."

"I guess we had better study these notes carefully," Sakura commented. Whatever medicine they had created would likely have completely lost all efficacy by now, but if something could devastate the Humtar population so thoroughly, they should probably learn everything they could about the disease and how to fight it.

****

Waves
Emerald City, New Eden

Viceroy Miles Hunt was extremely excited about eating at Waves, one of the highest-rated seafood restaurants on New Eden. After spending most of the last several years eating replicator food, he relished any occasion to eat a real dinner cooked by a human being.

Sure, he'd have to make small talk with several dignitaries, but Lilly would be there with him. She was great at running interference. Honestly, if he had intentionally gone into politics, he couldn't have married a better politician's wife.

The increased security for the evening managed not to detract too much from the spectacular coastal landscape. The floor-to-ceiling windows along one side of the restaurant provided the perfect view of the water as the suns began to set. This time of day, the light reflected off the sea to turn the waves the most amazing emerald color—it was where the city had gotten its name from.

Hunt found the menu a bit daunting. He had never heard of half of these things. New Eden had its own versions of fishlike creatures and shellfish, but he had never tasted any of them to know what to order. When Lilly asked the waiter for some suggestions, he handed her a companion to the menu that gave the nearest Earth equivalent of each item.

When his plate arrived, Hunt marveled at the bright colors. Everything on New Eden seemed so vibrant—even the food. He took his first bite and felt like he was having an out-of-body experience.

When Hunt had fully reveled in his hot meal, he excused himself to the restroom. A shorter man with dark hair walked in right before him and headed over to the urinals. Hunt scanned the room to make sure no one else was present and then walked over to the other urinal.

"Everything on track with the Kites, Mudo?" Hunt asked.

"The Kites are almost ready to fly, sir."

"Excellent."

Dr. Arief Mudo zipped up his pants, washed his hands, and walked out.

Now I just have to figure out what their first mission is going to be, thought Hunt.

****

Jacksonville, Arkansas
Earth, Sol System

Dakkuri read the report about ship movements one more time to make sure he really understood what he had read. A knot tightened in his stomach. As Ashurina had suggested, a large Republic fleet had indeed formed up near Sol. However, a new report from one of his other assets stated that the entire Seventh Fleet had suddenly become ghosts— disappeared into the wind. And there was no available intelligence to suggest where they had gone.

He slammed his fists on his desk. "Damn it!" he growled.

The Zodarks are probably walking right into a Republic trap, he realized. *All this buildup around Earth was to keep us away from there while they hatched their real attack elsewhere.*

Dakkuri thought back to a strange message he had recently received directly from Mavkah Otro, the head of the Zodark Malvari. Never before had he been contacted by someone who was effectively the most powerful Zodark other than the Council themselves. Otro's words repeated in his head. *There are forces who may wish to put me at risk. I need to be sure that I am receiving all pertinent intelligence.*

Since Dakkuri did not know *where* the ships had gone, he couldn't be certain of the Republic's exact strategy. However, he knew he needed to move this up the chain rapidly. He composed a message:

NOS Heltet,

> *The Republic's Seventh Fleet, which had formed up around Sol, is now unaccounted for. The destination of this*

mass movement of ships is unknown. It is my strong belief that the Fleeters intend to ensnare the Zodarks in a trap, although I cannot give further warning since I have no further intelligence to share at this time. Proceed with caution and may Lindow guard you.

Dakkuri, your Kafarr

Before he prepared to send the message to Heltet, Dakkuri decided to make another copy of it, which was specially encrypted and only able to be opened by Mavkah Otro. He debated for a moment whether this act would make him a hero or a traitor, but then he sent it anyway. His loyalty was to the Zodarks as a whole, not just to Heltet, and if this warning didn't make it to the appropriate decision makers, there could be a gruesome slaughter.

Chapter Twenty
A Well-Deserved Break

Kite Safe House
Emerald City, New Eden

"I can't believe this is it—we're finally going on our first mission," said Jessica.

"I can't believe they're giving us forty-eight hours off," laughed Amir.

They had been pushing pretty hard since they'd come back from the dead. Their initial training at the Titan Military Complex had been brutal, but it was a necessary process to allow them to adjust to all of their newfound enhancements and abilities. They'd drilled endlessly on high-altitude drops, combat diving, sniper training, combatives, and the use of countless weapons. However, David ultimately found the training on New Eden more challenging. Here they had learned interrogation techniques, covert movements, surveillance, countersurveillance, and how to cultivate a source. A lot had been crammed into a very short amount of time.

"Well, David, you and Catalina may just want to make this your personal honeymoon, but the rest of us weren't lucky enough to find our soulmates in the afterlife...so what's there to do for fun around here?"

The question struck David as a bit odd. He'd spent months and months training with the four other Kites, and while he knew a lot about their real backstories, they hadn't really had much downtime. Sure, they had enjoyed plenty of Somchai's delicious homemade Thai food, and Amir had handily won plenty of poker games, but this presented a unique opportunity.

"I've seen people kitesurfing along the coast," Jessica offered.

"That sounds kind of fun," David agreed. It reminded him of his home in California, less than half an hour from Morro Bay. "There's also some really good restaurants by the beach."

"There's a fight tonight, you know," said Amir.

"Do you think we can still get tickets?" asked Somchai.

Amir pulled out his Qpad. "Actually, yes. We'd have to get the more expensive tickets, but when's the last time we were able to spend any money?"

Catalina offered, "You know, I used to be a dancer—maybe there's a club where we could dance."

"Yeah, and Somchai could finally lose his virginity," Jessica teased.

Somchai laughed good-naturedly. "Look, I will neither confirm nor deny my status as a virgin," he replied with a wink. "But honestly, I'm not in for a hookup. That's just not me. And frankly, the only people in the world that I really trust right now are all in this room."

"Aw, Somchai. That's so sweet," said Jessica.

There was a weird awkward pause. David knew there was a sort of brother-sister vibe going on between Somchai and Jessica, but with them being stuck together for the next thirty years, who knew what might happen?

"Why don't we do all of it?" asked Somchai. "The fight, the dancing, the kitesurfing and the restaurant by the beach…it sounds like a great forty-eight hours."

"That does sound like a good plan," David agreed. "Wait—what's your contribution to our two days of freedom?" he asked.

"You guys are going to think I'm nerdy," Somchai declared.

"We already do," Amir said, grinning.

"There's a museum over in Alliance City where there's a wing for each of the alliance members. I think it would be neat to see what they have on display."

"OK, I could go for that," Catalina agreed.

"Five for five?" asked David.

"Five for five," Amir agreed.

****

Galactic Empire Cultural Exchange
Alliance City, New Eden

"Whoa, these Altairians are kind of weird," Amir remarked as he took off the earphones that had been provided for listening to a sample of Altairian music. "That sounded more like crickets chirping than any kind of melody I've ever heard."

"I mean, I'm not surprised that they don't seem to be very fun," said David, looking at a model of Altairius Prime. "Everything I know about them tells me that they're serious sticks in the mud."

"Maybe their music is like some sort of meditation tune," Jessica postulated. "Like they're syncing up their rhythms or something."

"That's an interesting thought," said Catalina. "But I agree, Amir—I certainly couldn't dance to this."

"I wonder what the Altairians do for amusement?" asked Somchai. "We were able to come up with several entertaining things to do rather quickly—what is it that they can't wait to do on a weekend?"

"I heard that they don't really take days off," said Amir. "Maybe that's just rumor, but it doesn't seem all that farfetched. They certainly have large libraries and learning institutions…do they *learn* for fun?"

"Well, I know that they have restaurants on Altairius Prime that have foods from all the alliance members…maybe they're foodies," David offered.

Jessica walked over to another display. "Guys, I think I know what they do for fun," she announced.

"Oh?" asked Catalina.

"Check this out. It's like some weird 3-D chess-like game. I mean, there's not a king or a queen or anything, but the pieces all seem to have very specific rules. Look," said Jess, pointing to a holographic simulation of two Altairians engaged in a rousing match.

"Of course that would be their pastime," said Somchai with a laugh. "They always have to be three steps ahead in their plan for galactic domination."

The group snickered.

"All right," said David. "Are we ready to move on to the Tully wing?"

****

Emerald Stadium
Emerald City, New Eden

"Dude, Amir, these seats are amazing," said David.

"Money can occasionally buy happiness," Amir replied with a smirk.

They were only three rows up from the ring, and the seats in their row were extremely comfortable—nothing like the ones in the nosebleeds.

"Ha! You can even heat or cool your rear end if you like," Jessica announced in amusement.

Amir addressed the group over the neurolink. *Hey, I heard that the Sumerian fighter in this matchup actually used to be Mukhabarat*, he explained. *If that's true, I really can't wait to watch his fighting technique.*

Are we here for research or to have fun? asked Somchai. *I thought I was the only nerdy one in the group.*

They all smiled at their shared thoughts.

Before the fight got started, they all grabbed a beer or two and enjoyed some of the Sumerian snacks the stadium sold. The Sumerians were apparently fans of food with a lot of flavor—each snack had a different blend of spices mixed into it or a sauce to dip it in.

When the referee hit the buzzer to begin the match, they all watched with rapt attention. The ex-Mukhabarat was *fast*. The Fleeter almost didn't stand a chance—he got a few good punches in, but the Sumerian seemed to absorb them as if he were being hit by a small child. The fight was over before the end of the first round, when the Fleeter's arm was nearly broken before he tapped out.

"What the hell was that?" yelled Jessica. She was apparently one of those sports fans that got extremely loud, a side of her that David hadn't had the chance to see yet.

"Yeah, I've never seen anyone take a hit like that before," said Amir.

Don't worry, guys. Your resident nerd recorded the whole thing so we could analyze it later, said Somchai over the neurolink.

David wished he had thought of that. He hoped he wouldn't run into any Mukhabarat anytime soon. Now he wanted to study their techniques. He wondered if there was any way to connect with the fighter.

Two down. Get ready for beach day and dancing, said Catalina as they exited the stadium.
****

Kite Safe House

Emerald City, New Eden

David and Catalina snuggled up next to each other, trying to soak in the last moments together before their mission the following day, when they would split up for the first time since coming back from the dead.

"The last two days have been really fun," said Catalina.

"I could apparently use a few dance lessons from you, though," David replied, remembering his less-than-coordinated performance.

"That's OK. At least you got out there with me," Catalina responded, pulling in tighter to him. "I'm really glad to have a dance partner."

"Jess sure did dance with a lot of guys, huh?" David observed.

Catalina laughed. "Yeah. I saw her making out with one of them, but ultimately, I think she wanted to play it safe before the mission."

"That's probably smart, honestly. I'd hate to see her get into a bad situation."

"David…I feel bad for the rest of the Kites. I mean, I just feel so incredibly grateful to have you here with me. But what about Jess, Somchai and Amir?"

"Well, I'm not entirely convinced that Somchai and Jess won't get past their 'friend zone' at some point," said David, half-joking. "But I think they're all right on their own, at least for now. Maybe they'll meet someone on our sabbaticals…but in a way, we were all alone before we died. We had to be OK with that."

"That's true, I guess. I hadn't thought of it that way," Catalina mused. She was quiet for a moment. "You know, thirty years used to be most of someone's adult lifetime. Now we can live so long…and women can have children much later in life. Jessica could always get married and have a family after we serve our time in the Kites—provided we survive, of course."

The comments were sobering. David didn't want to think about the possibility of losing Catalina, or any of the other Kites. He decided to focus on the first part of what she'd said. "Do you want to have kids one day?"

"Yeah, that's always been the dream," said Catalina. "Obviously, I'll have to wait, but there's still time."

David ran his fingers through her hair. "I think maybe I'd like to take that journey with you one day," he told her.

She started to tear up. "I love you, David...come home to me."

Chapter Twenty-One
Setup

Palette 22
Arlington, Virginia
Earth, Sol System

Dakkuri had told Ashurina to wear her DARPA pin on her lapel. It was subtle enough, but since most people didn't really wear pins anymore, it would stand out. She was looking forward to the meal at this restaurant almost as much as she looked forward to finally washing her hands of those insidious bombs—she'd heard great things about the tapas here. Some of the menu items actually reminded her of the food on Sumer.

Ashurina went to her table and sat facing the entrance so that she'd be visible to the Ani that was coming to meet her. The server came by, and she ordered a drink and waited.

At 8 p.m. exactly, someone she recognized walked through the door, and her heart skipped a beat. She waited in her seat to make sure there wasn't some confusion, but sure enough, her half brother sat down in front of her.

Ashurina's eyes welled up with tears. "Rayan…it's been so long," she remarked. He reached into his pocket and handed her a handkerchief. "I wasn't expecting it to be you," she stammered. "How are you?"

"I'm doing well, little sis," said Rayan calmly. "Work has been successful."

"How long has it been since you've been home?" Ashurina asked quietly. "I get little bits and pieces here and there, but of course, everything is heavily filtered."

Rayan reached over and grabbed her hand. Ashurina couldn't tell if he was trying to comfort her or get her to stop being so emotional. In either case, she took a deep breath and took control of her emotions.

"I was back about two years ago," he told her. "My wife Chadia had twins." Her brother had three wives, as was common in their culture, which highly valued children.

"Congratulations, Rayan," said Ashurina. She felt her eyes tearing up again at the thought of all the nieces and nephews she'd never been able to hold. "Twins—what a blessing. Boys or girls? I trust they are all healthy."

"One of each this time," he replied. "All healthy. Zinab and Atika are also well. Altogether I have twenty children now."

"Father must be very pleased," Ashurina remarked. "Were you able to see him on your last visit?"

"He is well. He loves his grandchildren, but of course, you were always his favorite," Rayan remarked with a wink. The comment wasn't made out of spite or jealousy, but her father had never hidden that fact from any of his children. Ashurina's mother had been unable to have children for many years, so her father had married a total of four other women, but he had always had a special place in his heart for his first wife. When Ashurina had been born, she had become the apple of his eye. It was because of his position as an elder on Gurista Prime that she'd been able to become a part of the Mukhabarat and not been relegated to a life of constant child-rearing.

"I know he was very proud of you too, Rayan. He was not always the best at speaking such things out loud, but I am sure the work you are doing here would please him very much."

They ordered their food and had a long conversation. Ashurina had to check her emotions many times. This was the first dialogue she had had with anyone in years that she could point to as two people simply reconnecting without any ulterior motives. Eventually, they'd have to get to the actual purpose of this chat, but for now, she was soaking up the time with her older brother.

She casually found a way to ask if her husband, Andre, was interested in any of the other Gurista women, and she managed to conceal her relief when she learned that he was focused on the duties of being a father to their three children.

When Ashurina had completed her Mukhabarat training, her first assignment as a deep cover agent had been to infiltrate a specific community on Gurista Prime and root out any potential dissension within the ranks. It was during this assignment that she'd met Andre. She hadn't intended to fall in love; it had just happened.

Once she'd obtained special permission to marry Andre, he'd been vetted and given a security clearance in secret, then he'd been made aware of who his wife really was. Andre had known she came from a powerful family on Gurista Prime and that her father was the clan leader of one of the founding clans of the planet. When he'd found out who she really was, *what* she was…it had nearly ended their relationship. To this day, Ashurina still didn't know if Andre had truly wanted to stay married to her after he'd found out or if he had somehow pieced together what would likely happen to him if he opted to dissolve their marriage and leave her. Once you were part of the Mukhabarat, you never really left. You remained and served until either you died of old age…or you died of what the state would declare "natural causes."

Ashurina was still hoping that somehow there was a way to play out this role of double agent without getting herself or her family killed. Her mind went down a dark hole. She was also filled with sorrow that her brother had been roped into the Mukhabarat.

"Are you still with me?" Rayan asked.

"Uh, yes. I'm sorry. I just haven't seen anyone in the family in so long…" Her voice trailed off.

"Time and distance change a lot of things," Rayan commented. He leaned in. "Ashurina, I can't really speak my mind with anyone else," he said quietly. "I've been here for a while now and, well, I know that the Galactic Empire is evil, but what are these humans doing fighting for them?"

"I ask myself the same question, regularly," Ashurina admitted. "And I'm not quite sure how the Republic was dragged into all of this. Those Altairians especially are conniving bastards—maybe they have a very convincing deception they employ."

"Well, unfortunately, I think my work must continue in order to advance our cause," Rayan commented.

"I think you're right," Ashurina replied. "I guess I'd better give you the tools you need to complete your next phase."

Suddenly, her palms began to sweat as she was hit with the sudden realization that the bombs, which had been marked with a kind of tracker that would completely evade Gurista technology, would directly put Rayan at risk. When this plan had been hatched, she hadn't pictured the Ani contact being one of the brothers she had grown up with.

Regardless, she had no options here that would allow her to leave without passing the explosive canisters on to Rayan. She explained that she had rented out a locker at Shillington Station, a bus station less than a five-minute walk away. Ashurina gave him the code to the locker and then explained how to open the false bottom in the box he would find inside.

"Listen, little sister, this is just the beginning," Rayan told her. "After the Republic has been crushed, we launch our new war against the Orbots. Those cyborgs have served their purpose, but soon the Zodarks and the Guristas will assume control of the Milky Way."

This speech caught Ashurina off guard. She hadn't realized that the Guristas were on such a massive war footing. The news was alarming.

"You must have a better view of the bigger picture than I do," she conceded, hoping he would say more. "My mission has me focused on a very small window."

"Oh, it's going to be brutal," Rayan said with a mischievous smile. "There's ships galore being built, and tons of soldiers are being recruited and trained. I am but a small cog in the machine, but the plan has been set in motion, and it cannot be stopped."

"Lindow watch over you, Rayan," she said quietly as they stood to leave. It took everything in her not to hug her older brother or chase after him and tell him not to do it.

I need to get in touch with Drew, she realized.
****

Drew Kanter listened as Ashurina provided the details of her meet with her Ani contact. He was frankly not all that surprised about the Guristas' preparations for war, although he would definitely be bringing up the tensions with the Orbots to the Viceroy. Still, none of this seemed to have the urgency she had conveyed before this meeting.

"You know, we could have done this the regular way," he told her. "Unless I'm missing something, your information is important, but not exactly urgent."

"It's urgent for *me*," she replied. "Look, what I haven't told you yet is that I *know* the Ani that came to meet me. He's one of my half brothers. I grew up with him."

"Ah..."

"Yes. Look, I know you can't save my husband and kids right now, but I know you are going to follow the cylinders...if you could manage to take my brother *alive*, it would go a long way for me. The only thing that makes me get up in the morning is trying to save my family—well, here is your chance to save one of them."

Drew leaned back and crossed his arms, staring up to the ceiling for a moment as he considered the situation. On the one hand, her half brother was an out-and-out terrorist. However, Ashurina's intel had proven to be not only accurate but extremely useful. This was a small price to pay to keep the gravy train rolling.

"Well, I'm certain you know that your brother will be heavily armed and very motivated to fight," Drew began, attempting to temper expectations. "But I will push this forward. I can't guarantee his safe capture, but we will certainly try."

Drew saw a rare show of emotions from Ashurina as he wiped a tear off her cheek.

"Thank you," she replied.

"Now, I think it would be helpful if you tell me everything you know about your brother," said Drew.

****

Austin, Texas
Earth, Sol System

Loni O'Brien was hoping for some redemption after what had happened at the safe house in Munich. It had been very difficult to process the loss of so many good people, and she had even voluntarily gone to the department shrink several times. But now her head was clear, and she was ready to take down some Ani terrorists.

Loni had placed trackers on the explosive cylinders before Ashurina had passed them on to her Ani contact—they were completely untraceable using any known Mukhabarat or Zodark technology. That had made identifying the location of this particular Ani safe house relatively easy, and there was no question as to the validity of the information. She suspected that the proposed target of this particular cell was the Tesla factory there in Austin—taking out the production capacity of the factor would cause serious problems for the Republic.

Once the safe house had been located, Loni had set up surveillance using high-altitude drones. They were visually and digitally tracking each person that entered and exited the building. Her team had successfully identified six individuals who were staying in this particular building. It was not going to be a walk in the park to take them down.

When she had received orders to try and capture the Ani alive, she'd initially balked at the idea, but Loni quickly realized this was an opportunity. If they did this right, it would reduce the risk to her people and also garner some high-value individuals for interrogation.

A plan was hatched. Hopefully, they would be able to accomplish their mission before the Ani enacted theirs.
****

Ani Safe House
Austin, Texas
Earth, Sol System

Rayan noticed some unusual activity on the surveillance footage surrounding their house and zoomed in. There was a man going door to door down the street with some kind of rolling container. He wore a uniform with a hat that read "DJ's BBQ." As he continued to monitor the situation, Rayan realized that the man was giving out samples of food.

Free food was popular, apparently. Some of the neighbors were even coming out of their houses to greet him before he knocked. The man continued steadily toward them, and Rayan decided to bring it up with the team.

"We could pretend we aren't home," one of his fellow Ani offered.

"Yeah, but we have two vehicles in the driveway. Plus, Rayan just got back from the store a couple of hours ago. Remember, you two went out and helped him carry the food in," countered another teammate. "Don't you think it would draw more attention to have someone ringing and knocking on our door multiple times knowing we're here than if we just answered?"

"Look up the restaurant," said another.

Rayan felt that was a good suggestion. A quick search revealed that DJ's BBQ had just had a "soft opening" two days ago and would be having their grand opening this Friday. Databases for the county showed that the restaurant had all the proper food permits.

"No red flags here," Rayan explained. "There's even a photo online of this man with his family, identifying him as one of the owners. I'm looking into his backstory right now..." There was a pause as he cycled through some of the available information. "He seems clean."

"I say we open the door and get the free food," said their team lead.

No one objected. Barbecued meat here was quite tasty, and somewhat reminiscent of food they had grown up eating back on Gurista Prime. Not everything about this assignment on Earth had been horrible.

About ten minutes later, their doorbell rang, and their team lead answered.

"Good eve'neen, sir. My name's Quentus, and my paw, DJ, and I just opened up a new barbeque restaurant down the street a few days ago. We have our grand opening on Friday, and today is your lucky day because I'm giving out some free samples."

"Oh, that sounds nice," said their team lead warmly.

"Yes, well, we have a feeling that once you try our amazing sauces, you'll be hooked. Here's a coupon for twenty-five percent off your first order. We figure after that, you'll be a lifetime customer."

Quentus handed the team lead the coupon and then held open a take-home tray of food. "This here is a sampler of our finest offerings—you've got some brisket, chicken, cornbread that's to die for, baked beans, fried okra and mac and cheese that will make you see God. Plus, we have some of our sauces here. We have ribs that are heavenly, but you'll have to come on in to try those."

"Well, thank you," said the team lead, accepting the tray. "What do I owe you?"

"This one's on me," said Quentus warmly. "If you don't think you can make it to our grand opening, I can offer you a takeout menu."

"Oh, actually, that would be nice. We do order in quite a bit."

"Perfect," Quentus replied. "Well, I hope y'all have a great night. If you like our food, please pass on the word."

"Will do. Thank you again."

With that, the door closed, and the group gathered around the free grub. There was quite a bit there for it being a free offering, but still, with six men in the house, each person was only going to be able to get so much.

They were in the middle of arguing over who was going to get some of the cornbread when Rayan noticed something in the container. Panicked, he grabbed it away from the group and went to run with it, but he didn't have time to formulate a plan. It was too late.

A gas emanated from the small device, and in seconds, they were all out cold.

****

Loni was ecstatic over their win. They'd managed to capture all six Ani from the safe house without a shot fired, and they'd removed their suicide devices safely, so now they had several high-value detainees who would hopefully provide a wealth of information. Not to mention, they'd safely recovered the two explosive cylinders that had led them to the safe house, which meant an untold number of lives had just been saved.

Loni had been made aware that the Ani named Rayan was related to a double agent. Ideally, they would bring his sister in and try to get her to flip him, but they might be tight on time right now and she needed to get something from them sooner rather than later.

She walked into the Conex box where they were conducting their interviews and sat down across from Rayan. The room was pretty sparse—just a table, a chair for her and one for her analyst, a single light overhead, and that C-100 standing in the corner. A one-way mirror allowed for observation and, of course, cameras recorded the whole thing.

She opened up the conversation casually. "Hello, Rayan. You can call me Loni. Ya know, today is actually yer lucky day." Her Irish lilt was especially strong in this moment.

"How do you figure?" asked Rayan, shrugging his shoulders. His hands were handcuffed in front of him, and his feet had been restrained to his chair, which was attached to the floor.

"Yer free," Loni announced. She saw the confused expression she'd been anticipating. "You no longer have to serve those hideous monsters, the Zodarks," she explained.

"You all are the monsters!" Rayan shot back.

"Is that so?" asked Loni. "Have you seen what your precious benefactors did to Sumer?"

She pulled out her Qpad and began projecting holographic footage of the horrors that had been discovered there: mass graves, children with gash marks on their faces, and horrible poverty.

"I know that you all have very sophisticated imaging technology, as we do. You can make up anything," Rayan countered.

"I wish I were making this up," said Loni. She pulled up footage of the first meet with the Zodarks. "We came in peace. They started this war," she explained.

"You're a liar!" Rayan shouted.

"It's not easy to admit that you've been used," Loni countered calmly. She pulled up footage of humans fighting each other on Sumer. "You see? They sent your people in like cannon fodder. They don't care at all if you die. They don't care if *humans* die…so long as they maintain control."

"I don't believe you!" Rayan raged. "You all are serving the evil Galactic Empire. You are on the wrong side of history." His face turned red and he clenched his fists in anger. "A great wave is coming your way, all over the Republic…you can't stop it. You may have captured my team, but the attacks are already underway. You will pay for your treachery!"

****

Space Command Headquarters
Jacksonville, Arkansas
Earth, Sol System

Fleet Admiral Chester Bailey looked at Viceroy Miles Hunt, unsure if this plan was truly the best course of action. If it worked, it would likely destroy the Zodarks' fleet—maybe even create the kind of strategic opportunity they had been looking for in order to capture Tueblets. Hell, the *Freedom* might even be able to drop them right on the Zodarks' home world, Zinconia. However, if the plan failed, Earth would be left wide open, especially if the Orbots assisted the Zodarks by using their wormhole bridge.

"It's a good thing you came here in person to talk about this," Bailey finally told Hunt after he had finished briefing him on the grand strategy. "This isn't the kind of conversation you want a recording of lying about."

Hunt shrugged before responding. "I'm not a politician, Chester. My only goal is ending this fight—securing a future for humanity that doesn't result in us being enslaved by a foreign power or made extinct like the Humtars. It's risky. If it works, though…"

"Agreed—*if* it works. But what if it doesn't, Miles? What if the Zodarks invade Sol instead? Then what?"

"You're right. It's risky. But it's a calculated risk based on facts," Hunt insisted. "The Orbots are the only ones outside of the Altairians and now us to a limited extent that have the technology to bridge two systems together. However, it is only our ship, the *Freedom*, that truly has nearly unlimited range. There isn't a system in Orbot or Zodark space that puts them in range of opening a bridge directly to Sol. This plan will work."

"Humor me, Miles. What do we do if the unthinkable happens and a Zodark fleet suddenly appears in Sol and you have Halsey's new fleet plus our other fleets hiding in the Rhea system? How would we defend Sol?"

"OK, I think I can help alleviate that concern," Hunt countered. He pulled out his Gallentine version of a Qpad and looked for something. Then an image appeared, floating on the coffee table in front of their chairs.

"This little ship is the one I came here on. It's a unique little bugger in that it has its own wormhole generator. It can jump about the same distance as an Orbot or Altairian ship can. It doesn't have the power generation capability to allow other warships to jump through or have the range the *Freedom* does, but it creates a micro wormhole essentially just big enough for it to jump through. I'll leave this ship here with instructions for the pilot that should the Zodarks or the Orbots appear in Sol, he's to return to the Rhea system and alert us to what's going on. Then I have the ability to open a bridge and we can move the fleet we had lying in ambush back into Sol to smash the Zodarks. Does that sound like a fair compromise?"

"Yeah, I think that could work. I feel better knowing we would have a way to call for help should we need it. Oh, and by the way, brilliant idea, calling Halsey's fleet the Seventh Fleet. That ought to throw the Zodarks and Orbots off-kilter," Bailey said, still amused at their little ruse with the fleet numbers.

Hunt laughed at the mention of Halsey's new fleet. "Yeah, well, I'm not the original author of that idea. A guy by the name of Richard Marcinko had a similar plan. He was the naval officer who founded the Navy's Special Warfare Development Group or DEVGRU. People commonly knew of them as SEAL Team Six, but at the time, the Navy only had two of these SEAL teams. When he got the go-ahead to create this new highly specialized SEAL team, instead of calling them Team Three, the next number, he labeled them Team Six. This was designed to give their adversaries at the time reason to believe they had more SEAL teams than they did. I figured we could do the same thing with our fleets—make the Zodarks think we have more than we do."

Bailey smirked. It was clever, and it just might work. Sun Tzu always used to say, "Appear weak when you are strong and strong when you are weak."

"OK, Miles. Let's set this trap. That interrogation summary I shared with you about those Anis we captured has me on edge. Best we spring our trap first instead of waiting for them to sit back and punch us in the face first. Fighting back with a bloody nose stinks."

Chapter Twenty-Two
Shakedown

Year 2112
Seventh Fleet Flagship
RNS *Ark Royal*
Republic Naval Shipyard
Between Earth and Luna, Sol System

"That was a beautiful commissioning ceremony, Chester," said Admiral Abigail Halsey. "I've thoroughly enjoyed my time at Space Command, but I won't lie and say I haven't longed for a final command back with the Fleet—to embark on a warship once again, to lead a fleet once more. Thank you for this, Chester. This means a lot."

They continued their walk through the hangar deck. The chairs, stage, and banners from the change of command ceremony were nearly gone, the hangar deck once again being made ready for use.

Admiral Chester Bailey waved her thanks off. "Don't thank me, Abi. I'm the one who should be thanking you. While I've been trying to balance the whole of Space Command, the task of rebuilding and growing our fleet largely fell on your shoulders. Now that we are ready to form the Seventh Fleet, I can't think of a better, more capable commander for such a force. Once this fleet is fully assembled, you'll command the largest naval force in our history. I also thought it fitting that the admiral that discovered the Zodarks should be the same one who defeats them."

"I'm always glad to hear you say that, Chester—defeating the Zodarks. I had feared when the war ended we would lose that focus— that drive to go after them in their own space. It's easy when a war has ended to turn inward and focus all our efforts on peacetime concerns, like colonizing these new moons and planets. Domestic affairs are critically important and cannot be ignored for the sake of creating some military-industrial state, but if we don't settle this issue with the Zodarks and the Dominion Alliance permanently…none of it will matter. We'll find ourselves conquered, subjected to a future of slavery and servitude like the Sumerians.

"I'm not sure how you managed to convince the Senate to stay the course—to keep our society on a wartime footing. But we need warships—lots and lots of warships, Chester. It's taken us a long time to build the kind of shipyards and industrial base needed to support something like this, but now that we've done it, we're starting to see the payoff, with multiple ships being commissioned weekly. Speaking to that very issue, Chester," Abi said as they continued to walk through the hangar deck, "I'm glad you stuck with Costello for my replacement. He'll make a great Director of Fleet Operations and second-in-command to you. He has been instrumental in aiding my efforts to make sure the Fleet has a steady stream of new warships entering service and the entire training apparatus behind it to ensure we have the crews to man them. This Seventh Fleet we've created…it's going to need a steady supply of replacements once we begin offensive operations."

Bailey nodded in agreement as they continued to walk along the outer edge of the hangar deck. "Hey, that room there looks empty," he said, pointing to what looked like a small maintenance room. "Come on. There's something I want to make sure you're fully aware of before you start this multimonth-long certification process."

As the two of them walked in silence toward the room, he knew this would be the last time he'd likely see her in person for months, maybe even years, depending on how long her fleet was gone. They had worked together at Space Command for more than fifteen years, seeing each other on a near daily basis. He had come to value her as one of his closest friends. Losing her to command a grand fleet like this—it was going to be a personal loss, no way around it.

Identifying someone who could take over the operational side of managing Space Command had been daunting. Her recommendation for Admiral Scott Costello to replace her had come as a surprise. If all he was evaluating was the man's service jacket, then Costello wouldn't have been Bailey's first choice. Hell, he wouldn't have even made it to the pile for consideration.

Walking into the maintenance room, Bailey spotted a couple of chairs near a workstation and made his way toward them. As they sat down, he looked at the protégé he felt most capable of serving as his successor once the time was right. He had thought that would be Hunt one day. Now Hunt was the Viceroy in charge of them all.

"Now that we're in private and away from the possible ears of those in the hangar, I have some things I wanted to say that wouldn't do us any good for someone else to overhear," said Bailey. "It's important we keep our concerns about senior leadership held close to the vest. Rumors can spread if we talk too loosely. Your choice of Costello as your replacement…I'll admit, Scott wasn't my first choice, and I was advised by many others not to choose him. I won't share their names, that's not relevant. But like them, I wanted someone with similar experience to you, someone who had led a squadron or fleet of warships in battle—a person with recent experience that I don't have. But you reminded me and my confidants about something just as important if not more critical than direct experience in the war—"

"Oh, I did?" Abi playfully interrupted.

Bailey could tell she was going to miss the banter between them as much as he was. As the smile broke his serious look, he began to explain. "Abi, you're a lot smarter than you give yourself credit for. What you reminded me is that this war will likely be won through logistics and our ability to scale up ship production. We have to become *the* dominant power if we have a snowball's chance in hell of not being conquered, wiped out or turned into some sort of slave caste society like the Sumerians were. Costello oversaw the construction and initial operations of the sprawling naval shipyard—a herculean effort few could have accomplished, considering it took place during the war. That's the same kind of grit you showed when you took over as the head of Fleet Operations.

"Space Command doesn't need another admiral who wants to regale his subordinates and the Senate with tales of combat and victories against the Zodarks. What we need are industrialists, logisticians, and innovative entrepreneurs to help us develop new technologies and weave various alien technologies into our own for the betterment of the Republic. So, while I was ready to dismiss someone like Scott out of hand, you made me realize that he's *exactly* who we need. In fact, we need a hundred *more* Costellos."

Bailey paused for a second when someone from his staff back at the hangar messaged him over the neurolink. *Sorry to interrupt, Admiral. We're supposed to head out in ten minutes so the* Ark *can begin final preparations to leave the shipyard*, the staff officer said.

Annoyed at the interruption of their conversation, Bailey held a hand up to stop Abi from replying. "Hold on, Abi. I need to remind my staff they work for *me*. If I want to spend another ten minutes or two hours conferring with one of my fleet admirals, I will, and they'll adjust *their* schedules accordingly."

She seemed amused as she gave him a moment to let the powers that be know he'd tell them when he was ready to leave—not the other way around.

Bailey sighed as he shook his head in annoyance. Staff seemed to forget that departure times could be changed. In-person consultations with the newly appointed fleet commander weren't as easy to arrange once the fleets were underway.

"Listen, Abi, there's something else I need to tell you. It's about a plan the Viceroy has been working on the past few years," he explained. "It's a high-risk, high-reward kind of strategy. Miles firmly believes it will put an end to the Zodarks, if we play our cards right."

Judging by the cautious look on her face, he wasn't sure if she liked these kinds of strategic plays Hunt had been utilizing more and more as of late. There were certainly those who thought he was being a little too aggressive, leading to enormous casualties and a great loss of warships in the process.

Abi leaned forward in her chair, closing the distance between them. "OK, Chester. You've piqued my interest. Let's dish. What's so special about this plan Miles cooked up? Does it have something to do with Seventh Fleet?"

"You always were sharp, Abi," Bailey replied. "That's why I can't think of a better person to be in command of this new fleet we've assembled. As I explain the plan to you, please understand, it's likely I don't know all the details either. Miles plays it close to the vest, as you know. He's a brilliant tactician, so it's likely he's got more than one plan up his sleeve right now, especially with all these foreign spies and the espionage craziness of the last three or four years.

"Republic Intelligence has captured several Mukhabarat spies over the past few years. What most don't know is that they managed to turn a few of them—now they're double agents working us, feeding their handlers the intelligence we want presented to the Zodarks—"

"Whoa, you've got to be kidding me," Abi replied in shock. "They managed to flip some of these people? They're really working for us now?" She seemed happy at the information, but still, as the number two person at Space Command, she was also probably a bit upset that even she hadn't been included in on this.

"Yeah, they did flip a few," Bailey replied with a nod. "I can't tell you any more than that. But here's the deal. The Viceroy has been feeding them intelligence to make them believe things aren't as they appear in the Republic. He's attempting to guide them into a trap, to lure them into a battle he knows we can win and soundly defeat their fleet. However, this requires creating an apparent vulnerability—something to prod the Zodarks into seizing the opportunity he's giving them."

Bailey then went into the details of the Qatana and Rhea traps with which Hunt was baiting the Zodarks. The more he explained, the more surprised and concerned she appeared.

"Sorry to interrupt, Chester," she finally said. "What happens if his plan goes south? Say the Zodarks don't bite and instead of going for the Rhea system or Qatana, they go for Sol—they attack Earth. Is Seventh Fleet still going to maintain its status as the home guard? Would we be able to defend against them?"

"Good questions, Abi. As Miles explained it to me, the Zodarks don't have a warship capable of generating a portable wormhole—not like the Orbots, Altairians, and us with the *Freedom*. That said, the Orbots lack the ability to cross the vast light-years of distance between Dominion-controlled space and Sol. That basically means Sol is beyond their direct reach. That's why the trap is being laid for Rhea or Qatana, at the edge of their travel range. As to the Seventh, your fleet—yes, you're still home guard. Miles said that if or when the Zodarks take the bait and initiate their offensive into one of these systems, then he'll send word for you to bring your fleet and join. He wants to thoroughly crush them."

"OK, I feel better about that," Abi replied, visibly relaxing. "Oh, by the way, you know Admiral McKee and Second Fleet are due to return to Sol toward the end of our certification process. Her fleet is scheduled to begin retiring the last of their *Rook*- and *Ryan*-class warships. I've got a dozen cruisers and battleships nearly done and ready to be commissioned and handed over to their new crews once she gets back."

Bailey smiled at that. He'd actually forgotten about McKee and 2nd Fleet returning home. They had been gone from Sol for nearly a decade at this point, forward deployed to the Primord planets Intus and Kita. With Alfheim fully under Primord control, there wasn't a reason to keep that large of a naval presence so far from Republic space.

"That's true, Abi. It'll be good to have Fran back. She's been gone a long time, you know."

"She has. I'll admit I kind of picked her for that assignment more to get her out my hair and all, but the reality is, she kicked ass over there with the Primords. She's seen more combat and fleet battles than I have."

"Yeah, she has," Bailey replied matter-of-factly. "I always thought there was a little tension between you two. Maybe once your fleet returns to the John Glenn from Titan, you two can sort things out and move on." He squeezed her hand and stood. "But hey, it's time for me to get going. I've shared what I needed to with you about Miles and the plans he has underway. Abi, if it doesn't work out, or somehow, someway, a Zodark fleet finds its way to Sol while you're out at Titan, you need to do whatever is necessary to get back here. I think the Sentinels will hold out for a little while. But without fleet support, they're only going to last so long. OK? You got this?"

Abi smiled as she stood. "Of course we've got this, Chester. You can count on me and the Seventh Fleet. I'll gladly save your butt should it need saving. It'll look good on my resume when I petition to be your replacement after you age out of your current posting," she concluded with a wink.

The two laughed. Bailey was starting to feel every bit his age and then some. Sure, medical nanites could help slow the aging process or reverse it. But mentally and emotionally…he was rapidly becoming a spent man. There was only so much more he could take. Eventually, it *would* be time to retire. Someday he promised himself he'd learn how to fly-fish, mastering that craft in the rivers of Montana, Wyoming, Idaho, and Utah—God's country as he liked to call it.

As they exited the maintenance room and Bailey walked toward his staff, he felt envious of Halsey's accomplishments. She'd led a fleet into combat multiple times and been victorious. In contrast, his career was drawing to a close, and he'd essentially spent the entire time stuck riding a desk. Sure, he'd led Space Command and had essentially overseen the war, but he'd never served in combat. Truth be told, part of him was scared to death about leading a ship or fleet into battle. The thought of dying in the vacuum of space or some fiery explosion sent chills down his spine. Yet hundreds of thousands had died just like that. On the ground, the losses had been even more gruesome.

His staff guided him to the shuttle waiting to take him back to Earth. For now, the best thing he could do was to make sure those defending the Republic had everything they needed to fight and win. That was his job, his war—facing down those senators who wanted to cut his budget or reallocate funds to some useless pet project in one of their districts. His battle was different—but it was just as important.

He turned to look back at the cavernous hangar deck one final time and briefly watched the crews working on various tasks as they got the ship ready to get underway. He hoped like hell the *Ark Royal* would never have to see combat. If it didn't, that meant they'd done their job of keeping the enemy at bay, appearing strong when they were weak, far away when they were close.

Your plan had better work, Miles, Bailey thought. *We're all depending on it.*
****

Seventh Fleet Flagship
RNS *Ark Royal*
Joint Training Center, Titan Military Complex
Saturn VI, Sol System

Captain Ethan Hunt sat opposite the captain of the *Ark Royal* and the fleet admiral, reviewing yesterday's fleet-wide exercise results. Following his time at the Top Gun academy, he'd been given the opportunity to become the first Commander, Flight Operations or C-FLO for the Republic's newest star carrier, the *Ark Royal*. The *Ark* also happened to be the flagship for the fleet commander, so that meant a lot more brass and eyeballs on the daily happenings aboard the ship.

Captain Gregory Carr shook his head as he placed the summary of the report down on the desk. "Commander Hunt, these results look like crap. Your command embarrassed the ship—and not just the ship, the admiral here as well. I've read the report. It's missing something."

Ethan raised an eyebrow at that. "I don't follow."

"The truth."

"The truth? Ah, you mean what's not in the report? OK. You're curious why this fairly experienced group of pilots did so poorly against the *Lexi*?"

"Pretty much, Captain. When you got this assignment, you got pick of the litter for squadrons to comprise the Fleet's flagship. So how is it that a premier group of squadrons got so thoroughly smoked by the *Lexington* and their carrier wing?" griped Captain Carr.

"Sir, the way I saw it, this was a training opportunity, a chance to test theories and tactics to see if they'd work in a real battle or if they'd fail spectacularly. In this case, Commander Mikhail Pushkin wanted to test a theory, a tactic involving us stacking three fighter squadrons up at multiple layered degrees to press home an attack against a—"

"Let me stop you there, Captain. I know you've spent the last few years at the schoolhouse teaching students and practicing all kinds of cool tactics, theories, and ideas. That was the past—this is the present. You are back with the Fleet, not in the schoolhouse. You want to practice experimental tactics, then you do them in the sim pods. We have another week here at the JTC before the evaluators come aboard to finalize our certification declaring us ready for the fleet. The only thing I want you to focus on right now is making sure we get through that certification process. Got it?"

Ethan felt his cheeks flush at the rebuke. He knew the captain was right. His gut had told him not to let Flattop test another one of his harebrained ideas during the big exercise.

"Copy that, sir. You've refocused me; I'll refocus them. I can guarantee it, or you can bust me down to commander. Carrier Wing Three *will* pass its certifications."

Carr snorted at his cocky attitude. "OK, Captain. I'm counting on you to make this the best, most savage wing in the fleet. You do that, and you and I won't have any issue. You got me?"

Ethan smiled at that. He liked a challenge, and he'd heard Captain Carr was one of those ruthlessly aggressive ship captains. He'd lost a cruiser and then a battleship during the last war and managed to survive both losses. He was a warhorse of a commander and someone Ethan was immensely excited to serve with and learn from. He knew if he played his cards right, one day he'd get a shot at commanding one of these carriers himself—maybe even the *Freedom* if he really lucked out.

"Yes, sir. I'll get them focused again. No more unorthodox ideas to chase or test. We'll stick to the book when we're in the cockpits and test in the sim pods."

"Excellent, now get out of here," Admiral Halsey said, speaking for the first time during their meeting. "We got more commanders to chew out before the day's done."

When Ethan left the office, he saw a row of ship captains, their XOs, and the typically salty COBs or Chiefs of the Boat. As the ships' senior enlisted members, it was usually they and their chiefs that could make or break a ship's efficiency and effectiveness. His dad had told him during his commissioning ceremony—never cross a Chief or COB unless you know beyond a doubt they're wrong. "They run the boat, you just sign the checks and tell 'em what needs to be done."

Ethan made his way past the next group on deck to meet with the admiral. He didn't envy their conversations with her. He knew Admiral Halsey tangentially via his father. She'd pinned a medal on him during the New Eden campaign. She had previously been the Director of Fleet Operations, the number two position at Space Command. Assuming command of Seventh Fleet was essentially a demotion. But he knew something most didn't. Halsey was going to be the one to lead the Republic to its final victory against the Zodarks.

As he reached the end of the corridor and the last of the officers and COBs waiting to see the admiral, it finally hit him what he'd just been told during his own meeting. He'd done something incredibly stupid during his first real chance to shine as the ship's new wing commander. He'd embarrassed the ship. He'd embarrassed the admiral, and he'd called into question his own maturity and ability to hold the leadership position he now held.

The admiral was trying to certify and prepare an entire brand-new fleet and the captain was still trying to work out the bugs in his new carrier. Instead of doing his part to help them both along, he'd allowed himself to be manipulated by his junior officers into testing some wild tactics they should be testing in the sim pods instead of ruining an exercise when they needed to perform specific duties—duties his squadrons had utterly failed to perform.

Come on, Ethan, time to step up your game. You're not on the Freedom...your dad isn't the captain anymore. It's time to step out of his shadow and lead.

****

Éire – Belters' Planet

Liam was mostly happy these days. The exhaustion of having a baby was very real, but so was the joy of watching his son smile and giggle. He had long forgotten the simple pleasures of a child, but now, as a man who once would have been considered old, he was rediscovering them again.

He found himself concerned with things that hadn't really been a priority for him before, such as how the schools were shaping up. The system that had been developed was very localized—each community got a say in how their school was operated. However, the funds for each student were provided by the Sovereign Wealth Fund, and a family could choose to send their child to any school on Éire if they wanted something different.

This had led to some groups congregating in different regions of the planet and forming cohesive communities, such as those who were formerly Sumerian, or the Primord sector. All of these groups interacted peacefully, but there was a certain benefit to allowing people to retain their traditions. Liam referred to it as a salad—each ingredient kept its own flavor, but together they made a fantastic dish.

The Primords had integrated better than Liam had anticipated, and he couldn't remember exactly why he had been so hesitant to have them immigrate there. The old *Gaelic* in the Belt had been turned into an immigration center for Éire, and that way, Liam and the council had maintained a certain level of control over who'd settled here. They didn't take just anyone—it took a special kind of person to make it out in the Wild West, and there was no room for freeloaders. Safety nets were there for emergencies or tragic events, not intended to be a lifestyle.

One day, Liam and Sara took their son, Sean, to the hilltop overlooking St. Patrick, and as their son crawled on the blanket they'd brought with them, Liam began to reminisce. "So much has changed, Sara," he said. "Remember when this place was basically a tent camp? We've created a world that I'm proud to have my son grow up in."

Sara smiled. The capital had grown, but they'd taken great care to keep green spaces for everyone's enjoyment, and they'd designed the place with the future in mind, so there would be room for expansion of the infrastructure later on, if needed. "St. Patrick is pretty much everything we dreamed of, isn't it?" she asked.

"I guess so. I suppose there will always be challenges, but for now, we can hold our heads high."

Sara hesitated. "Speaking of challenges…I suppose there is something I should bring to your attention."

"Oh?" Liam laughed. "I guess we can't have a perfect paradise," he joked. "That would be a bit hard to achieve. Human nature almost requires us to have some struggles…so what is it this time?"

"Well…I was at the market today, and I overheard some of the scuttlebutt," she explained. "Apparently, one of the Belter men has married a Primord woman."

Liam was taken aback. "I…well, we hadn't really thought about that happening, but I suppose it was inevitable."

"You're taking that more calmly than I anticipated," Sara replied with a laugh.

"I guess fatherhood has softened me up," said Liam.

"Speaking of fatherhood, that was one of the things people were murmuring about. No one really knows if a Primord and a human can *have* children. Everyone wants to know whether the DNA is compatible, and what one of their kids would look like. There hasn't really been any kind of laboratory study on crossbreeding our species—something about it being unethical."

Liam was deep in thought. Maybe the Primords and the humans were related, somewhere way back, and their genetic codes were compatible enough to have children. If not, that couple would simply live a happy life together and that would be that.

"I guess we'll just have to wait and see," he finally responded.

"Fatherhood *has* made you soft," Sara said. "But you know what? I kind of like it."

****

Office of the Viceroy
Alliance City, New Eden

Hunt listened to the video message from Admiral Bailey, a smile spreading from ear to ear.

The Seventh Fleet is off to Titan for certifications. That'll keep them out of sight and out of mind for months. It's time to put this deception plan into motion.

Hunt opened a secured messaging app, typed up a coded message and sent it off to his Republic Intelligence operative. It was time to put this final piece of intelligence into play, to really convince the Zodarks that now was the time to strike.

He sat back in his chair and ran his fingers through his hair. He hoped he'd made the right calculation. The Rhea system would now be wide open.

Chapter Twenty-Three
Investigation

Altairius Prime

David and the rest of the Kites had each taken separate transports to the Altairian home world in order to limit any sightings of them together. Republic Intelligence strongly suspected that the Ani were using the East India Trading Company as a front to move dangerous materials, but since Viceroy Hunt and others in the Republic leadership had reason to be suspicious of the Altairians, Hunt wanted to run an investigation of this operation without alerting the Altairians to their presence.

Drew had set up "jobs" for them at various cover companies on Altairius Prime. They had to show up from time to time to put in some face time, but they had no real responsibilities. They could use the offices when it was beneficial to them, or they could come and go as they pleased. In their off time, when they needed to sleep, they would be staying at various corporate-owned condos. They could keep up communications through the neurolinks, of course, but if the occasion did arise for them to meet in person, they could gather at one of the locations where Earth expats liked to play poker.

David had been observing the emporium for a few days now, mostly focusing on the trucks being used for shipments and collecting photographs and other biometrics of anyone that worked there for comparison to their databases. Finally, by using the stealth mesh on his exoskeleton suit, he'd managed to slip a tracker onto one of the trucks, and he dispatched Somchai and their drone to find out where it was headed.

Jessica had done quite a bit of shopping inside the store, capturing images of all of the workers and casually asking about shifts and job availability.

Catalina was using their secure search protocol to search through all available data on each person David and Jess had identified.

There's definitely something fishy going on, she told David.

What did you find? he asked.

Well, John Rigby's fingerprints match with the ones on file, as does his iris image...but his facial recognition analysis is only a close match, not an exact match. She sent over a few photos for comparison before she directed, *Look at his eyes.*

David pulled up the images and studied them carefully. They were very close. A casual observer would definitely not have been able to tell the difference. However, the man in the newer images had eyes that were set a little farther apart. It was subtle, but noticeable upon scrutiny.

I think the only way we're going to know for sure is to get a DNA sample, David said. *We have to verify this for the higher-ups.*

Let me set something up with Amir, Catalina responded. *No one has seen him yet, and I'm sure he'll love to be pulled off financial forensics for a while.*

Sounds good. Let me know what you find, David replied. *Oh, and what about his business partner, Rand Wilson?*

So far, he seems clean, said Catalina. *No red flags, and his biometrics perfectly match what was collected in the past.*

I wonder what level of knowledge or involvement he has in whatever's going on here, said David.

I guess that's what we need to figure out, Catalina replied.

One person can't run an operation by themself, David realized. *How wide does this web go?*

****

Once they'd identified a warehouse where the delivery trucks were going, Somchai and Jess set up observation there and went to work pulling up the plans for the building—the Altairians were meticulous about their permitting processes, which made their job a bit easier.

The warehouse had two distinct entrances, and the design specs showed that there would be a wall in the center partitioning off the two sides. Their assumption was that John Rigby and his business partner kept things separate and had two inventory systems for their different business streams. Somchai set up along the side that Rigby and his crew seemed to be using, and Jess took the side with Rand Wilson's crew.

It took a little bit of effort for each of them to find good places to set up using their new Gallentine scanning technology without being detected, but it was worth it. These devices weren't available to anyone in the Republic except for the Kites—even Republic Intelligence didn't have access to them. They came directly from Hunt, and they were more powerful than anything else available.

The first truck that Somchai looked inside already yielded some results.

Kites, we definitely have something going down on John Rigby's side, Somchai told the group over the neurolink.

What do you see? asked David.

Well, I can see everything in these trucks with the Gallentine tech...except that there's a black hole on two of the crates on this one, Somchai explained. *It's like there's some kind of shielding involved.*

That's definitely suspicious, Catalina agreed.

What about you, Jess? asked David. *Anything interesting?*

Sorry. Other than the fact that this tech is amazing, I'm bored over here, she replied.

Keep up your surveillance for a while, David directed. *Maybe just that one truck is clean, but you'll have some contraband coming in.*

You got it, David, Jess confirmed. *I'm here until you say otherwise.*

Somchai—I think you should see if you can find a way to use your scanner on the actual warehouse, David suggested.

Good idea. They seem to have a break in their activities right before morning, Somchai explained. *It would probably work best to try it then.*

Several hours went by fairly uneventfully. There were a lot of trucks moving in and out throughout the night. In every one on his end, Somchai noticed at least one or two boxes that were shielded.

When Somchai was relatively certain that he had hit that lull around dawn that he'd expected, he went to work. At first, the warehouse seemed just like any other he'd ever observed: shelves, crates, boxes, and loaders. There were definitely a lot of bottles of alcohol in this facility, and there were additional air conditioner units to keep the warehouse temperature controlled. Somchai was starting to wonder where all those shielded crates had gone.

Hey, team...I definitely have something here, Somchai announced.

What do you have for us? asked Jess.

There's a four-foot shielded space that's been walled off on Rigby's side of the warehouse, Somchai explained. *They're hiding a whole lot of something in there.*

****

Amir confidently walked into the East India Trading Company and asked to speak to the proprietor. A few minutes later, John Rigby appeared.

"What can I do for you, sir?" Rigby asked amiably.

"Well, you see, I work down at the port. I'm one of the main foremen there, and I've got a crew of about five hundred that I oversee. The guys all have a hankering for Stims. Do you think you could get some here?"

"Stims?" asked Rigby.

"Yeah, you know—the gum that you chew that has caffeine and some other pick-me-ups in it. Keeps the workers productive. You've never had any?" he asked, pulling a pack from his backpack. "Here, try a stick," he offered.

Rigby took the gum and chewed it for a moment. He shrugged. "I mean, it's not exactly my thing, but you say you have five hundred guys—how much of this do you think they would buy?"

"My guess is, if you could keep it in stock, you're looking at a minimum of two thousand purchases a month, and that's just from my guys," Amir offered. "No telling how many other people would want to buy some too."

The man twiddled his fingers as he seemed to be doing some mental calculations. "How much did you pay for this pack?" he asked.

Amir told him the price back on Earth but explained that his men realized imports would cost more.

"Well," said Rigby, "it'll take me a little while to work out a supplier back on Earth, but I think we could start carrying Stims here soon."

Amir stuck out his hand, and the two of them shook on it. As Amir turned to walk out, he watched Rigby out of his peripheral vision— just as he thought, he took the stick of gum, wrapped it in the wrapper it had come in, and disposed of it in the trash.

We have our DNA sample, Amir announced. *Just need to make sure I catch it on garbage duty.*

****

The Kites sat at various tables, playing poker as they used their neurolinks to plan for what was next. As they had suspected, the man posing as John Rigby was an impostor. Now they just needed to figure out what exactly he was hiding in that warehouse.

You know, it's not fair that these clubs play poker, joked Somchai. *Amir is going to wipe the floor with us as usual.*

Just try to stay in long enough for us to make a plan, said Jess.

So what are we going to do? asked David.

I think our best option is to go up on the roof, offered Catalina. *We can drill a hole and get a fiberoptic camera in there.*

We should bring some of that tracking mist, Amir offered. *I still don't understand exactly how that stuff works, but it'll make it a lot easier to pin down who's handling whatever is in there.*

Among the Gallentine technology available to them was a new spray that functioned somewhat like a radioisotope would in a PET scan—once it was released, special scanners would be able to trace these particles, but they wouldn't be visible or traceable by any other means than the specific tools given to them by the Gallentines.

That sounds like a good idea, Amir, Jess agreed.

So how are we doing this? asked David.

****

A few hours later, David and Somchai had donned their magnetic boots and were ready to scale the warehouse wall. Jess was providing overwatch, along with Amir, who was operating a drone, and Catalina remained nearby to assist if things went crazy.

How are we looking? asked David.

You are clear from here, Jess announced.

Drone footage is uneventful, said Amir.

The magnetic boots had gotten quite a bit quieter through the years. They shimmied up the side of the building with barely a sound at all.

Using the scanner that Somchai had previously utilized, they located the shielded area again and marked a spot right in the middle of it. David pulled out his laser cutter, which was not only silent but was programmed to stop as soon as it cut all the way through the roof. Even

227

if there were someone inside, it would be extremely difficult to notice what they were doing.

Somchai fed a very small fiberoptic camera into the shielded room, and they started to look around.

We're in, said David over the neurolink. *So far, just a lot of crates.*

Angle over to the right, David, said Somchai. *I think one of those crates is open over there.*

All right, David replied, complying with the request. *It looks like bottles of alcohol so far, in very fancy dark glass. Not sure why they'd go through all that trouble for some booze...wait...what is that?*

It looks like one of the bottles is split open on a workbench, Somchai replied. *Zoom in...*

We have explosives, David announced.

Sure would be nice if we could just bring in the bomb squad and eliminate it all, said Amir.

Yeah, but the problem is we don't know where it's coming from or where it's going yet, said Catalina. *If we don't disrupt the supply chain, they'll just find another way to move their explosives.*

Catalina's right, agreed Somchai. *Let's use the tracking mist and see what's what.*

****

As David and the rest of the Kites continued their observations, they found that at least some of the explosives made their way into the main storefront, where they were stored in the back in a shielded safe.

It wasn't long before they found a "customer" that came into the store and walked out with two of these special bottles. It was tempting to rush in and apprehend that individual immediately, but they wanted to see where he was headed and if there were any more of them. Following the tracing mist, they were able to determine that this man had boarded a ship headed to the Tully capital.

Jessica and Amir had placed several untraceable bugs within the walls of the East India Trading Company during their visits, so they were able to go back and find the audio at the sales counter right before the runner had come into the store. The man had come in and asked to speak to the proprietor, then requested two bottles of a very specific vintage of wine. The man impersonating John Rigby had then gone "into the back" to pick up the requested items.

After a couple of weeks of watching the store, the Kites were able to identify twelve different runners who were taking these explosives to various locations in the Galactic Empire. They had collected biometrics on those individuals and had started to piece together not just where those people were going but where they had been before coming to Altairius Prime. However, it became clear that this was bigger than the five of them could handle alone.

David got in touch with Drew and recommended that they present the information they had gathered to the Altairians and let them continue on with the investigation.

Unless you have several more Kite Program classes that are ready to go, you just don't have enough bodies to run an investigation this broad, David had explained.

Let me run this up the chain to the Viceroy, Drew replied. *In the meantime, I'd like to send you back to New Eden. There's some pretty big things coming down the pike, and we may need you for something else.*

Chapter Twenty-Four
A Change of Plans

Nefantar
Tueblets System

Mavkah Otro stared at his deputy, skeptical of the report he'd just received from a cousin within the Groff. *Is this some sort of final test by Utulf before he nominates me to replace him on the Council? If I fail this test, is Irhes supposed to relieve me of command?*

"NOS Irhes, explain to me again your relationship with Vukenda."

The large Zodark grinned as if he knew what Otro was concerned about. "Deputy Director Vukenda is a member of my clan. More importantly, he is a member of my tribe. He married my brother's daughter—he can be trusted. He stands to gain much when I become Mavkah and you become Zon. That is why he is sharing this."

"If what Kafarr 11 Alpha says is true—New Eden appears to be a trap. If we continue with the orders from the Council, then we are likely to fall into a carefully planned ambush and be destroyed."

"Perhaps that is why Vak'Atioth did not bring this to the Council. He knows it is a trap—he wants you to die in battle. If you die a glorious death for the Empire, then he is likely to be chosen to sit on the Council in your stead—right?"

Otro grunted at the blunt assessment. Irhes was likely right. Vak'Atioth would be the most likely candidate if Otro were to meet a premature death in battle. *But would Vak really sacrifice the* Nefantar *to prevent me from being appointed to the Council?*

"You may be right. But the Council's orders are final. We are to launch our invasion in days. There is simply no time to arrange to meet with the Council to try and convince them to delay the attack or allow us to move forward with the Malvari's original plans."

"If you can't meet with the Council, then what about the Zon? Send the report to Zon Utulf and see if he will alter our invasion plans. He has the authority himself to make that decision if necessary."

Otro stared at his deputy for a moment, impressed by his cunning. It was a risky plan. If it worked, though...he might be able to convince Utulf to let him proceed with their original invasion plans.

Dismissing Irhes to continue preparing two invasion forces, Otro prepared a message to send to Utulf. He attached Kafarr 11 Alpha's report along with his recommendations for a modified version of the Malvari's original invasion of Sol. Instead of lingering in the system waiting for the Republic's Gallentine warship to appear so they could destroy it, he proposed that they be allowed to jump into the system just long enough to wreck the Republic's massive naval yard, then turn their weapons on Earth and deliver a devastating orbital barrage across hundreds of their cities. Then the *Nefantar* would open a bridge and the fleet would jump out. They would be in Sol for no more than two or three days, tops.

Once the message had been sent, he went back to work getting the fleets ready for action. No matter what the Zon ultimately decided, they were about to go back to war and it was his job to make sure they were ready for it.
****

Office of the Zon, Private Study

What is this? Why would the Groff keep such important intelligence from the Council...from me? Zon Utulf thought angrily as he read the urgent message from Mavkah Otro.

At first he thought this might be a trick by the Malvari to convince him to change his orders. Then he saw the official communiqué from 11 Alpha, Heltet's Kafarr in Sol. His intelligence had been spotless up to this point. Now he was warning them that Sol was not in fact heavily built up and defended as they had been told. It was the Rhea and Qatana systems that had been greatly reinforced.

This Kafarr and Otro both believe these other two systems are a trap...then why would the Groff not share that with me and the Council?

After reviewing the modified plan Otro had attached for him to approve, he saw he was no longer advocating to wait around and look to fight the *Freedom* once it showed up. That actually made him feel better about the situation. It was highly unlikely the Republic had another ship that could cause severe enough damage to the *Nefantar* that it wouldn't be able to use its wormhole generator. With the fear of trapping their fleet in Sol removed, he would give Mavkah Otro permission to modify

231

his orders and invade Sol instead of Rhea and Qatana. His only caveat was that his fleet could only stay in Sol for no longer than seventy-two hours. Should that ship the *Freedom* show up, then he was to have the *Nefantar* open the bridge and jump away as many warships of the fleet as possible. Under no circumstances was the *Nefantar* to get in a fight with that Gallentine ship, not until they could engineer their own ambush to destroy it.

With his decision made, he called an emergency meeting of the Council. He wanted to brief them on the new intelligence and the new plan the Malvari had come up with given what they now knew, and then determine why the Groff had failed to present this intelligence to them during their last meeting. The meeting was short, at least by Council standards. By the end of it, they had five votes in support of the modified Malvari plan and two votes against. A majority had been reached, and Utulf had been spared invoking Lindowee and potentially tarnishing his legacy in the process. When he returned to his office, he sent the order, approving the invasion of Sol.

****

Two Days Later
Nefantar
Tueblets System

Otro looked at the communiqué with delight. His message had worked. Zon Utulf had not only approved of his new plan, he'd gotten four Council members to agree as well.

"They approved the plan?" Irhes commented.

"They did indeed. NOS Vesren, it is time to prepare the ship. I want to open the first bridge in one hour. Irhes, send the new orders out to the fleet. I am going to speak with the commanders for the first jump. I have special orders for them," Otro declared, then dismissed his senior leaders to go about getting everything ready.

The time to end this Terran Republic has arrived. After today...nothing will ever be the same.

For the rest of the hour, the ship and the fleet were a flurry of activity. The original fleet that was going to invade the Qatana system and look to cause havoc on Sumer or one of its colonies was now marshaling around the *Nefantar*, waiting for the bridge to be opened for them to follow through. While that wave of ships was preparing to cross the bridge, the primary assault force, the one the *Nefantar* would be crossing over with, was making their own final preparations.

When Mavkah Otro walked onto the bridge of the *Nefantar*, he saw the crew running through their checklists and final preparations with practiced precision. NOS Vesren, the captain of the ship, had drilled his crew hard for months in preparation for this very deployment. Today would mark the first time in history their people had reached technological parity with their Orbot patrons. The wormhole generator was a technological wonder that would free their fleets from being constrained to using only the stargates.

Otro made his way over to the workstation that controlled the wormhole generator and saw the technicians preparing it for use. "How soon until we can open the bridge?" he asked, seeing the countdown clock approaching zero.

"We are ready to begin the sequence now, Mavkah."

"Mavkah, the fleet reports ready to begin operations," announced Irhes.

Otro turned to look for NOS Vesren. The captain nodded; his people were ready. It was time to begin. Standing tall, Otro held a communicator up as he prepared to speak to the fleet.

"This is Mavkah Otro, the head of the Malvari. In a few minutes, the *Nefantar*, through the use of Humtar technology, will open a wormhole, creating a bridge connecting Tueblets and a system you likely have never heard of called Sol. This is the home system of the Republic, and the Terran home world, Earth. The intelligence operatives of the Groff have obtained last-minute intelligence alerting us to a Republic trap to lure us into the Rhea and Qatana systems so they could destroy our fleet and the *Nefantar*.

"With this newly acquired intelligence, the great Zon Utulf sought the guidance of Lindow on whether we should proceed with the plan or whether he had another one for us. The god of our people showed favor upon Zon Utulf and gave him a divine plan for us to pursue instead. In a few moments, the bridge will be opened—our assault will begin. The first group will be dropped near a planet they call Mars. This force will have the responsibility of wrecking the shipyard in orbit of the planet along with assaulting the colony down on the planet below.

"Once the first assault force has crossed, the bridge will be closed and a second opened near Earth. The second assault force will be led by the *Nefantar* itself. We will target the Republic home world and destroy their shipyards, heavy industry, and government. Our invasion will not be a long one. We do not intend to stay beyond three days. The Republic's fleet is five days' travel from Sol. By the time they know their home world is under attack and are able to respond, we will already be home, celebrating our great victory and plotting our next attack to finish their fleet and end the Republic as a military threat to the Empire. Ship commander, troop commanders, prepare your forces for battle. The war between the humans and the Zodarks is about to begin."

Otro saw the faces of those on the bridge beaming with pride as he concluded his speech to the fleet. They were eager to get the war going—to feel the thrill of battle once again.

"NOS Vesren, open the bridge. Let us begin."

Chapter Twenty-Five
The Zodarks Are Here

Space Command
Jacksonville, Arkansas
Earth, Sol System

Admiral Chester Bailey had just finished reading Admiral Halsey's official report on the operational status of Seventh Fleet when the alarms blared. He nearly jumped out of his skin when the warning klaxons sounded throughout Space Command and alerted the officers and senior NCOs who had a neurolink implant.

Alerts began to show up via his neurolink, followed by emails with bold red lettering demanding his immediate attention. *Oh my God...these are coming from the early-warning systems. God help us, the Zodarks are here! But how?!*

Bailey connected himself to the base's command center and demanded to know what the hell was going on. Standing near his desk, he listened to a report they'd just received from the Mars Orbital Station. They were reporting multiple Zodark warships emerging from a wormhole that had appeared out of nowhere. One minute the area had been empty; the next, ship after ship emerged from this strange anomaly.

The base commander activated the station's defensive weapons along with the planetary Sentinels and other ground-based defensive systems. He was scrambling their alert fighters and doing what he could to get them ready for action, but it was clear the force he had was no match for the number of warships he was reporting. They had already counted fifty-six warships, and more seemed to appear every few seconds. Then something even scarier happened. A new report came in detailing not just additional Zodark ships—it was now detecting transports. Dozens of troopships emerged, adding to his near-panicked state. This wasn't a raid; this wasn't an attack. This was an invasion. The Zodarks had found a way to bypass the stargates, appearing directly in Sol.

As the situation unfolded and the gravity of what it all meant set in, his military training kicked in and he began issuing a raft of instructions. He ordered the planet's defensive weapon systems online and started activating every emergency contingency they had for a situation such as this. One of the contingencies was the vaults of C100s he had located across Earth, particularly near critical infrastructure and densely populated civilian centers.

If the Zodarks were able to land their invasion force before the transports could be intercepted, then the vaults of C100s closest to those landing sites would be activated. The combat synthetics would be given orders to advance to contact and move to eliminate the threat. As Bailey's orders were being pushed to the vaults across the planet, the personnel manning them began arming the Synths and preparing the facilities for war.

While he was busy getting their ground forces ready for what would come next, the Sentinels in high orbit had transitioned from sleep mode to active as they prepared to give the Zodarks one hell of a nasty surprise. While the grid covering the planet had not been fully completed, they had more than enough Sentinels to cause some serious damage should an enemy warship come within range. Likewise, the defensive weapons on the portions of the Ring Station that had been completed went live as well, preparing to repel any invaders or attackers that got within range of their weapons.

Bailey paused for a moment. He knew Halsey would have gotten the alerts about the Zodarks and would likely be responding. Still, he wanted to make sure she knew as much as he did. He crafted a quick message, attaching all the information he had at the time, along with a short video message. He told her to rally her fleet and prepare to defend Earth and the naval shipyard. He knew that meant leaving Mars on its own, but protecting Earth and the billions of people living there was far more important.

He sent a message to the Gallentine shuttle pilot to leave Earth, head for New Eden, and alert the Viceroy of the sudden appearance of the Zodarks. He made sure the messenger knew to convey that somehow, the Zodarks had acquired the technology needed to open a wormhole and had bridged their fleet into Sol. He urgently pleaded for the Viceroy to bring the *Freedom* back to Earth and help him repulse this invasion. As he hit send on the message, he hoped that the shuttle pilot would be able to make the jump to Rhea. Depending on how long it took Hunt to react, their hopes for survival might hinge on the ability of Admiral Halsey and the Seventh Fleet to somehow defeat the Zodarks on their own. He

prayed it wouldn't come to that, but if it did, then at least her fleet had the bulk of their new warships available for this fight.
****

Seventh Fleet Flagship
RNS *Ark Royal*
Saturn, Sol System

Admiral Halsey's eyes went wide when she saw the message from Admiral Bailey. *Zodarks are in Sol...how can that be?* she started to ask herself as she read the header to his email. Then a flood of alerts started filling her inbox from the early-warning sensors they had scattered about Sol. The tiny listening posts began reporting contacts tightly packed in the vicinity of the Mars Orbital Station. Five of the active listening posts had reported the contacts, triangulating the precise location the ships appeared to be emerging from.

It's a wormhole...that's how they're getting in, she realized as she pieced together what the contact reports were telling her.

Clicking on Bailey's message, she saw he was ordering her to head directly for Earth, not the MOS. *He's concerned they may drop a new fleet above Earth...my God, they really found a way to circumvent the stargates and jump straight to Sol.*

Halsey nearly jumped out of her skin when Captain Carr burst into her office, shouting, "Admiral! The MOS is under attack. We're also getting reports from Sector One and Sector One Alpha of possible wormhole activity. That's Earth, Admiral!"

"I know that's Earth, damn it! Send a fleet-wide endex! Let them know this isn't an exercise, this is the real deal. I want all fighters and bombers recalled to their home ships and the fleet made ready to FTL to Earth. We'll jump as one force once we're ready."

Captain Carr nodded in agreement as he started relaying orders via his neurolink. As the two of them made their way out of her office to head towards the bridge, the gravity of the situation set in.

Halsey could sense the man's apprehension as they approached the bridge. She reached for his arm, grabbing it to force him to stop just before the automated sensors would have opened the blast doors leading to the bridge. "Bill, before we go in there—it's important they see nothing but resolute strength from us both. Regardless of how this all happened, they need to know that you and I have everything under control. Got it?"

"I agree. Maybe once this is over, we'll be able to learn how they managed to arrive here so unexpectedly."

When they entered the bridge, they separated, heading to their respective workstations. Captain Carr moved to the ship's central command section while she made her way over to the workstations to the left of the bridge, the section designated for the fleet commander to use.

The next ten minutes went by in a blur. The starfighters that had previously been participating in one exercise or another were being pulled back to their respective ships. Crews across the ships in the fleet and the *Ark Royal* were going about getting themselves ready for battle.

Catching her eye, Captain Carr motioned for her to come to his workstation. "Admiral, I'm not sure if you are aware of this, but our ship, along with half the others in the fleet, isn't ready for combat. I just received a message from my weapons officer letting me know that as of right now, we don't have any ammunition on board."

Bunching her eyebrows, she replied, "What?! We don't have any *ammo*? What do you mean we don't have any ammunition? How the hell is that even possible?!"

Captain Carr countered defensively, "What I mean, Admiral, is we don't have our ammo loadout for kinetic weapons and missiles yet. The ship just got commissioned. We haven't fully completed our carrier operations, weapons, and flight operations qualifications to certify the *Ark Royal* as ready to deploy to the fleet. Once a ship is certified for fleet duty, that's when you can report to either the Titan munitions depot or the munitions depot on Luna."

Halsey faltered for a second in her response, trying to comprehend what he had just said. Then it came flooding back—she'd written these very rules he was now reciting back to her, years ago.

Carr seemed to catch on to her sudden realization of what this all meant. He went on to add, "Admiral, technically the *Ark Royal*, along with nearly half the ships in Seventh Fleet, hasn't fully completed certification process yet. Until we can take on munitions from Titan, we can't send half the fleet to Earth if we don't have any missiles or ammo."

Halsey stared at him for a moment before cursing under her breath in frustration. *Earth is under attack by the Zodarks and my ship and nearly half the fleet don't have a proper loadout of ammo...*

"All right, Captain. You're right. Let's assume half the fleet is in the same situation we're in. If we jump back to Earth now, how bad will this hurt our combat power if we have to rely solely on just our direct energy weapons and forgo our missiles and kinetic ammo?"

Carr looked panicked by the question. He tilted his head to the right while he did some mental calculations. "Ma'am, we'd have full use of our turbo lasers, all twenty-four turrets of them, so we'd still pack a punch. But we'd lack ammo for the twenty magrail turrets, the antiship missiles, the antistarfighter missiles, and the ships' point defense weapons. We'd also lack missiles and torpedoes for the space wings' fighter and bomber squadrons. In short, we could provide some help and certainly punch pretty hard. But we'd be down more than sixty-five percent of our combat power. We'd also be left virtually defenseless. Admiral, if you'll give me some more time, I can get us at least a basic load of ammo from depot on Titan. We could dispatch every cargo shuttle and Osprey across the fleet to head to the depot and start pulling whatever ammo their ships need and get it to their respective hangars. This short delay will let us get in the fight with our ship's full capabilities," he explained.

"Damn it! This isn't good, Greg. Admiral Bailey is screaming for us to haul ass back to Earth and the best I can tell him is we're out of bullets and we need time to take on ordnance or we won't even be much help once we do show up."

Then Captain Bill Cunningham walked over and joined their conversation. "Admiral, there is an alternative."

"Oh? Do tell."

"Not all the ships in the fleet are in the same ammo situation we are. I propose we detail off the ships that have ammo and send them to Earth ASAP while we work to take on ammo. This way we're not leaving Earth defenseless. It shouldn't take us but a few hours at most to get the ammo aboard. After that, we can put the crew to work moving it about to where it needs to go while we jump the ship back to Earth," Cunningham offered, giving her the best alternative she'd heard up to this point.

Halsey thought about that for a moment. Reluctantly, she agreed. She told him to go ahead and start figuring out what ships would jump to Earth immediately. If they couldn't go as a combined fleet right now, then she'd do her best to send Admiral Bailey what help she could.
****

Carrier Wing 3 (CVW-3)
Aboard *Ark Royal*

When Captain Ethan Hunt's F-11 Gripen fighter came to a halt and his canopy opened, he didn't wait for the ground crew to help him out. He jumped out of the cockpit and tossed his helmet to his crew chief. "Get the birds ready to fly again, Chief. I'm going to talk to the old man and see about getting us back in the fight."

"Getting us in the fight? What are you talking about, sir?"

"Just get the birds ready and your crews ready to transfer to the *Lexington*. Don't ask questions, Chief. Just do it," Ethan ordered as he took off to the elevators that would lead him up to the bridge. Some ideas were best discussed in person and not over the neurolink.

Walking onto the bridge, Ethan made his way over to Captain Carr, the ship's commander.

"Sir, can I have a moment to talk with you?"

Carr looked up, annoyed at the interruption, but he nodded, motioning for them to step to the side, out of earshot of everyone else. "What's going on, Ethan?"

"Is it true? Earth is under attack by the Zodarks?"

"Yeah, it's looking like that. At least the MOS is right now. Not sure about Earth yet, but the early-warning sensors in Sectors One and One Alpha detected a wormhole, so it's likely the Orbots are bridging in a Zodark fleet there too."

"Damn. Wow. OK, so I heard we're going to have to wait around a few hours until we can take on some ammo before we can fly to Earth. Right?"

Carr just grimaced, nodding slowly.

"Sir, requesting permission to transfer my wing over to the *Lexington*. If they're going to jump back to Earth, then we can join them and add our weight and numbers to their wing. Once the *Ark Royal* has ammo and jumps back to join the battle, then we can transfer back to your command and resume flying out of the *Ark*. But at least this would get us in the fight right now," Ethan explained, making his case.

Carr was about to shoot the idea down when Admiral Halsey walked over to them. "Approved. Get your wing moved over to the *Lexington*. I'll order them to stand by and wait for you. The more combat power we can send to Earth right now, the better."

"Admiral, what about our own security?" Carr countered. "We need to keep some fighters here with us."

Halsey turned to Ethan. "He's got a point, Captain. Detail off a squadron of fighters to stay behind. Once we jump to Earth, your wing will fall back under operational control of our *Ark Royal*. Got it?"

"Aye, Admiral. Captain, I'll send you a message once I figure out which squadron is staying back," Ethan replied.

Heading back to the flight deck, he connected with Lieutenant Mikhail Pushkin and gave him the bad news. Pushkin's squadron was the best in the wing. As much as he wanted to bring them along, if the ship was only going to have one squadron for protection, then he wanted it to be their best squadron doing it.

For the next half hour, Ethan's wing left their home and made for the *Lexington*. It was going to be a crowded flight back to Earth, but they'd nearly doubled the combat power of the carrier. Ethan just hoped it'd be enough to make a difference.

Chapter Twenty-Six
Sentinel One-One-Five

Sentinel 115
GEO Nagpur, India
Earth Orbit, Sol System

This has got to be the most boring job in the Army. How I got stuck operating planetary defense weapons is beyond me, Lieutenant Rama Mahidol thought to himself as he stared at the monitors in front of him. All ten towers were showing green—fully operational.

Rama had joined the Army voluntarily. Like most people who weren't drafted against their will, he'd wanted to see new worlds and actually have a chance to live on them. Instead, he'd spent his first two years rotating between the ground control station directly below him in Nagpur, India, and Sentinel 115, maintaining a high geosynchronous orbit above the Indian subcontinent. One week floating in the tower, two weeks down on terra firma. *What a life...*

"Hey, LT. Just finished running that diagnostic you asked me to. Looks like you were right. Circuit five is toast. Maybe it was that solar flare from a few days back, but whatever it was, it needs replacing ASAP," Master Sergeant Dayga explained as he pulled himself up through the porthole below, holding the fried circuit in his hand.

Turning to look at his more experienced partner, Rama saw the card he was holding and concurred. It was toast. "Just great. Good thing these towers are still under warranty, eh?"

The two of them busted out laughing before Rama turned serious again, reminding him of what would likely have to happen next.

"That was a good job figuring that problem out. The last crew couldn't find it and here you did it our second day up here. Now we'll have to see if Team Pink is going to get sent up here a few days early or if Major Dikksweed can accept not being able to take control of our entire field at a moment's notice."

"Oh, man. It's really Team Pink on deck to replace us?"

"Yup. Sure is. But Tanya isn't so bad once you get to know her a bit," Rama said defensively.

"Ha ha ha—that's hilarious, sir. You haven't been around her long enough to say that yet. That gal is psycho. If we have to ask Captain

Hardy to replace us even a few hours early, let along four whole days—she'll lose her mind. You may think I'm joking, but I'm not. That crazy nutjob has a countdown for the number of hours she has left in uniform. And, no, I don't mean her assignment here working for Command Sergeant Major Fleet of the Admiralty of the Galactic Empire—Major Dikksweed. I mean the Army itself. She wants out—she's crazily desperate to leave the Army behind and start her new life. You tell her she'll have to spend a few extra days up here in the tower and I'll tell you what—when she gets back down to the ground, she'll make our lives a living hell. We'll be begging to swap rotations with someone else just to get away from her before she kneecaps us."

Rama chuckled to himself, trying not to draw the ire of one of the few friends he had. He didn't mind Tanya Hardy; she was one of the few people who had actually been nice to him when he'd first gotten here. But he also knew she hated this job. She'd been drafted during the final two years of the war, part of the group of reinforcements sent to Alfheim to retake the planet. She'd been there for the official surrender too. Try as he might, he'd never gotten her to talk about what had gone on during that deployment. All he knew was once the war had ended, she'd chosen to change career fields to something that would allow her all the time in the world to work on her graduate studies so that when she did leave the Army, she'd leave with management experience as a captain and a graduate-level degree.

To be honest, prior to graduating basic combat training, he'd never heard of this officer career field they called Area of Concentration 14 Alpha, Planetary Defense Command and Control Systems Officer. Once he'd shown up, he'd suddenly realized why damn near every officer and enlisted person enrolled in either an undergraduate or graduate degree program. With no war, this was arguably one of the most boring jobs someone could have, and it left you with a *lot* of time on your hands.

As an officer, Rama was put in charge of a platoon, but given its size—five enlisted, one officer—it felt more like a fire team or small squad. They were similar to the older US Air Force missileers, the people who manned the underground command module on orders from the President and would be responsible for arming, then firing their assigned Minuteman III ICBMs. In their case, each platoon of six personnel was responsible for ten towers. Each company had four platoons each controlling ten Sentinel towers and a fifth dedicated service platoon that repaired and maintained the Sentinels and rearmed them should they run dry on munitions during a battle.

That meant each company controlled a total of forty Sentinel towers. Instead of being broken into battalions like most Army units, they were structured around the same regimental system as the orbital assault divisions were. Each regiment had a total of two hundred and forty towers. Across Sol, there were six regiments of Sentinels, with a new regiment being created every eighteen months. It was steadily becoming a formidable defensive grid they were building in hopes of never actually needing to use it.

Ultimately, the goal was to build eight to ten of these Sentinel regiments spread across the star systems that had a habitable planet or sizable military presence. In the long term, that meant if Rama wanted to stick around, he'd likely have the chance to move up the ranks as few officers either knew about the job or wanted to cross over into it.

Floating his way to the empty chair next to his, Master Sergeant Dayga took a seat and proceeded to strap himself in. Turning to look at Rama, he asked, "Hey, LT, not sure if you saw the latest job postings on the battlenet or not, but if you're looking for a chance to travel outside Sol and actually get to see another planet, then you should check it out. It just came out maybe an hour ago, so it's still fresh. All you have to do is find one you qualify for and apply. Then it's just a matter of waiting to see if your career agent picks you over someone else."

"Really? Huh, I didn't realize they had posted them already. Let me jump on it right now," Rama replied as he opened the internal jobs and transfer portal.

His eyes suddenly went wide when he saw that eighty-six new slots had opened in the Qatana system—the same system the Sumerians were from and where the Belters had apparently created their own little society away from the rest of humanity...at least until they'd discovered Bronkis5. Now they were a heavily guarded system just like Sol.

"Damn, Dayga. You weren't joking. That's a lot of slots."

"Yeah, if I was you, I'd apply now and not wait around for the major. Better to ask for forgiveness than for permission in this case. Besides, you get selected, it's not like he can say no or deny it."

"Huh. Yeah, I guess you're right. Hey, in that case, why don't you keep watch on the scanners for me while I apply for this? Make sure the other guys are staying on top of watching their scanners too."

Dayga smiled as he nodded. "No worries, boss. It's not like anything can jump into a system that's not friendly. We'd get an alert from Rhea if a hostile fleet was inbound, and only the Altairians and the Viceroy's ship, the *Freedom*, have the ability to port into Sol directly, so we're good."

"I get it—just do as I ask. I don't need Dikksweed on my ass for anything more than leaving his command."

As Rama thought about Major Jules Dikksweed, he had to admit, he was a true jerk to work for. He was likely the reason Captain Hardy had a countdown to when she'd be able to leave the Army. The major had lost both his legs during the Alfheim campaign, and while he was eligible for a medical retirement considering his days in the infantry were effectively over, he'd opted for a transfer to the Army's Air and Space Defense branch instead. Now he spent his time making life miserable for anyone and everyone who happened to be assigned to his command.

Still, as bad as working for that guy was, he couldn't complain about the view he had when he was up here on rotation. If you looked out the windows, you could see the whole world just floating out there below you. You could also see the John Glenn Orbital Station, the shipyards surrounding it, and the space elevator connecting it to the continent below. He'd grown up in Narathiwat, a small city in the south of Thailand, near the Malaysian border; the Army had given him a unique opportunity to travel abroad and see some amazing things. Perhaps this time he'd get lucky and his application for a transfer to the Qatana system would get approved. Then he'd finally have achieved the ultimate goal he'd had when he'd joined up—a chance to see new worlds and travel the stars.

Warning—Zebra One—Warning—Zebra One—

"Hey, what the hell is a code Zebra One?" Rama asked Dayga. He had heard a few alerts during his time up here, but never this one.

"Uh, check the book if you don't know. Oh wait, I'm showing something appearing on the scanners…oh crap, that looks like a wormhole opening up."

"A wormhole? Do we have a scheduled Altairian ship dropping by, or the *Freedom*?" Rama asked, his heart skipping a beat at what this could possibly mean.

"Eh, not that I'm aware of—holy crap! Those aren't friendlies coming out of that wormhole. Oh my God, those are Zodark warships!" Dayga shouted, fear in his voice.

Holy hell, this is it. This is really happening! Rama thought as he reached over and smashed the red button that would sound the alarm not just on his tower but on all the other towers in orbit and the ground stations below. The enemy was here, and now they were invading their home space.

"Dayga, get on your soldiers below to go active with their guns. I want every gun system firing on those intruders *now*! I'm going to start engaging those smaller corvettes and frigates they warned us about. Got it?"

"Yes, sir, we're on it!" Dayga yelled to be heard over the warning alarms.

Once Rama saw all six seats in the tower go green, meaning each member of the crew was strapped in and ready to rock, he activated the tower's safety protocol. Fractions of a second later, the seats they were in retracted towards the wall closest to them. A paneled door withdrew to reveal a podlike chamber kitted out with a near 360-degree curved targeting monitor.

When everyone was tucked inside their chamber, Rama activated the automated eject option. If the tower started taking too much damage and was in danger of blowing up, the tower's safety AI would eject their pod and a pair of reentry rockets would light up, shooting them straight down towards the surface like a bullet. As they neared the surface, another set of rockets would turn on and slow their descent. If that final stage failed, a series of parachutes would deploy, slowing the pod enough to allow its final, much larger parachute to land the pod softly without killing the operator.

"Corvette, six o'clock! Engaging now!" shouted one of the privates, Olaf Lambrecht.

Rama saw the blackness of space around the Sentinel towers erupt in brilliant streaks of high-powered yellow laser bolts. The tower's four double-barreled antiship turbo lasers started lighting up the space around the Zodark ships charging towards them. He watched in awe as one of the corvettes fired what had to be a magrail gun system at a Sentinel near the Blue Origin shipyard connected to the far side of the John Glenn station.

He called it out to his teammates in case they missed what was going on. "Whoa, looks like those intelligence reports about the Zodarks integrating magrails into some of their newer ships are real. I need you guys to make sure you readjust our PDGs to engage those slugs if they fire at any of our towers. In the meantime, we need to take those corvettes down ASAP!"

"You hear that, everyone? Get those PDGs reset to go after any magrail slugs aimed at the towers. We need to keep as many towers online as possible so our other weapon systems can stay alive to keep firing on those larger warships," reiterated Master Sergeant Dayga.

It was times like this when Rama thoroughly enjoyed having an experienced noncommissioned officer. In a pinch, the guy knew how to run the whole team and operation without him should it be necessary.

Returning his gaze to the corvette attacking Tower 097, Rama saw the tower take multiple hits from the magrail. To his amazement, the slugs didn't punch a hole right through it. Instead, they appeared to glance off the tower or shatter upon impact. He was aware of the armor upgrades the Sentinel IIs had over the first version, but he'd had no idea the armor had been improved upon this much. It made him feel good that his field of ten Sentinels were of the newer variety.

The platoon of ten Sentinels his command tower oversaw was now clearly in a target-rich environment. Anywhere Rama looked, there was a charging Zodark corvette, frigate, or cruiser. Further behind the frontal assault and closer to the wormhole was a battle line forming up of their larger, more formidable battleships. It seemed like every few minutes, another wave of warships would emerge from the wormhole, adding to the already immense fleet arrayed against them.

Then Rama stomach tightened further when saw the kind of ships he had really hoped wouldn't emerge from that wormhole—star carriers. And there weren't just one or two of the giant vessels, but a string of them that continued to emerge from the bridge connecting his homeworld to whatever Zodark hell they had emerged from. *Holy Mother of God...that's twelve of them so far...*

"Lieutenant, are you *seeing* all those star carriers? What are we supposed to do now?!" Private Lambrecht lamented. Everyone saw them forming a secondary battle line behind the now forty-three battleships that had emerged from the wormhole so far.

"Shove it, Lambrecht! That goes for all of you bastards! We are the *last line of defense* protecting Earth, protecting our families—protecting our very existence from these murderous savages! If I see *one* of you slacking off, freezing up at the very moment of Earth's survival and our own, I'll grab you right out of your chair and beat you senseless!" roared Master Sergeant Dayga to his underlings. "We are sitting in the toughest, most advanced Sentinel towers ever built. These things are made with Bronkis5, and that means we're tough as hell to destroy. We're going to blow these bastards to hell and gone and send them packing right back through that wormhole. Now man your guns! Find a target and pulverize it! You got me?"

"Hell yeah, baby!"

"Bring it on, you Zodark bastards!"

Dayga then opened a private channel so just the two of them could talk briefly. "Sorry if I was a bit blunt back there, sir, but these guys needed a good kick in the nuts to remind them of how important our job is right now. I can't say for certain if we're going to live five more minutes or a few more hours, sir—but come hell or high water, we've got to hold the line for as long as possible until help arrives."

"I agree, Master Sergeant. How do you think we should approach this?" Rama asked, seeking the advice of the more senior tower operator.

"Sir, you're in charge, so we'll do as you tell us. If I were you, I'd place me and Lambrecht in charge of the PDGs. We've gotta intercept those missiles and magrail shells they're going to start throwing at us. Have the others take charge of a single turbo laser on our tower and then slave a single one from the other nine to join in. By focusing ten turrets on a single target, we'll be much more likely to take it down quick. With you and the three others working in tandem like this, we could knock some ships down in quick order. Me and Lambrecht will do our best to try and keep the tower in good shape, but at some point, we'll likely have to punch out and hope for the best."

Rama listened to Dayga, almost numbed by what he was saying. He couldn't believe this was actually happening, but at the same time, it was everything they had trained for. Dayga was right. He needed to break them down into teams and get them focused on taking down individual targets as quickly as they could.

All we gotta do is hold out long enough for reinforcements to arrive. That's right, Seventh Fleet is out at Titan. That's a big-ass fleet of warships I'll bet the Zodarks don't even know we have. Yeah…we just have to hold the line until they can jump back here to Earth…

"OK, Master Sergeant. That makes sense. Let's get it done. You keep those bastards off our tower, and I'll work with the guys to start taking those corvettes and frigates down. They look like the ones that'll do the most damage to our Sentinels."

Switching over to the coms channel the rest of the tower was on, Rama relayed what he and Dayga had gone over and got everyone tasked with what to do. Now it was time to start earning their pay and buy the fleet the time they needed to jump back from Titan and get in the fight. Hopefully someone would be sending a message back to the Rhea system. If they could get the *Freedom* to jump back to Sol, that could be the deciding factor in defeating this Zodark fleet that seemed to have appeared out of nowhere.

Taking a breath in now that he had issued his orders, Rama felt a strange surge of adrenaline course through his veins. He suddenly felt bulletproof, like his Sentinel tower was indestructible. He wasn't sure why or how he suddenly felt this way, but he wanted to ride the emotional high for as long as he possibly could. If his platoon of ten Sentinels could hold it together—hold the line—maybe the others could as well. If enough of them could hold out long enough and cut down their numbers, then when the Seventh Fleet did arrive, they'd be able to make short work of this Zodark fleet that thought they could just waltz right into Sol and wreak havoc on their world.

Well, you guys messed with the wrong group of humans. We're the Sentinels, the last line of defense…you shall not pass! Rama thought to himself as a wicked smile began to spread across his lips.

Tapping the side of his helmet, he activated the tower's virtual reality weapon controller. This was the whiz-bang multibillion-credit program that made the Sentinel IIs so damn formidable, aside from their Bronkis5 armored shell. As soon as he activated the system, a clear visor slid down from inside his helmet to encompass his entire field of view.

Then it turned on, instantly vaulting his mind into the metaverse of what almost felt like a virtual reality gaming system—only this wasn't a game. These weren't computer-generated aliens. This was the augmented reality system that allowed him to take control of one of the tower's four turbo laser antiship turrets and then slave one of the four other turrets from each of the nine other towers to his own. As he was doing this, the three other enlisted guys he'd assigned to the other turrets were doing the same.

Once the four of them each had full control over ten turrets across the towers, their targeting AI began assisting them in identifying the nearest Zodark corvette or frigate for them to engage. The AI would lead their targeting reticle just enough so that, as they fired their guns, the laser bolts would be right where it predicted the enemy warship would be fractions of a second later.

Rama saw that the warship his AI was directing him toward was a corvette that was attempting to take out one of the Sentinels stationed a few dozen kilometers above the John Glenn Orbital Station. He depressed the firing stud and watched a barrage of yellow streaks of light fly out towards the corvette from multiple directions—all converging on where the Zodark ship was going to be fractions of a second later.

The corvette that moments earlier had just delivered a devastating barrage that looked to have heavily damaged the Sentinel tower was now being pummeled by Rama's guns. A few laser bolts missed and streaked off into the blackness, but most of them found their marks, hammering the hell out of the smaller Zodark ships. Maybe five or ten seconds into his murderous barrage of laser fire, a few lucky shots appeared to have ripped the right rear engine port clean off the vessel. This put the ship into a spin, causing it to lose control. It took fractions of a second for the targeting AI to aid him in reacquiring the crippled ship and landing a few dozen more shots before it blew apart in a brilliant flash that winked out as fast as it occurred.

Rama didn't even have time to register that he'd just killed the entire crew of an enemy warship before his targeting AI had already identified another warship for him to start engaging.

Everywhere he looked, he saw bright yellow streaks of laser lights coming from Sentinel towers blasting away, red streaks coming from the station's self-defense turrets, and green flashes from the squadrons of starfighters flying up from Earth to get into the upper orbit and beyond to engage the swarms of Zodark starfighters the carriers were now starting to unleash. The John Glenn's own squadrons of starfighters had already formed a battle line and were heading towards the incoming swarm of enemy fighters. Soon they'd be in optimal range of their smart missiles and then they'd unleash the opening shots of their individual wars.

"Oh, damn! We just lost Tower 107. One of those frigates just nailed it with half a dozen plasma torpedoes or something," Private Lambrecht announced.

"Don't worry about the tower. We're going to lose some in this fight. Just focus on taking out those missiles and torps they keep firing at us. LT, it's on you and the others to keep thinning them out for us. Good job on taking that corvette out, by the way. Sally, damn good shooting, nailing that frigate. You blew that sucker to hell and gone. Keep shooting like that. Remember, the Seventh Fleet is out at Titan. You can bet your asses they're on their way back here right now. We just gotta hold the line until they get here," Master Sergeant Dayga encouraged, continuing to rally them on to victory.

Man, did I get lucky having an NCO like Dayga as my platoon sergeant, Rama thought as he squeezed the trigger, this time on a frigate that was making a move on Tower 108—one of his platoon's towers.

Mashing his thumb against the firing stud as his targeting reticle turned green, he sent shot after shot into a frigate that was angling in for an attack run on one of the older *Rook*-class battlecruisers. Rama's guns had finally found their mark as he stitched the side of the frigate with blaster shots. When he'd reached the rear midsection of the warship, he held his targeting reticle on the position, focusing all his fire on that one spot on the ship. As he was hammering the armor of the ship, it cut loose string of plasma torpedoes at Tower 108 while its lasers cut a gash into the side of Republic battlecruiser. Moments later, a gash tore open in the frigate, exposing the inside of the vessel to the vacuum of space. In fractions of a second, the frigate lost power and began floating adrift, helpless and out of action.

"Plasma torpedoes inbound on Tower 108! Dayga, see if you can intercept them before they convert!" Rama shouted. He was hoping like hell Dayga would have enough time to blow them up before they converted to their plasma form. Once that happened, they became an unstoppable streak of flowing plasma that'd plow right into whatever it impacted against.

"I'm gonna try, LT. Good job nailing that frigate. Maybe try and get it a few seconds sooner next time," Dayga joked, his voice sounding strained and tense.

Rama watched as the PDG or point defense gun began spitting out a torrent of the Bronkis3 coated magrail slugs in the direction of the plasma torpedoes. They were still in guidable mode as they attempted to course correct for their terminal approach, when they'd convert to their plasma form.

The hail of slugs zipping through the space around the torpedoes was mind-boggling to watch. Each round had a slight orange hue to it, which allowed the gunner and the targeting AI to better track the trajectory of the slugs in order to course correct the near-constant stream of shells the rotary gun barrels were spitting out. One torpedo exploded. Then a second, then a third and a fourth. The fifth took a glancing blow just as it converted to plasma form, its aim now off as it would sail harmlessly by the tower. The sixth torpedo managed to convert as it reached its terminal velocity and impact trajectory.

The torpedo plowed into the lower section of Tower 108, ripping the lower turbo laser turret and three of the tower's PDGs clean off. Sparks shot out from the missing bottom half of the tower as it vented what little oxygen had been exposed to the lower section of the Sentinel. Had that been a manned tower like their own, three of the six operators would have just died. Then again, the auto eject system might have reacted fast enough to send them on a one-way journey back to the surface too.

"It's still operational. We'll have three turbo lasers operational and half of the tower's PDGs. Refocus, everyone, and stay in the fight!" Master Sergeant Dayga continued to encourage, reminding them this fight wasn't over.

"Hey, it's the cavalry! Seventh Fleet is starting to arrive, guys! Let's keep smoking these corvettes and frigates and let them handle the big guns!" Rama shouted excitedly as elements of the fleet appeared a few tens of thousands of kilometers away. They had exited FTL almost directly to the enemy's rear and the backside of that wormhole that for whatever reason continued to stay open.

Then, Rama's jaw nearly dropped when he saw the most ungodly thing begin to exit the wormhole. It wasn't that it was a warship he hadn't seen before. It was that the warship just kept emerging from the wormhole—like it didn't have an end to it. As much as he wanted to continue to stare at it, to see what kind of strange new war machine the Zodarks had just brought to the battlefield of Earth, his targeting AI was telling him he had another corvette lining up to attack another one of his platoon's towers He needed to refocus on the immediate battle at hand and destroy this corvette before he lost yet another tower—another layer to their defense of Earth.

Chapter Twenty-Six
The Home Guard Returns

RNS *Lexington*
Between Luna and Earth, Sol System

Captain Ethan Hunt, call sign Paladin, shot down the launch bay of the RNS *Lexington* in his F-11 Gripen just seconds after the giant star carrier exited slip space and its FTL bubble. As his Altairian-Human hybrid starfighter exited the giant carrier, he got his first real picture of the situation they had just jumped into. If his helmet hadn't been fastened tightly to his face and head, his jaw would have dropped open at the sight of what his starfighter had just been hurled into.

To his complete shock and utter horror, their carrier had somehow dropped out of slip space practically on top of the enemy fleet. Normally a battle line between the two sides would be formed with hundreds of thousands of kilometers' distance between each other. The Republic, which was notorious throughout both alliances for their electronic warfare capabilities, would immediately jam the communication and sensor frequencies used by the various races within the Dominion Alliance. If they stumbled across a new one they hadn't encountered before, it'd take them just seconds to add it to the jamming hell they would unleash on their adversaries. Until the enemy was able to close the distance or manage to increase the signal strength of their targeting sensors, they couldn't gain an effective lock on the Republic warships or the allies they were fighting alongside.

When Ethan Hunt saw his Gripen had been launched less than a few hundred kilometers from what had to be the largest Zodark warship he'd ever seen, he instantly knew they were in serious trouble. Until the giant nose of the *Lexington* turned away from the Zodark fleet, every squadron they launched would be flying into a maelstrom of enemy fire being directed at the *Lex*.

Knowing the immediate danger his squadron, Number 3 Squadron of the *Ark Royal*, faced, he shouted into the squadron's coms for everyone to immediately go to maximum power and form up into a loose formation. They needed to position the carrier between themselves and this massive, unknown Zodark warship before their blasters tore them to shreds. By the time he pulled hard to the left on his Gripen and cleared the exiting path of the flight deck, Number 1 Squadron was already barreling out the front of the ship. He was rapidly relaying the same order to their squadron as a torrent of blue laser fire, indicative of Zodark blasters, unloaded on the front of the *Lexington*.

Two of the sixteen Gripens of Number 3 Squadron were shredded before they had a chance to get out of the way and begin positioning the giant carrier between themselves and this enormous warship shooting at them. Ethan cut into the command net for the *Lexington* and started screaming for them to abort the launches of his remaining squadrons until the carrier had repositioned the launch bay. Unfortunately, Number 1 Squadron had launched before he could yell for them to abort. In fractions of a second, nine of the sixteen Gripens were torn apart before they even got a hundred meters from the carrier. The few that survived the initial onslaught of fire broke in all directions as they pushed their engines to maximum power, trying to evade the enemy guns that were attempting to swat them from existence.

As Captain Hunt saw three more of the remaining seven fighters explode into a pile of flaming debris, he cursed himself for demanding a coin flip to determine which carrier strike wing would get the honor of leading the *Lexington* into battle. In less than three minutes, he'd already lost fourteen out of thirty-six fighters—nearly an entire squadron—without having fired a single shot in combat. Pulling the throttle back on his Gripen, he added some altitude, separating himself from the outer hull of the carrier.

As his Gripen and his remaining fighters continued to fly ahead of the *Lexington*, Ethan craned his neck around just enough to catch a glimpse of the opening salvo of the giant carrier's main guns. The twenty-four large turrets housing the ship's twin-barreled ship-to-ship turbo laser locked on and fired at near point-blank range. With the carrier's main guns having engaged, the gunners began laying into them as quickly as the capacitors recharged enough to fire the next volley. Given the ship's power output, it could sustain a maximum firing rate of almost three shots a minute, or one every twenty-one seconds.

Ethan angled his fighter slightly so he could catch a better glimpse of the battle beginning to unfold. As the nose of the carrier had finally pivoted away from the Zodark battle line and as more Republic battleships and cruisers began joining the battle, Number 4 Squadron was finally released and launched into the blackness of space to join up with the rest of his fighters. Again, less than a minute after Number 4 launched, Numbers 5 and 6 were hot on its heels, getting aloft and into the fight.

Ethan began calling out formations and ordering the six fighter squadrons to form up a combat air patrol to defend the *Lexington* and the surrounding battleships while they got their own squadrons launched. Next out the chute came Squadrons 7 through 10, his strike bombers— B-11 Valkyries. As he was leading Squadron 3 to escort the strike package in on whatever target the *Lexington* ordered them to hammer, he assigned Squadron 2 to assist them. Each of the Valkyries could carry either eight plasma torpedoes or fourteen Havoc-2 antiship missiles, or a mix of the two, giving the bombers a uniquely versatile capability.

One weapon Ethan insisted on each strike bomber carrying was the newly issued SM-98C or Casper-Ghost missiles. This was a third-generation upgrade to their venerable electronic warfare missile. Once fired at an adversary, the missile's warhead would separate into twenty smaller missiles able to project the same physical characteristics and electronic signature of the standard Havoc-2 antiship missile. This electronic spoof of the enemy targeting systems would cause them to target the wrong missiles, giving the real ones a slight edge in getting through the enemy's defensive screen to land a hit. If his electronic warfare strike fighter couldn't jam the enemy's point defense weapons inside of three hundred kilometers, then the 98Charlies were his best bet to land a few extra punches.

While his strike packages continued to form up and the *Lexington*'s own squadrons began launching and preparing to join him in their charging assault against whatever target package they were given, his eyes lingered on the carrier's most potent weapon—at least at these kinds of ranges. As the carrier approached a thousand kilometers between it and that mysterious warship that was still tearing into them, Ethan caught sight of the ship's twenty triple-barreled turrets unloading their thirty-six-inch projectiles at a rate of one round every forty seconds.

The sight of the projectiles racing across the distances at speeds of one hundred kilometers per second was incredible to see. It was slower than a laser bolt and not nearly as bright, but he could follow the projectile if he really watched it, and seeing it impact against the hull of a warship was a sight to behold. In some cases, the round would hit at an angle as the enemy ship rolled to one side or the other, seeking to throw the typical barrage of incoming slugs off-kilter by having them glance off the armor as opposed to slamming directly into it. The first-generation Mark-8 projectiles had a habit of bouncing off a hull if it hit at the wrong angle, or its warhead would prematurely detonate on the outer shell of the ship when it hit. The Mark-10 was an improved second-generation warhead that incorporated a spinning motion as well as several riveted grooves in the rear of the round with tiny steerable fins that would deploy once it left the barrel. Then a small compressed air canister in the base of the shell could provide it with just enough steerable change in velocity to make minor adjustments to help ensure a near miss would become a solid hit.

But seeing this new round, the third-generation Mark-12, punch through the armor of the mystery warship told Ethan all he needed to know about whether the newly improved warhead was worth the expenditure of the synthetic Bronkis3 material they had begun coating the penetrator tips with. Ensconcing the warheads' tips in Bronkis3 gave them the necessary density to punch a hole through even the toughest armor the Republic would likely face. But it was the five thousand pounds of high explosives and chemically generated incendiary gelatin that exploded inside the guts of its prey that made these new warheads so deadly. The blast from the high explosives would open a hole between the decks of the warship. Then the incendiary gelatin would be scattered throughout the cavernous space the explosion had just created. The instant flash temperature of the blast would then ignite the gelatin, which had already stuck itself all over inside the ship. The sudden incendiary component, burning at temperatures of greater than five thousand degrees, would then melt through the vessel's internal wiring, HVAC systems, and decks, creating all sorts of nastiness inside the ship until either it was chemically extinguished, or it simply burned through the available atmosphere and died from asphyxiation.

Hot damn! There has to be a way for us to work that kind of incendiary nastiness into these Havoc missiles…that stuff is the new gold standard as far as I'm concerned, Ethan thought as he looked on in awe at the damage the *Lexington* was inflicting on the giant Zodark warship.

"Paladin Actual, Blue Ghost Actual. Your target package is that lead battleship closing in on the Ring Station in GEO overtop of Europe. It's imperative that your strike package succeed in taking that battleship out before it can further damage or destroy the Ring Station. How copy?"

Ethan could hear the anguish in the captain's voice as he gave him that order. It likely came from someone higher than him, as he himself probably would have directed them to go after that large Zodark ship that was pounding the hell out of the carrier.

Damn it. We should be allowed to defend our ship! Ethan demurred silently, knowing orders were orders no matter how much you disagreed with them.

"That's good copy, Blue Ghost. If we have any ordnance left from our run, we'll look to dump it on that bastard pounding on you. Out.

"Mighty Ark, Mighty Ark. I'm sending our strike packages now. We've been tasked with taking out a Zodark battleship currently attacking a section of the Ring Station in GEO over Europe. Squadrons 4 and 5, you've got the tough duty of cutting us a whole through their defenders. Squadron 6, you're going to cover our rear and make sure no Vultures manage to slip in behind us and snipe at us from behind. Everyone else, stay in a loose formation around the Valkyries and let's get 'em in to deliver their packages. Paladin out!"

With the orders issued, the squadrons began taking up their different attack positions. Several additional squadrons from a couple of the newer battleships had joined them for this attack run as well. Whoever was directing this attack really wanted this particular battleship dead. Ethan just wished they could deliver their munitions against the large mystery warship. He wasn't sure how that damn thing was doing it, but every few minutes, it would fire some sort of particle beam weapon that would slam into one of their battleships and practically bore a hole right through it. If the ship didn't explode outright, it usually drifted off course as internal fires and atmospheric fluids and gases initiated a rapid decompression event across the ship. He saw more than one battleship go dark within minutes of being hit, its crew likely sucked out into the vacuum of space or simply trapped in a wing or compartment of the ship, unable to move without exposing themselves to the vacuum.

At least, if my autoeject failed to pop me out of this can before it blew up, my death would be swift...

Zipping through the Zodark battle line that continued to fall further and further into disarray as the Republic Navy was giving as good as it was taking, he saw the fighters of Squadron 5 chasing after a handful of Zodark Vultures. He'd seen plenty of these in his last battle in a starfighter in the Sirius system some six years ago. He was glad to see it didn't look like they had improved upon them since. The Zodarks were, if nothing else, slow to adjust to radical technological changes. They seemed to prefer the more brutal frontal attack every time instead of using the space between their ears to aid them in outfoxing their adversaries. He'd learned from his Gallentine mentors that the Zodarks were a bit of a copy and steal race as opposed to an invent your way out of a problem kind of species. They were essentially the complete opposite of the humans, or as he was steadily coming to call his race, the Terrans.

"Look out, Paladin! On your nine o'clock, break right!" yelled a voice over his coms. He instantly yanked his flight control to the right and automatically pulled up tight, hammering his body with seven g's as he maneuvered out of the way of a streak of blue flashes where his Gripen had just been.

Damn, I miss my old Hellcat! Ethan thought as he grunted from the pressure of the g-forces. That wasn't something you typically had to handle too much of when flying one of the Gallentine Hellcat fighters. They had that immersive tank in the cockpit that essentially enveloped a pilot's entire body, absorbing the g-forces instead of their bodies. *Ha ha, we'll figure that out one of these days*, he snickered to himself as he caught sight of the Vulture that had nearly zapped him.

Angling in for the attack, he gave chase to the fighter, who made a dash for one of the Valkyries his squadron was escorting in. The Vulture fired, but his shots went wide and to the left as he broke off his attack to dodge a string of shots Ethan had just fired at him. *Wow, I can't believe I missed that guy*, Ethan chided himself. He was generally a pretty good shot, but he'd overcompensated on this one, trying to lead the target more than his AI had told him to. He had a nasty habit of trusting his gut over his AI more than he should. That computer could calculate things faster than he could, even with his Gallentine neurolink implants.

Closing the distance between his Gripen and the Vulture, he got his targeting reticle to dance across the enemy starfighter a couple of times before he depressed the firing stud, sending a string of blaster bolts across the distance between them. He saw four or five of them hit across the center mass of the fighter, blowing it apart. As the ship separated into pieces, Ethan pulled back on his throttle, dropping his speed by fifty percent as he angled his fighter to the right, realigning into an escort position.

As they continued to approach the battleship, Ethan saw the ship was taking a beating from a handful of those Sentinel towers anchored nearby. He was kind of surprised the Zodarks hadn't taken them all out before they'd moved in on the Ring Station. Judging by the hits it was taking, the ship captain was probably pissed at whoever had told him those towers wouldn't pose that much danger to them. No sooner had he had this thought than a Zodark corvette zipped right past the battleship, unloading a barrage of plasma torpedoes at the offending tower. The Sentinel blew apart moments later from the impact, and the threat to the larger warship was neutralized.

"Red Four, Red Five. Zodark corvette coming around at your seven o'clock. Looks to be making an intercept run on our packages. Move to intercept."

"Copy that, Paladin. We're moving in," came the quick reply from two of his veteran pilots.

They angled in to intercept the corvette, whose captain must have suddenly realized they were being targeted. The corvette changed course and unleashed a slew of laser fire at them, causing Ethan and his fighters to split off and divert from their original attack vector.

While the corvette had momentarily been distracted by Ethan's fighters, two of the Valkyries had slipped past it and gotten in close to the battleship and unloaded their plasma torpedoes at near point-blank range.

The four torpedoes fired by each Valk made a couple of course corrections as the battleship attempted to roll to one side and change its course trajectory to dodge the incoming threats. By the time the torps had converted to plasma, they were practically on top of the massive warship. Whoever had programmed those warheads had done a damn good job in Ethan's mind. All eight of the flaming darts of death plowed into the side of the ship, ripping its guts open to the vacuum of space.

Secondary explosions began rippling across portions of the lower half of the warship. Then another pair of Valks swooped in to make their own attack runs on the now-crippled ship. This time, its point defense weapons were a bit more effective in throwing out a wall of flak fire at the diving intruders. One of the Valkyries took a couple of hits when the ship's autoeject shot the pilot right out of the airframe before it blew apart. The other Valk managed to dodge its way through the enemy fire to deliver four more flame darts into the already damaged battleship.

"Yellow Five, Six, you're up. Let's finish this bastard," Ethan called over the coms to Squadron 7, the group of strike fighters they were escorting in.

"We're on it, Paladin."

Ethan smiled as he saw the next two Valks circle in to begin their own attack runs. They were vectoring in from a different angle than the last group that had run into the wall of flak fire. That was the last thing a fighter bomber or bomber pilot wanted to try and fly their ship through—too many ways to get nailed and blown apart.

Suddenly, Ethan felt like he should look up and behind them as they were accelerating to maximum speed to try and avoid the ship's defensive guns. He realized that two Vultures had somehow snuck their way past Squadron 6 and were angling in for an attack from their rear.

Ethan flipped the master arm on the four JATM missiles he was still carrying, and his targeting AI acquired both the Vultures within seconds of activating the missiles. Once he heard that magical tonal signal letting him know they were locked on, he depressed the pickle button next to his gun stud and sent the first missile on its way. Then he sent the next one after the first. In what was either inactive flying on the part of the Zodarks or sheer determination to nail both those Valkyries closing on that battleship. Neither of the Vultures appeared to acknowledge the threat racing towards them at speeds in excess of six thousand kilometers per hour.

Come on, you can hit them, you can hit them...splash one! Ah, damn it, he got a shot off before he blew up, Ethan cursed as the second Vulture fired off two missiles of his own at the Valkyries angling in to release their torpedoes, having maneuvered their way through the various defensive turrets trying to swat them from the existence.

Ethan watched helplessly as the two missiles closed the distance between the strike fighters in seconds. One of the Valkyries began popping flares and chaff canisters in hopes of spoofing the missile closing in. The other Valk's rear defensive gun fired a series of shotgun-style blasts behind the fighter in hopes of shredding the missile when it flew through the debris field.

The missile shot right through the chaff cloud, then ignored the bright shiny flares detonated near the rear of the Valkyries. It ripped the back half of strike bomber right off and sent it spinning out of control down into the planet's atmosphere. Ethan saw the pilot eject moments later. He'd have a somewhat long and choppy flight back to terra firma, but it did look like he'd make it.

The other missile flew right into the shotgun blast of debris and blew apart too far behind the Valkyrie to cause it any damage. The pilot, having evaded death now many times over in the span of a few minutes, fired off his four torpedoes at almost point-blank range. He barely had time to pull away from the warship as he practically skidded across the outer hull of the vessel as it sped right across many of the defensive turrets still trying to blast him apart.

The four torpedoes instantly transformed into their flaming darts of fire and plowed into another section of the warship that likely thought it might escape unscathed. These last four torpedoes managed to rip somewhere near the reactor rooms to the ship; a series of large explosions erupted that nearly tore the back half of the ship apart. It didn't take long before a series of secondary explosions erupted, separating the vessel into a handful of large chunks of charred, floating debris. Sparks flew as the remaining bits of atmosphere fed the fires. Many of the dark, dead segments of the ship would likely get pulled down into the Earth's atmosphere to burn up as a bright comet-like feature in the sky.

While Ethan had been so focused on escorting his package to the target, he hadn't seen a sudden rush of these elongated warships racing to get into either high or low Earth orbit. As he thought about what it all meant, it suddenly dawned on him he'd seen these kinds of ships in the past, in the Sirius system, over Alfheim.

Oh my God. They're going to try and land troop ships. Holy crap, we have to take those landers out before they start dropping Zodarks all over the planet! he thought. He was filled with sheer terror at the thought of what a handful of Zodark warriors could do if they managed to land in an urban environment. They were savage animals in a fight. Ethan would hate to see local law enforcement trying to battle it out with a Zodark warrior.

"All Ark elements. All Ark elements. We have Zodark troop ships moving in to start dropping landers on the surface. I want all Ark elements to disengage whatever target you're currently attacking and rally on my position. We're going lander hunting!" Captain Hunt ordered across his carrier wing's com channel.

At this precise moment, he didn't care if he was overriding some order from Space Command or the *Lexington*. Once those Zodark transports got in position, they'd start dropping landers all across Earth. If his squadrons could cut down on their numbers, it would greatly aid the defenders on the ground and likely save the lives of tens of thousands of their fellow humans. It was worth the ass chewing later for overriding other orders, if it came to it.

"Paladin Actual, this is Republic One. If you can intercept those landers, that would be greatly appreciated. How copy?"

Republic One? Who the hell is that? he thought to himself as he quickly replied. "That's a good copy, Republic One. We're on it. Paladin out."

Accelerating to maximum power, Ethan pushed his Gripen to its limits as he raced across the distances to close the gap over a group of eight transports that appeared to be settling in low Earth orbit over the center of North America.

Damn, they're going in for low orbit. That's going to make it hard as hell to swat their landers down without diving into the atmosphere.

He suddenly realized why they hadn't started releasing their landers yet. The lower into Earth's orbit they got, the less time the landers had to spend outside of the planet's atmosphere. They were a lot safer once they got inside the atmosphere as most starfighters didn't perform well in both kinds of environments. Sadly, while Gripens were able to fly inside Earth's atmosphere, they weren't exactly the nimblest of creatures. A P-97 Orion unmanned combat fighter drone could maneuver inside the atmosphere a hell of a lot better than their Gripen could.

Then his radar started showing new contacts rising up from the direction of Space Command Headquarters, the IFF signals indicating a lone squadron of exactly what they needed to start taking to the sky. Sixteen P-97 Orions appeared to be holding in a racetrack pattern around twenty thousand feet.

Damn, I wish we could contact those pilots. Try and coordinate our attack on these landers that are about to start dropping from the sky like snowflakes in a blizzard. It's about to get real, people.

At first, it was just a couple of landers that made their appearance. Then it became a tsunami of Zodark troop landers disgorging from their assault ship. In a way, the movement of ships was very organized, similar to how their own orbital assault divisions would invade a planet. First, they concentrated their force to hit several land zones at once. Then they'd establish a perimeter, expanding it as rapidly as they could while awaiting follow-on forces bringing with them your armored vehicles and heavy artillery support.

As his targeting AI counted the number of landers descending below, Ethan activated his two remaining JATMs and highlighted two landers for elimination.

Easiest kills I'll get all day, he thought.

He fired off the first one, then the second one. In seconds, God only knew how many Zodarks he'd blast from the sky before they ever made it to the surface. Now it was time to switch back to guns. He was going to get up close and personal and see how many more landers he could zap before they reached the surface or he got shot down himself.

Then he heard a call he'd never thought he'd hear. "*Ark Royal*— Broken Arrow—*Ark Royal*—Broken Arrow," came the call from a voice that sounded a lot like Admiral Halsey herself.

Broken Arrow...how in the hell could the ship be going down? Didn't they just get here?

Chapter Twenty-Seven
This Is Not Going to Plan

Nefantar
Between Luna and Earth, Sol System

Mavkah Otro had gone from absolutely elated and supremely optimistic just sixteen hours ago to near panicked that both his worst fears and those of the High Council might be coming true. The first fleet the *Nefantar* had dropped near the planet they called Mars had encountered little to no resistance in the form of enemy warships—just as the intelligence reports had suggested. The majority of the Republic Navy appeared not to be in system.

However, when the battleship *Shantri* had attempted to utilize the specific kind of electronic infiltration against the Sentinel defensive towers that had been identified by their recent intelligence reports, the ship had come under a reverse cyberassault. Within seconds, the *Shantri* and three other battleships that had been networked together had lost control of their weapons systems.

Damn it! thought Otro. Their intel had specified that there was a risk of the vulnerability being closed the longer they waited to press forward with their attack, but the Republic had done more than just employ defensive measures.

While the remainder of the *Shantri*'s battle group continued their assault against the orbital station and the planetary defensive weapons, the *Shantri* and the three other battleships representing the bulk of the battle group's combat power remained locked out of their weapon systems. It wasn't until the commander, NOS Yantar, ordered a full electronic shutdown and reset of the four ships' entire systems, to include a hard reset of the ships' reactors, that they were able to regain control of their weapon systems.

Meanwhile, five precious hours of tactical surprise had been lost. To compound the loss of surprise and time, Yantar's battle group had lost eight cruisers, sixteen frigates and twelve corvettes when his less-powerful ships had to carry on the main assault against the Mars facilities without the support of his four battleships. By the time the planet's defenses had been defeated, he'd lost more than half his warships in the process. While he hadn't lost any of the Malvari's precious battleships, he'd effectively lost three-quarters of his escort vessels.

With the pathway cleared to begin landing his ground force and capturing the sprawling colony, he gave the order to initiate the next phase of the operation in earnest. At this point, the main assault against the Republic's home world, Earth, had finally begun.

Once Otro had overseen the last of the troop transports and the final star carriers had crossed the bridge into the Sol system, he ordered the *Nefantar* to join the Grand Fleet: the largest congregation of Malvari warships ever assembled for a single military operation.

As the *Nefantar* crossed hundreds of light-years in what felt like a fraction of a second, his ship and the view he had of everything around them began to stretch—elongating itself like a piece of sticky tar before he felt a slight shudder beneath his feet. Then everything snapped into place and his ship reappeared in an entirely new section of the Orion-Cygnus Arm.

It took a couple of moments for the ship's sensors to begin receiving returns and painting a visual picture of their immediate surroundings. As the *Nefantar* connected to the battle groups already in system, their collected returns and the digital picture their sensors had created of the Sol system populated the giant warship's own navigational and combat systems.

Looking to the ten-meter-by-ten-meter monitor that covered a wall of his command center, Otro watched as the picture of the battle unfolding around him came into focus. Next came a tidal wave of situational updates and progress reports on the various invasion objectives the Malvari war planners had outlined years ago as they had prepared for this very day.

Turning to his second-in-command, Otro directed, "NOS Irhes, I want a status update on the progress of the invasion in ten minutes. Put your best people on this. We have a lot of information we need to assimilate and decisions that need to be made. It is time that we take charge of this invasion and decisively defeat these Terrans once and for all."

Irhes nodded in approval and began barking orders to his underlings to put the Mavkah's orders into motion.

Otro then looked to his ship captain, focusing his attention on the man who now wielded the most powerful warship in the system.

"NOS Vesren, begin launching your starfighters. Command your weapons officers to target at will any threats to the *Nefantar* and see to the immediate destruction of the Republic's starships, shipyards, orbital space stations and military outposts. It is time to bring this new superweapon of ours online and demonstrate the power of the *Nefantar*!"

NOS Vesren smiled a devilish smile as he turned to his own officers, issuing a slew of orders. He put into motion a series of events that would soon see this massive warship become a veritable wrecking ball of death and destruction across the Sol system.

While Otro let his subordinates continue on with their taskings, he viewed the main battle map, taking the information in and analyzing what it was showing them. What he immediately found concerning was the situation unfolding with NOS Yantar's battle group near the Terrans' Mars colony. Aside from the apparent cyberattack his ship had somehow fallen under, his ground force was now encountering unusually stiff resistance. He recalled the Groff's intelligence reports on the Republic Army's garrison on Mars; they had insisted that the size of the garrison was no more than five thousand soldiers. If that report was correct, then why was NOS Yantar's ground force, numbering some thirty thousand battle-hardened warriors, struggling to subdue them?

Something is not adding up here...

Otro was beginning to think that either their Kafarr had been fed faulty information, or he had turned against them. *Could this be a baited trap we have been carefully led into?* The very thought made his stomach tighten. He felt his pulse quickening, his body becoming sweaty at the idea of the Groff and the Malvari having been duped into believing Sol was virtually defenseless.

Then he saw another report. This one spoke of a great achievement. A border party of warriors had breached the orbital space station and was even now working to establish a gateway for them to bring aboard additional warriors to help them seize control of the station. Pushing aside his doubts and worries about this being a trap, Otro focused on the successes they had achieved thus far and looked to press home their advantage while they had it. *So long as we can open a bridge to escape should we need to, this invasion will still be seen as a great victory...my seat on the Council and then my ascension to the role of Zon will be all but certain...*

Then a series of alarms blared, accompanied by lights flashing. A warning was being sounded throughout the command center.

"Mavkah, we're detecting a group of warships dropping out of FTL warp. They're arriving...they're arriving almost on top of us!" NOS Vesren practically exploded in anger at his officers. They had failed to detect that an enemy fleet was somewhere else within the Sol system, and they were only just now finding out about it.

Otro growled as he stared angrily at his ship captain and his officers who had failed to properly prepare the fleet to meet these enemy warships. "I suggest you get your ship and your warriors ready for battle! This had best not be a large fleet that somehow hid under the noses of your officers."

"Yes, Mavkah. I shall deal with this failure personally once we have destroyed these warships," Vesren replied, then angrily dressed down his officers, who had missed what should have been found given the capabilities of the *Nefantar*. If they hadn't found this enemy fleet, then the battle groups that had already been in system for many hours prior to their arrival should have.

Turning to look at the battle map, Otro reached a hand out to steady himself and grabbed the back of a chair. The ships dropping out of FTL warp weren't some small ragtag group of ships being cobbled together from some far-flung outpost in one of the asteroid belts. This was a massive fleet of warships. Not only that, once again, he felt the Groff had seriously miscalculated the number of advanced Altairian-Human hybrid warships that this sprawling shipyard had apparently been producing en masse—somehow directly under the nose of NOS Heltet's Kafarr.

As ship after ship dropped out of warp, falling in line directly behind their battle line, almost on top of their troop transports and their star carriers, Otro berated NOS Vesren for his officers' failure to spot such a massive force apparently lingering about somewhere in the system.

Orders were being given to hastily move the troop transports to the opposite side of the *Nefantar*. They'd look to use the sheer size of the warship itself to block the Republic from picking them off. Similarly, they redeployed their star carriers while at the same time ordering them to release their swarms of starfighters and attack bombers. The Vultures in particular were very capable fighters that had given the Primords and

Terrans fits during the last war. If they could get their attack bombers, the Glaives, properly deployed, then they could likely make short work of these Republic battleships. They didn't appear to be equipped with many starfighters and looked like they would be rapidly overwhelmed by the swarms Otro was about to unleash on them.

Then a new threat appeared—a wrench thrown into a hastily redrawn plan.

A warship came into focus, painted in a black, blue, and yellow striped pattern appearing to match the same color scheme he had just noticed on all the other warships that had recently appeared. Only unlike the previous ships that were randomly dropping out of FTL warp, this beast of a machine looked to be three thousand, two hundred meters in length and represented the most clear and present danger to Mavkah Otro's years of planning and scheming to become the next Zon of the Zodark Empire.

After staring at the image for a moment, he raised a hand, pointing a finger at the image and demanding, "What the hell is *that*?!"

For a moment, no one responded. This was not something any of them had seen or read about in any of the previous intelligence reports from the Groff, and it was abundantly clear it should have been mentioned. Then a lone voice spoke from among those who kept their heads held slightly down, hoping to go unnoticed.

"That, Mavkah, looks to be a star carrier. In fact, it looks almost identical to those Altairian carriers. I would go so far as to say this…is likely an Altairian-Human hybrid warship, just like these new battleships we are encountering. Judging by the apparent matching color scheme these warships look to be using, they are likely part of some sort of new battle group our Groff have apparently *failed* to identify until *we*, the *Malvari*, stumbled upon them during *your* brilliantly led invasion of our greatest enemies' home territories."

Otro observed that the NOS that spoke looked to be one of the junior officers on Vesren's staff, but clearly he saw the picture more clearly than those in higher stations around him. The fact that he would speak so confidently to Otro told him this was the kind of warrior around which they needed to focus on building the new Malvari once he had assumed his new role as Zon.

Then, as if on cue, this Altairian-looking carrier began launching its own starfighters, likely wanting to go after his vital troop transports carrying the best and bravest of their warriors for the next phase in the operation.

Otro faced NOS Vesren as he ordered, "Engage those fighters as they're launching. I want that carrier destroyed immediately!" He then pivoted to his deputy, Irhes. "Order the ground invasion to begin immediately. We must get our warriors down on the surface before the Republic can organize some sort of effort to go after our transports. Remind the ground commanders one more time—they have forty-eight hours to cause as much damage as possible. Then they must withdraw their forces to rejoin the fleet. If they are unable to accomplish that, then they must prepare to be left behind and continue to wage a reign of terror on our enemies while we will write tales of their exploits to be told for all to hear of their sacrifice."

"Yes, Mavkah. It shall be done!"

With Irhes and Vesren moving to execute his orders, Otro returned his attention to the battle map, studying the continually evolving situation. The sudden appearance of this new fleet they hadn't known existed presented him with a unique challenge. His modified plan to invade Sol might need to be adjusted yet again. Where he had thought they might have seventy-two hours to unleash a wave of terror and devastation across the Republic's home system, he now knew he might have substantially less time.

He knew from past experiences that these Altairian carriers were incredibly tough and hard to destroy. They employed some kind of secret armor that gave even the Orbots' deadliest warships a hard time. What caused him more alarm was the thought that this ship, like the other Altairian-Human hybrid ships, had been greatly modified to employ only the best aspects of the Altairian navy while integrating the parts of the Terran navy that had proven so effective against the Dominion Alliance. If he was being honest with himself, these new warships represented an even graver threat to the *Nefantar* and the greater Zodark Empire than the ships they'd encountered in the previous war with the humans. What galled him the most was that the Groff and even this Kafarr had failed to warn them of such a ship, or even that a fleet of this size was being built in secret, likely for a moment just such as this.

When I return from this mission, someone is going to pay for this failure...

Chapter Twenty-Eight
A Rook for a Queen

RNS *Ark Royal*
Near Luna, Sol System

Admiral Abigail Halsey grabbed the edge of her chair as the *Ark Royal* shook violently. Sparks and debris rained down across the bridge. Smoke started to fill the bridge as electrical fires broke out—cries for help rang out over the chaos.

As Halsey's faculties returned, a piercing pain spread down the right side of her face. She wasn't sure why, but several of her upper molars hurt, like a needle was being driven into the roots of those teeth. Then she felt a tear, or at least she thought it was a tear. Reaching to her temple to investigate the source of this newfound yet growing pain, her fingers felt something sharp. It suddenly dawned on her—she'd been stabbed in the side of the head by something metallic. Yet she wasn't unconscious, at least not yet. She felt pain, but it seemed to be more localized to her teeth. The injury was proving to be shockingly painful. But she could still function; she could lead.

Searching for Captain Gregory Carr, Halsey looked through the smoke still filling the bridge and saw a chair knocked over to the side, ripped from its anchor to the floor. As she looked down, where the smoke was less thick, she saw Greg, the man she'd come to call friend, lying there, still strapped into his command chair, unconscious, unmoving.

Is he dead? Please let him not be dead...

"Admiral, you're injured," someone called out to her. "Let me get a medic for you."

When Halsey heard the word "admiral," it was like a switch had suddenly been flipped. The mental fog she'd felt herself drifting inside of dissipated. In her newfound moment of clarity, she felt the sudden urge to take charge of the ship and the situation. Turning to face the direction of the voice, she couldn't see who had spoken to her since the smoke from an electrical fire near the tactical station still clouded her view. So she just spoke loudly, hoping to be heard.

"No, not until the others have been taken care of," Halsey insisted. "Right now, I want someone to get this smoke vented out of here. Get the air system back online and let's get the backup bridge crew brought up to fill in for those who were killed or who are too injured. *Now!* I also want a damage report. We need to know how badly we've been harmed, and by the way, what the hell just hit us?" Halsey spoke loudly, issuing a raft of orders as she sought to reassert control on the bridge.

"Uh, we're still trying to figure that out, Admiral. I…we just received a warning from the *Lexington* moments after we came out of FTL about some kind of new superweapon on that giant Zodark ship. It…uh, sorry, ma'am. I'm trying to recall what it said…"

Turning to look for the familiar voice, Halsey saw the young officer she'd taken an interest in mentoring, Lieutenant Phillips. He was the lone person surrounded by a station of dead and gravely wounded comrades in what had been the *Ark*'s CIC section. Then she saw blood pulsating from a compound fracture on his upper left arm, the limb being loosely held together by exposed strands of muscles and tendons as spurts of blood oozed from the wound with each beat of the heart.

"Captain Mitchner warned that the weapon was in some cases almost destroying an entire battleship in a single shot. He said the *Lexi* has taken three hits…uh, he said he's not sure they're going to last much longer," Lieutenant Phillips barely finished speaking before his head slumped to the side as he passed out.

"My God, medic! Someone get a tourniquet on Lieutenant Phillips's left arm before he bleeds out!" Halsey called out.

A team of medics had just arrived on the bridge when they heard her words and sprang into action. Then another group of damage control personnel and a dozen engineering Synths emerged from the stairwell and joined the medics in treating the gravely injured bridge crew. The newly arrived spacers and Synths had eventually made their way to the bridge via one of the emergency exit stairwells that connected the various decks of the ship should the turbo lifts ever go down during a battle like they just had.

As a medic ran over to Phillips to render aid, an engineering Synth near one of the control panels fiddled with something. Moments later, the HVAC kicked back on, pulling the smoke and burning electrical smell toward the ceiling. That was when Halsey saw just how bad the situation on the bridge really was. Whatever that new weapon was packing, it had managed to score practically a direct hit on the bridge and CIC. Crazily enough, the entire bridge and CIC section of the ship had been purposely built near the center of the *Ark Royal*, specifically to provide the ship's leadership a higher degree of protection.

A voice called out to grab Halsey's attention. "Ma'am, we're getting a report from the *Lexington*," said Lieutenant Commander Linderri. "The CO, Captain Mitchner, said to inform you that they've sustained critical damage to their reactor room. They've had to conduct an emergency shutdown of reactors two and six. Reactor one went critical, and they had to eject it. Reactors three and four also took damage and are operating at less than twenty percent capacity. He's requesting permission to attempt a withdrawal from the battle line, in hopes of saving the ship. What should I tell him?"

Halsey stared for a moment at Linderri. She wasn't puzzled by the question he'd asked; she was puzzled by why *he* was the one asking it. Linderri was the *Ark*'s chief electronic warfare officer. Then it dawned on her that he must have been the next in line for command should all the others above him become incapacitated.

"Go ahead and tell him permission granted," Halsey replied. "Tell Mitchner Godspeed and good luck. They put up one hell of a fight, but we'll take it over from here."

Linderri seemed puzzled by what she meant but went ahead and relayed the message. He then set about trying to figure out what kind of working controls they still had on the bridge. It might become necessary to transfer operations to the alternative bridge—that was, if it was still *there*. The alternative bridge was located in the tower section that housed the bulk of the ship's electronic warfare and communications equipment, atop the rear quarter of the ship.

"Admiral, you've got a piece of metal lodged in the side of your head, ma'am. Please let me at least see how bad it is and if there's anything I can do about it," one of the medics pleaded with her as he approached her chair. A medical synthetic stood there with him, medical scanner in hand.

She nodded and sat back in the chair as the Synth approached her. It slowly moved the scanner up and down as the device performed a series of maneuvers that would feed data into the medical AI on the device.

Judging by the concerned look in the young medic's eyes, it was serious.

You'd make a terrible poker player, Petty Officer, she thought.

Boooom!

A violent explosion rocked the ship once more. The thunderous roar was so loud, Halsey could feel it vibrate the air itself.

That damn weapon just hit us again, she realized as the bridge was plunged into darkness for a second time. Thankfully, the lights kicked on a little faster this time and the bridge appeared to be no worse for wear.

"Where's my first damage report, damn it? Now we need an update on that one!" she roared in anger, hoping to spark a fire under someone's ass to get this ship back in the fight before they were ripped apart.

"I've got it, Admiral. Let me read it off for you…"

****

Nefantar – Bridge

"Mavkah, I recommend opening the bridge now. Our ships can organize a fighting withdrawal while our ground forces begin the process of withdrawing. We cannot predict when or if additional Republic warships will arrive. Should that ship the *Freedom* arrive in system, evacuating the ground force while protecting the *Nefantar* from their superweapon will be difficult," NOS Vesren suggested.

Otro narrowed his eyes as his gaze bored into his ship commander. He was trying to determine if it was weakness in the face of battle or something else leading the man to propose this idea. "Is the damage to our ship so severe that we must withdraw now…before our primary objectives have been achieved? Or is there something more?" he pressed.

Vesren appeared uncomfortable with the question. He held his upper right hand up as he replied, "Mavkah, you have achieved a great victory for the Malvari and the Zodark people. My suggestion is for us to capitalize on that victory by regrouping our fleet back in Tueblets, where we can properly assess the damage we have inflicted. Then, if you agree, I would like to suggest we launch a second invasion immediately—this time to the Rhea system, so we can deliver a decisive blow against this Alliance City of theirs where the Galactic Empire has moved their seat of power."

Otro grunted at the response, not finding any fault in his logic—pivoting rapidly from one battle to another had been a key Malvari doctrinal strategy prior to their joining the Dominion. They had quickly conquered territory and other species via this pivot, attack, repivot, reattack strategy. Now it was the Orbots who dictated more and more of the Malvari's tactics—something Mavkah Otro firmly planned on changing once he became the Zon.

Otro growled in frustration. He didn't want to stop just yet. The ground force had just landed. Their twenty-four hours of terror had just started. How could he now order them back into their landers to rejoin their transports—their tails tucked between their legs like a six-legged wartle?

"If we open the bridge, how long will the ground force take to recover?"

This question seemed to catch Vesren off guard. That little hesitation told Otro all he needed to know about his ship commander's true reasons for wanting to open the bridge. He wasn't interested in the pivot, reattack strategy—he was scared they might become trapped here. *That* could why he wanted to open the bridge and begin their exit out of Sol.

"Mavkah, it took the ships an hour to get into position. Another hour to deploy the landers to the surface. If we issue the order now, I believe the transport can rejoin the fleet to exit as one force within the next six hours. Six hours is still plenty of time for our warships to continue wrecking their facilities. We could hit them with a limited orbital bombardment on our way out of Sol if you would like?"

Six hours...perhaps he is right, Mavkah Otro considered. *Perhaps it is best to consolidate our achievements now.*

"NOS Vesren, you speak wisely in this moment. I have considered your suggestion and cannot find fault or weakness in it. Go ahead and issue the recall. Prepare the ship to reopen the bridge. Let's begin to withdraw our forces. It is time to return home—as Victors of the Empire!"

Otro saw a smile form on his face. Victors of the Empire was a battle honor rarely awarded to a fleet. It was an honor his warriors would welcome.

"Yes, Mavkah. The Zon will be proud of your achievements. They will write tales and great songs of this triumph you have achieved for the Empire today, Zon Otro," Vesren said, letting slip the title everyone knew he was destined to achieve.

"I see a bright future for you, NOS Vesren. Perhaps you will take a seat at the table of the Malvari soon enough. I hear an opening is going to materialize soon…"

****

Ark Royal – Alternate Bridge

"Admiral, we can't take much more of this. That superweapon is popping our battleships like bloated pimples. We must withdraw the fleet while we still have a fleet to withdraw," pleaded Lieutenant Commander Linderri.

"No, Commander!" Admiral Halsey insisted. "We cannot abandon Earth. If it means the destruction of our entire fleet to save the people of Earth—to save the Republic—then that is the price that shall be paid! We will stand and we will fight until our very last breath. I will hear no more about retreating to fight another day. It is live or die, win or lose right here, right now in this very moment!"

Linderri looked apoplectic at her response. Halsey could see in his eyes that the fear of dying was overtaking his duty to his oath, his duty to defend the Republic to the death so long as he remained a naval officer. It was a duty she planned on ensuring he adhered to—either that, or she'd have him shot as an example to anyone who thought otherwise.

"Wait a second! Admiral, something is happening near that Zodark ship," the replacement tactical action officer declared loudly, demanding the attention of everyone on the bridge.

Halsey looked in the direction of the officer who'd broken into her conversation with Linderri. He'd likely saved him from being removed right there and then for cowardice.

"What is it, TAO?"

"Ma'am, I'm not one hundred percent certain what it means, but there appears to be a spatial disturbance near that ship. It's a similar kind of disturbance as the one's we've seen around the *Freedom*—the kind that happens prior to activating a wormhole," explained Lieutenant Commander Abe.

Halsey bunched her eyebrows at the explanation. "Are you implying this Zodark ship…is preparing to open another wormhole—another bridge between Zodark space and Sol?"

As the words left her mouth, a look of sheer terror appeared on the face of Commander Linderri. Then she saw similar looks on the faces of the others. The Zodarks had smashed the Republic. An invasion of Earth was already underway. If they were about to bring in more ships, more soldiers—this could be the end for Earth…maybe even the Republic.

"Admiral, it's not a perfect match to the *Freedom*. But it's close enough to lead me to believe that's exactly what they're about to do," Abe explained.

Halsey felt like she'd been punched in the gut. Her speech, so full of piss and vinegar, just moments ago—it all seemed wasted. The realization suddenly hit her—it wasn't their own demise, it was the acceptance that there was no hope of saving Earth. Not if that ship opened another bridge between their territories.

This can't be it…there must be another move, another play we can make? Halsey thought. Then a more vindictive idea welled up within her. A smile formed as she played the final move out in her head.

Yeah…there is one final move…

"Commander Linderri, Commander Abe, I am officially ordering you and everyone else on the *Ark Royal* to abandon ship," Halsey said firmly. "I alone will remain on the bridge to guide the *Ark* towards that Zodark vessel. It is my intent to ram that vessel with as much speed and velocity as I can push from the engines we have left. If I can damage that ship enough, maybe even destroy it, I can stop them from opening another wormhole. I can stop them from bringing more invaders into Sol. I can save the Republic."

She left no room for debate or questioning her orders. She was giving them a chance to live. A chance to get off before she drove the *Ark* into the guts of that damned ship that just might destroy humanity if she couldn't stop it.

"Ma'am, I'm staying with you," Abe declared. "You're going to need my help if that's what you want to do."

Halsey looked around to the others on the bridge to see who else would choose to stay behind and help see her plan through.

"Admiral, I have a better plan and you'll need to let me stay behind to make it work," announced a spacer she didn't recognize. He had replaced the two others who should have taken charge of the helmsman position.

"If that's your order, Admiral, then I will see to it," Linderri announced. "I will work to ensure we can evacuate as many of the crew and injured as possible before you ram the bastards."

Of course you'll abandon the ship—while others volunteer to stay on in your stead, thought Halsey. *You're only the acting captain of the ship! You should have been the first to volunteer to stay with your command, you bastard!*

"Very well, Linderri. Best get to it," she said bitterly to him. "Once we're ready to move, we're not waiting around for stragglers. The fate of the Republic is hanging by a thread. I will not let anything stand between us and our date with destiny!"

As Linderri left the bridge to see to the evacuation, the acting helmsman position explained his idea. The more she heard, the more she liked it. This was indeed a much better plan than simply trying to build up speed and hope they could hit the ship with enough force to damage its wormhole generator—or maybe even destroy it.

No…this plan has a real chance of success.

Admiral Abigail Halsey straightened herself up and took one deep breath, realizing the full weight of her decision. Fixing the helmsman with a steely gaze, she asked, "Course laid in?"

"Yes, Admiral," he replied, resolute.

"All right, then. Let's do this thing."

****

Nefantar—Bridge

"NOS Vesren, we have a problem!" someone called out.

Otro heard the panic in the officer's voice and turned to see what was happening. He couldn't hear their hushed words, but he didn't have to. He saw it on the battle map. An image of a Republic carrier they had left for dead. But it wasn't dead—at least not yet.

Otro watched as the giant ship with fires raging from the multiple gashes and tears across its armor turned to point in the direction of his fleet once again. Then he saw something else. Hundreds of tiny life pods ejecting across the vastness of the ship. It appeared the ship's commander had finally given the order to abandon the vessel once they could no longer hope to save it. But as the cloud of life pods moved away from the ship, Otro noticed something more. The bow of the ship was still moving—continuing to align itself with his fleet. *What are you doing...?*

As the fiery wreck slowly aligned itself, Otro's eyes widened. He realized what the bastard was going to do next. *He's aligning to ram us...*

Otro roared loudly, "Destroy that ship *now*!"

"Oh, Lindow! It is preparing to ram us!" someone shouted.

"We are trying, Mavkah. The particle beam is recharging now!"

Otro shouted urgently. "Order every vessel in the fleet to stop what they are doing and attack that carrier! Order our battleships to move in front of the *Nefantar*. Place themselves in front of us and do not allow that ship to ram us!"

A flurry of activity broke out across the command center as everyone now realized what was about to happen. If that ship was able to crash into them—if it damaged the wormhole generator...they would become trapped. Doomed to fight until the bitter end in Sol.

Otro stared at the image of that carrier as it looked to have finished aligning itself with the *Nefantar*—its forward velocity still remaining unchanged. In that moment, he realized the ship wasn't lining up to ram them. It was aligning to *enter warp* with them directly in its path. Before he could say or think anything further, he felt his body suddenly being hurled through the air—connecting against a wall moments later.

As his vision went black, so too did the lights around him.

Otro fought the urge to keep his eyes closed, allowing his mind and body drift away. To numb the pain that was spreading across his body. But that was not what a future Zon would do. He willed himself to get up, needing to know how badly his ship had been damaged.

As Otro struggled to push a fallen Zodark off him, the emergency lights flickered on and he could see what was happening around him.

"Mavkah, are you OK?" someone shouted as they approached him.

"I am fine," he growled. "How badly is the ship damaged? Are we still able to open the bridge?"

Otro was irritated that no one immediately responded to him, but as he looked around the bridge, he understood why. Everything that had not been extremely well secured during impact, from Zodarks to monitors, had been thrashed about with extreme force. Two of the chairs had detached themselves from the floor and flown against screens, breaking them. One of the panels in the ceiling had popped open, revealing a damaged HVAC system. Hot steam hissed, and a haze started to fill the room.

The force of the hit was still affecting Otro's ability to think clearly. There was a bit of a fog surrounding his vision, and he was forced to sit down. He looked around for the officer responsible for the damage control parties and finally spotted him—his body impaled by something that had broken free and now nailed him against the far wall.

Soon medical personnel rushed onto the bridge along with damage control sailors and replacement officers needed to get the bridge and the ship back operational. Many of the wounded appeared to be suffering from broken bones and severe fractures. Looking towards the chair from which NOS Vesren commanded the ship, he saw the man lying in a heap, his body twisted into a form that left no question as to whether he was still with them or gone to meet Lindow.

"I need a damage report!" he shouted to whoever was taking charge of the ship for the moment.

"Yes, Mavkah. I'm bringing it up right now," called out a newly arrived replacement crewman.

Otro felt like an eternity was passing as he waited to hear how badly damaged the ship was. Given how hard they had just been rammed and also the fact that they were still here, it was possible that Republic ship had glanced them. Had it gone through them…he wouldn't be here to ponder that. Then a voice broke into his thoughts.

"Sir, the damage report is coming in now." He paused for a moment before continuing. "It…it is severe, Mavkah. The Republic ship did not hit the center of the ship, but it did connect with the front of the *Nefantar*. We are showing a five-hundred-meter section that looks to have been sheared off. Ripped from the rest of the ship."

The officer continued to read for a moment before continuing his report. "Damage control parties are sealing off exposed decks. Large sections had been exposed to the vacuum, causing a significant loss of life. They are reporting that additional decks may need to be sealed as they look to restore the ship's structural integrity. Engineering is also reporting that we are currently dead in the water. They are attempting to restart the main engines to get us moving again. There are also reports coming in of large pieces of debris clouding our path from that warship that rammed us. We may sustain additional damage as our engines attempt to push us through it once they have restarted."

"Thank you for that report. But right now we need to know if we can still use the bridge or, if it is too damaged, how soon it can be repaired," Otro said.

The officer gave him a confused look, as though he did not understand the question that had just been asked.

"Mavkah, that is not possible. The generator was in the forward section of the ship that was just ripped apart. Should engineering be able to restart the main engines, we will barely have the capacity to move. With no forward section to the ship, any debris we encounter will likely inflict severe damage and further compromise the ship's structural integrity. For all intents and purposes, Mavkah, the *Nefantar* is dead in the water—unable to safely move from our current position."

As those words were spoken, Mavkah Otro lost control of his emotions and let out a primal roar as he beat his chest with his four hands. They were trapped. There was no way to return to Zodark space—no way to escape at all. That flaming wreck of a ship had just doomed them all.

"Sir, our scanners are detecting multiple signatures just beyond the Earth's moon—several incoming FTL bubbles are appearing. More ships are starting to arrive."

Otro knew those would be Republic ships. They had no reinforcements coming. No other ships in that direction. Looking to the officer who had spoken, he asked the question he knew was on everyone's mind. "It that Gallentine ship killer among them?"

"It is too early to tell, Mavkah. We will know soon enough."

A sense of defeat and despair rose up within Otro. So too did a burning rage at how this situation had come about. Had the Groff provided them better, more accurate intelligence of the system, he would not have altered the plans. Had that Kafarr not betrayed them with faulty intelligence, his fleet would not be trapped. Had that intelligence about those Sentinel towers not been a trap, his ships would not have sustained such devastating damage in those early hours of the battle. Had Director Vak'Atioth not failed them, this defeat would not have happened.

If my forces are trapped...if we are going to fight until the bitter end...then we are going to do our best to destroy this planet they call Earth and leave it a burning cauldron of death...unlivable for centuries to come.

Turning to look to the officers waiting to hear his next orders, Otro calmly declared, "If this is the fate Lindow has bestowed upon us, then let us not let him down. Let us not let our Empire down. Let us prepare to do everything within our power to kill every last Terran on that planet they call Earth. Order our transports to land our ground forces once again, and order them to wage a campaign of extermination across the planet. Our honor will be restored as we destroy the beating heart of the Republic—ensuring our deaths will not be in vain."

Looking for NOS Irhes, he found his deputy cradling a broken arm but looking on proudly at him. "Come, my friend. It is time for one last battle before Lindow welcomes us into his warm embrace. Let us board a transport and join our warrior brothers in a battle, leading them in a final battle to honor Lindow—to honor the Empire."

From the Authors

Miranda and I hope you have enjoyed this book. If you are ready to continue the action, the preorder for the next book in the series, *Into the Terror*, is already live. Reserve your copy today and continue the story as soon as it's released.

If you would like to stay up to date on new releases and receive emails about any special pricing deals we may make available, please sign up for our email distribution list. Simply go to https://www.frontlinepublishinginc.com/ and sign up.

If you enjoy audiobooks, we have a great selection that has been created for your listening pleasure. Our entire Red Storm series and our Falling Empire series have been recorded, and several books in our Rise of the Republic series and our Monroe Doctrine series are now available. Please see below for a complete listing.

As independent authors, reviews are very important to us and make a huge difference to other prospective readers. If you enjoyed this book, we humbly ask you to write up a positive review on Amazon and Goodreads. We sincerely appreciate each person that takes the time to write one.

We have really valued connecting with our readers via social media, especially on our Facebook page https://www.facebook.com/RosoneandWatson/. Sometimes we ask for help from our readers as we write future books—we love to draw upon all your different areas of expertise. We also have a group of beta readers who get to look at the books before they are officially published and help us fine-tune last-minute adjustments. If you would like to be a part of this team, please go to our author website, and send us a message through the "Contact" tab.

You may also enjoy some of our other works. A full list can be found below:

Nonfiction:

Iraq Memoir 2006–2007 Troop Surge
Interview with a Terrorist (audiobook available)

Fiction:

The Monroe Doctrine Series
Volume One (audiobook available)
Volume Two (audiobook available)
Volume Three (audiobook available)
Volume Four (audiobook available)
Volume Five (audiobook still in production)
Volume Six (available for preorder)

Rise of the Republic Series
Into the Stars (audiobook available)
Into the Battle (audiobook available)
Into the War (audiobook available)
Into the Chaos (audiobook available)
Into the Fire (audiobook still in production)
Into the Calm
Into the Terror (available for preorder)

Apollo's Arrows Series (co-authored with T.C. Manning)
Cherubim's Call

Crisis in the Desert Series (co-authored with Matt Jackson)
Project 19 (audiobook available)
Desert Shield
Desert Storm

Falling Empires Series
Rigged (audiobook available)
Peacekeepers (audiobook available)
Invasion (audiobook available)
Vengeance (audiobook available)
Retribution (audiobook available)

Red Storm Series
Battlefield Ukraine (audiobook available)
Battlefield Korea (audiobook available)
Battlefield Taiwan (audiobook available)
Battlefield Pacific (audiobook available)

Battlefield Russia (audiobook available)
Battlefield China (audiobook available)

Michael Stone Series
Traitors Within (audiobook available)

World War III Series
Prelude to World War III: The Rise of the Islamic Republic and the Rebirth of America (audiobook available)
Operation Red Dragon and the Unthinkable (audiobook available)
Operation Red Dawn and the Siege of Europe (audiobook available)
Cyber Warfare and the New World Order (audiobook available)

Children's Books:
My Daddy has PTSD
My Mommy has PTSD

Abbreviation Key

AI	Artificial Intelligence
ASAP	As Soon As Possible
AT	Assault Troops
C-FLO	Commander, Flight Operations
CAS	Close-Air Support
CCTV	Closed-circuit Television
CIC	Combat Information Center
CO	Commanding Officer
COB	Chief of the Boat
CT	Counterterrorism
D2	Dagger Badge (specialized training)
DARPA	Defense Advanced Research Projects Agency
DFO	Director of Fleet Operations
EMS	Emergency Medical Services
ETA	Estimated Time of Arrival
EWO	Electronic Warfare Officer
FTL	Faster Than Light
G2	Intelligence Officer
G3	Operations Officer
HALO	High-Altitude, Low Opening
HQ	Headquarters
HTAS	Heavy Troop Assault Ships
HUD	Heads-up Display
ICBM	Intercontinental Ballistic Missile
IMS	Interstellar Marshals Service
JATM	Joint Advanced Tactical Missile
JBR	John Bentley Reactors
JSOC	Joint Special Operations Command
LMG	Light Machine Gun
LT	Lieutenant
LZ	Landing Zone
MG	Machine Gun
MRE	Meal Ready-to-Eat
NCO	Noncommissioned Officer
NGA	National Geospatial Agency
NOS	Zodark leadership

OAD	Orbital Assault Division
OAR	Orbital Assault Regiment
ODA	Operational Delta Attachment (Special Forces)
PDG	Point Defense Guns
QRF	Quick Reaction Force
R&D	Research and Development
R&R	Rest and Recreation
RA	Republic Army
RD	Republic Dollar
RI	Republic Intelligence
RHIP	Rank Has Its Privileges
RNS	Republic Naval Ship
S2	Intelligence Officer
SAC	Supervising Agent in Charge
SF	Special Forces
SOF	Special Operations Forces
SOP	Standard Operating Procedure
TAM	Tactical Action Map
TAO	Tactical Action Officer
TAS	Troop Assault Ships
VR	Virtual Reality
XO	Executive Officer

Made in United States
North Haven, CT
21 May 2023